PRAISE FOR *WHAT SHE KNEW*

"AN AMAZING, GRIPPING, BEAUTIFULLY WRITTEN DEBUT."
—LIANE MORIARTY, *NEW YORK TIMES* BESTSELLING AUTHOR

"A CLEVER, TAUTLY PLOTTED PAGE-TURNER
FROM A TERRIFIC NEW WRITER."
—*GOOD HOUSEKEEPING*

PRAISE FOR *THE PERFECT GIRL*

"[A] PAGE-TURNING THRILLER."
—*REAL SIMPLE* MAGAZINE

"FOR ANYONE WHO LOVED *GIRL ON THE TRAIN*,
IT'S A MUST-READ."
—ROSAMUND LUPTON

PRAISE FOR *ODD CHILD OUT*

"SUBTLE, NUANCED WRITING AND A COMPELLING, TIMELY STORY."
—SHARI LAPENA, *NEW YORK TIMES* BESTSELLING AUTHOR

"IMPOSSIBLE TO PUT DOWN."
—*SULLIVAN COUNTY DEMOCRAT*

"A master of the written word." —MARY KUBICA, New York Times bestselling author

Praise for *Odd Child Out*

"Subtle, nuanced writing and a compelling, timely story taut with tension—*Odd Child Out* is a hugely satisfying and thrilling read. Highly recommended!"

—Shari Lapena, *New York Times* bestselling author of *The Couple Next Door*

"In this engrossing novel . . . the action builds to a shattering conclusion."

—*Publishers Weekly*

"Macmillan excels at getting into the minds of terrified, brokenhearted parents . . . this mix of police procedural and thriller will satisfy fans of the author's previous work as well as those looking for something after Tana French."

—*Booklist*

"With characters who are sympathetic and believable, Macmillan's latest will keep readers in suspense to the very end. Highly recommended."

—*Library Journal* (starred review)

"The story is emotionally compelling and Macmillan nails the complexity of adolescent friendship."

—*Kirkus Reviews*

"This is a fascinating book focusing on the aftermath of the Somalian concentration camps and the effect it held on those who were involved. . . . Macmillan changes the course of direction of the story several times, which makes for interesting reading. The characterizations are vivid and come alive on the page."

—RT Book Reviews

"Hard to put down the book. . . . The storyline is intriguing, full of twists and turns, and readers will become fully invested in these characters, all of whom are interesting in their own right."

—Bookreporter.com

"[A] taut psychological thriller."

—*Birmingham Magazine*

"Intricately worked out and impossible to put down."

—*Sullivan County Democrat*

Praise for *The Perfect Girl*

"Gilly Macmillan deftly explores the intricacies of relationships and the bonds that tie families all while ratcheting up the suspense in this page-turning thriller."

—*Real Simple* magazine

"With tightly drawn characters, a fascinating storyline, and absolutely exquisite narration, *The Perfect Girl* is sure to keep readers up all night. Gilly Macmillan proves once again to be a master of the written word and is quickly becoming one of my go-to authors."

—Mary Kubica, *New York Times* bestselling author of *Pretty Baby*

"A wonderfully addictive book with virtuoso plotting and characters—for anyone who loved *Girl on the Train,* it's a must-read."

—Rosamund Lupton

"As the suspenseful, serpentine tale unreels from the alternating perspectives of several key players, readers will be rooting for the resilient, resourceful Zoe all the way to the perfectly executed final twists."

—*Publishers Weekly* (starred review)

"A compelling read for fans of psychological suspense."

—*Library Journal*

"I DEVOURED *The Perfect Girl.* An incredible page-turner with awesome characters and suspense. Bravo."

—Kate White, *New York Times* bestselling author

"Macmillan captivates readers with a story just as addictive as her first . . . [and] shines when exploring the intricacies of relationships. . . . Fans of Tana French, Ruth Ware, and Gillian Flynn will become completely entrenched in the unfolding details."

—*BookPage*

"With lovely prose, depth of character and an intelligent narrative, Macmillan lifts the level of suspense with stiletto-like precision: a tiny graze here, a shallow cut there and, eventually, a thrust into the heart. At once profoundly unsettling and richly rewarding."

—*Richmond Times-Dispatch*

Praise for *What She Knew*

"A clever, tautly plotted page-turner from a terrific new writer."

—*Good Housekeeping*

"Heart-in-the-mouth excitement from the start of this electrifyingly good debut . . . an absolute firecracker of a thriller that convinces and captivates from the word go. A must-read."

—*Sunday Mirror*

"Macmillan peppers her debut with subtle red herrings and a variety of potential suspects, ratcheting up the tension slowly but oh so deliciously."

—*Booklist*

"Gilly Macmillan introduces some smart variations on the [missing child] theme in her debut mystery . . . Macmillan enlivens the narrative with emails, newspaper headlines, passages from professional journals, even transcripts from Inspector Clemo's sessions with a psychotherapist. But her best move is to include vicious blog posts that go viral."

—*New York Times Book Review*

"Tightly focused and fast-paced. You won't rest until you really know what happened."

—Lisa Ballantyne, author of *The Guilty One*

"One of the brightest debuts I have read this year—a visceral, emotionally charged story . . . heart-wrenchingly well told and expertly constructed, this deserves to stay on the bestseller list until Christmas."

—*Daily Mail*

"This accomplished, intelligent debut should come with a warning—it's completely addictive. A nail-biting, sleep-depriving, brilliant read."

—Saskia Sarginson, author of *The Twins*

"An engaging debut."

—*Kirkus Reviews*

"Readers will have a tough time putting this one down."
—*Publishers Weekly*

"A terrific debut."

—*Reader's Digest*

"What an amazing, gripping, beautifully written debut. *What She Knew* kept me up late into the night (and scared the life out of me)."

—Liane Moriarty, *New York Times* bestselling author

"A nuanced, completely addictive debut."

—*People*

I KNOW
YOU
KNOW

Also by Gilly Macmillan

Odd Child Out
The Perfect Girl
What She Knew

I KNOW YOU KNOW

A Novel

GILLY MACMILLAN

wm

WILLIAM MORROW

An Imprint of HarperCollinsPublishers

P.S.™ is a trademark of HarperCollins Publishers.

HarperCollins books may be purchased for educational, business, or sales promotional use. For information, please e-mail the Special Markets Department at SPsales@harpercollins.com.

FIRST EDITION

Designed by Diahann Sturge

Library of Congress Cataloging-in-Publication Data has been applied for.

ISBN 978-0-06-269860-5
ISBN 978-0-06-286919-7 (library edition)
ISBN 978-0-06-287014-8 (international edition)

18 19 20 21 22   LSC   10 9 8 7 6 5 4 3 2 1

For Jules

I KNOW
YOU
KNOW

The weather is raw. Horizontal rain spatters Fletcher's glasses and slaps his cheeks.

He saw the pit from the motorway. He had a bird's-eye view from the overpass and another glimpse from a meaner angle as the car came down the exit ramp. The wipers were going like the clappers. He saw the backs of the gathered construction workers. The pit was a muddy gash in the car park in front of them, and the sticky clay soil inside it a dull dirty orange. Fletcher and Danny parked near the entrance to the superstore, at the end of a line of cars in disorderly formation. Danny didn't open the passenger door until he'd cinched his hood tight around his face like a girl's bonnet.

Inside the pit the men have discovered a nest of bones. Fletcher stands unflinchingly beside it as the weather assaults him. He takes in the scene. He sees fresh black tarmac, shiny with surface water. Rainwater has collected in every undulation and the puddles are pockmarked and squally. They offer wobbly reflections of the rectangular building and the sky behind it, where a streak of sickly yellow light cowers beneath clouds pregnant with more rain. One of the workers tries to light a cigarette. His lighter sparks and dies repeatedly.

"What are they doing here?" Fletcher asks.

"They're expanding the store," Danny says.

"Is it not large enough already?"

The superstore is a behemoth, as big as a city block. The tarmac flows around it like a moat, and from its black edges, streets of Victorian terraced houses radiate away in lines that track the ancient curves of the landscape, rising to colonize a natural bowl in a steep ridge behind. Parkland runs along the top of the ridge, a telecom tower lodged amongst the trees.

On the other side of the superstore, dominating the horizon, Fletcher can see six high-rise towers that form the housing estate called the Glenfrome Estate. He can't believe it has escaped the dynamite. It's a relic. Fletcher and Danny have history there, but Fletcher likes to look forward, not back, so he won't be the one to mention it.

The pit is deep. Seven or eight feet, Fletcher estimates as he stands at the edge of it. He quells a mild lurch of vertigo. He's perturbed by the sight of the bone—the tip of a femur, he guesses from the size of it—and by the depth of the pit, and the way it resembles a grave. The digger is abandoned beside them, the huge scraping tool quivering above. Danny shakes the hand of the site foreman. Beads of water hang like pearls from the edge of his hood. "We need to get this covered up," he says. Water is accumulating in the bottom of the pit, a few inches already. It'll be lapping the bone before long.

To Fletcher, he says, "It's probably another fucking Julius Caesar."

"Could be." Fletcher shudders. It's because of the weather, not the body. The cold has finally got to him. He can feel it in his bones. This isn't the first time he and Danny have investigated the discovery of suspected human remains. Once it turned out to be a Roman burial, another time a plague pit. This body is definitely not going to be fresh. So far as Fletcher knows, it has been twenty years or thereabouts since the superstore was built and the land under the deepest layers of tarmac was last dug.

"Could be the missing link," he says to Danny. It gets a laugh.

There's nothing much more to do until somebody can get out here to examine the bones and date them. Deciding how much of the car park to cordon off is probably the extent of it. Fletcher feels a wave of heartburn: hot tongues of stomach acid defying gravity just when the rest of his body's giving up that fight. He extracts a strip of antacid tablets from his trouser pocket. It's not easy. The wind nearly takes them. He chews three as he and Danny watch the men in high visibility jackets fetch a tarpaulin. The tablets taste unpleasantly of chalk dust with an overtone of spearmint.

"Do you know what?" Danny says. He's swiveling on his heel, looking around.

"What?" Fletcher replies.

The men struggle to spread the tarpaulin over the pit. Its edges flutter so violently it could have been caught on a line and dragged fresh from the sea, and before they can get it in place, a chunk of clay detaches stickily from the wall of the pit and falls.

"Wasn't it here that we found the boys?"

"Hold on!" Fletcher shouts. "Stop!"

Where the clay has dropped away, it has cleanly exposed more bone. Fletcher can see the curve of a skull. Eye sockets gape and it looks as though the bone of the forehead has caved in, or been staved in. He can also see what looks like the end of a large metal spanner. He would bet fifty quid it was buried with the bones, and he thinks there might be some sort of material matted on it. It's definitely not a Roman artifact.

"See that?"

He turns to catch Danny's reaction,

but Danny's puking a few feet away, bent double right behind the stand. The tips of long grasses obscure his head and tickle his ears. The heat intensifies the smell of his vomit.

"He's still alive!" Fletcher shouts. He tries to drag the heavy roll of carpet, wanting to move it, but not wanting to hurt the boy any more than he already is.

"Help me! For fuck's sake, Danny."

Danny comes, stumbling, wiping his mouth, still retching, and together they get the carpet off the lad who still has some rise and fall in his chest. Fletcher is sweating buckets into his brand-new suit. His wife brushed nonexistent dust off the lapels before he left this morning and admired the expensive cut of it, but the suit doesn't cross his mind as he kneels on the bloody dirt. Nothing does apart from this kid. It's too late for the other one. His body's motionless, without breath. His face is pulpy. That's what set Danny off.

Yards away, the stand at the dog track is deserted. It's Monday morning and there are only enough people in the stadium to fill a few tables at the bar terrace opposite. Three bookies have turned out, though, and set up in the morning sunshine, their black bags already full of notes. A sign says the minimum wager is two quid.

While they wait for the ambulance, a tractor skirts the track twice, smoothing the sand. Fletcher cradles the lad's head in his lap and carefully wipes his hair back from his forehead, avoiding the wounds. He takes one of the boy's small, soft hands in his own and tells him over and over again that he's all right now, that they've found him, that he's going to be okay, that he needs to hang in there, that help is on its way and it won't be long.

A leaning corrugated metal fence separates Fletcher and the boy from the back of the uncovered bleachers. The fence has gaps in it a slight man might be able to squeeze through. People have dumped rubbish here: building site rubble, bits of metal, furniture carcasses, cracked old tires with no tread, a mattress, and the carpet roll, all marooned in the corner of half an acre of unmade ground that otherwise resembles a moonscape. Here and there, Fletcher sees remnants of an old coating of asphalt: peeled-up pieces and sticky black clods oozing in the heat.

From the dog track a public address system plays a startlingly loud trumpet fanfare. Through a gap in the fence and the bleachers, Fletcher has a view of blue-coated handlers leading the dogs onto the track. Some of the men wear flat caps in spite of the heat, or maybe because of it. Fletcher wipes his brow. A gobbet of blood appears at the edge of the boy's mouth and drips down the side of his cheek. Fletcher wipes it away.

"No you don't," he says. "No, no. Hang in there, son."

There is such a struggle in the child's eyes. He retches and more blood appears. Fletcher gently pulls the kid further onto his lap and wraps his arms across him, willing some of his own vitality into the child, yet trying not to squeeze him too tightly. The track PA announces the names of the dogs that are ready to race. The words boom into the intense blue sky above Fletcher, and when they fade, he hears the whine of ambulance sirens from the overpass. Finally. Five minutes left to place your bets, the voice on the PA warns. The boy's eyelids flutter. Flying insects buzz and whine at an unbearable pitch.

"Come on, son!" Fletcher says. "Hang in there. Do it for me."

Danny has run back to their car. He sits in the passenger seat, door open, one leg out, foot on the ground. He's talking on the radio. His mouth is making the shapes of urgent words, but Fletcher can't hear them. He squints. Behind Danny the ambulance is circling down the exit ramp, lights flashing.

"Ambulance is here!" Fletcher roars at Danny. "Meet them at the gate. Bring them over here!" He and the boy are screened by a drift of California poppies growing amongst the rubbish. They're so fucking orange. A fly lands on the boy's nose and Fletcher waves it away. The boy blinks, too slowly. He attempts to speak, but his throat catches and his eyes fill with tears. He tries again and this time he rasps something.

"What did you say?" Fletcher asks.

With lips as parched as the boiled air, the boy's mouth forms a word, but a gargle from inside his throat distorts it.

"Ghost?" Fletcher asks. "Did you say ghost?"

From the track comes the sound of the gates crashing open and the dogs running. The commentary's a drone. In response to Fletcher's question there is only fear in the boy's eyes. He dies seven seconds later, as the dogs fly past on the other side of the stand. The speed of them: silky coats flashing by and clumps of sand kicked up behind.

The paramedics are only halfway across the asphalt when the boy dies. Running. Too late. The air shimmers behind them. It takes them a few minutes to persuade Fletcher to let go of the boy so they can ascertain for certain that their services aren't required.

Danny calls the coroner's office while Fletcher pukes.

IT'S TIME TO TELL

EPISODE 1—THREE DEATHS
AND AN ARTICLE

A DISHLICKER
PODCAST PRODUCTION

"You are listening to *It's Time to Tell,* a Dishlicker Podcast Production. This podcast contains material that might not be suitable for younger listeners. Your discretion is advised.

"Twenty years ago, two boys were brutally murdered, their bodies abandoned on wasteland. What happened to them remains a mystery to this day.

"Award-winning filmmaker Cody Swift, haunted by the murder of his two best friends, now returns to the Bristol estate he grew up on to find out if, for the people involved, it's time to tell."

My name is Cody Swift. I'm a filmmaker and your host of *It's Time to Tell,* a Dishlicker Podcast Production.

Two months ago, on 7 February 2017, a man called Sidney Noyce died in prison. The coroner ruled that Noyce took his own life. He made use of his bedsheets to form a noose. He tied one end to a bedpost and asphyxiated himself with the other.

On the day of his death, Sidney Noyce had been incarcerated for just over twenty years since his conviction for the brutal murder of my two best friends—eleven-year-old Scott Ashby and ten-year-old Charlie Paige—back in 1996.

Not everybody believed Sidney Noyce was guilty. Here's Owen Weston, a reporter who covered the original murder trial:

"Sidney Noyce was a bird in the hand for the police. Or a sitting duck. Take your pick. He had confessed to hurting the boys, but I for one questioned his guilt from the moment I saw him in court. Noyce had substandard intelligence. He didn't seem to know what was going on. For me, that was the first red flag, but there were others."

The police took a different view. This is Chief Constable David Tremain (who was a detective chief superintendent at the time) issuing a statement to the press on the day of Noyce's sentencing:

"This has been one of the most deeply harrowing and disturbing cases myself and my colleagues have worked on in all our years of service. Sidney Noyce's actions on the night of 18 August imposed a life sentence on the families of Charlie Paige and Scott Ashby, when he ended the boys' lives in cold blood. It is my sincere hope that Noyce's sentencing today will help the community to feel safeguarded and reassured going forward, though it can never bring the boys back and our thoughts remain with their families."

When the judge in the trial sentenced Noyce to life imprisonment, he said the following:

"The crime you committed was brutal and pointless. I am in no doubt that your mental difficulties have held you back in life, but I believe you well understand the difference between right and wrong. On 18 August Charlie Paige and Scott Ashby were out playing on a beautiful summer evening. They may have been on their way home to their families when they encountered you. You subjected both boys to a brutal beating, an ordeal that must have terrified them. Scott Ashby died that evening, but Charlie Paige remained alive overnight. His suffering must have been dreadful. The word *monstrous* seems inadequate when describing what you did."

Who to believe? Was Noyce a monster or did he have clean hands? During the twenty years Sidney Noyce spent in prison, he never stopped proclaiming his innocence. After Noyce died, Owen Weston published an article expressing his sadness and frustration and describing once again his long-held concerns about Noyce's conviction.

I came across the article by chance. I opened the newspaper one Sunday morning and there it was, illustrated with head shots of Scott and Charlie. Seeing their faces after all these years was like getting a punch in the gut. Reading the article gave me a similar feeling because twenty years ago my family and I were not aware that there was any possibility that Noyce could have been innocent. We were delighted by his arrest and his conviction. On the estate where we lived, the predominant feeling amongst the other families was relief that he had been taken off the streets. Kids began to be allowed to come out and play again after months of being kept in by nervous parents.

The thought that Noyce could be innocent overturned everything for me. I wondered how my family and neighbors and friends from back in the day would feel about it. I wondered if they would even want to know. It kept me up at night. Having avoided any mention of the case for all these years, I began to look into it. I contacted Owen Weston and spoke to other individuals involved in the original investigation, and a story emerged. It pulled me in.

As I got deeper into the research, I shared my findings with my girlfriend, Maya, a producer. "If you really can't get this out of your system," she said, "why don't you do something with it?" She mentioned a true crime podcast she'd been listening to. "It would be the perfect format for a story like this," she said. "And," she added, "isn't it possible that after all these years, if somebody who knew something about the murders that they didn't want to share at the time, perhaps because they were afraid, or overlooked, or because they didn't know it was useful, might they not feel that now could be the time to tell?"

So here we are. *It's Time to Tell* is my personal investigation into the murders of my best friends and this is how the story began for me.

It was the summer holidays of 1996. August 18 was a Sunday. I spent the afternoon getting up to mischief with my friends Charlie Paige and Scott Ashby on and around the estate where we lived. Charlie, like me, was ten. Scott had just turned eleven. In the late afternoon, we were hanging around the estate's play area. It was constructed from unwanted building materials that a local firm had donated and concreted into place. I remember a rusting climbing frame, a honeycomb arrangement of huge tires laid on their sides, and rough-edged concrete tubes in different sizes that you could crawl through if the urge took you. None of it would pass a modern health and safety inspection.

I had gone out earlier that day in a brand-new Atlanta Olympics T-shirt my uncle had sent me from the United States. It was my pride and joy. We didn't have much money, so most of my clothes were hand-me-downs from cousins or neighbors' kids, and a new item of clothing was something to show off. Mum told me that if I was going to wear it, I mustn't play in the concrete tubes. But I rarely did what my mother told me to do, so I did play in the tubes—it was the best place to smoke the cigarette butts I used to nick from my dad's ashtray. I remember how mesmerizing the smoke looked as it curled around the rough inside of the cylinder. By the time Mum called us in for tea at five, my T-shirt was ripped and filthy.

Mum fed me and Charlie and Scott jam sandwiches and squash. We were jostling one another in the doorway, getting our shoes on, desperate to head out to play again, when she noticed the rip in my T-shirt. I tried to cover up the damage and slip away, but she caught me by the arm, pulled me back into the flat, and made me take the shirt off. She grounded me as a punishment, and for the rest of that night I had to stay in our sweltering flat with her.

Charlie and Scott went out without me, into the evening where the tower blocks were throwing long, deep shadows across the estate and the sun was a sinking ember behind them. That was the last time I saw my friends, because they didn't come home that night or ever after. A rip in my T-shirt saved my life.

The following morning Charlie and Scott were found brutally bludgeoned beside a pile of rubbish on a bit of unkempt land behind the dog track. Scott was already dead. Charlie survived overnight, and lived for a few minutes after the police arrived—long enough to say just one word—but he died before the ambulance reached them.

The loss of my friends and my guilt that I survived is a darkness I've lived with since that night. I'm not the only one. Digging up the past for my research into this case has not been easy for me, or for some of the people I've been speaking to.

But—and this is a big *but*—if the reporter Owen Weston is correct and Sidney Noyce didn't kill my friends, then somebody needs to ask questions about that. And if Noyce didn't commit the murders, somebody must know who did. Charlie and Scott's killer went home bloody that night and had to live with what he or she had done in the days and weeks afterward. That kind of thing surely doesn't go unnoticed. Maybe now, twenty years on, keeping a secret like that will have burnt enough of a hole in that person's conscience that he or she will be ready to tell. Or perhaps circumstances have changed, and this person will feel able to speak up now without fear of reprisal. Loyalty is a slippery thing.

If that somebody is you and you are ready to talk, I am ready to listen, because those of us who were close to Charlie and Scott need to know what really happened. We need certainty and we need closure. It wasn't just the lives of two families who were shattered by these murders, it wasn't just their friends; it was an entire community, including Sidney Noyce and his family.

So if you're out there and you know something, please—for the sake of all of us who are still remembering, and still struggling with the darkness—it's time to tell.

J ess stops off at the supermarket on her way home from yoga. She heads directly to the bakery aisle and takes a few moments to select candles for Nick's birthday cake. She opts for one fat one instead of forty-six spindly ones. The packaging promises it will burn and sparkle like a firework. Nick will love it. Beneath his serious, hardworking front beats the heart of a big kid. Not many people know that, but it's one of the things Jess loves most about her husband. She believes Nick is a good man through and through.

Decision made, she cruises down the wine aisle and grabs a bottle of bubbly. She splurges on a brand Nick likes. At the end of the aisle, she spends a couple of minutes looking at magazines. Jess is a student of lifestyle. She selects her two favorite titles—one fashion, the other interiors—and puts both in her trolley. She will spend hours poring over them later. She and Nick don't have lots of money, but there's enough to make them and their home look nice if she budgets carefully.

Jess checks her watch and hums as she makes her way toward the checkout: plenty of time to get home and get everything ready for Nick's return. She feels relaxed. It's a good day.

She notices the newspaper headline when she's waiting in line to pay. She snatches the local rag from the shelf above the conveyor belt and tries to read it, but she doesn't have her reading glasses with her and the small print is a blur. The headline is not. It's crystal clear.

LOCAL BOY CODY SWIFT RETURNS TO BRISTOL TO INVESTIGATE DOUBLE MURDER OF BEST FRIENDS

Head shots of the victims are printed below, side by side. They appear slightly out of focus to Jess, just as the small print does, but she doesn't need her glasses to recall every detail of these faces as if she last saw them yesterday, because the boys in the photographs are her son, Charlie, and his best friend, Scott. They are the same pictures that were plastered across the front pages of the local and national papers in the weeks after their murders and during the trial, twenty years ago. They are bland school photographs and the boys have the flattened, startled expressions of the flash-lit. Both wear red school sweat shirts, and somebody, the school nurse perhaps, must have brushed their hair roughly and forced it into an unfamiliar parting seconds before the pictures were taken.

This is it, Jess thinks: *game over.* Over the past twenty years, she has learned to organize the different stages of her life into distinct strata: the lonely childhood full of foster families she can barely remember; then what she thinks of as the dirty years before and after Charlie was born; after that, the desolate ones following his murder, a time that brimmed with anger and self-destruction until she met endlessly kind and patient Nick, who coaxed her onto a path toward sanity; and now. Now is good and wholesome. It has been like this ever since she learned to trust Nick, and it has only got better since Erica was born. It has been so good, in fact, that it might be perfect if it hadn't been for Jess's guilt about what happened all those years ago.

Jess's hands begin to shake and the paper trembles. Cody Swift has lit a stick of dynamite that could blow everything in her life to smithereens. She knows already that his podcast could be a new and dark dawn in her life.

She ignores the man behind her who is nudging her trolley with his and asking if it belongs to her. She leaves the things she has carefully selected in the bottom of it and hands just the newspaper to the cashier. The cashier talks to Jess, but Jess doesn't reply. She grabs the paper and her change and hurries back to her car.

When she gets home, Jess goes straight to the computer in the office she shares with Nick, scooping up her glasses on the way. She studies the newspaper article in detail and discovers there's not much more information to be found online, only a short CV for Cody—it's impressive, who knew he'd do that well for himself?—and a brief recap of the case. Of course, there's not a single detail Jess is not already aware of. Her stomach plunges as she reads.

Jess gets up and crosses the hallway to her daughter's room. Erica's belongings are scattered on the floor, her bed is a rumpled mess, and there's not an inch of surface space to be seen on her desk or dressing table. Her bulletin board is a lovingly curated montage of every good time Erica has ever had. Jess sits on Erica's bed and picks up a pillow. She holds it tightly to her chest and the pressure releases the sweet smell of her daughter. Sunshine peeks through the shutter slats, casting lines of shadow across the room. *Erica is my everything,* she thinks. *She and Nick are my whole world.*

Jess doesn't want Nick to find out about the podcast because he'll go mad. He considers himself her protector. He knows about Charlie, because he has known Jess almost forever.

Nick and Jess met in the darkest times after Charlie's murder. He literally picked her up off the street one night, about a year after Charlie's death. She had fallen off a curb, dead drunk. She had a black eye and a broken wrist. Nick didn't care. He said he saw something in her, even in that moment, and he took her to the hospital and stayed with her that night and afterward, fighting tooth and nail first to persuade her to trust him enough to let him be part of her life. If it hadn't been for Nick, she doesn't know where she would be now. Dead probably. Maybe. Either by her own hand or somebody else's. She had sunk that low.

There is not just Nick to consider, but Erica, too. She doesn't know about Charlie. Back in the late 1990s when the murders happened, the internet was too new to be a widely used news source. When the media lashed out at Jess at the time of the murders, and again later, when she was in the public eye, they did it in print. News one day, fish-and-chip paper the next. Jess has relied on this to hide her past from her daughter.

Years ago Jess flirted with telling Erica the truth, but when is a good time to tell your beloved daughter that her half brother was murdered and that you were accused of negligence in the aftermath? Never. So Jess has kept her past packed away and clung to Nick's mantra, which is that loving and raising Erica to a gold standard represents the chance for Jess to put things behind her and create something good.

Jess forces herself to stop remembering. The guilt her memories induce takes many forms, but it is consistently powerful enough to make her feel as if she has a mouthful of ashes. It can cause her to retch. It is complicated and exhausting. She glances at the clock on Erica's bedside table. *Pull yourself together,* she thinks. She has two hours until Nick gets home. He's been working away for a few weeks. His favorite stew has been simmering in the oven since this morning. They'll have to do without the bottle of fizz she abandoned in the supermarket trolley. Never mind. She's got some red wine they can share instead.

She takes herself downstairs and lays the table. She concentrates on the task to block Cody Swift and the article out of her mind. She has learned over the years how to anesthetize her emotions with practical activity, especially with creating a home. She gets out the good silverware, linen napkins, napkin holders, best candlesticks, and wine bottle holder. There is a vase of fresh flowers on the mantelpiece. She arranged them this morning. She loves flowers. Except for poppies. Never poppies. Not even red or white ones. In the days after Charlie's murder, she visited the spot where his body was found. She saw the bank of orange poppies that marked the spot where he died and knew the brightness and vigor of their wafer-thin petals would haunt her forever.

In the kitchen, she takes a chocolate mousse cake out of the fridge and decants it from the box it came in onto a glass plate with a gold rim. She remembers she also left the spectacular candle in the trolley at the supermarket and feels disappointed. Luckily, the pâtisserie she ordered the cake from has done some lovely writing on the top. It reads *Happy birthday, Nick,* with all sorts of curlicues and fancy italics. It'll have to do.

She puts the cake back in the fridge and thinks it's a shame Erica isn't able to be with them on Nick's birthday, but the plan is to celebrate again on the night she returns from her school trip. They'll have a special meal out. Even though it's Nick's birthday celebration, he let Erica choose the restaurant, so it's going to be nachos and mocktails all the way— the more straws, umbrellas, and colors in the drinks, the better.

Upstairs, Jess dithers over her outfit. She wants to look right. Like her guilt, this impulse to please has traveled with her for the past twenty years. She lays out a simple, pretty shift dress and a pair of silver ballet flats. She showers and expertly puts together her hair and makeup at her dressing table. A fresh look is what she's after.

Brand-new underwear goes on: matching and silky. If Erica's not home, Nick sometimes wants to get cozy almost as soon as he's stepped in the door. Jess doesn't mind because it probably means he's kept it in his pants while he's been on set; she understands the temptations of that world better than most. She also doesn't mind because she has missed him sorely while he's been away. In Jess's world, you can be both a pragmatist and a romantic.

She jumps when she hears the double hoot of Nick's car horn. He's early. Her shoes clatter as she trots down the stairs. She opens the front door and stands framed in the doorway, offering him a side view of the slender curves she works hard to maintain. She places one foot in front of the other and hikes her chin up. "Hello, darling," she says.

"You're a sight for sore eyes." He always says that; bless him.

He gets his duffel off the back seat of the car. He looks tired. He's been away all week: fourteen-hour days minimum. It's the way it is on set. He's a first assistant director. They work like beasts. He hugs her and plants a kiss on her lips, but no wandering hands this time.

"I filled up on the M32," he says. It's a petrol station that's only a couple of miles away, and she thinks, *Oh, crap,* because she suspects she knows where this is going.

"Have you seen this?" He gets the local newspaper off the passenger seat and holds it up to show her the article about Cody, the podcast, and the murders.

"I'm not going to talk to Cody Swift. He's not getting a single word out of me." She says it tough as old leather, like she would if she was playing a mob wife, and Nick nods, but a sob escapes her. "Charlie," she says. Spoken aloud, there's no other word that can make her feel as raw as this one. She loses herself in Nick's chest and arms. She feels heat, a heartbeat, and takes comfort from the firm pressure of his embrace.

Later, she pulls herself together and he tells her more than once how much he loves his birthday meal. She holds his hand across the table and keeps her real feelings behind her smile as she proposes a toast: "Happy birthday, darling. Here's to being another year younger!"

The sign on the door says WET LAB.

Fletcher didn't have to come here in person, but he likes to see things for himself. Back in the day, it was a tactic that helped fast-track him up the ranks.

Dr. Mary Hayward, senior forensic pathologist, is waiting for Fletcher in the lab. Her red hair is on the turn to gray, but her clear green eyes pack a punch that Fletcher feels somewhere in his stomach, just like he did the first day he met her. She wears pearl earrings and red lipstick, and her eyes are rimmed lightly in black. She appears to have grown even more groomed, glossy, and successful over the years, while Fletcher feels as if he has been incrementally fraying at the seams.

"Mary," he says.

"John." They shake hands and her cheeks dimple as she smiles.

"Amazingly, we've got a full set of bones," she says. "Shall we?"

She pulls on a pair of plastic gloves and they move to a table where the bones found in the car park have been laid out on a thin foam sheet. The bones have been cleaned and reassembled into a two-dimensional skeleton. At the head of the table the skull rests upright, supported by a white ring that reminds Fletcher of a vicar's dog collar. Mary picks the skull up carefully. Fletcher's always liked that about her: the way she has respect for the dead.

"There's obvious trauma to the skull," she says.

This confirms what Fletcher thought he noticed in the car park. She swivels the skull so he can get a close view. The front looks to have been caved in with a single deep blow. The bone surrounding the fissure is riddled with hairline cracks as if it were no more robust than wall plaster.

"Somebody took a good swing at him," Fletcher says.

"It's consistent with a blow from the spanner that was found with him."

"Anything else?" To Fletcher, most of the bones on the table look like old brown sticks, but he knows Mary will have found clues to the identity and lifestyle of this person in every piece.

She talks him through it. "He's male. Approximately forty to fifty years old at time of death and approximately six feet tall. Large frame. Caucasian. Historical fracture to his tibia and collarbone, probably sustained in childhood."

"Do you know when he died?"

"We're working on it."

"It'll be before 1997," Fletcher says. "The car park he was found under was dug up and relaid then."

"So I gather. We also have some scraps of clothing and footwear remnants. They'll help."

"At a guess?"

"You know I don't guess."

He nods. He knows. Mary places the skull back onto its foam ring. "There is one thing you might like," she says. She hands him a small object in an evidence bag. Fletcher holds it up to the window. The object glints dully through the plastic.

"A signet ring," he says. "What's engraved on it?"

"Initials," she says. "And a four-leaf clover."

"A four-leaf clover?"

"Looks like it."

They both allow themselves to smirk. They share a love of gallows humor.

"Not so lucky, then," Fletcher says. One of them had to.

"The initials are *PD*," Mary says. "Obviously, we'll run his DNA, but they might help you get you an ID sooner."

Fletcher feels hopeful. He'll input details of the ring into the missing persons database when he gets back to the office and see if it throws up a link to anybody.

Mary strips off her gloves and bins them. "I heard about Jane," Mary says. "I'm sorry."

The comment takes Fletcher by surprise because he likes to keep his private life private, and it pains him to think that the recent breakdown of his marriage might have become the subject of gossip. He manages a response. "Happens to the best of us."

His reply acknowledges that he knows Mary's marriage has also ended. Fletcher could say more, and knows he probably should, but he's reached his limit on personal talk, so he changes the subject.

"Do you remember the boys who were murdered by the dog track?"

Mary nods. "Difficult to forget that one."

"We found this guy a hop and a skip from there."

She raises an eyebrow. They both know better than to read

anything into the coincidence, yet also realize that it should be kept in mind.

"And weirdly, something else happened related to that case . . ."

Lately, Fletcher has developed a habit of giving up on what he's saying in the middle of a sentence. It's usually because something has occurred to him. Mary prompts him. "Enlighten me."

"I had a phone call at the end of last week from a man who said he was called Cody Swift."

The name is a challenge to her powers of recollection, but Fletcher knows Mary has a superb memory for detail, and sure enough, it takes her only a moment to place the name.

"He was the best friend of the victims."

"Exactly."

"What did he want?"

"He's come back to Bristol to do an investigation of his own into the case."

"An investigation of his own?"

Fletcher shrugs.

"What did he want from you?" Mary asks.

"Cooperation. Information."

"But you can't share anything."

"I told him that. And I told him what he's doing is going to upset a lot of people. With consequences, potentially."

"Why's he doing it? Why now?"

"He wants closure." Fletcher understands that a longing for closure can become a noose that cannot easily be lifted from the necks of the victims' families.

She exhales audibly. "Closure. Wow. Good luck to him. But I think it's a Pandora's box. He's crazy."

"He says he's going to speak to Howard Smail."

"Smail won't talk."

"That's what I told him, but Swift said he'd already approached him and got an encouraging response."

"Do you believe him?"

"No."

"Me neither."

"But never say never."

Mary pauses before she says, "Well, shit."

Fletcher doesn't think he's heard Mary swear before, but if ever there was a reason to, it's the possibility that disgraced ex–Detective Superintendent Howard Smail might be spilling the beans in public about this case. Mary is still shaking her head in disbelief as they move out of the lab and into her office next door. "Coffee?" she asks.

Fletcher accepts because he always does, though when she turns her back on him to prepare it, he grimaces in anticipation of the fact that she won't add sugar. He didn't have the courage to ask for it when he first met her, twenty years ago, and now it's way too late to correct that mistake.

"Get Detective Inspector Fletcher a coffee, will you, Mary," the senior forensic pathologist says. She glowers at him and Fletcher badly wants to say, "No, it's okay, I'm fine, I've changed my mind," but the truth is, he's asked for a coffee to delay having to enter the room where the autopsies are conducted. He's witnessed autopsies before, but this time it's different because the child died in his own arms.

"Are you asking me because I'm a woman?" Mary replies. She's already partway into getting gowned up. Lab technicians are moving purposefully around the autopsy room behind them. Through the

windows set into the door, Fletcher can see one of them preparing equipment and the other rolling a gurney over to the bank of numbered refrigerators to retrieve the second body. The first lies under a shroud on one of the tables.

"I'm asking you because you're the most junior person in the room," the senior pathologist tells her. He's devoid of charm and humor and known to be a misogynist. Mary Hayward's got her work cut out with him as her boss, Fletcher thinks.

She exudes a quiet fury as she marches down the corridor to a room where a hot water tap dispenses scorching steam into a mug. When it's full, she dumps two scoops of instant coffee and a teaspoon into it and hands it to him ungraciously. She watches as he blows the liquid cautiously and takes a sip because he feels obliged to show gratitude. It scalds his mouth. He wants to ask her if there's any sugar, but he doesn't dare.

"Drink up," she says. "We're about to start. Excuse me, please."

He shuffles aside and follows her out of the kitchenette and down the corridor. "Sorry," he says as he struggles to keep pace with her. "I could have got this myself."

"Well, why would you do that when there's somebody in a skirt to do it for you? I'll see you in there."

He is about to follow her through a set of doors that lead back toward the autopsy room when she points to a sign on the wall that says NO HOT DRINKS. He looks around for somewhere to dump the coffee. A potted plant that seems as if it's already leading a dismal life does the trick. He empties the liquid out and lodges the mug into the steaming soil before following her through the double doors.

The mood's grim in the autopsy room. Sometimes there's a bit of banter between the pathologists, their assistants, and the technicians, but not today. The bodies of the two murdered boys are laid out on tables set at right angles to each other. Nobody's expecting any other result than confirmation that the boys died of the brutal beating they received.

Fletcher volunteered to be here because he wants to be part of every stage of the boys' journey until whoever did this is brought to justice. The sight of the bodies on the tables stokes the fire that their discovery lit in him yesterday. He's only a year out of Bramshill—the police training college—and already a detective inspector. He didn't earn a fast-track promotion by sitting around scratching his ass. He's known to get results. He doesn't know the meaning of working hours. He lives the job.

It feels crowded in the room. It helps him cope. The pathologists and their assistants move methodically around the bodies as they work in a well-rehearsed choreography. They periodically obscure the boys' bodies from Fletcher's view. He's able to breathe relatively normally only when that happens. Otherwise, he's mostly holding his breath.

He experiences the autopsies as a collection of unpleasant sensations: the rasp of the pathologist's scissors as they cut through skin and the more businesslike sound of the clippers that they use to tackle the small rib cages; metal trays and implements clashing and water gushing. There's blood. One of the taps squeaks as it's turned on and off. The pathologists record their findings verbally in an incantation of technical jargon that partly alleviates the violence of the examinations, but not enough. Fletcher can't keep his eyes fixed on anything that's happening on the tables. He tries to because he doesn't want to lose face, but his gaze flutters away and settles anywhere else: the drainage channels set into the floor, the stained grouting, the pale white shins of Dr. Mary Howard, reluctant maker of coffee, who's assisting at the table where they're working on the boy Fletcher now knows is called Charlie Paige. The boy who died in Fletcher's arms.

By the time the pathologist working on Charlie confirms that from an initial inspection the child does appear to have died as a result of his head injuries, Fletcher's on the point of having to bolt, wondering if the potted plant on the other side of the door will accommodate the contents of his stomach as well as his coffee. He is pathetically grateful when a lab administrator beckons him out of the room.

In the corridor a man leans against the wall. He's tall, sinewy, and dapper. Fletcher draws in breath sharply and hopes the intense nausea he's been feeling doesn't show on his face. He respects this man.

Detective Superintendent Howard Smail is talking on a mobile phone. They haven't been issued at Fletcher's rank, but the top dogs have them. Smail finishes the call promptly when he sees Fletcher and says, "Take a walk with me."

They step outside. It's only 6:30 A.M. The boys' autopsies have been fitted in before the scheduled ones. The hot weather broke overnight. Thunder and rain rattled the city during the dark hours, and although the storm has moved on, the air still feels heavy and oppressive. Since Fletcher's been in the autopsy room, a thin band of light has broken the night's darkness beyond the hospital car park, but it is feebly pale and only just bright enough to describe the turbulent clouds overhead. Fletcher watches Smail carefully, wondering what he wants. It's unusual for somebody of his seniority to attend an autopsy.

"Brutal in there?" Smail asks. His crisp features are tempered by a profusion of deeply pitted acne scars spread across both cheeks.

Fletcher nods.

"I'll be working this case as senior investigating officer," Smail says.

Fletcher is not surprised. This is going to be a high-profile case: a Category A murder investigation, the most serious kind. He figures he's about to be sent on his way, but Smail says, "I'd like you to join me on the case as my deputy. I've heard very good things about your work."

Fletcher tries not to let his surprise show. There are officers with years more of service whom you would have put your money on to get the role. His nausea and fatigue vanish instantly, replaced by a feeling of triumph.

"Thank you, sir. I'm delighted to have the opportunity. It goes without saying that I'll do my very best. Thank you." I've arrived, he thinks. A drop of rain hits the concrete pathway they're standing on.

"The murder of a child is the hardest sort of case," Smail tells him, as if Fletcher didn't already know it, as if that child hadn't died in his arms.

"I understand, sir," he says.

"When a kid gets murdered, it's never just about one life. It's about everybody. It hits people at their core. It makes every aspect of life feel unsafe. Until I catch who did this, it's going to feel as if the bogeyman has moved in with every family on that estate, and probably in the rest of this city, too."

"Yes, sir."

"My investigation will not stop until we find who did this. It will be meticulous; we will leave no stone unturned. All my men are going to live this until we solve it." Smail has intense blue eyes. Fletcher feels as if he's being pinned against a wall by the other man's gaze.

"Yes, sir!" he agrees, though it bothers him that Smail is referring to the case as my investigation and referring to the team as my men. Most officers use the terms we and us, Fletcher included.

"Get back to the station and do what you have to do so you can make an immediate start on this. I'll speak to the pathologist and join you there. I'll be working on selecting the rest of my team."

"What about DC Fryer?"

"Danny Fryer?"

"He was with me when we found the bodies. He's a good detective, sir."

"If you say so, that's enough for me, but everybody on my team must pull their weight. No exceptions."

"Understood. Thank you, sir."

After they part, Fletcher feels good about getting Danny on the team. He's always looked out for Danny Fryer. They've been friends since school. They have a strong bond. Fletcher plans to have a word with Danny as soon as he gets to the office. He'll warn Danny that Smail seems to be a stickler and tell him now is the time to put his best foot forward.

Fletcher finds his car and begins the drive to Southmead Police Station, where the Criminal Investigations Department is based on a small campus of redbrick buildings that are no longer fit for the purpose. As he cuts into the city traffic, still light because of the early hour, his hands tighten around the steering wheel. For the first time in his professional life, he has landed in the arena where the big boys fight, and if he knows one thing, it's that he's ready to prove himself.

IT'S TIME TO TELL

EPISODE 2—HOME, BUT NOT HOME

A DISHLICKER
PODCAST PRODUCTION

"Good morning. It's seven o'clock on Monday, 19 August. The headlines. Police were called last night to the Glenfrome Estate in Eastville, where two boys, ten-year-old Charlie Paige and eleven-year-old Scott Ashby, have gone missing. The boys were last seen at around eight P.M. walking down Primrose Lane on the estate. Police and residents have been searching through the night to find them. Our reporter, Joshua Ankers, is at the scene."

"*Good morning. The Glenfrome Estate has had its share of troubles over the years as residents and local police have not always seen eye to eye, but this morning, scenes here tell a story of cooperation. Residents and police have been working together throughout the night to search for missing boys Charlie Paige and Scott Ashby, who we believe were last seen walking down this lane at around eight P.M. yesterday evening. Police are issuing an urgent appeal to the public for anybody who might have seen the boys, or know of their whereabouts, to come forward.*"

My name is Cody Swift. I'm a filmmaker and your host of *It's Time to Tell*, a Dishlicker Podcast Production. What you just heard was a clip from the BBC's local news service on the morning of

Monday, 19 August, around seven and a half hours after my friends Charlie and Scott were reported missing.

I have a question for you: what does *going home* mean to you? And by that, I don't mean the home you've built for yourself or found yourself in since you've become an adult. I mean your childhood home. Was it a refuge? A sweet, safe place where you felt loved? Or was it a place of uncertainty or even fear? Whichever it was, there are doubtless a whole host of complicated memories you have to deal with whenever you return.

I'm standing in front of a small bungalow in a suburban area of Bristol I'm not very familiar with. Most of the properties on this street are occupied by elderly people. It's where you might choose to spend your twilight years if you want a manageable property, a driveway to wash your car on, and a patch of lawn to tend out front. It's peaceful. Under my feet is a green mat swarming with plastic tendrils. It has the word *Welcome* picked out on it in white. As I wait for the door to be answered, I'm being watched by three small ceramic garden gnomes painted in garish colors. They're pretty creepy.

After I went away to college, my parents moved here from the Glenfrome Estate, the place I was born in and grew up in, and where the murders happened. This compact, tidy space is my family home now, even though I've never lived here. Even so, whenever I visit, my parents and all of their familiar belongings exert a strange bittersweet pull on me, tugging me back to the past. I'm home, but not home.

"Come on in, my love. Tea? Coffee? Down, Muffy!"

That's my mum talking and it's Muffy you can hear barking. Muffy is a little white fluffy dog that is about as big as my shoe.

She doesn't like me. Mum settles the dog and makes tea. We sit by a window through which we have a view of an immaculate back garden. There's a many-tiered fountain constructed out of shiny bowls and smooth pebbles, and flowerbeds packed with shrubs and bulbs. The plot is enclosed by a shoulder-height wooden fence, and the neighbors' properties are close by.

My dad, Ted, had a stroke a few years back and my mum is his full-time carer. He's sitting with us, but he struggles to move and talk.

I start by asking Mum why they moved away from the estate, to live here, ten years ago.

"I don't know why we didn't do it earlier. The estate was never the same after the murders. Even though they put that Noyce fellow away for it, the place felt different afterward, sort of unhealthy. Before the murders, you felt like it was a place you could raise a family. It wasn't perfect, I'm not saying that, there were problems, but people did look out for each other. You could have a decent life there."

I want to talk to Mum about the murders because she knew most of the people involved as well or much better than I did, and I'm curious to know what she remembers and how she feels about it. This will be the first time we've discussed the murders since I've become an adult.

I ask Mum to start by telling me about the day it happened.

"It was a Sunday, and it was such a hot day. You'll remember that. Hot enough so as you'd stick to the chair if you sat down for too long and your blood felt like sludge in your veins. Morning time, we had bacon butties for breakfast because your dad got paid on the Friday."

My dad's head shifts slightly. It is the best he can do to nod his acknowledgment of what she's saying. Mum reaches out to pat his arm before continuing.

"Scott and Charlie called round after lunchtime, and you went off with them, and I said, 'If you're going to wear that T-shirt, don't go hanging around that playground,' but of course that's exactly where you went, trust you. I stayed home, up to my arms in strawberries because your dad brought home a crate from the market the night before. Do you remember, Ted? You got them for a quid because they were on the turn, but it started to rain when you were bringing them home and all that red juice leaked out the bottom of the crate and down your trousers. It looked like blood. You didn't even notice until you got home. We laughed about that, how it made you look like a bloody serial killer, but of course it didn't seem so funny later."

Scott and Charlie's injuries were horrendous. They were so brutal that I won't be describing them in detail on air. As a kid, I wasn't aware of this. The adults kept that information from me for as long as possible. Mum continues:

"I spent the afternoon making jam and thinking that only a fool would be doing that on such a hot day, but the strawberries would have spoiled if I didn't. Your dad went down the club for a snooker game in the afternoon. You and Charlie and Scott came back to the flat at five after I called you in. I made you some sandwiches . . . Sorry, love, this is hard. Anyway, after you had your tea, I saw that rip in your T-shirt when the three of you were putting your shoes on to go back out. You were trying to hide it, but you weren't doing a very good job. I felt so cross with you about ripping it, I didn't let you go back out with Scott and Charlie. I thank God for that every day."

These are difficult memories for both me and for Mum. She dabs at her eyes with a lace-edged handkerchief and fingers a small gold cross hanging on a narrow chain around her neck. She's been a churchgoer all her life, though she struggled to persuade Dad or me to join her. Dad agreed to a church wedding only on condition he never had to set foot in the place again.

"We watched television that night, do you remember? It was too hot to do anything else. I remember we had the door onto the balcony open and all the windows, but it was still baking inside. I wanted you to help me with my crossword puzzles because you were good with words, but you wouldn't answer when I read out the clues because you were cross with me for grounding you. I remember the cat was trying to catch flies in the window and there were hot air balloons in the sky because it was the balloon festival that weekend. Your dad got home just after dark—just before ten, I think it was. He sent you to bed and me and him weren't sat there long before the phone rang. It was Annette."

Mum is referring to Annette Ashby, Scott's mother. Annette was one of Mum's best friends on the estate. As I was listening to Mum, it occurred to me that memory is a funny thing. I remember some of the things she mentions, but not all of them. I don't remember the cat or the crossword puzzles. I do remember feeling hard done by because I was stuck inside with her. I remember the estate dogs barking at dusk like they always did and the lights coming on in the building opposite. I remember the sounds of other people's TVs and the smell of barbecue. I don't remember the phone call. I fell asleep to a small, noisy fan in my bedroom. It drowned out the noise of the phone.

"Your dad answered, and he passed the phone to me. Annette asked had we seen Scott or Charlie at all. I said no, not for hours. I asked her why. She said they hadn't come home yet. She said Jessy was supposed to be looking after the boys, taking them to the lido over at Portishead or something, but she wasn't answering her phone and there was nobody at her flat. Annette thought you'd been with them, too, but I explained that I kept you in."

The Jessy whom my mum is referring to is Jessica Paige, Charlie's mother. She married later in life and took her husband's name, so she's called Jessica Guttridge now, but for the purposes of the podcast we're going to refer to her as Jessica Paige, to avoid confusion. You'll hear more about her in Episode 3. Here's Mum again:

"Annette told me she convinced herself not to worry at first when they were late, because Jessy was a really bad time-keeper, but she was panicking by then. 'It's Sunday night,' she kept saying. 'Where could they be this late on Sunday night?' My heart started going like the clappers when I realized it was over an hour since they were supposed to be home."

It had been Annette's specific understanding that Scott would be back home before it got dark. Scott and Charlie had assured her they would be when they left her house at lunchtime. At that point, there had been a plan for Charlie's mother to take them for a swim at the lido. I had known about it, too. Jessy's boyfriend was supposed to be driving us, but the swimming plan went nowhere. To our disappointment it fell through in the early afternoon before I even mentioned it to my mum. It fell through because Jessy and her boyfriend realized they needed to be elsewhere. Nobody told Annette.

On 18 August 1996, in Bristol, dusk was officially recorded as being at 9:01 P.M., so by the time she phoned Mum, Annette's anxiety had been mounting for a while. Mum and Annette went out into the estate to look for the boys. Nobody they talked to had seen Scott or Charlie since around eight, when a neighbor said she'd spotted them walking down a path in the estate. The neighbor had assumed they were on their way home. She hadn't spoken to them. That was the first clue Annette had that the lido plan had gone awry.

Here's Mum again:

"When we realized they probably hadn't gone to the lido we started to get really worried. We searched in all the places we could think of, and then we went back to Annette's and phoned everybody we knew—and I mean *everybody*. We kept phoning Jessy's flat, but no answer. Your dad went back round Jessy's flat as well, didn't you, Ted? He came with us the second time we went."

Another partial nod from my dad. He croaks something. I find it hard to understand him nowadays, but Mum can interpret.

"Nobody was in. That's right. We were getting proper worried because it was gone eleven by then, but as we got back outside, we saw a taxi pull up. Nobody said anything, but we was all thinking the same thing: this'll be them and we're going to feel like silly buggers for running around the place and waking everybody up looking for them. I was all ready to give Jessy Paige an earful for making us worry like that, but when she got out of the taxi, the awful thing was that she was alone. And I tell you, if my heart was going like the clappers before, it felt like it stopped at that moment. Annette gripped me so hard there was a bruise there the next day, and you had to support her, didn't you, Ted? She collapsed."

I can imagine this scene. The estate at night could be a scary place. Nighttime was when you suddenly became aware of the empty properties and the great stretches of darkness between the towers. The brightest communal lights hung above the main entrance to each tower block, but even they didn't cast much more than a halfhearted glow about the place, as if they were underpowered or exhausted. I can imagine my mum, my dad, and Annette Ashby standing under one of these, the tops of their heads and shoulders glowing, their shadows pooled underfoot. I can imagine them watching the taxi disgorge Jessy Paige in front of her building, the noise of the slamming car door echoing between the buildings and the sound of its tires as it accelerated away swiftly, the way taxis always did after dark.

"Jessy didn't see us at first. She was hardly able to stand upright. She vomited. She had sick on her face and hair. Annette ran over to her and went mad. She was shaking Jessy, shouting at her, even though Jessy was all floppy. Annette's asking 'Where are the boys? Where's Scott and Charlie?' The state of Jessy, though, she was so drunk or drugged we couldn't tell which. It was awful. Do you remember, Ted? Once we got a few words out of Jessy, it turned out she hadn't taken the boys anywhere. She thought they were with us or Annette. We called the police then, Annette did, and we pulled people from their beds to help search. By the time it got to midnight, the crowd had grown and loads of people on the estate was searching around the place, walking the paths, checking the stairwells, and calling for Scott and Charlie. It was so hot, everybody who was awake was asking out their windows 'What's going on?' So we told them and word kept spreading. Lots of people came out to search, but there was no sign of Scott and Charlie. It was like they'd disappeared off the face of the earth."

I interrupt to ask a question. It has become quite dark in the house now, but none of us has bothered to turn on the lights. The dog is asleep on Mum's lap. This is a question I have been nervous to ask. There is something I want to know because it has preyed on my mind over all the years since Charlie and Scott were murdered. I'm not nervous because I think Mum might be angry, but because it's a question she has probably asked herself many times, too. It's a what-if question, and they often come with regrets.

"Why didn't you wake me up and ask me where Charlie and Scott might have been?"

Mum strokes the dog for a moment or two before responding. Then she sighs.

"Love, I wish we had. I don't know why we didn't. I suppose we got caught up in the search, and all the panic. How I wish we had, though—I do wish that. Every time I think about it."

If they had asked me, at least one of my friends might have survived, because I would have told them to search by the track. It was one of the places we hung out, even though we weren't supposed to. Instead, my parents left me sleeping and got a neighbor's daughter to babysit while they went out searching.

Mum picks up the story again.

"We searched all night. It was about eleven the next morning when they found Scott and Charlie. All that searching, but nobody thought to go around the back of the dog track until then. Them two detectives found them. They tried to save Charlie, but Scott was already dead. That was when all hell broke loose."

She makes a minute adjustment to a coaster that's on the polished table beside her. She turns on a reading lamp, and the bulb is reflected in the film of tears on each of her eyes. As I prepare to leave, Mum says she has a question for me.

"Have you thought about what you're doing, digging up the past? People might not like it. They might have learned to live with their feelings by now, but the feelings haven't gone away. They never will. Be careful what you stir up."

I've thought a lot about this, about the pros and cons of revisiting something so painful after all these years. But the conclusion I came to is this: isn't it better, always, to have answers? Mum and I are going to have to agree to disagree on this one.

As I'm leaving, Mum hands me something.

"It's the last photograph I've got of the three of you to-gether. Your dad took it the week before the murders. I never gave this to the press, even when they came banging on the door asking for photos and stories, offering money. It felt wrong. I wanted you to have it when you were ready, but I forgot about it over the years, until now."

The photograph shows me, Charlie, and Scott sitting on one of the concrete cylinders that I was forbidden to play inside. Behind us, you can see the back end of an ice cream van. We are sit-ting shoulder-to-shoulder and each of us is holding a 99 Flake ice cream. Charlie is holding up his cone, pretending it's the Olympic torch, and the chocolate flake is hanging out of the edge of his ear-to-ear grin. It's typical Charlie. He looks like a mob boss who just heard some good news.

I find the photograph very moving. We were the best of friends. It reminds me in the strongest possible way why I should pack away any moments of doubt about pursuing this investigation because Charlie and Scott deserve the truth.

The photograph reminds me of something else, too. It reminds me of the title of this episode. After the violence of my best friends' murders, my home never felt the same again. Not the estate, not our community, not the families we knew, not the flat, not any-thing. The violence of the crime ripped everything apart. It was home, but not home.

Thanks so much for listening to *It's Time to Tell*. In the next episode, we're going to meet two very important people, both of whom lost a son on the night of 18 August 1996. Here's Annette Ashby, Scott's mother, who'll be talking more next week:

"We let you boys run around the estate that summer and all the summers before it because life felt more innocent back then. We believed we knew our community and you boys were brought up to be streetwise. More fool us. The next time I saw Scott was at the morgue."

On the evening Erica is due back from her school English trip to London, Jess and Nick go to collect her. Nick has a new job lined up, but shooting doesn't start for a few days. He and Jess have been trying to relax after the shock of the news about Cody Swift and his podcast. They have gone about their normal routines and tried to enjoy Nick's downtime. They have been out to breakfast together and shopping. Jess has cooked something nice for them every night. The house feels empty without Erica.

So far Cody Swift hasn't tried to contact Jess. She and Nick have decided not to listen to the podcast and not to mention it to Erica. They're hoping it'll stay under her radar. Nick has looked the podcast up on iTunes and seen that it has fewer than fifty subscribers. It feels like less of a threat than it did at first, but since she became aware of it, Jess's nights have involved bad dreams interspersed with violent awakenings in which she finds herself gasping for air, as if she were being throttled.

When they arrive at the school to collect Erica, Jess and Nick join a group of parents waiting at the gates. Erica looks to be in fine form when she emerges from the coach. She drags her bag and assorted items she's failed to fit into it. Once she's navigated her way through the throng of kids, she drops everything and throws herself into Nick's arms first. *That's my girl,* Jess thinks, and her heart fills.

Erica is a bundle of energy; she wears every emotion on her sleeve. She is Jess's greatest achievement. She is also a daily reminder of the child Jess failed to keep alive, which means that on a bad day Jess feels unworthy of having her. *Who,* she thinks as she watches Nick and Erica embrace, *deserves the daughter they always wanted when they couldn't do enough to keep their son alive?* The thought nags distractingly and the familiar taste of ashes fills her mouth, but she is practiced at keeping her composure and manages to hold the smile on her face.

It's Jess's turn for a hug next. Erica smells strongly of a new perfume and Jess wonders how much shopping her daughter has managed to fit in between "cultural experiences" in London. Quite a lot, judging by the amount of stuff she has.

"What the bloody hell have you got in here?" Nick asks when he picks it up. "How much spending money did you take?" Jess smiles. Nick was the one who pressed a wad of twenty-pound notes into Erica's hand before she left.

Nick and Jess wait in the car while Erica says goodbye to her brand-new boyfriend. They learnt about this relationship via a series of excitable text messages from Erica while she was away. They know the boyfriend is called Olly and he's in the Upper Sixth, but not much else. Jess assesses him through the car window: tall and skinny, with floppy brown hair. Shades of a young Hugh Grant. Nick's also watching him like a hawk, though Jess doesn't think he has much to worry about. From the look of Olly, she doubts he's got it in him to do a single thing that Erica doesn't want him to. Her daughter is nothing if not strong-willed.

Jess winds down the window as Erica approaches, dragging Olly by the hand.

"Can we go straight to Pete's Cantina?" Erica says.

"Now?"

"I'm *so* hungry."

"Don't you want to go home and take a shower first? And change your clothes, maybe?"

Erica's wearing sweat pants and a hoodie. Her long blond hair looks as if she used it as a nest to sleep in on the coach. Jess would like Erica to give it a brush at least. Her daughter has other ideas: "I really want to go straight there. Then Olly can come, too. Please?"

Jess and Nick exchange glances and she shrugs, because what Erica wants, Erica usually gets. It's not the way Jess brought Charlie up, but that's the point. It must be different with her daughter. *Everything* must be different.

"The more the merrier as far as I'm concerned," Nick says. "Jump in, both of you."

At Pete's Cantina they are seated in a corner booth. Erica and Olly slide into the banquette and Jess and Nick take chairs opposite. The teenagers are full of giggles and sit pressed up against each other.

"What did you like best in London, then?" Jess asks.

"Literally *everything*!" Erica says.

"*Hamlet* at the Barbican was a highlight," Olly says. He's got a surprisingly deep voice.

"Can I get you something to drink?" The waitress rattles through the list of specials. She's just audible above the pumping mariachi soundtrack. Erica and Olly order elaborate mocktails, Nick asks for a bottled beer, and Jess treats herself to a pink cocktail with a sugared rim. As Jess listens to the kids choosing their food, she notes how this whole experience seems as normal as tying a pair of shoelaces for them.

Not that Jess really knows what "normal" is. She relies on Nick to tell her or show her, because nothing she experienced when she was growing up gave her a "normal" road map.

The closest Jess ever got to eating out in a restaurant when she was a teenager was eggs, beans, chips, and a tea at a Little Chef restaurant in a service area just off the A361. She was on her way to a caravan park in Devon with her last-but-one foster family. It was 1986. She turned sixteen on that holiday, and she'd just found out she was pregnant.

Jess remembers how her foster dad's upper lip shone with grease as he ate his strips of bacon and how he moved his foot underneath the table until the tip of his shoe made contact with Jess's skinny, razor-nicked calf.

She already knew she was carrying his baby. She'd spent her holiday cash on a pregnancy test and done it in the loo while they waited for the food.

She kicked her foster dad's shin as hard as she could and watched him try to suppress his reaction to the pain in front of his family. He would be grateful to her very soon, Jess knew, because she would never admit he was the father of her child.

She wanted to keep the baby for herself, because she had nobody else. Her mum was a drug addict who overdosed and died when Jess was four years old. Her dad disappeared before she was born. She never learned his name. There were no siblings. For as long as she could remember, Jess had lived with a gnawing sense of rejection and separateness.

As she shoveled her food into her mouth that morning, her mind grew full with rich, unrealistic thoughts of the baby—how she and it would become a family of their own. Her heart swelled with hope. She could belong to the baby, and the baby could belong to her. It would, she felt sure, be a girl.

"So, Mrs. Guttridge . . ."—Olly interrupts her thoughts—"Erica told me you used to have a role on *Dart Street*? Like, the girlfriend of a gangster or something? Regular cast?" he asks.

Jess feels the smile freeze on her face. She hates talking about the past, even the good bits. She feels as if she's already spent too much time thinking about it and they haven't even got their main courses yet.

Nick got her the role on *Dart Street*. He was working on the production in its earliest days. It was a brand-new soap set on a street in Bristol, about the lives of the families who lived there. They were struggling to cast the role of Amber Rowe, a feisty newcomer to the street and the love interest for one of the main characters. Production had already rejected dozens of actresses when Nick suggested they take a look at Jess, and they auditioned her in spite of her lack of experience. She was a perfect fit: right look, right voice, and right attitude. She saw the opportunity for what it was—a once-in-a-lifetime chance—and threw herself into the role. It helped bring her back to life after Charlie's death.

"I might have done," she says.

"What was that like?"

"Well, it was a job. I loved it, but the schedule was relentless. It's why I quit after I had Erica, because I wanted to spend time with my baby." Jess pats the back of Erica's hand and gets a smile in return.

Neither Nick nor Erica know this is a half-truth. Jess did want to spend time raising Erica herself, but she might have stayed on *Dart Street* for longer if the media hadn't taken an interest in her past once the show became successful. She got the story quashed, but it frightened her into quitting.

"See! That is why I would want to work in film!" Olly says. "Because otherwise it must be really difficult to develop as an actor."

Bloody hell, Jess thinks. The sense of entitlement and possibility some of these kids possess astounds her.

"I totally agree," Erica says. "He's right, isn't he, Dad?"

"Acting's a tough job whichever way it rolls. Amber Rowe was a great role, which *did develop.* Your mum played it brilliantly, she was amazing, *and* it guaranteed her a steady income. You can't ask more than that." If Olly works out he's being gently chastised, he doesn't show it. Jess, as ever, gets a warm feeling from Nick's loyalty.

The fajitas arrive on sizzling platters. As the waitresses place them on the table, Jess rubs her daughter's shoulder. "It's good to have you home, love," she says. Erica leans her flushed cheek on Jess's hand before tucking in to the food and turning her attention back to Olly. Jess smiles. She knows when she's been upstaged. She wants her daughter to enjoy these precious moments that Jess never had. An unwelcome thought occurs to her: *But what if I have sheltered Erica too much? Might it be better if she knew everything? If I'd told her about Charlie and tried to explain what my life was like? Is she too naive because we've wrapped her in cotton wool all these years?* She glances at Nick, wanting reassurance. He's laughing at something Erica said. Jess drains the last half-inch of her cocktail and tells herself to lighten up. The podcast has got under her skin, and dwelling on the past hasn't helped. The answer to this evening, she thinks, is to lighten up and not worry about everything, and the way to do that is to have another drink.

"You driving?" she asks Nick.

He nods. He knows what she wants and he signals to the waitress. Jess is halfway down her second cocktail and feeling nicely mellow when her phone vibrates. It's a call from an unknown number but she decides to take it because it's an excuse to escape the Olly Show for a few moments.

"Hello?" she says. She can't hear what the caller's saying because the noise in the restaurant is loud. Drink in one hand and phone in the other she gets up and weaves her way through the other tables to the door. Once she's outside, she apologizes: "Sorry. I couldn't hear a thing in there." It's dark. She stands beneath the restaurant's awning. It glows a dull red, lit by strings of bulbs hanging from its underside. Jess is alone.

"Is that Jessy?"

Nobody calls her Jessy anymore. Very few people ever did. "Who's this?" she asks, but she thinks she knows.

"It's Cody Swift, Charlie's friend."

She hangs up and downs her drink, although she's never felt so sober. She stares back into the restaurant, seeking out her husband. As if he has a sixth sense, Nick turns and meets her eye. She beckons and he gets up instantly.

"That was Cody Swift on the phone. From the podcast," she says once he is outside. She hands him her phone as if it's tainted by the call.

"What did he say?"

"I didn't give him the chance to say anything. I hung up."

"Good girl. Well done. Don't cry. Come here, love."

Nick ushers her into a shop doorway, out of the snappy wind and out of Erica's and Olly's line of vision. On her phone, he goes to recent calls and presses the number at the top of the list. He puts it on speakerphone as it rings.

"Cody Swift."

"Cody Swift, you little runt," Nick says.

"Who's this?"

"Never you mind. You just listen to me for a minute, and listen really, bloody carefully, because I won't warn you twice. Do not telephone Jessica again. Do not try to approach her. If you do, you'll have me to answer to, and it won't be pleasant. Do you understand?"

"Who is this?"

"Do you understand me?"

"Is that Mr. Guttridge? Are you Jessy's husband?"

"It doesn't matter who I am. Listen to me carefully, because I'm not going to tell you this again. Keep. Away. From. Jess."

"Or what?"

Nick hangs up and hands the phone back to Jess. "Don't answer if he rings again."

She shakes her head. She's got no intention of doing so. She was off her guard. With shaking fingers she blocks Cody Swift's number.

When they return to their seats back inside, Erica frowns as if she's the grown-up and they've been truant. She signals the waitress and some staff gather, one of them holding a plate loaded with a tower of brownies topped with whipped cream and candles. He sets it down in front of Nick, and Erica beams as everybody sings "Happy Birthday." Nick smiles and thanks his daughter, but underneath the table, he clutches Jess's hand tightly and doesn't let go. She loves that he does it, but beneath the smile she has plastered on, she's very afraid Nick might not be able to save them from this Cody Swift thing, no matter how much he wants to.

As they walk back to the car, the kids ahead of them, she says, without thinking first, "Do you think I should call Felix?"

Nick stops dead. "Are you joking?" He keeps his voice down, but only just.

Jess knows she's made a big mistake. Neither of them has mentioned that name for years, and that's the way it should be. The cocktails have loosened her tongue. Nick made only one condition when they got together: that Jess never have contact with Felix Abernathy again. Ever.

"I don't mean it. I don't know why I said it. I've had too much to drink. I'm being silly."

"Felix Abernathy doesn't interfere with you or our family. What's the matter with you? Have you forgotten what he's like? I'll sort out Cody Swift. Leave him to me."

"You're right," she says. "Sorry. You're right, darling." She kisses him tenderly and is relieved to sense him letting go of some of his outrage. "I really am sorry," she repeats. She doesn't want to hurt him. "I'm a bit pissed and the phone call stressed me out. I don't know where that came from. Forget I said it." She kisses him again.

"Gross!" It's Erica, fifty yards ahead, standing beside the car with her hand on her hip. "Come on! It's freezing!"

Nick unlocks the car and its lights wink brightly. The kids scramble in. He looks at Jess with an expression that is both hurt and wary before putting his arm around her and squeezing her shoulders as they walk to the car. Her apology is accepted. She is so relieved.

She never told Nick it was Felix who helped her before, when *Dart Street* got the media interested in her. It was early days for Felix's PR business at the time, but he already had good contacts and other, juicier stories he could trade for silence. Jess would have turned to Nick if she could have—God knows she knew better than anyone the dangers of involving Felix Abernathy—but there were and are some things Nick is just too good and too nice to handle effectively. That's when you need somebody like Felix. Somebody who is prepared to bark and bite.

In the car on the way home, Jess is glad it's dark because nobody notices her blinking back tears as they drive. It's not like her to let her emotions overwhelm her in public—control is something she has had to learn to be very good at—but Felix Abernathy is one person who truly frightens her, and she's got a feeling she's going to face a choice very soon: call him or see her family ripped apart.

letcher is lost in thought as he waits to speak to Chief Constable David Tremain about the Cody Swift podcast. Since reporting that Swift contacted him, Fletcher has been summoned—as he knew he would be—to discuss it.

He has given a photograph of the signet ring found with the skeleton to Danny and asked him to run a search on the missing persons database. The four-leaf clover on the ring has predictably earned John Doe a nickname: Lucky.

It's quiet in the waiting area. The DCI's secretary is typing up an audio recording, so the only sound is the clatter of her nails on the keyboard and the huffy noise she makes when she needs to pause and rewind.

Fletcher likes quiet. He didn't used to. He used to feed off noise and chaos as if it were a silvery bait ball and he an ocean predator gorging on it. Not now. He's become more reflective over the years, though he knows his silences can be frustrating. "I'm not a bloody mind reader," his ex-wife used to snap at him, rapping her fingernails on the kitchen island, staccato sharp so that he winced. "I can't know what you're thinking unless you communicate it to me! It's a form of torture, John, honestly. It's not like I've got a spare husband I can chat to." Until she did.

She never understood how Fletcher grew to need the silence because he believed the things he dealt with day to day were best kept to himself. What would their life have been like if he'd gone home every evening and told Jane and the boys exactly what he'd been doing that day? How do you sit at the table and tell your family about the day's rape or murder or beating as you pass the vegetables and mashed potatoes? Why would any man do that? It would have destroyed his marriage just as the silence did in the end, though probably quicker.

"He's ready for you now," Tremain's secretary says. She watches out of the corner of her eye as Fletcher makes two attempts to get up.

Tremain indicates Fletcher should sit. He's a dapper man, always has been. He has starched collars and crisp creases in the front of his trousers. Being around Tremain makes Fletcher hyperaware of his own dishevelment, though he doesn't attempt to adjust any part of his appearance.

Neither man speaks at first because the first episode of the podcast is playing on Tremain's computer. Cody Swift's voice comes through loud and clear: "I find the photograph very moving. We were the best of friends. It reminds me in the strongest possible way why I should pack away any moments of doubt about pursuing this investigation because Charlie and Scott deserve the truth."

Tremain lets the last few minutes of the podcast play out. He turns it off and sighs. "Did you listen to this?"

"I did."

"What did you think?"

"So far, so mediocre."

"That's a more relaxed approach than I was expecting."

"Cody Swift chatting with his mum doesn't worry me too much."

"I'm going to disagree, John. I think we have to be proactive. Any ideas?"

"Leave him be. He'll hang himself if we give him enough rope."

"I'm not sure about that."

"Nobody on the Glenfrome Estate will talk to him."

"I'm not so sure about that either. Did you read Weston's article?"

Fletcher nods. As far as he is concerned, the article said nothing that should worry them. He remembers Owen Weston from the courtroom. The reporter got under Fletcher's skin with his moral outrage and his persistence, but it didn't get him anywhere in the end and Fletcher doesn't believe things will be any different this time around. "Weston's blowing smoke. He's trying to get attention by coming up with an innocence theory because it's all the rage."

Tremain's expression suggests he is doubtful, but Fletcher has said what he thinks and he doesn't feel the need to elaborate or defend his position. He looks steadily at his superior officer. Tremain has been around in the force for as long as Fletcher has, but he stepped away from detective work to seek promotion ten years ago. In Fletcher's opinion, that dulls your street instincts and has an effect on your psyche like agar does for bacteria, breeding neurosis and self-regard in equal measure. For twenty years, since the day Tremain dealt an immutable blow to Fletcher's career, they have coexisted professionally with the mutual admiration of cats and dogs.

Tremain sighs. "Hoping Weston and Swift spontaneously

go back down their burrows is not what I'd call a proactive approach. I'd like you to talk to Swift. Cooperate with him, or appear to cooperate. Obviously, it'll have to be within the restrictions on what we can legally share." Tremain tweaks the knot of his tie. "Swift told you that he was expecting to get Howard Smail on the record?" he adds, and Fletcher nods. "So, if we don't cooperate with Swift directly and Howard Smail breaks his silence, his voice is going to be the only one representing the police. It's the kind of PR we could do without, don't you think?"

The smile he offers Fletcher is a rictus grin. Power dances behind his eyes. Fletcher has no choice but to agree. Privately, Fletcher believes Smail fell too far from grace too long ago for anybody to pay attention to him now, but it would be unwise to argue with Tremain.

"Of course, boss," he says.

When he gets back to his desk, he's hoping to find out if there's been an ID on John Doe, but Danny's away from his desk. Fletcher calls Cody Swift and bows to the pressure that Swift applies to meet in person. There's no need for a face-to-face, they could easily do this over the phone, but a meet in person is a bone that's easy to throw, and Fletcher knows there can be value in giving what you can easily afford to. He's also curious to clap eyes on Cody Swift after all these years. He wants to know who that grubby little kid with the sharp eyes and bruised knees became.

Fletcher makes sure to control the venue of the meet, though. If you can control where an interview takes place, you are part of the way to controlling the interview itself. Location matters. Fletcher's wife announced she was leaving him when they were in the Costco car park. He didn't see it coming. He remembers acutely the humiliation of loading bags into the boot of the car while she explained across the laden shopping trolley that their marriage was over.

"Well, why are we buying in bulk then?" was all he could think to ask.

"Because I'm taking it with me to Almondsbury!"

Fletcher stopped packing the car. He detected a hint of possibility in his wife's eye as she described how she had a new love and how they planned to build a new life together. Listening to her, he was seized by a feeling of disorientation and loss, as if he was being left behind in life's gloaming.

Fletcher tells Cody Swift they can meet in his car, in one hour, in the underground parking area of the middle-class mecca that is the Cribbs Causeway shopping mall on the out-skirts of the city. It's a good location because it's bland and offers an illusion of subterfuge that Fletcher feels Swift might enjoy if he's playing private investigator. Fletcher's been told to get Swift onside, so he'll do his best. He sets off for their meeting immediately in order to arrive early. He's already parked and watching the entrance when Swift appears exactly on time.

Swift is driving a battered old Land Rover. He parks it badly. Fletcher signals to him and Swift climbs into Fletcher's car carrying an armful of recording kit. He's taller than Fletcher thought he would be, and he looks nervous.

"Thanks for meeting me," Swift says. He takes a good look at Fletcher, almost drinks him in with his eyes, before he catches himself and starts to fuss with the kit.

"Wait a minute, son," Fletcher says. "We're off the record in the first instance, as we discussed on the phone. Nothing's changed."

Swift's hands fall still. "You're right. I want you to know that I respect the boundaries."

Fletcher narrows his eyes but doesn't reply with the sarcastic rebuttal he's composing in his head in case Swift is recording secretly. Twenty years ago he found Cody to be a smart but slippery sort of boy, and Fletcher believes that nobody changes too much over the years, no matter how much they want to or claim that they have.

"What can I do for you?" he says.

"Honestly?"

Fletcher nods.

"All I want is the truth, Detective."

Fletcher's heart sinks a little. Not because this isn't a noble aim, but because he wonders when the hell Cody Swift lost the streetwise skills he was honing when he was a kid and became such a cliché. "Son, you need to be careful when you look under stones. This case was solved twenty years ago."

"I've come back here to discover the truth."

"There was an arrest and a trial and a verdict. That's the truth."

"Not everybody believes that. Did you read Owen Weston's article?"

Fletcher is too experienced to let it show that Swift's words provoke a small but unwelcome feeling of foreboding in him. He has to work to keep his tone even when he replies. "The article is conspiracy theory nonsense. Justice was served. The outcome of that case was sad and the murders might have been avoidable, but sometimes we have to live with that. It's best to leave it alone."

"I believe I owe it to myself and to the other families to try to get to the truth. What's the harm in trying?"

"Because other people might not want to relive this."

"But I'm not police. I'm one of them. I was there. I think people will be willing to share with me."

Fletcher sighs. "You need to be very careful."

Swift's hyped up now and takes this as encouragement. "But you think it can be solved?"

"It has been solved."

"Unless somebody tells me something new," Swift says. "Unless they want to talk after all these years."

Fletcher sighs again. "Even if they talk, you need to ask yourself why. Ask yourself what they have to gain. And watch your back. Look, son, people have been getting on with their lives. Is it fair to make them relive the past based on what boils down to fantasy-based suspicions from one individual? Weston is retired now. He never broke a big story. He is a bitter man."

"The truth is worth fighting for," Swift says. "Isn't that why you do what you do and why you're here?"

"I'm here to explain there's very little I can share with you. I would love to, but my hands are tied."

Cody reaches for the door handle. "That's exactly the response I was expecting, but thank you for your time."

Fletcher doesn't like his tone or the way he slams the door shut behind him. *That is all we need,* he thinks as he watches Swift make his way across the car park. That weaselly kid he and Danny interviewed all those years ago has got himself an education and a good job, and now he thinks he's on the side of the angels.

Danny speaks quietly and calmly. His mischievous quality, which doesn't do him any favors professionally, works well with youngsters. The boy is folded up in a corner of the sofa, all skinny limbs and wide eyes. Fletcher thinks he looks semi-feral.

"Now here's the thing," Danny says. "The more you can tell us about what you and your friends were up to yesterday, the better the chance we have of finding out who did this to them. I reckon you'd like to help us catch that person."

The kid's name is Cody Swift. They are gathered in his family's tiny living room in a fifth-floor flat on the Glenfrome Estate. Fletcher estimates the room is only about eight by fifteen feet maximum. It's dominated by an easy chair, an oversize sofa, and a TV that sits on a chipped, mahogany-effect cabinet. A perilously narrow vase stands in the corner of the room, containing dried feathery grasses dyed in unnatural colors.

Cody's wearing shorts and a Magpies football shirt. The soles of his bare feet are grubby, and he's suntanned enough that Fletcher can tell he spends a lot of time outside. The back of his neck is dark bronze. He's got mud-brown hair, buzz cut. His little face has a stubborn quality that's slightly mitigated by a delicate freckled nose. He's clasping a cushion across his abdomen. His parents sit beside him. Danny has perched on the edge of the coffee table and Fletcher's standing in the doorway. The window is wide open, but the room's as hot as a toaster.

Fletcher wouldn't be here at all, because the deputy investigating officer wouldn't normally be expected to do interviews, but he had no choice. "We're going to be under scrutiny," Smail told him that morn-ing. "The detective chief constable has requested that somebody senior is present at all important interviews." The expression on Smail's face made it clear that while they were going to obey the order, he thought it was an overreaction. Fletcher wasn't surprised to hear it. The DCC was a nervy, press- and politics-sensitive sort.

Smail did his bit by visiting the bereaved parents personally to as-sure them that everything possible would be done in "his" investiga-tion. He wasn't lying. "Everything's being thrown at this," he said after emerging from a meeting with the top dogs. "Unlimited budget." Fletcher thought Smail sounded self-important, as if he himself was the reason the money was flowing, not the two dead boys.

Now Smail has tucked himself in back at the station and sent Fletcher out onto the front line in his place. Fletcher is frustrated. He feels he's wasting his time standing in on an interview that a well-trained detective constable could easily handle. He should be sit-ting down with Smail right now, making decisions on how to direct inquiries and proceedings. The beginning of a major investigation is always chaos, but this is the first time Fletcher's borne any personal responsibility for creating order out of the mayhem. He wants to prove his worth and he can't do that standing here watching Danny interview Cody Swift, the third boy in the friendship. The one who got away.

"Can you tell us what you did yesterday?" Danny asks the lad. "With your friends."

The mother starts to answer for him, but Danny says, "In his own words, if you don't mind."

"We went to the dog track," Cody says.

"You went to the dog track?"

"Yes." He keeps his gaze fixed on Danny like a hard little man, *though he flinches almost imperceptibly when his parents chip in with recriminations.*

"You're not bloody allowed there, you know you're not," his dad says.

The man's skinny but looks strong. He's wearing a pale gray V-necked T-shirt. A few white chest hairs emerge at his neckline. The skin on his face is red and rough, and what remains of his receding hair has been slicked back. It's so oiled that the tines of a comb have left furrows in their wake, revealing the dull white of his scalp. Deep lines score his forehead and his cheeks sag and bristle with a few days' worth of stubble. His eyes are dark, sharp, and wary. He's smoked nonstop since Danny and Fletcher arrived, lighting one cigarette from the last. Fletcher estimates he's ten years younger than he looks.

"We told the boys not to hang around there. Time and again we said it," Mrs. Swift says.

"Charlie likes the dogs," Cody says. He doesn't look at either of his parents.

"Does he? That's nice. Is there one dog in particular he likes?" Danny asks.

"He likes them all."

"You said you was at the play area." Mrs. Swift isn't happy. "That's what they told me, Detective."

"That's okay," Danny says. Fletcher is willing her to shut up so the kid can talk uninterrupted, but she's a bag of nerves. Danny keeps his eyes on Cody. "What do you do when you go to the track, then?"

"You can get in round the back. Where the fence is split."

He's describing the area where we discovered his friends, Fletcher thinks. Danny will be thinking the same, but he doesn't give it away. *"How do you know about that place?"*

"We just found it."

"Do you watch the races from there?"

"Sometimes we hide under the stands and watch. Sometimes we go to the kennels."

"Did you go into the kennels yesterday? You can tell me. You won't get into trouble."

The kid gives a tight nod and a half glance toward his dad.

"The kennels are in a locked area, aren't they? So who let you in?"

Cody's dad's hand moves from his belly to his belt buckle. It's a subtle movement, but Cody clocks it and reacts to it. He tenses up. Fletcher can't decide if the man's movement is a coincidence, an innocent gesture, or a warning for Cody. Ted Swift looks like the kind of man who wouldn't think twice about giving a kid a thrashing.

"I don't know," Cody says.

"You mean you don't know his name?"

"I don't know."

"But this person let you into the kennel area?" Danny asks.

Cody nods again.

"So he must have recognized one of you?"

"He recognized Charlie."

"Just Charlie?"

"Charlie knew lots of blokes there."

"What did you do at the kennels?"

"We hung around for a bit. Charlie was helping with the dogs, but after a bit the track boss came. He doesn't like us there, so we had to scarper and he bollocked Sid. After that, we went to the play area. Then Mum called us in for tea and we had a sandwich."

"And I grounded him," she chips in. "Because he ripped his new T-shirt. But he never said they'd been at the track. Never mentioned a word of it."

"Bloody little liar," his dad says. Cody swallows, but he keeps

*his gaze on Danny. He's a brave kid who's going to be a hard man.
Fletcher has seen it happen before. If you get to know them well
enough, their skin thickens right in front of your eyes.*

*"Why did the track boss bollock Sid?" Fletcher asks. "Was he the
one who let you in?"*

Cody shakes his head, but they both know he has let that slip.

"What are the names of the people you saw at the track?"

"I don't know. Only Sid."

"Sid who?"

He shrugs.

"Is Sid a trainer?"

"He helps the stewards."

"Do you know his second name?"

"We call him Sid the Village."

*Our confusion must show, because a small smile flashes across
Cody's face. It is slightly cruel. "Because if Sid's out, it means somewhere there's a village short of an idiot," he says. He cackles. His dad
gives an amused snort at first, but catches himself and cuffs the back of
Cody's head. That cuts Cody's laugh short and he tries to shrug off
the blow by giving his head a rub. He attempts to give Danny good
eye contact again, though Fletcher thinks there's a touch of defiance in
his gaze and a thin wash of tears.*

*"I'm sorry, Detective," Mrs. Swift says. "We brought him up bet-
ter than that, honest."*

*Fletcher looks at Cody with interest. He thinks there may still be
something the boy's not telling, but he doesn't think Danny's going to
get it out of him here and now.*

*Danny senses this, too. He tries a soft touch. "Son, you've been
really helpful. We'll talk again, maybe tomorrow. I'm really sorry
about your friends."*

The kind words release tears from Cody's eyes. He looks up at Fletcher. "They said Charlie was alive when you found him."

Fletcher nods. He has no idea how the kid knows that. He wants to say that Charlie died peacefully, but he can't lie. Not about the death of a kid.

"I was with Charlie when he passed away," he manages. "He said a word to me. He said ghost. I think that's what he said. Does that mean anything to you, son?"

Cody shakes his head and his chin trembles. All traces of his bravado disappear as he covers his face with both hands and sobs so hard his shoulders shake. Danny stands, signaling an end to the interview, and Fletcher is relieved to see Cody's mother take the lad in her arms. Ted Swift's head hangs low and heavy. A slender trail of smoke rises from the cigarette between his fingers and disperses in curls and tendrils into the stifling air.

IT'S TIME TO TELL

EPISODE 3—THE OTHER MOTHERS

A DISHLICKER
PODCAST PRODUCTION

OPERATOR: Police, emergency?

CALLER: Yes, I'm calling to report my son is missing.

OPERATOR: Okay. How old is your son?

CALLER: He's eleven.

OPERATOR: When did you last see him?

CALLER: This morning. Late morning.

OPERATOR: Have there been any arguments at home today or this morning, anything like that?

CALLER: No, everything was fine. It was normal.

OPERATOR: Have you been in touch with your son's friends or other family members or anybody like that?

CALLER: We've called everybody. Nobody's seen him. We think he might be with another boy who is also missing.

OPERATOR: Have you searched all the places you think they might be?

CALLER: We've searched everywhere. We can't think of anywhere else. We're worried because it's dark now. They said they'd be in before it got dark.

OPERATOR: Have either of the boys disappeared before, that you know of?

CALLER: No. It's the first time, for Scott, anyway. I don't know about Charlie. It's like they've disappeared off the face of the earth.

My name is Cody Swift. I'm a filmmaker and your host of *It's Time to Tell,* a Dishlicker Podcast Production. What you just heard was a clip of a 999 recording made to police on the night of Scott's and Charlie's murders. The call was made by Annette Ashby, Scott's mother, at 23:37 on Sunday, 18 August 1996.

In the last episode of *It's Time to Tell,* you met my mother, Julie Swift. This week I'll be introducing you to the mothers of Charlie and Scott, my two best friends whose lives were brutally cut short on the day that call was made.

If Scott and Charlie and I were inseparable friends, the relationship between our mothers was more complicated. Mum and Annette Ashby got on well. Here's Mum talking about Annette:

"Annette was lovely. She was very caring; she was sensible. She tried to bring her kids up right. It wasn't easy for her because she was on her own, but she worked hard to give them everything they needed. At one time, she was working three jobs at once. She kept up good relations with Scott's dad even after he walked out and moved in with that woman who worked for the council. Annette did it for the children. She said she could change husbands, but they couldn't change their dad, so she was going to do her best to make sure they all got along together. That was Annette all over. She'd take the coat off her own back if she thought you looked cold. Lovely lady. She didn't deserve what happened."

My own recollection is that Mum and Annette would always have a chat when they came across each other, and a laugh. They laughed a lot. But things were different with Charlie's mum. Here's my mother again:

"Jessy Paige. Oh, yes. There are words you don't like to use, and a few of them spring to mind. A stunner, she was, and I think it went to her head. She had Charlie when she was a teenager, but as far as I could tell, she didn't do much with herself since she had him apart from sit around the estate living off benefits. I know it's not easy being on your own with a kid, especially when you're young, but you've still got your two hands, and there's no excuse for not keeping things clean and tidy and teaching your kid right from wrong. Jessy didn't seem to care about anything apart from her social life. She let Charlie run wild. I don't think she knew half the people that boy hung around with. Annette and me took him under our wings a bit, whenever we could. We had to be careful not to make it obvious, because Jessy would have bitten our heads off if she thought we were showing her charity. She was proud in that way, lazy but proud, and she went out too much. She was always begging people to babysit Charlie for free. People said she ran with a fast crowd and there was talk about how she got the money to go out all the time when Charlie was always in shoes and trousers two sizes too small for him. People talk. We knew each other's business on the estate, and the way she behaved attracted attention. And in the end it was the going out that was the problem, wasn't it? If Jessy hadn't gone out and left the boys that night, they'd still be with us. I have no doubt about that."

My partner and producer, Maya, and I have made efforts to get in contact with Jessica Paige since we began work on this podcast, but she hasn't returned our calls. On one occasion I managed to speak to her briefly, but she hung up on me. I completely understand why she might not want to revisit the case, and I respect her privacy, but her story is so central to this podcast that I made the decision to try to approach her in person. I'll be honest, invading her privacy in that way took me some way out of my comfort zone, but overriding my concerns was the hope that she might agree to tell her side of the story.

We had heard that Jessica volunteers at an animal rescue shelter once a week, so I took a trip over there. The shelter was in a one-story building in a car park on the edge of a main road outside Bristol. It was surrounded by fields. I arrived a few minutes before the end of Jessica's shift and waited outside the building. She appeared not long afterward. I ran over to intercept her. You're about to hear a clip of our conversation:

"Jessica?"
"Who's asking?"
"It's me. Cody Swift. Do you remember me? Can I help you with that?"

Jessica was carrying a basket containing a bruiser of a tabby cat. She put it down. She wore her long hair in a neat ponytail. She looked trim and well dressed in dark jeans, knee-high leather boots with a low heel, and a short, quilted jacket. Her makeup was discreet and flattering. She looked every inch the yummy mummy. She stared at me in a slightly brazen way, and that was the moment when I caught my first glimpse of the old Jessy Paige.

"I remember you, Cody Swift. You always could put on those perfect manners, but I'm not talking to you no matter how nicely you ask. I've told you that."

"Please, just a quick chat, a few minutes of your time? I'm investigating the murders of Charlie and Scott for my podcast and I want to make sure that the listeners get to hear your voice and your side of the story."

"The case was solved."

"I don't think it was solved. I think they might have put away the wrong guy. Sidney Noyce could be innocent. That matters to me, and it should matter to you, too. It's why I'm doing this. I want to hear from people who were involved at the time. That's why the podcast is called *It's Time to Tell*."

"And I've said all I'm saying."

She picked up the cat basket, the weight of it making her lop-sided as she walked toward a snazzy red Mini parked on its own about seventy-five yards away. I followed and called after her.

"Can I give you one of my cards, Jessy? So you can get in touch if you change your mind? You're the only person who can speak for Charlie."

She stopped suddenly, surprising me. I skidded to a halt beside her. For a moment I felt hopeful she might open up to me, because she looked as if there was a lot bottled up inside her, but she decided against it and walked away.

"Please! Get in touch whenever you want, Jessy! Jessy! I'm here to listen, Jessy!"

Her car backed out of its space fast, gravel chippings flying. It's a shame that Jessica didn't want to talk to us. Not everybody thought she was a bad person or a bad mother back in 1996. I was only ten years old, but I was one of her biggest fans.

Back then, all of us called her Jessy, Charlie included, because she said she hated being called "mum" or "Miss Paige." She acted more like a friend to us than a mother. She told terrific jokes, she had a big laugh, and she talked to us boys as if we were adults. She didn't dress like the other mums, and she let us play ball in her flat. Sometimes she joined in our games. Once she bounced with us on Charlie's bed until the mattress fell through the base and she laughed so hard she cried. We loved her, no matter what our parents thought. We saw a side to her that perhaps, in retrospect, she never showed the other adults. Not the ones I knew, anyhow.

When people described Jessy in derogatory ways after the murders, they weren't describing the Jessy Paige I knew. I heard the talk, as kids do, and I thought: why don't they talk about how funny she was, and how nice? It goes without saying that I was judging her from a child's perspective, and my standards probably fell far short of the adults', but I couldn't see the bad in her.

I asked my mother if she thought that people, and some of the women in particular, might have been jealous of Jessy.

"Might have been. Perhaps because she did all the things you weren't supposed to do. She went out, had a good time; she got involved with a few fellas along the way, though none of them seemed to hang around. But in the end, you've got to ask yourself, do you behave like that when there's a kid to raise? Family comes first, son. Family always comes first. Look what she lost because of it."

Mum wouldn't say much more, but it sounds to me as if Jessica Paige broke a code of respectability. The estate may have had its share of social problems, but many people there adhered to a set of standards and a way of life they were proud of.

We'll keep trying with our efforts to start a conversation with Jessica Paige so she can tell her side of the story.

I had better luck when I contacted Annette Ashby, Scott's mother. When I first approached Annette she was already aware of Owen Weston's article expressing doubts about Sidney Noyce's guilt, and she admitted to harboring doubts of her own about his conviction. Doubts she hadn't wanted to voice until now. This is what she said on the phone:

> "I knew Sidney. I used to chat to him in the Tesco car park sometimes. I didn't think he would harm a fly, but when something like that happens you doubt everything you ever knew. By the time he was convicted I was sure he'd done it."

Annette agreed to meet so that I could record an interview and suggested we get together in a coffee concession in a shopping outlet center on the outskirts of Swindon, the town she lives in now. The coffee bar is in the middle of the mall. When I arrive, I don't spot Annette at first. It's not until a woman approaches me that I realize it's her.

Annette has changed a lot. Physically, she's smaller and frailer than I remember. She still has a spark in her eyes, but it seems dimmer than before. That's time and grief, I suppose. She still gives good hugs, though. It reminded me how she would throw her arms around Scott at any opportunity, though by the time he died, he'd grown old enough to perfect the art of wriggling away.

What follows are clips from a recording of our conversation.

"Annette, hello! Is that really you?"

"You're all grown up, Cody Swift. Look at you!"

"You recognized me right away?"

"You've still got that up-to-no-good look about you."

"Really? I'm not sure that's a good thing!"

Over coffee, Annette and I get reacquainted. She tells me she moved away from the estate in the immediate aftermath of the murders. She went to Swindon because she had a brother there and she's done well for herself. She tells me she's recently retired. She does a bit of voluntary work and spends time with her daughter Cally— Scott's younger sister—and her grandchildren. She describes how Scott's death still affects her:

"It feels like a part of me is missing, like I got broken and I can't be fixed until I join him again on the other side."

"Can you talk to me about the day of the murders?"

"Apart from the heat, the day felt normal. I was watering my pots on the balcony when Charlie called round about mid-morning to ask if Scott wanted to come and play. Course Scott did! You three were like the Three Musketeers that summer. Inseparable."

"Did Charlie and Scott say what they were going to do?"

"They were going to call on you, of course. Then there was the plan to go to the lido. When they told me about it, I thought it was nice that Jessy was bothering to have a family outing for Charlie. I didn't ask questions. Nobody had a mobile back then, so it wasn't so easy to double-check plans. Jessy had a landline, but I didn't want to disturb her and her fella. I should have."

"Once they'd gone, did you see Scott again that day?"

"I never saw him again. I thought he was having a nice day out swimming. They said they would be back before dark, and that was good enough for me. Scott never let me down before. He might have been naughty in other ways, but he was always home when he said he would be. We let you boys run around the estate that summer and all the summers before it because life felt more innocent back then. We believed we knew our community and you boys were brought up to be streetwise. More fool us. The next time I saw Scott was at the morgue."

That word sinks in for both of us, and as it does, it seems very odd to be in this random coffee shop in this unfamiliar town, talking about the murders. Wrong, somehow, yet a reminder of how life shuffles on past any event, however traumatic, and you need to try to hold on to its coattails and keep moving with it, even if you feel as if that's the last thing you want to do.

"Can you talk me through what happened for the rest of the evening?"

"Sorry, Cody, love, this bit's hard. Even now."

"Take your time."

Annette describes a timeline for the evening that dovetails with the one my mother described. She mentions one complication that was missing from Mum's account:

"Once I realized they weren't with Jessy, I thought the boys might have gone to Scott's dad's house. It was only a twenty-minute walk away, you'll remember, he lived up by Purdown."

Purdown is the parkland you can see if you drive into Bristol on the M32 motorway. It runs alongside the motorway between Filton and Eastville and is dominated by a tall communications tower and a yellow mansion house. Both are local landmarks. Annette continues:

"I went up there, to his house, because nobody had answered the phone all evening. It was after I rang the police that I went. I didn't want to wait for them to arrive and I didn't have a car, so I ran. Malcolm—that's Scott's dad—he wasn't in. Nobody was, and I don't know what got into me, but I thought they might have taken Scott. You know, kidnapped him, like you read about. It was just so odd for Malcolm and Sal to be out on a Sunday night. No car in the drive, no lights left on, I couldn't hear the dogs barking, nothing. It was gone midnight by the time I got back to the estate and I was so stupid, I told one of the police officers what I was thinking."

I spoke to Scott's father, Malcolm Ashby, about this. Here's a clip from our conversation. Malcolm is speaking from his home in Australia, about that night:

"I was at work and my partner Sal was at a barbecue. She took the dogs with her. I don't know what got into Annette. First thing I knew about any of it was when I arrived back at the depot at the end of my shift and a squad car and two coppers were waiting."

Scott's dad was a coach driver. He had been out all day and evening taking a sports team halfway across the country for a tournament and arrived back at the depot at half past midnight. He continues:

"The police drove me back to the estate and I joined the search. I can't really describe how desperate it felt. Every time somebody came back with no news, you felt as if a piece of you had been taken away. We searched all night and into the next morning. We weren't going to stop until we found them. We concentrated on the estate, and the area around the sluice gates and under the motorway overpass. Some people went up to Purdown to search the old gun pits. Nobody thought to look by the dog track that night, and I wonder if that was my fault because I told them Scotty used to like to take our dogs walking on Purdown with me, so the police concentrated the search on that area. I wish I'd never said it. If I could take one thing back in my life, it would be that. It might have saved Charlie's life even if it was too late for Scotty."

"Were you angry with Annette for pointing the finger at you?"

"She could point the finger at whoever she liked if it would have got our boy back. No, I wasn't angry. What would be the point? I knew how she was feeling. We had that in common that night and we still have it in common now. Nobody else can understand what a parent is going through."

Malcolm Ashby's words tell us everything. This isn't just a story about a brutal crime; it's a story about people who will have to live the greater part of their lifetime with grief and with regret.

It might also be a story about people who thought they'd got closure, because the police and justice system had worked for them, but who could be wrong.

After our conversation, Annette and I parted a little awkwardly. It had been an intense couple of hours. As we stood in the car park outside the mall, ready to say our goodbyes, Annette rubbed my arm awkwardly and I was struck by how difficult it must be for her to see me as a grown man when her son's life was cut so short. We exchanged a few more words before we went our separate ways.

"What about you, Cody? How have you fared over the years? I see you've done well for yourself jobwise and all that, but what about in yourself?"

"I still miss them."

"I'm not surprised. Thick as thieves, you were. They'll always be with you, Charlie and Scott. They always will. Just not the way you want them to be. They'll be in your heart, though. That's how I think of it and it helps me."

"Thank you."

"Do you have a girlfriend? Kids?"

"I have a girlfriend."

"Keep her close, darling. Keep her close."

"I will."

"Take care now."

"You too, Annette."

Next week on *It's Time to Tell,* we will be moving away from the personal and taking you right into the heart of the official murder investigation. In Episode 4 we meet the detective who led the investigation and hear what he has to say. I promise you, it will be gripping.

Before we go, we have news. I'm also happy to report that our little podcast has been steadily growing in popularity since we launched it. Episode 2 of *It's Time to Tell* was downloaded an amazing fifteen hundred times and has been recommended on Overcast! Heartfelt thanks from Maya and me to Overcast and to everybody who has taken the time to listen. Please continue to listen, share and recommend using #TimetoTell on your social media channels. You can spread the word the old-fashioned way by telling friends and family, too.

More good news is that *It's Time to Tell* has found a private sponsor. We are delighted to be bringing you future episodes in conjunction with this sponsor, who wishes to remain anonymous, but to whom we extend our most heartfelt thanks. With our sponsor's help, we've been able to set up a simple website where you can find timelines of the case, photographs of some of the people involved, and other information that we'll post as and when it's relevant. The website address is www.timetotell.com.

If you have any information about the case you'd like to share with us, the website also has our contact details, and we would love to hear from you.

To finish, here is a clip from Episode 4. This is ex–Detective Superintendent Howard Smail, the man they said would never agree to speak to us, talking about why he decided to break his silence:

"I'm not as vulnerable as if I was in the UK, but people can reach you. They won't like me talking about the case at all, let alone about internal decision-making. It's not what you do. Ever. It's taboo. I'm persona non grata anyway, but this will make it worse. Ask yourself if that's something you would willingly bring on yourself."

Jessy doesn't know what Felix's surname is until he slaps his gold Amex card down. From where she's sitting, the card's upside down, so it's hard to see, but she thinks it reads *Abernathy.* F. G. Abernathy. *Posh,* she thinks, *or Scottish.* Not that he sounds as if he's either.

Jessy is sitting at a table in the private members' area of a nightclub. She and Felix have shared a bottle of champagne. "Enjoy the Silence" by Depeche Mode is playing loud enough to make you feel like your eardrums are going to burst. "I love this song," she says, but she doesn't know if he can hear her. She snuggles closer to him, rubbing her arm against his. "What's your middle name, then?" she says. This time she shouts right up close to him, brushing his ear with her lips. It's velvet soft.

He looks at her with a hint of a smirk. He doesn't seem drunk at all, though she knows if she stands up, the room will spin around her. "That would be telling," he says. "What do you think it is?" He's been like this all night. Coming forward, backing off, treating her keen, treating her mean. She loves the game of it. It makes her feel something: little fireworks are going off inside her body.

All day long, she's been sitting with Charlie. It's what she does every day of her life. She hasn't even got a TV to keep them both occupied. The only thing to look at in her living room is a gas fire she can't afford to turn on. Her benefit check scarcely covers food, rent, and utilities. The flat they've been allocated on the Glenfrome Estate is as crap as the last place they had to leave because the building had been condemned. There's not enough room indoors, there's nothing to do within walking distance, and the elevators break so often she has to lug everything up flights of stairs almost every time she goes shopping. At least Charlie doesn't need a pushchair anymore.

She tried to play with Charlie today, but he was being annoying. He'd been up since half past five and she managed to ignore him until eight, but then he went manic. Wouldn't listen to her, talked back to her, refused to eat the cereal she got for him even though there was nothing else, so she ended up screaming at him, wishing she was anywhere else except stuck in that flat with him. She said that to him, she was stretched so tight she couldn't help herself, but she felt guilty about it afterward. She wishes it were better between them, like she imagined it would be when she was pregnant. She wishes he had been a girl. She thinks a girl would have been easier. More fun. She wishes she had money so they could go out and do something nice. The zoo, maybe. She wishes people on the estate didn't look down their noses at her because she had Charlie when she was a teenager. *Slut,* one of the married mothers hissed at her the other day outside the butcher. *Slag.*

In the end she had to get out of bed and improvise to keep Charlie entertained this morning. She found a can of fruit salad in the cupboard and laid out a row of the little fruit cubes on the table. "Watch this," she said and she sucked the cubes up one by one, without letting her lips touch them. Charlie loved it, but he couldn't do it himself. Not enough suction. It made him smile, though, and after that they were friends again and made a fortress out of what little crap they could find in the flat, but inside she was screaming that her life must be worth more than this. Has to be. Or what is the point?

So, as much as she loves Charlie, this grown-up game with Felix feels like a different world. It feels like the kind of thing she should be doing at her age. Faster, better, more brightly lit. Electric.

"Gabriel?" she says. "Like the angel? Is that your middle name?"

Felix likes a bit of a tease, up to a point. That's her sense, anyhow. Living with multiple foster families has helped her judge the limits of others pretty well. She smiles in return when she sees Felix's lips twitch. They're full lips; they look right on him. He's got one of those timeless faces: strong bone structure, cheeks flat and broad, prominent eyebrows that frame dark, teasing eyes. If Jessy saw him on the street, she'd swear he was Italian, because he looks like she thinks a Roman emperor should look, though his accent's pure West Country.

"Gabriel!" he says. The lip twitch turns into a laugh and he downs his drink. He puts two cigarettes in his mouth and lights both at once. The ends glow as he inhales. They mesmerize her. He passes one to her. They're French. Unfiltered. She knows to take only a small toke or she'll end up coughing half to death like she did the first time he offered her one. That set him off laughing as well, a proper belly laugh. They smoke together and he puts his arm around her shoulders and she leans right into him. It feels nice. His hand falls over her shoulder and she's hyperaware that his fingers are resting on the top of her breast. She turns her face to his.

"I'll bet you're no angel, though," she says.

It's a cheesy line, she knows it, but she gets what she wants because his answer is to bend his head down and kiss her so hard she almost gags at first, before she gives in to it. It's a drunken, Gauloises-flavored, teeth-clashing filthy sort of kiss. It's sort of gross, but she knows she wants it more than anything she's ever wanted.

"Who are you, anyway?" she says when the kiss breaks off. "What do you do exactly?"

"Wouldn't you like to know?" he says. He puts his finger under her chin and lifts it. As he studies her face, she realizes Felix Abernathy is the first person she's ever met who feels like he might offer a ticket out of her life.

"You ever done any modeling?" he asked her earlier that evening. She was arguing with the girl who was tending bar, because the bitch shortchanged her and Felix appeared right beside her as if from nowhere and smoothed the situation over, pressing cash into Jessy's hand to make up for what she was short. She tried to refuse it and was too embarrassed to admit she was especially bothered because it had been the last of her child support money. Her friend Kirsty had helped her justify a night out: "That money's for you, too. It's no good to Charlie if it's doing your head in staying in all the time." It was all the encouragement Jessy had needed.

Jessy and Felix go outside when they've finished their cigarettes. Felix's car is parked in a dark corner. He takes her around the front of it where they're in the shadows, and leans her against the bonnet and kisses her hard. When the kiss breaks off, he doesn't say a word. He flips her around, bends her over, lifts up her dress, and pulls down her panties. He crunches his hand tightly into her hair at the nape of her neck, and gives her what he calls a "good seeing to." He says that to her while he is going at it. She feels crushed against the car by the weight of him, but she wants him enough that she doesn't care.

Jessy can tell it isn't the first time he's done this with a girl. She's not stupid. She knows what men want. She's heard words like these before, though she's never understood why men want to talk to her like that. Felix finishes up with a grunt and a shudder, and a hard squeeze of one of her buttocks that hurts. He smokes while she puts herself back together and then he gives her a lift home. On the drive back to the estate he has one hand wedged deep between her legs as he rolls the wheel with the other, and he promises to pick her up the next night.

She is relieved he doesn't want to come up to the flat. She doesn't want him to see how she lives. She takes a moment to make herself look respectable before she lets herself in because Doris from next door is minding Charlie. Jess opens the door to find Doris asleep on the couch, leaning at a diagonal, mouth open as if she is dead, still in her housecoat.

Jessy pulls off her heels, trying not to stagger too much. The sex is still making her body thrum, or maybe it's the

Bacardi and Cokes she's had, probably both. She takes a hard look at Doris before she wakes her. *I don't want to end up like that,* she thinks. Doris had four kids of her own and would be the first to tell you they'd sucked the life out of her.

Jessy wakes Doris and hustles her out of the flat before Doris starts chatting unstoppably. She finds Charlie splayed out across her bed. He doesn't like sleeping on his own. Jessy smiles at the sight of him and gets in beside him, careful not to wake him. His little face looks perfect. His thumb is in his mouth. She kisses Charlie's forehead. She wonders what time he will be up in the morning. She feels dampness between her legs. She turns away from her son and stretches her spine and wishes she were in bed with Felix. A sudden lurch of her stomach sends her bolting for the bathroom, where she throws up the alcohol, the crisps from earlier in the evening, and the Gauloises-tinged taste of Felix, until there is only bile left. Slumped on the bathroom floor, she finds money falling out of her pocket. Three folded twenties. A fortune. From him.

When Felix Abernathy doesn't turn up to collect her the following night, even though she has spent ages getting ready, she refuses to take the hint that perhaps he wasn't as keen on her as she was on him. She doesn't think twice about the rough sex in the car park or the way he played games with her all evening. She thinks only of his looks and of the promises he'd made in the club when they were flirting. There were two that stuck with her: "I could get you some modeling work. I could introduce you to people in TV."

With the money he gave her, she goes out the next day and buys a new dress, a new push-up bra, a bottle of hair dye, and a lipstick. She borrows some killer heels from a mate. That night she returns to the nightclub. Felix Abernathy does a double take when he sees her, and that, she thinks as he pats the seat beside him and she walks over to take it, is a result.

have an ID on Lucky John Doe."

Danny sticks a Post-it note in the middle of Fletcher's computer screen. *Peter Dale* is written in the middle of it.

"Why does that name ring a bell?" Fletcher peels it off.

"Well, that's where it gets interesting," Danny says. "He was a con man. Pulled off a big property investment scam and was last rumored to be sunning himself on a beach in Venezuela, which is where everybody assumed he's been since then."

"Except that he was six feet under."

"Looks that way."

"Well, there's a turnup for the books."

Fletcher thinks for a minute, trolling his memory for details about Peter Dale. Dale's was a high-profile disgrace locally, so it doesn't take Fletcher long to come up with some. He can picture the unflattering photograph of Dale that ran in the papers and on the local TV news. It was a poor-quality holiday snap showing Dale standing beside a pool in swimming trunks. He was speaking on a mobile phone. He had his back to a young boy who stood behind him in tears. The image stuck with Fletcher because of that: the way Dale was ignoring the little fellow. The kid wasn't named, so far as Fletcher can remember, and Dale had no known children of his own, but that didn't matter. The picture made him look like as much of a lowlife as his crimes proved him to be.

"Bald guy," Fletcher says. "Big gut. I remember the case, but not when it was."

"Nineties, but let me check precisely. I'll get the details up," Danny says. The HOLMES database confirms what Fletcher remembers. He scans the information and feels a trip downstairs coming on.

In the archive store in the basement of Kenneth Steele House, Fletcher requests the case materials for Peter Dale. Compared to the buzz of the office upstairs, it feels unnaturally calm down here. It's a resting place for cold cases, and Fletcher thinks of it as an archive of failure. For every high-profile solve, there's an unsolved crime shelved here. In each tidily filed box, Fletcher thinks, there are not just papers, photographs, and other case materials, but other things, invisible things. There are traces of the open emotional wounds an unsolved crime leaves on the families and detectives affected by it. There is also the shadow of something more rotten: the person who got away with it. Fletcher shudders. Loose ends. He cannot stand them.

A lad who looks too young to have a job dumps a green crate containing the Peter Dale case materials onto the table in front of Fletcher. He glances quickly through the material and organizes the papers he's most interested in roughly chronologically so he can take a closer look. He wants to try to get a feel for events as they unfolded in real time.

The missing person report is the first document he studies. A woman called Hazel Collins made the report. It was recorded by a police constable named Joe Lansdown. Fletcher reads it closely:

I spoke to Hazel Collins at 7:47 P.M. on 20 August 1996. She called in at the police station on East Shrubbery to express concern that she hadn't heard from her boss, Peter Dale, for two days. She said he hadn't turned up at work since Monday in spite of having meetings arranged, and hadn't contacted her, which was very unusual. She said he has a mobile phone, but when she called it, it was going straight to a message service. She works with him in his office in central Bristol, and had been fielding calls from increasingly upset and angry clients who said that their money had disappeared. Hazel Collins had called at Peter Dale's home address, but there was no answer there, and when she looked through the letter box, she could see that mail had piled up in the hallway. So far as she knows, Peter Dale lived alone. Hazel Collins works as an executive assistant for Peter Dale. She is his only employee. She states that this behavior is out of the ordinary because Peter Dale is usually in touch with her many times a day, even when he isn't in the office.

The rest of the report consists of a list of actions that officers took in response to Hazel Collins's report. In the first instance, they were seeking to verify that Peter Dale was missing, not just away on a jolly for a few days.

Fletcher notes the date with interest. Hazel Collins filed the missing person report just two days after Charlie Paige and Scott Ashby were murdered. Again, rationally, it could mean either something or nothing, but the coincidences of both location and timing have piqued his interest a little more.

He picks up a slim brochure that's amongst the papers. It

looks very dated. It provides some information about Peter Dale's company and is obviously aimed at potential clients. It includes a head-and-shoulder shot of Dale and one of Hazel Collins. She looks to have been in her late forties or early fifties in 1996. It's hard to tell. She's wearing a white cotton top that dips low, almost offering a hint of cleavage, but not quite. She's overweight. The skin on her neck and chest is pale and putty-like. Her gold necklace looks cheap, and her hair, in all shades of gray, has been freshly brushed for the photograph. It's blunt cut at shoulder length around the back and sides, and an uncompromising fringe obscures both eyebrows. She was either without vanity, Fletcher thinks, or without money, or both. He'd like to speak to her as a priority.

Fletcher sifts through more papers. Some of them document the filtering of the case into the police's awareness and the public eye. It happened rapidly. As the days went by after the missing person report was filed, more and more people came forward to say they'd been victims of Peter Dale's scam. They weren't rich people trying to get richer, but families and small-business owners who had been seeking to invest their money well. They were angry, bitter, and in a few cases, depending on the extent of their financial exposure, totally ruined. One committed suicide. It made for sobering reading. Fletcher was a veteran of seeing security and safety snatched from people who are living good, ordinary lives, but the calculated nature of this crime appalls him especially.

For two or three days, as the extent of the fiscal and emotional devastation he'd caused became clearer, the police had searched for Peter Dale. It didn't take them long to discover that his passport was missing and so was his money. He'd emptied out his business accounts and transferred the money offshore. Tracking it down was going to be complicated, if not impossible. The chances of his victims getting a penny back from him seemed vanishingly small.

On Friday, 23 August, three days after Fletcher attended the murdered boys' autopsies, the investigation team on the Peter Dale case received a bit of information that confirmed their mounting suspicions. It was a sighting of him in Venezuela, at a marina. It was apparently from a trustworthy and independent source. At the time, Venezuela had no extradition treaty with Britain. Peter Dale was known to have visited the country previously. It was a place where a man could easily disappear and live very well if he had money, which Dale most certainly did. Fletcher flicks through the rest of the papers and wonders why police took the reported sighting so seriously, because in light of the discovery of Dale's body, it was almost certainly cobblers.

Fletcher takes a deep breath, fortifying himself for whatever this case will bring. He packs the papers away and signs them out. As he makes his way back upstairs, he thinks of the murdered boys again—how their case files will have been archived off-site, sealed, because their case was solved by Fletcher himself. He pauses on a landing to catch his breath and rests the crate on the banister. He feels a pulse of contempt for Cody Swift for trying to overturn stones that should be left as they are, settling quietly into the landscape until they look as if they've always been part of it.

The incident room is packed for Detective Superintendent Smail's briefing. For the first time in his career, Fletcher takes a seat facing the room. It feels good.

It is thirty hours since the bodies of Charlie Paige and Scott Ashby were discovered. So far, the investigation feels like an explosion that's hurling pieces of debris in every direction. News of the murders broke last night and the team have been fielding phone calls from the public ever since. Crackpots and pet theorists have been having a field day, calling in with tips, most of which everyone knows will turn out to be a load of rubbish.

Smail stands straight-backed in front of the team. On a desk between him and Fletcher rests his policy book, in which he records every decision he makes on the case and the rationale behind it. He's already filled a few pages as he and Fletcher have begun to impose order on the proceedings. They have formed teams to focus on victims, suspects, media, location, and vehicles. Fletcher has experienced a few moments of professional vertigo. He's acutely aware that his new position is a new opportunity but also a new level of exposure.

Smail addresses the team:

"The pathologist estimates time of death for Scott Ashby to be between eight and eleven P.M. on the night of Sunday, 18 August. Charlie Paige, as we know, died at eleven A.M. on Monday, 19 August—yesterday, in other words—but we must assume that he sustained his injuries at the same time as Scott. Given what we know of the boys' last movements, they are unaccounted for from approximately eight P.M., when one of the residents of the Glenfrome Estate saw them walking down a lane on the estate, until their discovery on Monday morning. We've talked to the boys' families and broken the news to them. Members of Scott Ashby's family have given us some helpful stuff for timelines, but Charlie Paige's mother, Jessica, was not in a fit state for interview, so we'll be trying to speak to her again today. We suspect that she was under the influence when we first spoke to her. Our priority now is

to talk to wider family and friends of the victims' families as well as neighbors.

"I want teams to divide up the buildings on the estate. I want every single door knocked on and a statement taken from every single person who knows the families or may have seen the boys. People are going to be scared. Mums and dads are going to be scared. Kiddies are going to be scared. Be sensitive to that.

"There's no racing at the track tonight, but we'll be interviewing there tomorrow, starting in the morning when it opens. I want statements from punters, trainers, track officials, and anyone else who knew or might have seen the boys. Particular attention needs to be paid to the kennels and the lads and lasses that work there. We'll talk to the builders on the site next door, to everybody who uses the community club between the estate and the track, and to the residents of the houses opposite. We need to cast our net as widely as possible, as quickly as possible, and see what we catch. I want this investigation to be efficient and effective. Don't let me down."

Fletcher wonders if anybody else in the room is catching a whiff of Smail's ego. He spies Danny at the back of the room, his preferred place to sit ever since he and Fletcher were in school together. Danny will have caught it, for sure.

The men and women disperse quickly after the meeting, once actions have been allocated and recorded. Their expressions are grim and determined. The case cuts close to the bone for everybody. Smail turns to Fletcher as the room empties.

"Lynn Rawlins has agreed to be FLO for Jessica Paige, Charlie's mother."

Fletcher nods his approval. The role of the family liaison officer is an important one, and Lynn Rawlins is perfect for it. She's sharp *enough to watch Jessica Paige like a hawk and emotionally intelligent enough to offer support.*

"Go with her to meet Jessica Paige, will you?" Smail says. "When I spoke to Ms. Paige yesterday I couldn't get a word out of her about where she was on Sunday night. She said she couldn't remember. Go easy on her. I want you to reinforce the message that we'll be doing everything we can on her behalf and on Charlie's, but try and get some sense out of her."

Jessica Paige's flat is on the fifteenth floor of one of the estate's six identical monolithic towers that loom against a turbulent cloudscape. There are two elevators in the lobby of Jessica Paige's building. One serves the odd-numbered floors, and the other the even numbers. After snatching only four hours of sleep last night, Fletcher is grateful they're working. He rings Jessica Paige's doorbell three times before she answers. She looks like crap. Fletcher wouldn't expect anybody to be looking together after losing a child, but his instinct is that there's a deeper level of neglect on display here.

Jessica's hair is greasy and her skin is pallid. So far, so understandable. She's wearing a vest top and a translucent sarong knotted around her waist so loosely it looks as if it'll fall at any second. Okay, she got dressed in a hurry. She's too skinny. You don't get skinny in a day. Fletcher notes a bruise on one of her upper arms. He wants to know who put it there. There are no visible track marks, at least. If she has a drug problem, she's not shooting up. That's something.

Fletcher and Rawlins follow Jessica into the flat. It's compact. Visible from the tiny entrance area is a child's bedroom, a bathroom that's seen better days, a poky kitchen dominated with a two-person table against the wall, and a living space where the window opens onto the balcony. Another door is shut. Fletcher assumes it's Jessica's bedroom.

She has minimal furniture. There's one small couch in the sitting room that looks as if it might have had previous owners over a couple of decades, a TV resting on a pile of magazines, and a plastic box upturned and in use as a coffee table. The carpet is covered with garish swirls in black and yellow. There are magazines, comics, dirty cups, plates, and cutlery on the floor. A flattened beanbag pools onto the carpet in front of the TV. Its black, plasticky cover is peeling off in places, and it sits in a puddle of polystyrene balls. Fletcher wonders if the dent in the middle of it was made by Charlie. Net curtains hang across the sitting room window, smudging the light. There's enough filtering in for Fletcher to see that the flat isn't much different in size from Scott Ashby's family's place, but the state of it is shocking in comparison. Nobody who lives here takes pride in their surroundings.

He thinks briefly of his own home. It's immaculate. There's not a day goes by when Mrs. Fletcher doesn't dust or clean the kitchen floor and surfaces or run the vacuum cleaner around the place. She manages to fit it in when the baby goes down for his nap.

On second glance, Fletcher finds one or two signs of domesticity in Jessica Paige's flat: a monochrome poster of Audrey Hepburn looking impossibly elegant has been tacked on the wall, so Jessica has aspirations perhaps, however unrealistic. Beside it there are some childish drawings. When Fletcher looks more closely, he sees Charlie has signed his name on most of them with varying levels of penmanship.

Jessica seems sober. She sits on the sofa and pulls a blanket over her, reducing what's visible of her to a pale face and large, dark eyes. Fletcher's relieved she's covered up. He's already seen enough of her underwear. It strikes him that she's very young to have a ten-year-old kid.

Fletcher introduces Lynn Rawlins, but decides to do the talking *himself. He's glad Danny's not here. Danny's got it in him to run a bit roughshod over female witnesses. Fletcher takes a seat at the other end of the couch from Jessica. Lynn takes a seat on the beanbag. It takes her a few seconds to settle. As the polystyrene balls move beneath her, they sound like falling sand. It sets Fletcher's teeth on edge.*

As soon as Fletcher mentions Charlie's name, Jessica starts to cry. He watches her carefully. Her grief seems genuine, but he knows that guilt can produce grief, just as loss can.

"Anything you can tell us could be helpful," he says. "You knew Charlie best. Has anything come back to you about Sunday night? Anything at all?"

"I can't remember."

"What, nothing?"

"I remember getting out of the taxi and everybody was waiting there for me, but I don't remember what happened before." Her voice is so low it might be a whisper.

"Did you black out?"

"I might have."

"Had you been drinking?"

She nods.

"What's your last memory before the taxi?"

She shakes her head and the tears come again and seem unstoppable. Lynn Rawlins excuses herself and beckons to Fletcher to follow her into the hallway.

"Let's give her some time," she says. "Leave her with me. I'll make her some tea and something to eat and take it from there."

Fletcher nods. He can't wait to get out of there.

"Any priorities?" Rawlins asks.

"Where she was on Sunday evening, and who she was with."

Jessica calls out something that neither Fletcher nor Rawlins can make out.

"What was that, love?" Rawlins asks. She and Fletcher move to the doorway. Jessica looks up at them from the sofa, shadows carving holes out of her face.

"Where I was," she says. She must have overheard them.

"Where were you, darling?" Rawlins asks.

"Paradise. I remember now." Jessica laughs. It sounds artificial and loud, and Fletcher's heart sinks. She's playing games with them. Maybe she's still high or drunk. The look on Rawlins's face tells him she's come to the same conclusion. "There's no point in both of us hanging around," she says. "Let me get on with it. I'll page you if I learn anything useful."

Fletcher takes his leave. On the way down in the elevator, he realizes Jessica might have been more helpful than she seemed.

Paradise, he remembers, is the name of a casino.

Jessica is fostering the rescue cat for the time being. She felt sorry for it at the shelter because it looked depressed in its cage. Its fur is cotton wool soft and it is generally a sweet old thing, though Jess has learned to beware when it rolls onto its back. If she tries to stroke its tummy, it strikes lightning fast with claws and teeth.

Two days have passed since Cody Swift ambushed Jess in the car park and she is still rattled, though not rattled enough to contact Felix yet. She has been working hard to push that impulse back into the cage it should never have escaped from.

She was too upset after the incident with Cody to hide what had happened from Nick. After she told him about it, she watched a red flush spread swiftly across his neck and cheeks.

"I'm going to call him again," Nick said, "and tell him—"

"Don't bother," she said. "Honestly, don't."

"I'll find out where he lives and tell him face-to-face."

"Don't lower yourself. He's not worth it. I told him to get lost. He got the message." She was already regretting letting slip what had happened. She learned years ago how to keep things a secret and to deal with them herself, but her instincts have got soft since she married Nick.

"I want to protect you from this," Nick said.

I don't want you to have to, Jess thought. She adores him when he says this kind of thing, but finds it uncomfortable, too, because whatever Nick says or does to prove how much he loves her, she will always believe she is damaged goods and not worth the ground he walks on.

"Darling, I'm fine," she said. "Please, don't get worked up. I told Cody he would have to answer to you if he comes near me again. He understood. He understands."

She leaned in toward Nick. He put his arms around her and kissed the top of her head and they stayed that way, still as statues, while Jess let her demons rage secretly inside her.

She kept her emotions carefully in check for Nick's last two days of leave, praying that Cody would not try to contact them again. She put on her best wife-and-mother game face and went out of her way to make everything as nice as possible for Nick and for Erica. This is something she's discovered she's good at: buffing her small family's domestic experience until it shines.

Now she waves Nick goodbye as a cab takes him to the station. He's on his way to London for days of preproduction meetings. Erica is out with Olly. As soon as Nick has gone, Jess shuts the front door behind her and bolts it. She lowers the slats on the shutters covering the front windows. The house darkens inside, but she doesn't care. She stands in the gloom and takes deep breaths. With Nick gone, it is almost a relief to allow herself to taste and feel her fear. Keeping it bottled up has taken a toll on her. She is exhausted, but she feels she has time and space to think now, and her first thought is that if Cody Swift is planning on coming to her house, she's not going to make it easy for him to snoop. She nips out to the bins by the back door and pulls out the two bags of rubbish that are in there. She puts them in the garage and double-checks that the up and over door is locked. She knows better than to leave anything around that a stranger can get their hands on. After the murders and during the trial Jess was stalked by reporters for weeks.

When Erica gets home she probably won't notice the extra security measures—she lives too much in her own sweet sixteen bubble—but if she asks about the gloom, Jess will say she has a migraine. *Or should I tell her what's happening?* Jess thinks. *Should I? Would Erica be safer?* She checks herself as soon as she's had the thought. *Erica is not in any real danger,* she tells herself. *Not yet. Not nearly. Not if I can help it.*

In Jess's wary mind, that train of thought leads inevitably to another. She can't help thinking how she herself was used and abused by men as a teenager and later, until she met Nick. That at least is a danger her and Nick's careful parenting has spared Erica from. That safety is something her daughter has that Jess never did.

The thought stirs pride but also a familiar swell of anger in her. She battled her anger so hard after Charlie's death: anger that he had been murdered, anger at what she had been through herself, anger at what people said about her, anger at herself for not being a better mother. Being safe with Nick let the anger rise. He encouraged her to feel it. "You need to," he said, "or it'll eat you up from the inside." How she raged.

Now that she feels less vulnerable in the house, she goes upstairs to her office and sits in front of the computer. She will resist looking up the podcast, she tells herself. She fears it. Instead, she types two words into the search engine: Felix

Abernathy. She clicks on the link to his website. When it loads she flinches. *Felix Abernathy Public Relations* scrolls across a black screen, and then she is face-to-face with an almost life-size head shot of Felix himself.

A photograph can't hurt me, she has to tell herself, though her heart has begun to pound and goose bumps are rising on her arms. She can hear her own breathing. *Calm down,* she thinks. The cat has begun to move in silky figures of eight between her feet; she reaches down and scoops him up onto her lap. She clicks further into the website. "Face your fears," Felix told her once, with a crooked smile that was part encouragement, part threat. She can hear his voice as she sits in her study today, even though he spoke those words to her more than twenty years ago. She shudders as she remembers how his fingertips were poised on the handle of a hotel room door when he said it, and how his other hand was in the small of her back, exerting pressure, ushering her into a room where a man was waiting. She has to shake her head to rid herself of the memory. The cat gazes up at her levelly as she does. "Waifs and strays, the pair of us," Jess tells it.

She takes a deep breath and explores the website further, but it contains minimal personal information about Felix. She didn't really expect to find any, but she can't help feeling a twinge of disappointment because while this is stressful, she can't deny she's also curious about what Felix is like now, perhaps morbidly so. Just the thought of him creates a pull in her gut even after all these years. She hates that it does. It feels like a dirty part of her, but it also keeps her finger on the mouse and her eyes on the screen as she clicks through each page on the website and examines every photograph of him.

In most of the pictures Felix has his arm slung around a client. The majority of his clients are instantly recognizable to Jess as celebrities. There will be others, Jess thinks, who are not keen to be on display and for whom Felix's discretion will be his greatest asset. He has always done favors for people who need those favors to remain a secret. It was how he rose so high and so fast, back in the day. He became very useful to some very influential people in Bristol. He facilitated their illegal habits and made sure those habits were kept out of the public eye and beyond the law.

The clients in the pictures are a type Jess also recognizes, because she was like that once. In the main, they are young women or reality TV stars. They are the most hungry and vulnerable, Jess thinks, the ones who'll use and abuse their bodies in every way imaginable, just to get their picture in the paper. They want fame and take any route to get it. Just like Jess did. How ironic that it was Nick who finally got her work in the industry, after all the promises Felix made.

She strokes the cat as her eyes rove over the images on-screen. Its purr sounds like an idling engine. There's no denying Felix has aged well. He looks good. Well groomed and well dressed in a way that only money can buy. He has a bright white smile and there's no sign of the gap between his front teeth she used to find attractive. "Your dream came true, then," she says aloud. She's not sure what it is, maybe the sight of all those desperate young women hooked on Felix's arm or the contrast between Felix's lifestyle and her own quiet domestic life, but suddenly she's had enough of snooping on him. She clicks the small red circle on the top corner of her browsing window and Felix disappears. She rests her eyes on the computer wallpaper: a professional photograph of herself with Nick and Erica. This is what she should be concentrating on. She stands up abruptly and the cat falls to the carpet, hissing its disapproval. "Tough luck," she says to it. "We can't always get what we want."

She will go for a run, she thinks. It will help her get rid of the tension she's been carrying around for days. She'll push herself and go for one of her longer routes. Ten minutes later she's changed and stepping out, earbuds in, house key zipped safely into a pocket, determination to maintain control of her life launching her run at a challenging pace.

The woman opens the door of her car as Jess is about to jog past. She's only a few yards from her driveway and getting into her stride. The door takes up most of the pavement and forces Jess to stop abruptly. "I'm so sorry," the woman says, and Jess grimaces, jogging on the spot and waiting for her to shut the door when the woman asks, "Are you Jessica Paige?"

Jess isn't sure she's heard correctly at first. Her music's on quite loudly. She turns. She'll run around the car if this stupid cow won't shut her door like a normal person, but the woman repeats, loudly enough that Jess hears it crystal clear this time, "Jessica Paige?"

Jess's heart skips a beat. She stops.

"I'm from the *Bristol Echo*. Have you got a minute?"

The small smile curling the edge of the woman's lip has a callous shape that Jess dislikes. This has got to be about the podcast. Jess pretends she didn't hear. She flashes the woman her best bland smile and runs as fast as she can, cutting down random roads and into narrow alleyways. She doesn't stop until she reaches her local park, and by the time she gets there, she's so out of breath she sinks onto a bench.

"Fuck!" she says. There's nobody close enough to hear her. At first she can do nothing more than wait for her breathing to slow and the pounding of her heart to subside. As they do, she becomes aware of the ache in her legs. She doesn't normally sprint that hard.

She tries to get her thoughts together. She needs to figure out how to get home without running into that woman again. She needs to know whether this was simply a random journalist trying it on in response to the podcast because there's no other news today, or if there's a bigger problem. She tries not to think about Felix. He must be a last resort. *Two days,* she thinks, *for two days it felt as if there was a chance things could go back to normal again, and now this.*

She turns off her music so she can try to think straight, but the noises of the park intrude immediately: dogs barking, the squeak of another runner's shoes, and worst of all, children's voices from somewhere nearby. It's a reel of playtime sound effects: shrieks, yells, the scuffs and shoe slaps of running and dodging, and laughter. It triggers a physical reaction in Jess. Her breathing quickens as if she's still running, and her chest tightens. She knows what's happening because it has happened before, though not for a very long time. It's a panic attack. Her vision blurs and she screws her eyes shut. She wraps her arms around her stomach and leans forward. It's as if the whole of her life is concentrated in this one moment and she can never move beyond it; it feels both painful and hollow. She moans. It's a feral sound, long and low and empty of hope. It expresses only a fraction of the guilt Jess has felt for the past twenty years. She'll never stop blaming herself for Charlie's death. Never.

Sometimes she wins the fight against the guilt—as the years have gone by, she's won more often than not, though even if she does, it still feels *close*—but sometimes she loses, badly. There have been weeks on end when she has felt as if the simplest things—getting dressed, taking a shower, making a cup of tea—require Herculean amounts of effort. During those weeks, she feels disengaged from Nick and from Erica. When she is at her lowest, all she knows for certain is that she's no better than a dirty, filthy thing, an unfit mother, a whore. She fully inhabits the names that people called her all those years ago, and she does not attempt to check the self-hatred she feels because she believes it is what she deserves.

In the park, when the first wave of panic begins to subside, she opens her eyes and sees a pair of neon trainers. Somebody is standing in front of her and speaking to her.

"Are you all right? Excuse me, are you okay?"

It's a young man. He has a hand stretched out toward her as if he wants to touch her, but knows that's not okay. She has a sudden urge to lash out and say something vicious to him, but she doesn't. She has spent twenty years training herself out of the aggression she sometimes had to use to protect or defend herself and Charlie on the estate.

"I'm fine," she says. "Thank you."

"Are you sure?"

"Very sure. Sorry. Thank you."

Jess gets up to demonstrate that she's fine, and he says, "Okay," though he doesn't look sure until she fixes on a smile and attempts a stretch. As soon as he's gone, she sits back down and stays there for a long time before she makes her way home at a careful jog. On the way, she thinks, *If that woman is still outside my house, I'll call Felix; if she's not, I won't.* It feels decisive. It gives her the illusion of control. It allows her to put one foot in front of the other.

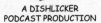

IT'S TIME TO TELL

EPISODE 4—THE DETECTIVES

"This case turned around and bit me on the ass. Fatally. Even if you've dedicated your life to justice and to the law, you can't survive something like that. I was set up."

My name is Cody Swift. I'm a filmmaker and your host of *It's Time to Tell*, a Dishlicker Podcast Production. Those are the words of ex–Detective Superintendent Howard Smail, the man in charge of the investigation into Charlie's and Scott's murders. I didn't meet him personally twenty years ago, but his name was on everybody's lips. Here's what his deputy on the case, John Fletcher, had to say about him:

"I looked up to Howard Smail. I wanted to learn from him and I was eager to work with him, but he behaved unacceptably and he paid the price for that when he lost his job. It was hugely disappointing, not just for me as his deputy, but for the team and for the families of Scott and Charlie. Thank God we were able to solve the case regardless. You say Howard Smail is living abroad now? I wonder if he remembers us. There are a lot of people here in Bristol waiting for an apology for what he did."

I was familiar with the police from a young age. It was not unusual to see a squad car pull into one of the Glenfrome Estate car parks, though unusual enough to attract interest. My mother would twitch back a curtain to better see where the officers might be headed. My dad would glance, then shrug and get on with what he was doing. In other households, the occupants might step carefully back from the window and think about alternative exit routes from the building. Depending on what they had done, neighbors might help cover their tracks. There was a code of silence on the estate: you protected your own. That code shattered if the crime involved children, though. People who hurt children were considered no better than scum.

So when Detective Inspector John Fletcher and Detective Constable Danny Fryer came to call on our family after Charlie and Scott's bodies were found, they weren't the first police officers I'd seen or spoken to, but they were the first detectives. The title had a sort of glamour to it. Perhaps that's why their visit is the only thing I can remember from that time.

Detective Fryer wore a business suit with creases in the trousers. He had brown eyes and a silky handkerchief in the pocket of his jacket. He looked sharp, but he was kind. I suppose Detective Fletcher was wearing a suit and tie, too, but I can't recall. All I remember about him is that he stood in the doorway of our living room and watched us. I felt as if I was on display, as if he could see right through me.

Fletcher and Fryer worked the investigation, but it was led, as I've mentioned, by Detective Superintendent Howard Smail. He was the senior investigating officer on the case, and his was the voice you heard at the start of this episode. Smail worked on the case for just one week before being forced to step down.

Since then he has been a recluse. He won't give interviews. Any reporters who have managed to track him down have had doors slammed in their faces and threats of legal action against them.

I contacted one of those journalists. This is what she had to say in an email:

> "I can give you an address for Smail, but I have two bits of advice. One: Pack your thermals. Two: He does not speak to anybody, even if you offer very good money. Don't think there's anything different about you."

I thought there was something different about me, though. Who else was as intimately connected to the case as I was? Which explains how Maya and I find ourselves in a hired car driving along a coastal highway that links an archipelago of islands off the coast of northern Norway. We have taken two flights to get here so far, and set out on a long highway, which stretches over a hundred miles. At the end of it we hope to meet and interview ex–Detective Superintendent Howard Smail.

To say that the place we are headed to is remote would be an understatement. Howard Smail has done *reclusive* in style. We arrive at his village in the late afternoon. It feels as if it is on the edge of the world. Old fishermen's cottages teeter on the edge of the land, held up on stilts that disappear into glassy water. Dominating the roadside where we stop is a large wooden structure that resembles the skeleton of an old chapel. Stockfish are draped over every horizontal beam, yellow-brown and tightly packed. They smell fetid and salty. There is snow on the ground, but not as much as I was expecting. We scramble across the rocks to look at the water in the inlet. It seems bottomless. Reflections of the dark mountains surrounding us float on the surface. Below, large jellyfish drift, transparent tentacles wafting unhurriedly. Everything we see is beautiful and mesmerizing, yet harsh.

Howard Smail's house is only two miles down the road. We park the car and I get out. I'm standing beside a five-bar gate at the entrance to the driveway of a modest traditional property. It's late afternoon and the light has almost faded completely. There's a sign on the gate. I can't read Norwegian, but the picture of a large dog tells me everything I need to know. Maya stays in the car. I open the gate and walk toward the door. I can see lights on inside the property and hear a dog barking. I ring the bell and chimes sound from inside the house. The door opens a crack.

"Hello?"

"Hello, Mr. Smail? Sir, my name is Cody Swift. I don't know if you remember me? No? Well, that's okay. I've come here to see you because I'm working on a podcast about the murders of Scott Ashby and Charlie Paige."

That sound you just heard? That was the sound of Smail's front door slamming in my face. I try calling out to him.

"Charlie and Scott were my best friends, Mr. Smail! I don't know if you know, but Sidney Noyce took his own life recently. I'm investigating allegations that police put the wrong man behind bars. Do you have a comment for me, Mr. Smail?"

He didn't. The door remains shut and the dog continues to bark. Maya watches from the car, her face white behind the windscreen. I retreated.

That night, as the northern lights snaked across the sky, Maya and I decided I should write Howard Smail a letter. We could afford to spend only one more full day in the Lofoten Islands before starting our trek back to the airport, so we hand-delivered the letter first thing the following morning. Howard Smail called early afternoon, just when we were beginning to give up hope. He said four words: "You can come now."

The sound of the dog barking is more distant when I approach his house for the second time. The daylight will not last much longer, but today there is enough of it that I can see his house is positioned on the rocky shore of an inlet and in the shadow of a sheer mountainside. Smail shows me in with few words and invites me to sit in a small lounge paneled in cream-painted wood and warmed by a stove. A fine antique telescope is mounted on a stand and points at the mountainside.

What follows is a recording of our conversation. Smail took control of the interview at the start. He immediately addressed what might otherwise have been the elephant in the room: the scandal that forced him out of his job during the investigation into Charlie and Scott's deaths.

"I'm going to say this once and I will not repeat it: I did not assault Jessica Paige. I exhibited no inappropriate behavior around her. Her accusation was entirely untrue. The charge was fabricated against me in order to ruin me and to halt certain aspects of the investigation. I'm prepared to discuss the investigation with you, because your letter was very honest, but on condition we don't talk about the accusation and you report that I maintain my innocence."

"Of course."

"So, what do you want to know?"

"I have a list of questions we can work through, or you can start by telling me what you remember and we can go from there?"

"Is that thing recording already?"

"Yes."

"The case was a Category A murder investigation. That's as serious as it gets. Resources were not a problem. I picked the best men for my team. I launched that investigation meticulously. This is the kind of case where you don't even care if you're paid or not, because it involves kids. Your only goal is to catch whoever took the lives of those two boys and you are prepared to do whatever it takes. Nobody wants to see this investigation fail. Nobody apart from the person who committed the crime."

"Can you tell me about your team?"

"My team was excellent. I picked John Fletcher to be my deputy because he'd come to my attention as a very bright up-and-coming detective, and I wanted to give him an opportunity. Plus, he was one of the officers who found the boys. He found them and Charlie Paige died in his arms. That's the kind of thing that stays with you your whole career, probably until your dying day. Even if he wouldn't admit to it—because he is not the type of guy to show emotions—I'm sure that moment still haunts John Fletcher today and will do so until the end of his own life. It meant that by the time I appointed Fletcher to deputy investigating officer, the case was already in his bones."

"Can you talk about the first few days of the case?"

"A murder case is a complicated thing. Always. The lead

detective must take his or her time at first, even though time is the one thing you haven't got. You need to ignore that. No matter how crazy the press is going around you and how much pressure is on you from families and senior officers to solve the case quickly, you cannot rush in. See out that window? Where the telescope is pointing?"

"The mountainside?"

"See how the clouds send shadows scudding across it, so one moment it looks black, then it's a dark green, then sunshine glints off one particular area, but that changes after a few seconds? There is snow, but it can melt or be replenished. It disguises the contours. To get the measure of that mountain, you need to look at it over time. You cannot make a swift assessment of the lay of the land. A murder case is like that. There are two sea eagle families who live around this fjord. Imagine one of them is hovering above the landscape, searching the water for signs of prey. He's assessing if the water is choppy or glassy, if he can see what he's looking for or not. That's the first stage of an investigation. You need an *overview of everything*. You are looking for facts. What are the facts? They will begin to emerge if you are patient, and if you don't form your own theories before the investigation has even begun. When the sea eagle is satisfied that he has a good overview of what is going on, he drops down lower. Maybe he's seen something that draws his attention to a particular spot. He's hovering closer to the water now, strategizing about how to make his catch, the speed he'll need, angles of attack, working out if what he thinks he can see is really prey or just a shadow or a piece of plastic floating in the water. If he drops down too early or the wrong way, he's blown it. The prey will get away and the eagle will go hungry. So he makes sure he knows what he's looking at. He makes sure he's sure. The first few hours and days of an investigation are all about establishing facts, finding out what is true and working with that, forming theories based on the facts. Then, when you are sure, and only then do you swoop down and bag your prey. That's the idea, anyway."

"Does that mean you were looking at a wide pool of suspects?"

"Families of victims are always of immediate interest. Statistics tell you a family member can be a likely perpetrator in any homicide. But we never assume. We were gathering information about the boys, their families, but also their friends, their neighbors, the community, people's habits and patterns, and so on."

By this point in our conversation, the light in the room has become grainy, smudging Smail's features. He gets up with a grunt to switch on a lamp and at the same time retrieves a sheaf of papers from a desk drawer. He sits down with the papers on his lap. I'm the first to speak.

"Was there agreement amongst the team about which leads you should pursue?"

"There may be repercussions if I discuss that."

"Even here? Now?"

"I'm not as vulnerable as if I was in the UK, but people can reach you. They won't like me talking about the case at all, let alone about internal decision-making. It's not what you do. Ever. It's taboo. I'm persona non grata anyway, but this will make it worse. Ask yourself if that's something you would willingly bring on yourself."

"I understand."

"I will say that there were disagreements, but I was the senior investigating officer, so I should have had the final call on any decisions. Unfortunately, I was not on the investigation for long enough to enforce those decisions."

"Because of the accusation made by Jessica Paige?"

"Because of that. I was set up."

"Who set you up?"

"I won't speculate about that on tape. But you might ask yourself who had the most to gain from my 'disgrace.'"

Smail looks agitated. He puts the papers down just far enough away so I can't make out what they are. He gets up and feeds the stove with a few logs that have been precisely chopped into small pieces. Flames surge around them after he closes the stove door. When he retakes his seat, he grabs the papers and holds them up.

"This is a copy of my policy book from the case."

"Can you explain what that is?"

"A policy book is kept by the lead detective on every case. He uses it to make a record of each of the decisions he makes and the rationale behind them. Obviously, this isn't the actual book. That will be under lock and key in Bristol with the original case files. This is a photocopy."

"Why do you have a photocopy?"

"I wouldn't be the first officer who took a copy of a docu-

ment that's officially police property and mailed it to himself.
It's an insurance policy."

"Why do you need an insurance policy?"

"I knew I was about to be under investigation for something
I didn't do. I wanted to keep a record of my decision-making
on the case to protect myself from further accusations."

"Are you saying you were concerned people might tamper
with your policy book after you left the investigation? In order to misrepresent your work?"

"If somebody is going to manufacture a sexual assault allegation, why wouldn't they also try to discredit my work?
Look, when things are going well, CID is the best place in
the world to work, but when they're not going well, it can
feel like the loneliest place on earth."

"Lonelier than here?"

"People think I came here to escape. But who really escapes these days? It's impossible unless you're willing to give
up everybody you've ever loved. No, I came here because it's
home. My mother is from this island."

"Are you willing to share the contents of those papers?"

"I might be. If I think it's relevant."

"Can I see the papers?"

"No. I want to listen to more of your podcast before I
decide what I might release. You have editorial control over
your material, which is a powerful thing, and I want to see
where you're going with all this."

"I have to prove myself?"

"We all have to prove ourselves."

"And how do I know you are telling the truth?"

"That's up to you to decide. Personally, I've nothing to prove."

"Except that the accusation against you was fabricated."

"Except for that, yes."

Howard Smail and I spoke late into the night and I'll share more of our conversation in future episodes. He continued to talk about the case with the same strange mixture of defensiveness, paranoia, and acuity. He had such good recall of the details it was as if it had happened yesterday. He gave me a lot to think about. He also agreed to keep in touch. Maya and I made the long drive back to the airport feeling elated.

On our return to Bristol, I made efforts to contact Detective Inspector John Fletcher. He is still in service in the Criminal Investigations Department and his rank hasn't changed. A little while ago, after a frustrating few days of leaving messages, I got a call back from him and we met in a mall car park, a location suggested by him.

It was very strange to see Detective Fletcher in person again after all these years. He still had the steely detective's gaze. He explained he was unable to share details about the investigation and could discuss only what is already in the public domain. He explained that the case remained closed as far as police were concerned, regardless of Weston's allegations, but that police would of course consider any new evidence, should it arise. He was utterly professional. He wished me well. I wouldn't have expected him to say anything different, however frustrating it might be, because his hands are tied. He also told me I could call him anytime, and it's good to have the lines of communication open.

In the next episode, we'll be discovering more about the prime suspect in the case, Sidney Noyce. He was charged and convicted of the murders of Charlie and Scott. This is Valerie Noyce, his mother:

"Sidney grew bigger than his dad before he was seventeen, but he never developed in his head. The doctors and the social workers told us he would only ever have the sense of a ten-year-old, and they were right. They call it mental impairment these days. Back then they said Sid was a retard. It's not a nice word, is it?"

Jess sits on the easy chair in the corner of the bedroom she and Nick share and watches him pack. She loves the way he does it so precisely: garments rolled or carefully folded and neatly tucked into place. He's finally off to Morocco for his six-week shoot and has managed to fit everything he needs into a modest-sized bag. He zips it shut.

"Done," he says.

"Good job."

Jess hasn't told Nick about the journalist who ambushed her outside the house when he was away before. She's worked hard to cover the agitation she felt in the aftermath of that. Nor has she mentioned the email she received this morning.

"Come and visit me in Morocco," Nick says. "Please. Maybe Erica could come, too, if you make it half term, and bring Olly. They could come to the set."

"I'll price up flights," she says.

"Do you mean it?"

"Of course!" She doesn't mean it, though. The email that landed in her inbox this morning has made a trip impossible, but she can't tell him. Once again, she needs him to leave so she has time and headspace to deal with this her way.

The email was from a woman called Maya Summers who described herself as Cody Swift's "life partner" and explained that she was working on the podcast with him. Would it be possible, the note had asked, if Jess didn't want to meet with Cody, for Jess and Maya to maybe get to know each other over email in the first instance, woman to woman? Jess felt her irritation mount as she read it. As if opening up to a woman podcaster was any less exposing than talking to Cody! They must think she was born yesterday. She snorted as she read the ridiculous email, but she also felt her dread ratchet back up because it wasn't looking likely that Cody was going to back off anytime soon. It's tempting to get on a plane to Morocco and hope the whole thing will go away, but what if it doesn't die down, but balloons instead? She wouldn't be able to stay away forever. She needs to act.

As soon as Nick has left, Jess finds Felix's website online once again and clicks through to the "Contact Us" page. She dials his office. Her call is answered by a woman with a clipped voice: "Felix Abernathy PR."

"Can I speak to Felix, please?"

"He's unavailable just now. Can I help you?"

"I need to speak to him urgently. I'm an old friend."

"Can I take your name?"

"Jessy Paige." Jess can hear a keyboard clacking at the other end of the line. "It's a bit of business," she adds, because she knows that money talks louder than anything else for Felix. She's pleased with how she's coming over. She sounds businesslike. She recites her phone number, says a polite goodbye, hangs up, and gives in to her nerves. Her forehead is still resting on the cool surface of her desk when her mobile rings. She sits up and looks at the screen. It's a London number. She takes a deep breath before answering. "Hello."

"Jessy Paige!" Felix's voice resonates down the line. It hasn't changed a bit. He sounds so confident, as if he owns her still.

She shuts her eyes. "Thanks for calling me back."

"I wouldn't miss a catch-up with you for the world. How are you? How's married life treating you?" The question is more harmful than it seems. Jess is pretty sure he is purposely echoing words she spat at him years ago, after she had met Nick and when she finally stood up to Felix and refused to take part in one of his sex parties. "I'm with someone now, someone good," she had said, prying his fingers off her arm. "I want normal. We're getting married."

"That doesn't mean you can't be nice to other men now and then," he'd replied. "Since when did you zip your knickers up and get so bloody bourgeois?" He'd followed that up with a direct hit: "Probably for the best, though, darling. I've had complaints about your dead eyes."

She used to be able to disarm Felix occasionally by being completely honest and she goes for that tactic over the phone now. "It's really lovely," she says. "I'm very happy. How about you?"

"Oh, I'm happy as a bloody bandicoot, darling, or I was until my girl said you had a bit of business for me, which makes me think you're in a spot of bother like last time you rang. What was that? Sixteen years ago?"

He's referring to the time when she was on *Dart Street* and he quashed the story about Charlie for her. It was before the millennium. Long enough ago that the internet didn't instantly deliver every news item straight to people's fingertips. She knows she won't be so lucky if the story goes big nowadays.

"Yes," she says. "Near enough."

"What's the problem? What can I do?"

"Do you recall the name Cody Swift?"

"Refresh my memory."

She tells Felix about the podcast, how she is afraid her life will be ripped apart if he can't help her put a stop to it. When she's finished talking, he remains quiet for so long she wonders if he's going to hang her out to dry on this one.

"Jessy," he says eventually, "I wouldn't do this for anybody, but you know I think of you as family. I can help you, but I think it would be best if we meet to talk about it. You know I don't trust phones. Can you come and see me tomorrow?"

She doesn't want to. The thought of it makes her skin crawl, but she doesn't see that she has a choice, if a meeting is what he wants. This favor is on a bigger scale than the last time. It'll be more difficult for him. They agree on a lunchtime appointment. It means she can be back in Bristol by the time Erica gets home from her course, which is something at least.

Once the call has ended, Jess goes to the bedroom and sits at her dressing table. She gazes at her reflection in the mirror, then gently pushes the skin on her cheeks back and upward and glimpses a version of her younger self.

She glimpses Erica in her own features, too. They look alike. She has raised Erica so differently from Charlie, and she wonders again if she should have taught her daughter to be more streetwise. It was a conscious choice for Jess not to raise her daughter that way, but to protect her instead. It was a decision she made because Charlie was more savvy and streetwise than he should have been and it didn't help him in the end, but for the first time Jess wonders if a different upbringing would mean Erica was less vulnerable to threat. Because a threat is exactly what the podcast feels like.

She releases her skin and it settles back into place. She wonders what Felix will think of her now. She wonders what she will think of him and whether there will be any attraction between them after all these years, and immediately feels guilty for the thought. She opens her wardrobe and begins to lay clothes on her bed, putting together outfits that might work for the trip to London. In the end, she narrows it down to two possibilities. Both cover as much flesh as possible.

letcher takes the Peter Dale case files home and dumps the crate on the dining table. The high sheen his wife used to rub into the table every week has been gone for as long as she has. The surface is dull and marked by a pattern of pale interlocking rings left by the bases of mugs, wine-glasses, and the noodle pots Fletcher has been eating most nights, interspersed with a bit of frying. Fletcher decants the contents of the crate onto the table and sits down before re-membering he's forgotten to take his coat off. He can't be bothered to get up again so he wriggles out of the coat and drops it on the floor. Since his wife left, he's found bittersweet pleasure in doing things she would have chided him for.

He fixes himself baked beans on toast and eats it at the table. He drinks a glass of wine with it and finds himself star-ing at the space on top of the upright piano where the family photos used to be. Two sons, he thinks, and neither one loyal to him after the divorce. He expected it of Theo, his younger child, always a mother's boy, but for his elder son, Andrew, to side with his mother feels like a sharp betrayal to Fletcher. Andrew is a son to be proud of. Fletcher tries to give him a call, but Andrew's voice mail picks up with its familiar and never-fulfilled promise that he'll return the call ASAP.

In the silence after he's left his son a message, Fletcher once again considers the photograph of Hazel Collins, the secretary of the missing man. He estimates she must be in her seventies by now. He hopes she's alive because she's a person of immediate interest to him. She reported Peter Dale missing and she worked closely with him. He pours another glass of wine and begins to go through each and every paper carefully. He intends to build a list of persons of interest. Hazel Collins is the first name he writes down.

THE FOLLOWING MORNING starts well. Good news and the buzz of the office help Fletcher shake off the blues after a sleepless night. Hazel Collins proves easy to track down even though she has moved from the address they had for her originally. Her new home is on a smart street overlooking the Clifton Suspension Bridge. It's the best view in town. Danny speaks to her daughter Annabel, who lives with Hazel, and learns that the older woman is in reasonable but not entire possession of her faculties and will be happy to see them at any time after eleven A.M.

At ten minutes past eleven, Fletcher and Danny climb the black-and-white-tiled front steps of Hazel Collins's address. It's a four-story Georgian house painted pastel blue. The original decorative balcony adorns the first floor and its black-and-white-striped awning has been freshly painted. Hazel Collins's property is on the ground floor. Inside the building, the staircase in the atrium is ornate. Wood paneling wraps around the space to waist height, with striped wallpaper above it. Three letter trays are neatly arranged on a console table, labeled with residents' names. Hanging above the table is a large watercolor of the suspension bridge in a gilt frame. This place isn't what Fletcher imagined based on the photograph he saw of Hazel Collins in the case notes. He wonders where the money has come from.

A woman stands in the doorway of the ground-floor flat. She's young but well dressed in ballet pumps, formfitting jeans, and a tucked-in shirt. "Annabel Collins," she says. Her handshake is firm. At her invitation, they step directly into a generous-sized sitting room. Fletcher takes in a grand piano and floor-to-ceiling windows offering a spectacular view of the bridge. Sunlight glints on the bridge's parabolic steel girders, and behind it, the sheer face of the densely wooded gorge is in shadow, creating a still, dark backdrop.

Annabel Collins shows them through a formal dining area and a midsize but grandly appointed kitchen to a courtyard garden, where an elderly woman is kneeling beside a bed of roses. She's mulching them carefully. Fletcher's nostrils curl at the mild whiff of manure. "She still likes to garden," Annabel says to the detectives and then, louder, says, "Mum! Do you want to come in and have a chat? About Peter? Remember I told you the detectives were coming."

Annabel Collins seats Fletcher and Danny in the sitting room, and they wait an age while she helps her mother get out of her coat and boots and the older woman washes her hands. When Hazel finally takes a seat opposite them, Fletcher can't help noticing the bloody wounds on her liver-spotted knuckles where the rose thorns have caught her. She's wearing a soft knitted turtleneck sweater in pale blue and a generous string of pearls. Her pure white curls look windswept after her gardening efforts, but they've been carefully tended at some point this morning. There's a hint of vacancy in her cloudy eyes. She looks very old to be Annabel's mother.

Annabel serves tea from a pot and milk from a solid silver creamer. She hands the detectives tiny teaspoons for stirring and Fletcher feels as if he's walked onto the set of *Downton Abbey*.

"Mummy!" Annabel says when Hazel appears to doze. "The detectives are here to talk about Peter. Remember?"

Hazel Collins looks from Danny to Fletcher and says, "Peter ran away to Venezuela."

"Well, that's the thing," Danny says. "I'm afraid we've got some news about Peter."

The old woman's expression remains blank. It's impossible to know how much she's taking in.

"Did you know Peter Dale?" Danny asks Annabel. She shakes her head. Danny focuses on the old lady and speaks exaggeratedly clearly. "Ms. Collins, I'm so sorry to tell you that Peter died."

"Peter's dead?" she asks.

"Yes. I'm sorry."

Hazel Collins shuts her eyes abruptly, as if the thin skin of her eyelids was a shield against reality. Perhaps, Fletcher thinks, that's what it comes down to at her time of life: your last line of defense is your eyelids. When she stays that way for a few moments longer than is comfortable, he and Danny exchange a glance and Fletcher can tell Danny is thinking the same as him: *Is she alive?* Hazel Collins's sweater lies loosely across her chest, held aloft by breasts that must be encased in a formidable bra. It makes it difficult to see if she's breathing.

"Mum?" Annabel Collins asks. "Mummy!" She pats the back of her mother's hand gently. Fletcher notes she's careful to avoid the bloody scrapes from the rose thorns. There's tenderness between these two. Hazel's eyes snap open. Her eyes look milky. Fletcher searches her face for signs of lucidity, feeling his frustration build. A cabinet clock ticks dully while they wait for her response. It comes in the form of a gesture. Hazel Collins reaches a trembling, liver-spotted hand toward Fletcher. "Was he murdered?" she asks. Fletcher feels as if he catches the words a few seconds after her mouth has formed them.

"What makes you say that?" Danny asks.

Like a nodding dog ornament on a dashboard, she moves her head laboriously to look at Danny. Everything she does is so slow it makes Fletcher's joints feel as if they're liquefying under the strain of being patient.

"Peter would have taken the rings off a dead man's fingers," she says. Annabel Collins's eyes widen. Her mother laughs, as if delighted. "He knew how to treat a lady in bed, though," she adds. Fletcher thinks he sees her wink, but he's not sure. Danny shuffles forward in his seat, paying close attention. "Is that right?" he says, all cheeky dimples and mischief in his eyes—nudge, nudge, wink, wink. Thank god he's got the energy to run with this. Fletcher finds it too surreal. Hazel Collins seems to live as if she were born with a silver spoon in her mouth, but talks like a bawdy fishwife. "Best lover I ever had," she says.

"Mummy! That's not appropriate. Really, it's not." Annabel flushes. "Sorry," she mouths to Fletcher.

Danny ignores her. He's totally focused on Hazel. "Were you lovers?" he asks.

But Hazel's eyelids have begun to droop, even though traces of a smile linger at the edges of her lips. She forces them open again and manages to answer with a bit of vigor. "Were we ever!" she says. "He wasn't much to look at, but then nor was I. But between the sheets looks don't really matter, if you know what I mean? It's what they can do for you."

"You're not wrong," Danny says, though Fletcher notices even he's pinking up a little on the cheeks now.

"Happy days," Hazel Collins says, "happy bloody days." Her eyelids droop once again and this time they remain shut. It's as if she's delivered a definitive pearl of wisdom and considers her work is done. Her mouth falls open wide as if her jaw pivots on a broken hinge, and Fletcher notices her dentures slacken. Within seconds, she's snoring.

"I'm so sorry," Annabel says. "I don't know what got into her. She's not normally crude."

The way Annabel says *crude* makes it sound as if it's a rude word itself. *She's prim,* Fletcher thinks. He can see her reflection in the raised lid of the baby grand piano as she stands up. Polished to a shine, it reminds him of his ex-wife.

"Do you play?" he asks Annabel. He's on his feet now, peering into the piano's guts, all of those taut, perfectly placed strings and orderly hammers that have the potential to create such wild, beautiful sound.

"I do," she replies. She doesn't elaborate and Fletcher feels a bit piqued. He knows his Chopin from his Beethoven well enough, but he also knows he probably doesn't give that impression. When he was young, he had a fire in his eyes that elevated him in people's estimation in spite of his scruffy appearance. They excused his sartorial failings as part and parcel of his brilliance—it was allowed when he was getting results—but age and the ebbing of ambition have robbed him of that exemption. Painful as it is to him, he understands how unappealing he can seem to the young, so he resists the temptation to say anything more.

Annabel walks toward the door, words tossed back over her shoulder as she does: "I'll get your coats. You'll have to come back if you want to talk to Mum. She'll be asleep for a few hours after the gardening and everything."

On the doorstep Fletcher wraps a scarf around his neck and buttons up his overcoat. He takes his time. No rush on this job, with the body being twenty years old. He sucks in the cold air.

"Did you notice?" he asks Danny as they walk.

"What?" The penny hasn't dropped for Danny, probably because he hasn't studied the file in as much detail as Fletcher.

"Annabel Collins is the spit of Peter Dale."

Danny stops. "No shit," he says. He forages around his mouth with his tongue as if he's got something stuck in his teeth, and the crease between his eyes deepens. "Did the original investigators know that Hazel Collins had a relationship with Dale?"

"It's not in the files," Fletcher says.

"Who ran the case?"

"A DS, I'll have to remind myself what his name is. He's long gone. He retired in 2003." *They'll be referring to me like that soon,* Fletcher thinks as he says it, *as if I never existed.* It pains him to think that the only legacy you could leave after a lifetime career in CID is to be a forgettable name in the archived file of an incompetently run case. "It would be good to speak to him."

"If you're right, it puts Hazel Collins front and center as a suspect," Danny says.

"It does. And she's come into money from somewhere. Her address twenty years ago was for a property worth a quarter of the value of that flat. She was working as a PA. It's not the kind of job that offers an obvious salary jump."

"Do you think Annabel Collins is aware of who her father is?"

"I don't know," Fletcher says. "But I doubt it."

He cracks his fingers one by one, and feels like he might finally be ready for the day. "Want me to drive?" he asks. Danny chucks him the keys and Fletcher catches them with one hand. "Gonna be a long, long sunshiny day," he croons as the car indicator thumps and he eases into the traffic. He takes a steep road down the side of the gorge toward the city center. Blades of sunlight cut through the trees and flash across the windscreen as they descend. "Gonna be a long, long drive if you keep singing," Danny says, but he's smiling all the same. There's nothing they like better than a break in a case.

"Is it nature or nurture?" Howard Smail asks. Fletcher can tell he doesn't want an answer because Smail doesn't even draw breath before adding, "You'd never know with a kid like Charlie Paige because his mother hasn't given him a chance, not a hope in hell. I'm not saying that kid is better off dead, God knows I'm not, but you know how he would have ended up, don't you, with a start like this?"

Smail selects a statement from the stack he has in front of him. "This one's from the woman who runs the newsagent's on the estate: 'Scott and Charlie and Cody were into nicking. They used to nick sweets from the shop and milk from the van in the morning, and from the stalls in the market. They were bold as brass.'" Smail plucks another statement from the pile. "This one's from a Mr. Dennis George. Runs a stall at the market. Says the same thing."

"I wouldn't trust Dennis George as far as I could throw him," Fletcher says.

"There are more. They're all variations on the same theme. It makes me think, did those boys do something to somebody that crossed a line? Did they push things too far and somebody snapped?"

"Could have," Fletcher replies. "Though might it have just been mischief? Boys being boys and all that?" He checks his watch.

"Time to visit Paradise?" Smail asks.

Fletcher nods. He's feeling stretched. This won't be the only moment during the investigation when he wishes he could be in two places at once. He could do with time to look over the sheaf of statements in more detail alongside Smail and to work on their evolving strategy. He's running on cups of instant coffee and canteen sandwiches that have been refrigerated long enough to turn the bread to rubber. A visit to Paradise Casino is important, though, and they're about to open their doors for the early crowd. Fletcher wants to be there when they do.

The casino is a single-story nondescript building that looks more like an industrial warehouse than a gambling mecca. It sits on a bit of undeveloped land beside the floating harbor and a stonemason's yard. The parking area is almost empty. At the door, Fletcher has a low-key word with a security guard who could have been picked out of central casting. Fletcher wants cooperation, so he's careful not to draw overt attention to the fact that he and Danny are police officers. Not that there are many punters to take notice.

While they wait, Fletcher takes a look around. It's lunchtime, but it could be the middle of the night. There are no windows. Everything *is artificially lit. Camera lenses glint amongst the mirrored tiles in the ceiling. There are rows of one-armed bandits and five blackjack tables. A game is already under way at one of them. The dealer's a kid who doesn't look old enough to have left school. He's wearing a bow tie and a waistcoat over a crisp white shirt that has picked up a blue hue from the lighting. His hair is slicked back with something oily. A middle-aged woman and a man in his twenties sit on the other side of the table. Smoke curls from a cigarette that's resting on an ashtray on the edge of the baize. The woman makes eyes at the dealer. Fletcher doesn't think she's here just for the gambling. The young man stares at his cards and plays with his chips. He cups them in his palm before dropping them onto the table, one upon another—a paltry stack. Dinner money. Beyond their immediate environs, Fletcher can see a bar and the entrance to at least one other room, where he suspects more serious gambling takes place. The bar is empty apart from a woman who's pushing a vacuum cleaner across the floor. A cascade of electronic sounds from the slot machines drowns out any noise it might be making.*

The security guard returns and deferentially ushers Fletcher and Danny through a door you wouldn't notice unless you knew it was there. The scene behind it is a world away from the casino floor. They walk down a bare-walled corridor. The walls have been glossed in off-white so long ago they've acquired a creamy hue and a greasy texture; the gray linoleum floor has seen better days.

They reach a door that has a paper sign pinned on it. It says THE BOSS. The security guard knocks, opens the door without waiting for an answer, and shows Fletcher and Danny into a decent-sized office. A man steps out from behind the desk. He is wearing a sharp gray suit jacket that he buttons up with one hand as he offers them the other. Fletcher suspects he's had a hair transplant. He doesn't smile, but Fletcher isn't sensing hostility either.

"Stuart Legrand. What can I do for you, detectives?"

"We're interested in some visitors to the casino on Sunday night, specifically a woman called Jessica Paige. Apparently she goes by Jessy."

"Don't know her." It's a quick response.

"Twenty-six years old, brunette, brown eyes, about five-four."

Legrand shakes his head. "Do you know what time she was here?"

"Any time up until approximately eleven P.M." This is Fletcher's best guess. It fits with her arrival time back at the estate and takes into account the fact that she may have gone somewhere else between the casino and home.

"Do you know what she played?"

"I'm hoping you can tell me that," Fletcher says. "It's likely she was drinking here."

"We'll start with the bar cameras. I hope you've got some time."

Legrand takes them back out into the corridor and through a chipped unmarked door into another room, where there's an impressive bank of CCTV monitors. A skinny guy has his feet up on the desk. He's eating crisps from a packet. An open newspaper is balanced on his thighs. He makes no move to adjust his position.

Legrand sets up the detectives in front of a different screen that's hooked up to a VCR. He inserts a tape of the bar footage from Sunday night for them to review. Danny offers to stay and look through it all and Fletcher agrees so he can get back to the office, but he hasn't even stepped out of the room when Danny says, "That's her!"

The quality of the footage is good. Jessica Paige is clearly visible sitting on a barstool. Or rather she's half sitting and half standing, perched on the edge of the stool with her legs stretched out in front of her as if to keep herself from falling. She's disheveled and looks drunk. Her dress is scanty and rucked up too high on her thighs; her hair is flopping over her face. Danny and Fletcher watch as a man approaches her. His face is partially obscured by a hat, but Fletcher feels an immediate tug of recognition. Jessy pulls her head up with some effort in response to something the man says and they exchange words. Her face falls as she listens to him and she lifts her glass in a mock toast when he walks away from her. He's carrying himself as if he's angry.

"Look at the state of her," Danny says.

Legrand is defensive. "She's an adult. We don't babysit our clients."

"Do you recognize the man?"

Fletcher licks his lips, which suddenly feel papery and tacky. He recognizes the man, but he remains mute as Legrand shakes his head with a tight, controlled movement. It strikes Fletcher as forced. Maybe he's not the only one in the room who knows it might be more than his life is worth to name this man in this context.

"You sure?" Danny asks.

"Sure I'm sure."

They watch more of the tape. Jessy gets up from the stool, staggers, steadies herself, and totters out of view as if she was being pulled by a string. Fletcher notes the time stamp: 22:13. This must be the start of her journey home, though according to witness statements she didn't arrive at the estate—which is approximately a fifteen-minute drive away—until 23:25. Unless she walked. "Have you got cameras in the car park?" he asks.

There's hesitation. Fletcher doesn't have time for it. The feeling of having the dying boy in his arms returns, hot and alive. The sounds of the autopsy follow. Added to those is the weight of recognizing the man who is with Jessy Paige on the tape. "We're investigating a murder, Mr. Legrand. Will you be helping us with our inquiries, or will I be making a call to our organized crime unit to let them know I suspect there's something to investigate in the way this casino is run?"

Legrand doesn't take his eyes off Fletcher's, but he says, "Get the car park tapes, Ray," and the skinny man jumps to it.

The quality of the car park tapes isn't as clear as the footage from inside—no need for it, Fletcher supposes—but they see well enough that a man exits the casino at 22:13 and Jessy Paige follows him thirty seconds later. It's the same man she was talking to in the bar. Once again, his face is partially obscured. Fletcher holds himself very still as he watches. On the tape the man strides to a car and gets into it. Jessy follows drunkenly, weaving her way between the few other parked cars as laboriously as if she was in a complicated maze. The car headlights switch on when she's at least thirty yards away. As she totters along, the driver aggressively backs out of the parking spot and accelerates toward her.

Jessy stops, blinded by the headlights, and puts her hand up to cover her eyes. She's standing a few feet in front of the car and looks as functional as a rag doll. Her hair is stringy, and in the shadow of her arm her eyes are dark bruises. The car lurches forward again, another few feet toward her. And then another. Jessy stands her ground lopsidedly. When the car has remained stationary for a few seconds, she walks toward it and slams her hands on the bonnet. Fletcher is certain the engine is gunning, but there is no sound on the tape, so he can't be sure. Jessy Paige stares through the windscreen at the driver. Fletcher has never seen anybody look so broken and so defiant all at once. He feels a small spark of admiration, but it's tempered by fear, because it's crystal clear that Jessy Paige was playing with fire the night her son went missing.

"Jesus," Danny says, "she's going to go with him, isn't she?"

They watch as she walks around the car, opens the passenger door, *and gets in. The driver reaches a hand toward her and grabs her by the back of the neck. She tenses and stays very still, eyes shut. Her face is obscured when he leans in and kisses her. The kiss doesn't last long. It is not loving, more a gesture of violent possession. The driver straightens up and accelerates away. As the car pulls out of the parking area the tape allows a quick final glimpse of Jessica's face, pale as a moon, turned toward the camera as she looks out of the window. Fletcher would give good money to know what she's thinking.*

"Fit bird," Danny says. "She's got some bollocks, too."

Fletcher bites his tongue. "Are you sure you don't recognize this man?" Danny asks again. It's a negative from both Legrand and his employee.

"We'll run the number plate," Fletcher says to divert Danny's attention, and because that's what Danny will be expecting them to do. "We'll take the tapes with us." Fletcher eyeballs Legrand with his best cop stare. "You can hand them over now or I'll be back in half an hour with a warrant and a few uniformed officers who might want a chat with your punters."

The detectives leave the casino five minutes later. Fletcher holds a rattling box of videocassettes in his arms.

IT'S TIME TO TELL

EPISODE 5—THE PRIME SUSPECT

A DISHLICKER
PODCAST PRODUCTION

"'Wednesday, 21 August, time: 09:45.

"'Priority to speak to the man known as Sid the Village. We believe his full name to be Sidney Noyce. Twenty-four years old. Lives with his parents in Nightingale Tower on Glenfrome Estate. Three reasons:

1. Cody Swift reports that he, Scott, and Charlie spent time with Sidney Noyce at the dog track kennels on the morning before Scott and Charlie disappeared.
2. An estate resident reports seeing Sidney Noyce walking down Primrose Lane in the path of Scott and Charlie at approximately 20:15 on the night the boys disappeared.
3. Estate residents report that Sidney Noyce and the boys were often spotted together around the estate during the summer.'"

My name is Cody Swift. I'm a filmmaker and your host of *It's Time to Tell,* a Dishlicker Podcast Production. What you just heard is ex–Detective Superintendent Howard Smail reading from the photocopied pages of his policy book. That's the book he made notes in during his 1996 investigation into the murders of my best

friends, Charlie Paige and Scott Ashby. Smail and I discussed what
he recorded in the book and the clip that follows is our conversation. You'll hear Smail's voice first.

"That's the first time Noyce's name appears in the book."

"Can you tell us about Noyce?"

"He quickly became a person of interest in the investigation, but it was complicated. We were not initially aware of
how acute his impairment was, but it turned out it was very
severe. Nowadays we would describe Sidney Noyce as having special educational needs. He was a twenty-four-year-old
man with the mental age of a ten-year-old boy."

"A boy in a man's body."

"Yes. Exactly that. Noyce didn't have a criminal record.
Estate residents we talked to who knew him said he wasn't
the sharpest tool in the box, and certainly when we began
our inquiries—before anybody had had ideas put into their
heads—nobody seemed to think him capable of harm. He
helped out on and off at the dog track, and he got the occa-
sional shift collecting trolleys at Tesco."

"Can you tell us a bit about the sighting of Sidney Noyce
on the night of the murders?"

"The last sighting of Charlie and Scott was when they
walked down a lane called Primrose Lane that divided one of
the high-rise blocks from the semidetached housing on the
estate. It went from east to west and led from a play area at the
center of the estate toward the dog track and the new Tesco
supermarket. Officers interviewed a resident of Meadowsweet Tower, which overlooked the lane, and she stated that
she saw Charlie and Scott walking along Primrose Lane in

the direction of the dog track at approximately 20:15 on the night of Sunday, 18 August. She was sitting out on her balcony, smoking a cigarette. She saw Sidney Noyce following in the path of the boys. He walked east up Primrose Lane a few minutes after them."

"Was the identification of Noyce secure?"

"The witness was credible. She'd come across Noyce before, so she could identify him. Additionally, Sidney Noyce's mother stated that her son went out to buy some ketchup at some point that evening, though she couldn't pinpoint the precise time because she went out for the evening, so nobody could tell us exactly what time he returned home either and what kind of state he was in when he did. Based on that information, I made Sidney Noyce one of our priorities for further investigation."

Maya and I have been working hard to try to find a variety of people to interview about Noyce in order to give you a balanced picture of him, but frustratingly, we haven't had much success. People were either unwilling to talk or impossible to find.

One success we have had is in locating Sidney Noyce's mother, Valerie. Noyce's father died a few months before Sidney took his own life. We'll play you my interview with Valerie shortly, but before we do, there is one other person who can tell you a little about Sidney Noyce.

That's me. I knew Sidney Noyce.

The reports in Smail's policy book of Noyce's hanging around with Charlie, Scott, and me in the summer of 1996 are true. But before I add my voice to the picture of Noyce that we've been building up, I need to be honest with you, because here's where things get awkward for me. In the interests of being completely transparent, I'm going to let Howard Smail explain why. This clip of Smail speaking is from my interview with him at his home in Norway:

> "You and Charlie Paige and Scott Ashby took advantage of Sidney Noyce, didn't you? You wound him up. We heard that from more than one person on the estate."

What Howard Smail said is true. The way Charlie, Scott, and I treated Sidney Noyce that summer is something I feel guilty about to this day. It is also why I felt particularly nervous about approaching Valerie Noyce, Sidney's mother, to ask if she'd be willing to be interviewed. She knew how Charlie, Scott, and I treated her son because it formed part of the prosecution's case against him and she attended every day of her son's trial. The prosecution vigorously asserted that it was our poor treatment of Noyce that goaded him into retaliating with the act of violence that ended Scott's and Charlie's lives.

We found Valerie Noyce easily. She still lives in the same flat in the Glenfrome Estate. It is to her credit that she agreed not only to see me but also to let me record an interview. At her request, I went to meet her in a park in Redland. That sounds more cloak-and-dagger than it was. Valerie has a cleaning job in a chapel beside the park, and it was convenient for her to meet me there.

I find the chapel quite easily. It is a little gem hidden in a corner of the city I'm not familiar with. It is a small Georgian building built from Bath stone and surrounded by a graveyard in which every headstone seems to be tilting. I turn the heavy handle of the main door and ease it open.

"Hello?"

"Come on in out of the wind, my love."

Valerie Noyce is holding a feather duster in one hand, and she shakes my hand with the other. We are the only people in the chapel. It has impressive stained-glass windows and a large painting of Christ on the cross above the altar, framed by ornate wooden carvings. Valerie sees me looking at it. Her breath mists in front of her as she speaks.

"They're a devil to dust. Are you cold?"

"I'm fine."

"It's always chilly in here, but I don't feel it when I'm cleaning. I'd offer you a tea, but the kettle's on the blink. Come on, let's sit down."

There are only a few rows of pews and we sit in one toward the back of the chapel. I ask Valerie if she would be willing to describe Sidney and talk about the relationship he had with Charlie and Scott and me. I ask her not to hold back. To hear her side of the story feels like a sort of penance for the way I treated Sidney. Valerie looks at me with dark, restless eyes as she speaks. In the following clip you'll hear one of the most challenging conversations I have ever had.

"Sidney grew bigger than his dad before he was seventeen, but he never developed in his head. The doctors and the social workers told us he would only ever have the sense of a ten-year-old, and they were right. They call it mental impairment these days. Back then they said Sid was a retard. It's not a nice word, is it? You taunted Sid something rotten, you boys did. Tormented him. Do you remember, you told him you would meet him at certain times and places? Then you wouldn't turn up. You encouraged him to steal for you. Milk bottles from the van or from people's steps, bits from the shop. You got him to buy you cans of Black Label because he was old enough—on paper, anyway. Did you know because of the stealing, Sid got banned from the corner shop on the estate, so he had to go all the way to Tesco if I sent him out to get something for me? They sound like little things, but they never stopped. It really affected him. I told him until I was blue in the face to keep away from you three, but he couldn't see the harm in you because the problem was, no matter how bad you treated him, he wanted to play. He was lonely. To him, it felt like you little daredevils should be his friends because you were into all the things he wanted to be into. He thought you were fun, and in his head he was just like you."

"I understand that now that I'm an adult and I'm not making excuses—because I'm very, very ashamed of what we did and extremely sorry for how we treated Sid back then—but I don't think any of us understood him or his condition."

"'Course you didn't. Sidney seemed disgusting to you because he was as big as a man, but he didn't act like one. That's not natural. You weren't the only ones who thought that, but you were the ones who truly made his life a misery. Do you remember one day you had him carrying an armchair somebody left in the foyer while they moved in, and putting it in the middle of the green by the estate? You sat on it like little princes, that Charlie smoking a cigarette bold as brass, and you told him to, you know, eff off, and threw stuff at him.

Stones! They left bruises on Sid. I witnessed that with my own eyes. You wouldn't treat an animal like that. You boys hurt his feelings all the time, but he couldn't keep away from you. He didn't have enough sense in him."

"I'm so sorry. I can't tell you how sorry I am. We were stupid and thoughtless and, well, I'm incredibly sorry."

"You were kids. Have I upset you? Did I say too much? You said I should be honest, love."

"I meant it. The listeners need to hear what Sidney went through."

"Ask me something else. Change the subject."

"Can you tell me about Sid's work at the dog track?"

"Sid loved them dogs, and he couldn't keep away from them either. Harry Jacks, one of the kennel stewards, was a friend of Sid's dad. He took Sid down there whenever he could. Sid was ever so good with them dogs. He knew how to take care of them before they raced and after. He tidied up and cleaned the kennels, he did the water bowls after the race. Me and his dad hoped he could get a permanent position there, a few hours a week maybe, but one of the trainers took against him."

"Why?"

"He said Sid couldn't be trusted. There's money riding on them dogs, of course that's why they're there, so the people who handle them have to be tight-lipped about what goes on in the kennels, and Sid wasn't. He didn't know how to be."

"Are you saying Sid might have known about some bad practice that was taking place? Illegal practice?"

"I'm saying that if you work close with the dogs you know their form better than anyone else and you know what goes on. I'm not accusing nobody of nothing illegal. Sid loved it when you boys came down the kennels. Not you and Scott Ashby, though, was it? It was Charlie Paige, mostly. Sid said Charlie loved the dogs as much as he did."

"Do you know where Sid was going when he was spotted walking down Primrose Lane on the evening the boys disappeared?"

"He was going to Tesco. To get some tomato ketchup. Like I told the police."

"Why didn't he go to the corner shop?"

"Because he got banned, like I said. They twisted that in court, of course, that sighting of him. Sid said he went to Tesco, but it was shut because of flooding, so he came back home and watched television, but the barrister made it sound like he was circling the block, looking for Scott and Charlie, wanting to hurt them. Like some kind of predator. Sid would never have done that. He was gentle as a lamb."

Valerie is upset. I reach out to her to try to offer some comfort; she takes my hand between both of hers and squeezes my fingers. Her fingers are bony and cold and her face is a mirror of the grieving Virgin Mary in the painting above the altar.

"Cody, you must think hard about what you are doing. For what it's worth, I don't think any good will come from this. You should walk away and get on with your life before it gets snatched away from you. Seize life while you can, dear."

"Don't you want justice for Sid?"

"I want peace for Sid."

"What if he was innocent?"

"He was innocent. I know that. I've always known it. I don't need the world to know it anymore. I used to want them to. I used to feel so much rage about it I thought it would eat me from the inside out, but what good would it do now that he's dead?"

"It could restore his reputation? It could give you closure?"

"I'm his mother. I know he didn't do it. Sidney didn't have a vengeful bone in his body. What you boys did upset him, but he never said he wanted to get you back for it. Never. That's how I know he's innocent and God knows it, too. That's good enough for me. I'll never have him back now, so the best I can hope for is to live my life in peace. It passes in a flash, Cody—you'll understand that one day. So don't be chasing dragons when you could be building foundations for a good life. Some people never have that opportunity."

I tread carefully as I take my leave, anxious to avoid stepping on the worn plaques set into the chapel floor, marking graves. I pause at the chapel door and turn back to face the altar. I watch as Valerie begins to move a mop across the flagstones in smooth, circular motions. When her back is to me, I dip my knee and make the sign of the cross, a memory of how to do so rescued from a decades-long dormancy with surprising ease. Outside, the wind is sharp and strong, shifting mountains of cloud above me and bending the branches on the trees. I shudder and feel foolish for genuflecting to a god I haven't believed in since I was a child, but I also reflect on why I did it. Any port, as they say, in a storm. Even for the unbeliever.

My interview with Valerie Noyce certainly unnerved me, but not for the reasons I thought it would. I had expected bitterness and rancor, accusations and recriminations, but found a raw yet gentle honesty in its place. Our discussion subverted many assumptions I had held about her. It reminded me to take nothing for granted. But it did not discourage me from continuing with this podcast. Why? Because Valerie Noyce might not want justice for her son, but I do.

I would like to deliver justice, through this podcast, to Sidney Noyce.

Why?

It's time I told.

I knew Sidney Noyce when I was ten years old. I didn't like him and we've established that my friends and I treated him badly. But—and this is a big *but*—I never really believed Sid was the person who murdered Charlie and Scott, because, as others have said, he didn't have a bad bone in his body. He never once lifted a finger against any of us, no matter what we did to him. Did I tell anybody at the time? No. Would they have listened if I had? Probably not. I was ten years old. I was not a nice kid. I was a liar.

But I believed Noyce was innocent then, and I still do, twenty years later. It's why Owen Weston's article asserting Noyce's innocence resonated with me so much.

Detective Inspector John Fletcher disagrees. This is a clip from a phone conversation we had:

"Sid Noyce may have gone out with the intention of buying ketchup, but that doesn't mean he didn't get a different idea along the way. The prosecution alleged that he walked around the block because he was searching for the boys to take revenge on them, and the jury chose to believe that. People can snap. Even the gentlest, sweetest people can snap if you put them under enough pressure. I've seen it many times during my career."

Fletcher's feelings about Noyce are crystal clear, and like mine, they have remained the same for the past two decades.

However, if you were listening carefully to that clip, you'll have heard John Fletcher say something important. Detective Inspector Fletcher says, referring to Sidney Noyce: "He walked around the block because he was searching for the boys to take revenge on them." But let me put this into context for you. This clip comes from the end of a phone conversation I had with Detective Fletcher. What you're about to hear is a recording of our whole conversation on this subject. It puts what you heard Fletcher say in the last clip into context. It is my voice you'll hear first:

"Can you tell us about the sighting of Noyce on Primrose Lane on the night the boys disappeared?"

"Detective Constable Fryer let us know that he'd interviewed a woman called Sonya Matthews as part of our door-to-door inquiries. She lived in Meadowsweet Tower in a flat overlooking Primrose Lane."

"You have good recall of her name."

"You don't forget the details of a case like this. Sonya Matthews told DC Fryer that she saw Noyce walking up and down Primrose Lane after 20:15, calling out the boys' names."

"Excuse me, did you say *up and down*?"

"No. I said *up*."

"So the witness saw Sidney Noyce walk up Primrose Lane once?"

"That is correct."

"And when she saw him on that occasion, he was walking in the direction of the supermarket, in the path of the boys?"

"Yes."

"And then she saw him walking back the other way?"

"No. That is incorrect."

"So, just to be clear, when she saw him the second time, he was walking the same way as the first time she saw him?"

"Correct."

"She didn't see him backtracking between those two sightings?"

"She did not."

"So how did he come to be walking the same way down the same alleyway at eight-fifteen P.M. and then again twenty minutes later?"

"We came to the conclusion he had walked around the block."

"You're saying he walked in a circle?"

"That was the assumption the prosecution made based on the sightings, yes."

"People don't normally walk in circles if they're on their way to buy ketchup."

"Sid Noyce may have gone out with the intention of buying ketchup, but that doesn't mean he didn't get a different idea along the way. The prosecution alleged that he walked around the block because he was searching for the boys to take revenge on them, and the jury chose to believe that. People can snap. Even the gentlest, sweetest people can snap if you put them under enough pressure. I've seen it many times during my career."

"Did you agree with the prosecution?"

"I did, yes. Especially when combined with the other evidence we had."

What Fletcher says is plausible, but it is his slip of the tongue that intrigues me. The reason I'm intrigued is because what the witness said she saw on that night became a crucial issue in the case against Noyce and is one of what Owen describes as "grains of uncertainty" surrounding his conviction for the murders.

Even Noyce's defense team—in what was apparently an unusual display of vigor—claimed that the witness had changed her story at some point before the case got to trial, and that she had in fact originally stated she saw Noyce going in the opposite direction the second time he passed down Primrose Lane. That is, away from the boys. That is, toward his home, where he said he went.

Here's journalist Owen Weston explaining why there was unfortunately no proof of whether Noyce ever made it to Tesco to buy ketchup, as he said he did.

"Sidney Noyce had bad luck. That night Tesco's air conditioning packed up and flooded the store, so it was closed down. He couldn't have bought ketchup even if he did go to the store, so there's no proof of whether he ever made it to Tesco or not. There were CCTV cameras in the Tesco car park that might have caught him arriving there, but by the time his defense team woke up and requested the footage from the store, it had been taped over."

Maya and I have tried very hard to gain access to the court records of Sidney Noyce's trial, but we weren't able to. They're not on the public record yet. Most of the information we have about what went on in the courtroom during Noyce's trial has come from the reporting done by Owen Weston when he covered the trial for the *Bristol Echo*. Like Valerie Noyce, he attended court every day.

In the next episode of *It's Time to Tell* we are going to talk to Weston about some of the other "grains of uncertainty" in Noyce's conviction and about where he thinks police should have been looking.

Before we leave you today, I have two brief news items. Maya and I are thrilled to report that the number of downloads of *It's Time to Tell* has doubled over the past week, taking us into the top ten for our category on Overcast, and what's more we are now a featured listen on iTunes, too! Thank you to each and every one of our listeners for your support. Please keep listening and keep spreading the word using #TimetoTell. It means the world to us!

Something we are less excited to report is a bit of negative news. We wondered whether to keep this from you, but decided, once again in the interests of transparency, to share it.

Yesterday, we received by post an A5 envelope containing three photographs of Maya and I: one of us leaving our flat, one of us in our car, and, most disturbingly, one of Maya in the bathroom of our flat, taken through a window. At the bottom of this photo, one word was printed in ballpoint: STOP. We have handed the photographs over to the police and are still processing what it might mean for us and for the podcast.

It certainly makes the following clip even more pertinent. Back to Owen Weston, the man whose article got me started on this journey in the first place. This is a clip from my interview with Owen. You'll hear more from this interview in the next episode of *It's Time to Tell*:

"The case the police built against Noyce is a classic example of detectives seeing a suspect who looked good for the crime and making the facts fit the face so they could get a quick and tidy result . . . Remember this, though: If Sidney Noyce was innocent, somebody else is guilty . . . there will be information you might be closing in on that they don't want uncovered. And that person has murdered before."

Jess emerges from Oxford Circus tube station and has to step away from the throng of pedestrians to get her bearings. Retail and advertising signs fight for her attention. Traffic surges through the junction. She hates looking like a tourist as she consults her phone to find her way to Felix's office, but it does the job, and a few minutes later she finds herself on a narrow street in Soho standing in front of a door beside which five buzzers nestle discreetly on a modest brass plaque.

Felix Abernathy PR is engraved next to one of them. Jess straightens her jacket and stoops to try to check her hair in the shiny plaque before pushing the buzzer. She announces herself and is buzzed in. Inside the building there's a small elevator, but Jess takes the stairs at a steady pace up all five floors. As she walks up, she is completely focused on the meeting ahead of her.

When she reaches the office, she's struck by how small it is. Cozy, almost. There seem to be only a couple of rooms, yet his website would have you believe Felix is running an empire. In the reception space, three women sit at desks. They are smartly dressed. A large window offers a partial view over Golden Square. One of the women rises, smiles nicely at Jess, and asks her to take a seat for a few minutes. "Felix is on a call, but he's expecting you," she explains.

Jess looks out of the window. It's lunchtime. Down in the square, young and pretty television types are eating, vaping, flirting, posing in the sun, and looking beautiful before they go back to their jobs running crappy errands for postproduction companies. Jess feels a pang for the things she might have done if she hadn't had Charlie when she was so young.

After a few minutes, Felix flings open a frosted glass door at the back of the room. He doesn't say a word, but smiles and opens his arms to her and Jess understands he wants her to come to him the way she used to. He always did like to make an entrance and control a room. She stands up and puts on a smile. She knows how to make her cheeks dimple. She walks steadily toward Felix and hugs him, and they kiss each other chastely on either cheek.

"You look a million dollars," he says. She endures the feeling of his eyes traveling down her body. "Come on in." Before he shuts the door behind them, he addresses the women at the desks: "I hope you've been looking after my Jessy. She's a very old friend of mine. Bring us some tea, would you, Sarah?"

My Jessy, Jess notes as the door closes.

"Take a seat. Get off your feet. Don't stand about on ceremony." Felix settles into his desk chair in front of the window and gestures to the seat opposite. Jess sits. He leans back and crosses his arms loosely. It is such a benign gesture and he's wearing an expression so affable—as if she's a pet he's very fond of—that out of the blue a sense of farce overcomes her and she feels as if he's her bank manager. The thought brings a smile to her face. Of all the things she didn't think they'd ever come to—after the terrible, filthy acts they were involved in together and inflicted on each other—it was this.

"What's so funny?"

"Nothing." But she can't help a smile. It's because he's presenting such a sanitized, successful version of himself. She knew he was capable of success—everybody knew it back in the day—but sitting here with him like this, she suddenly can't believe he's done so well. It's hard to take in the reality of it. She gestures to their surroundings, encompassing the office, the view outside. "All of this."

"It's all right, isn't it?" He tilts back in his chair. He looks smug, but he's watching her carefully.

"You've done well," she says. He always liked flattery.

"Thank you. And you have, too, by the sound of it."

"I've done okay." She feels her sense of unreality ebbing as quickly as it arrived. *He's faking it as much as you are,* she thinks. *Be careful.*

"We came from nothing, you and me," he says. "We should be proud of what we've achieved. Everything we've got, we built with our own hands."

She nods, though she doesn't exactly agree. *Me, not so much,* she thinks, but it's true that Felix clawed his way up to this all by himself. When she first met him, he was so proud to be driving for his boss, a local businessman with his hand in the TV business amongst other things. Felix remained proud when he moved on to doing more than just drive for the man. He started fixing things, and not the plumbing: parties, discreet rendezvous, drugs. Felix made contacts of his own as soon as he could, with powerful people, people in authority, and he stopped working for somebody else. He had his hand in so many things. She remembers how Felix used Charlie and his friends to run drug deliveries for him on the estate.

That was wrong. She can't believe she let Charlie do that. She smiles at Felix cautiously—she doesn't want her discomfort to show—and he says without any more preamble: "Cody Swift."

"I need him stopped." She didn't mean it to come out like that. She meant to say, "I need the podcast stopped."

There's a knock on the door. "Come in," Felix calls, and the secretary carries in a tray with a steaming teapot and two cups and saucers on it. Felix remains poker-faced, staring at Jess. "Would you care to clarify what you mean?" he says once the woman leaves the room, shutting the door behind her. Neither of them have acknowledged her, let alone thanked her. "Just so I'm sure I understand."

"I want Cody Swift to leave me and my family alone."

Felix pours tea. He moves to put a cube of sugar in her cup, but she covers it with her hand.

"All grown up now, are we?" he says. "I remember when you took three. Or are we just watching our figure?"

She doesn't rise to it. "I can't lose another family," she says.

"Because of Charlie," he says.

Their eyes meet, but she doesn't answer. She doesn't feel any need to explain. He's seen her rawest emotions before; to display them again now would increase her vulnerability.

"Do you have any thoughts about how to achieve this?" he asks.

"Don't hurt Cody."

"Isn't that what your husband threatened to do?"

"How do you know that?"

"Darling, you phoned me twenty-four hours ago. Don't you think I've done a little bit of due diligence since then?"

"Did you talk to Cody?"

"No. We don't want to make him nervous. I talked to somebody I trust. He got me some information. Sounds like your husband gave Cody Swift a real scare. Not."

Felix shouldn't criticize Nick, Jess thinks. *It's out of order.* She puts her cup down on the saucer and it chinks sharply. Felix tilts his chair back again, eyes on her, as ever.

"We need to discuss money," he says. "Some of my private clients prefer to make arrangements for a monthly retainer."

She can't believe he's got the brass neck to try this on. She leans forward. "We both know I'm not paying you a penny," she says. She takes a pointed look around his office so he can see her taking in the view of central London, the framed photographs and articles, the fancy clients and fancy china. "If Cody Swift digs as deep as he says he's going to, you might have as much to lose as I do, don't you think?"

Felix blinks, but otherwise doesn't move a muscle. *The cogs are turning,* Jess thinks. *Hold your nerve.*

Fletcher and Danny listen to the latest episode of the podcast in the car on the way to the prison. Fletcher winces when he hears the sound of his own voice. Both snigger when Swift quotes Owen Weston's *grains of uncertainty.*

"Thinks he's a poet," Danny says.

"Always did."

At the end of the episode, Danny says, "Who would be threatening them?"

"I have no idea. Somebody who doesn't like meddling, I expect."

"Let sleeping dogs lie," Danny says as he pulls into a parking space outside the jail.

"Correct." Fletcher looks at the high-security wall in front of them and thinks of the man behind it they've come to visit. "I'm looking forward to hearing what this paragon of virtue can tell us."

As they head between prison buildings, Fletcher ducks his head into his scarf, unsure of whether what's buffeting him is snow, sleet, hail, or rain. He and Danny follow the prison officer into B Block, a low-security wing where they're due to meet Damien Saint, whose criminal record shows a repetitive string of time-share frauds and an incompetent attempt at armed robbery.

Fletcher and Danny are shown into a small room where a table and four chairs are bolted to the floor and a panic strip runs across two walls, a blue neon glow threading through the center of it. They sit and wait for the prison officer to bring Saint to them. Through a barred window, the view includes a slice of the roof of another prison block, a section of the bladed wire that runs along the prison's external wall, and a metallic sky.

The prison officer ushers Saint in. Clean-shaven and sallow-skinned, he's a skinny fellow in a prison regulation pale blue shirt and beltless blue jeans that hang off his frame. He has buzz-cut white hair on the back and sides of his head and a shiny pate above. His chin is receding. His eyebrows are dark gray and bushy, and the skin under his eyes is baggy and loose. There's something unremarkable yet depressing about him that reminds Fletcher of a dozen other small-time criminals he's met over the years. The only notable thing about him is that he's missing two fingers on his left hand.

Saint sees Fletcher looking. "Motorcycle accident," he says. "Before you ask."

"You're assuming I'm interested." Fletcher takes off his glasses and rubs them clean on a corner of his scarf. He squints at Saint as he does so, as if that sharpens his view of the man. In fact, it doesn't. Without his glasses on, Saint's face blurs formlessly.

There was a time when Fletcher enjoyed the game of interviewing, when he watched his interviewee with the implacable gaze of a large cat who knows there'll be playing before slaying and is looking forward to it, but over the years he's become tired of the process, tired of the fact that if you get rid of one of them, another nasty piece of work just shuffles in to take his or her place.

A smile flickers and expires on Saint's mouth as he realizes this meeting might not be the interesting break in routine he'd been anticipating. Fletcher notices the dying pleasantry as he replaces his glasses and feels nothing but contempt for Saint because he's obviously weak. White collars are often like this: pleasers, ultimately, many of them. Wanting to do well for themselves to show off to friends and family, but without the smarts or the work ethic to achieve it legally. Even Danny can't be bothered to play nice.

"Peter Dale," he says to Saint. "Remember him?"

"I knew him back in the eighties. We did a bit of business together."

"What kind of business?"

"We had a share in a pub. He screwed me over when he took off."

Fletcher is roused to raise his eyebrows at the note of self-pity. "You think that's unfair, do you?" he asks. He plants his elbows on the table and leans toward Saint. Saint blinks and swallows and recrosses his legs but says nothing, and it's a sub-servient enough response that Fletcher loses interest in going in for the kill. He needs Saint to talk, not quiver.

"What was Peter Dale's setup?"

"He had an office on Cheltenham Road, above the barber's by the arches. I went there maybe once or twice, I think." Saint's voice slows as caution sets in. Obviously, Saint's not sure why he's here and he's too chicken to ask outright. Fletcher expects a bit of haziness to set in around his recollec-tions from this point.

Fletcher knows the barber's outfit Saint's referring to. It's still in business, but the frontage needs repainting, and the turning red and white signs out the front are encased in tubes yellowed by age and pollution. There are three or four chairs crammed into the narrow space inside. So far as he knows, the place has been owned and run for what seems like forever by a heavyset asthmatic called Wilfred Jones. It is well known to police as a money-laundering spot for his family's activities.

"Do you remember Dale's assistant?" Danny asks Saint.

"Yeah, I remember her. Good girl, she was. Name of Heather or Holly or something."

"Hazel," Danny says.

"That's right, Hazel. I remember she got us coffee from that Turkish place up the road. Peter loved that coffee. I used to wonder if he missed that in Venezuela, though he made off with enough that he could probably afford to have it shipped over. Thought of that as a line of inquiry, have you? Tracing shipments of Turkish coffee to Venezuela?"

Saint cackles at his own attempt at wit. *No wonder he got caught,* Fletcher thinks. *He's a fucking idiot.* "What was the relationship like between Dale and Hazel Collins?" he asks.

"Secretary. She did his typing. Answered the phone. Did the filing. Got sandwiches. That sort of thing."

"Anything more?"

Saint shakes his head. "Not that I know of."

"Nothing more personal?"

Saint snorts. "Peter didn't mix business and pleasure. He had prettier birds to chase, anyway. Hazel wasn't really his type."

"Who did he chase?" Fletcher asks. The case files suggested that police hadn't found evidence of a relationship at the time Dale disappeared.

"Seriously?" asks Saint. "You don't know this? I thought you lot investigated him?"

Fletcher waits for Saint's attempt at triumphalism to get back in the box where it belongs. To hurry the process along, he'd like to seize the guy by the neck and give him a shake, but he treats him to a hard stare instead.

Saint says, "If you wanted to find the money, you should have looked at the divorce. Pete got divorced from his wife about three months before he disappeared. She was a girl-next-door type called Rhonda. I can't remember her maiden name. Not his usual type, I don't know where he found her. But if you want to make money disappear, a sham divorce is how you do it. The authorities won't dig too deep. I always thought she'd made her way to join Pete."

Fletcher doesn't answer. He's thinking. He stands up. "Let's go," he says to Danny. He bangs on the door to request that they are let out.

Saint's face falls. "Is that it? You'll put in a good word for me, then. I've got a parole hearing soon."

"I think you've been watching too many TV cop shows," Fletcher says. "What makes you think I would do that?" When the guard has let him and Danny out, he enjoys the sound of the door shutting behind him and the way it blunts Saint's shouts of protest.

"Remind me who was running the Dale case?" Danny asks.

"DS called Chase. I had an email this morning to say he's six feet under."

"Helpful."

Fletcher nods. Sarcasm feels about right for today. As they walk to the car, he notices Danny limping. "Hurt yourself?"

"Training. Busted my knee."

Fletcher shakes his head. The problem with a new and younger wife, he thinks, is that they make unreasonable demands on a man in his late middle age. Danny has given the new Mrs. Fryer a baby and now she wants him running half marathons, too.

"Don't let her kill you off," he says.

Danny grins. "Better that than dying of boredom. You've got to live."

Fletcher doesn't answer. He supposes it depends what you mean by living. He thinks of his own empty home and feels a small stab of jealousy.

In the car on the way back from the casino, Fletcher holds the box of videotapes on his lap. The tapes rattle every time Danny steers the car around a pothole. He drives like a boy racer. When they reach Southmead Station, Fletcher lugs the tapes upstairs and oversees as they are entered into evidence. He knows when to follow procedure. As soon as they are logged, he signs them out and tucks them under his desk. Danny observes but doesn't comment.

Fletcher raps on the open door to Smail's office and pokes his head around it. Smail is on the phone. He looks shattered. The fingertips of one hand are buried in the flesh on his forehead. He indicates with the other that Fletcher should sit.

"What have you got for me, John?" he asks when he puts down the phone.

"*Video footage of Jessica Paige at the Paradise Casino on Sunday evening.*"

"Classy," Smail says. "While her kid's out running wild. Does it give her an alibi?"

"A partial alibi. She left the casino at 22:13, so about seventy-two minutes are unaccounted for between then and her arrival back at the estate. She left the casino in a car with an unknown male."

"Have you asked her who he is?"

"Not yet, but I will."

"Good. What did you make of her?"

"She was under the influence of something."

"Does she work?"

"No. Lives on benefits."

"Turns tricks?"

"Maybe. But if she does, I don't think she uses the flat. Danny will run the plate from the car that picked her up at the casino and go through the rest of the CCTV. I'll get somebody to see if any road cameras picked up the car she left the casino in. When she arrived back at the estate she was in a taxi, so she switched vehicles at some point."

"Do you like her for this?"

Fletcher balks at the question. Infanticide is vanishingly rare, even amongst unfit mothers. "Jury's still out, boss," he says. Smail nods.

"Sidney Noyce," he says. "Have you come across him?"

Fletcher has excellent recall. Sid the Village, *he thinks*. He says, "Cody Swift—the kid, friend of the other two—he mentioned a man called Sid when I interviewed him."

"A witness says she saw Noyce taking the same path the boys did shortly after them on Sunday evening," Smail says. He raises his eyebrows at Fletcher, who nods to indicate that he recognizes the significance of this.

"*Action for you,*" Smail says and Fletcher bristles, though he doesn't let it show, because he should be discussing action allocations with Smail in his role as deputy investigating officer, not being handed them.

"*Interview Noyce. Go and see him at home today. In fact, go now.*"

"*Can we discuss strategy when I get back?*"

"*Of course.*" The smile Smail gives him looks more like a wince. Fletcher feels like Smail is giving him responsibility with one hand and snatching it away with the other. The thought blackens his mood as he heads out, but he has a call to make that requires all his focus. He walks out of the station and down Southmead Road. There's a public phone box a quarter of a mile away, opposite the hospital. He yanks the door open and steps in. He dials a number he knows by heart and pumps a few coins in.

"*It's John,*" he says to the man who answers. "*Can you talk?*"

"*Is there a problem?*"

Felix Abernathy and Fletcher are, by arrangement, very careful about how they communicate and when. This phone call breaks the protocol they've agreed on.

"*I'm on a pay phone, don't worry. Can't you hear the fucking traffic?*" Fletcher shouts as an ambulance pulls out of the hospital, with sirens wailing.

Felix Abernathy has been a presence in his life since Fletcher took a bung from him six months ago. Fletcher was handsomely rewarded for burying a charge against a man who had hurt one of the girls working for Felix. He didn't hurt her badly, just a bit of roughing up, but it was a delicate situation, Felix explained, because the man had a public profile. He was extremely contrite. He would be very grateful for a blind eye. Fletcher prevaricated at first, but was assured Felix would be making sure this man didn't come near his girls again, and *that the girl would be handsomely compensated, too. In the end he felt that everybody involved would come out better off this way than if it was dragged through the system.*

Fletcher knew his loyalty had been bought that day, but he felt he could handle it. He had a feeling in his bones that Felix Abernathy might turn out to be a very good contact to have. Managing him felt like a similar challenge to managing some of the senior officers in CID: a game Fletcher would relish, and one he intended to win.

He's about to play an ace.

"What's happening?" Felix asks.

"It's a potential problem. There are CCTV tapes of you and Jessy Paige together at the Paradise on Sunday night." A truck brakes noisily beside Fletcher, and Felix's response is lost. "What's that?" Fletcher shouts.

"Lose them."

"Well, as you can imagine, that won't be easy. They're in evidence."

"Not my problem."

"I'm calling because it is your problem. Can you give Jessy Paige an alibi for the evening?"

"I can't be associated with this; I can't be anywhere near it. It would be damaging to business."

Fletcher catches his breath.

"I found him," he says, though he didn't mean to. "I found her boy."

There is a moment of silence on the line before Felix says, "I'm sorry. I didn't know that was you."

"It was all hands on deck. Every man out there searching, and I found them. Charlie was alive. There were these flowers. They were so fucking orange."

"Look, tell me when the tapes are gone. John? Are you there?"

Fletcher rallies. "Like I said, it might not be that easy. I was wondering what you know about Jessy Paige. Any reason to think she might harm the kid?"

"Drop it."

Fletcher hears the threat and backs down. "Okay," he says. "So I'm going to see what I can do about the tapes, but no promises. This was a courtesy call to keep you in the loop."

Fletcher hangs up before Felix can reply. Apart from having a bit of an emotional moment—unprecedented for him—Fletcher feels that went well. Smail might be trying to keep him on his back, but Felix Abernathy will not do the same.

Fletcher finds Danny leaning against his car smoking a cigarette and chatting to another detective on the squad and thinks that the pair of them look like flash gits. Fletcher sometimes feels an urge to shake his childhood friend off and find another partner, but loyalty is a trait he might not be able to replace, and he needs it like he needs oxygen, just as Felix does.

Fletcher takes the wheel for the drive from the station to the Glenfrome Estate. By the time they arrive the rain is bucketing down. Somebody has dumped two armchairs, a chipped bathtub, and a plastic Christmas tree in the middle of the grass. They remind Fletcher of desert flora that sprouts strangely and garishly after a downpour.

The tower blocks loom tall and bleak. They are lined up in two rows—one row of three slightly in front of the other—with uniform distance between them, like soldiers waiting for inspection. Fletcher and Danny pass under a crisp-edged concrete awning to enter Nightingale Tower. The foyer is tiled in sixties patterns that make Fletcher's brain ache. The colors are vile, amongst them a bright orange that drags his mind back to the discovery of the boys and those poppies that *hazed his view. He blinks the image away. He wonders when he'll ever be rid of it.*

Fletcher and Danny take the elevator to the thirteenth floor. They brandish their ID cards at the Noyces' door. Valerie Noyce glances at them anxiously before telling them who she is and offering a limp handshake, fingers held out cautiously as if she's not used to formal introductions or is expecting a slap on the wrist. Doe-eyed, Fletcher thinks as he studies her. The definition of. Her eyes are very dark brown, fringed with long lashes. She has a rosebud mouth and a crooked nose.

She shows them into the lounge. Danny crosses the room to look out the window and says, "Lovely view, Mrs. Noyce. Do you get good sunsets?"

"We do, yes, when it's not raining." She laughs. It's high-pitched. She's nervous. Rain hits the window like a shower of pebbles, and she jumps.

Phil Noyce is a bear of a man, taller and wider than both Fletcher and Danny. He gets up off a sofa and stands beside Danny at the window. He blocks a lot of light.

A large table fills at least a third of the space in the room. A sewing machine and some dowdy garments are laid on top of it. It looks to Fletcher like a bit of a cottage industry—repairs or alterations, maybe. Valerie Noyce shoves the garments out of their way and invites them to sit at the table. She offers tea. Fletcher doesn't want it, but it's good to accept hospitality because it oils the wheels. "Milk and two sugars, please," he says, and she smiles as if she's pleased with him.

"Were you both here on Sunday evening?" Danny asks.

"We went to the bingo," Valerie Noyce replies. "Down the social club."

"What time?"

"We must have left at about quarter to eight and we got home at half eleven. A bit later than normal."

"Was Sidney here when you got home?"

She nods. "In his room."

"Did you see him?"

"No. I just called out, 'You all right, love?' and he said, 'Yeah,' and I said, 'Didn't you get the ketchup, then?' because I seen he didn't eat his dinner. He doesn't eat lasagna without ketchup, so he was going to get some while we was out. And he said, 'No. Shop was shut because of a flooding, so I had cereal instead.' After that, we just said good night."

"Did you notice anything different about him?"

"Everything seemed normal. I washed up his bowl and spoon and we went to bed ourselves."

"We are hoping to speak to Sidney," Fletcher says.

The shadows in the room shift as Phil Noyce turns away from the window. "Sid's in his room watching his program," he says. "He won't talk to you until it's finished. There's no point in trying."

"What time does it finish?" Danny asks.

"Half past."

Fletcher looks at his watch. Only five minutes to wait, which would be the sensible thing to do if it avoids agitating Noyce junior. On the other hand, a bit of agitation can be helpful in an interview. You don't always want your interviewee to feel in control. Fletcher fancies getting a look at Sid Noyce's bedroom, too. "Do you mind if I go and say hello?" he asks in his best I'm-no-threat voice.

"It's your funeral," Phil Noyce says. "Second on the left."

Fletcher follows the direction indicated and takes a few steps down a short corridor. He knocks gently on a door where SIDNEY is spelled out in childish wooden letters stuck on at chest height. He can hear the television, but no answer. He knocks again and this time opens the door a crack.

Sidney Noyce is sitting on a single bed in a corner of the room. He's easily as big as his father and is surrounded by the accoutrements of childhood. Fletcher has a tenuous grasp on popular culture, but he recognizes the design on Noyce's duvet cover as the Ninja Turtles. Noyce glances at Fletcher and treats him to a glower that would have got Fletcher a sharp clip around the ear when he was a kid. Noyce's eyes return to the television screen.

Fletcher glances back down the corridor into the sitting room. Danny is standing beside Phil Noyce. Both have their arms folded. Noyce is nodding as Danny talks. Fletcher eases the door of the bedroom open a little more. He sees a couple of comic books on the bedside table and a well-loved copy of the Guinness Book of Records. *Noyce is sitting cross-legged on the end of his bed, a couple of feet from a television that's on a white chest of drawers.*

"What are you watching?" Fletcher asks.

"Supermarket Sweep with Dale Winton," Noyce replies readily. "They run and get things in the trolley. They can have anything they want." He glances quickly at Fletcher with eyes wide as saucers at the wonder of it.

"I like that one," Fletcher says, though he's never watched it. He eases himself into the room slowly and takes a seat on the side of the bed, keeping a good distance between himself and Noyce. Valerie appears in the doorway holding a mug of tea. She doesn't enter but holds up the mug, offering it to Fletcher.

"Thanks," he says.

"Don't come in!" Sidney says, though his eyes remain fixed on the TV set.

"He doesn't like me to come in his room," Valerie explains. Her

*toes are inches from the door's threshold. Fletcher stands up, takes the
tea from her, and sits back down. The mattress springs creak. The
bedding smells fruity.*

"Did your mum and dad tell you who I am and why I'm here?"
Fletcher asks. *Noyce shakes his head. His bottom lip protrudes farther
than the top one. It's moist with saliva. His back is large and powerful.* "I'm a police detective and I'm here to have a chat with you about
two boys who I think you know," *he says.*

This captures Noyce's attention. "A detective like Sherlock
Holmes?"

Fletcher nods.

"Do you solve mysteries?"

"I do. And sometimes people help me." *Fletcher can't see Valerie
Noyce any longer but a shadow on the hall carpet tells him that she's
standing just out of sight.* "People like you help me," *Fletcher adds as
the credits roll on* Supermarket Sweep. *A voice-over announces the
upcoming entertainment.*

"The next program is boring," *Noyce says. He presses a button on
the TV, extinguishing the picture, and shifts round to face Fletcher.*
"Hi, mister detective."

"Hi. Now, tell me, do you think you can help me find out what
happened to Charlie and Scott? Because they got hurt."

"They're not dead," *Noyce says matter-of-factly, as if he's informed, and Fletcher catches his breath.*

"What makes you say that?"

"Because they was breathing when I put the carpet on them."

*From the landing outside, there's the sound of fabric scraping
against a solid surface, as if Valerie Noyce is sinking to her knees, her
back against the wall. Rainwater washes down the window behind
Noyce, liquefying the view of the sky, the city, and the green hills*

beyond. *The sudden pounding of Fletcher's heart tells him that he—* *John Fletcher—is holding all the cards in his hand, right here, right* *now.* Tread carefully, *he thinks.* Fuck Howard Smail, *he thinks,* and anybody else who thinks they own me. I have this. This could be mine.

He stretches his fingers out and relaxes them. He allows himself *no other movement. He is walking on eggshells, but his concentration* *is perfectly sharp.* "Where were Charlie and Scott when you put the carpet on them?" *he asks.*

"Behind the track."

"Were they hurt?"

Noyce pauses before answering, apparently considering this. "I didn't know if they were pretending or if it was real."

"What did you see? Can you tell me how they looked when you saw them?"

"Scotty had blood on his hair," *he says.* "They looked cold, so I pulled the carpet on them." *Jesus, Fletcher thinks. He draws in* *a deep breath to keep control. Noyce tears viciously at a fingernail* *with his teeth and looks out of the window.* "It's raining," *he says.* *He flattens the pad of his index finger on the glass, leaving a greasy* *smudge.*

"What else did you see?" *Fletcher keeps his voice even and calm* *and drops it almost to a whisper. Trust is everything. This moment* *must not be broken.*

"I didn't touch them."

"Why do you say that?"

"I'm not allowed to talk to them or touch them or follow them."

"Who told you that?"

"Scotty and Charlie and Cody."

"Do you know why they said it?"

"*Because I want to play with them, but they don't want me to.*"

"*How does that make you feel?*" Fletcher asks. "*When they tell you they don't want to play with you?*"

Noyce shakes his head and turns away from Fletcher. The set of his jaw is truculent. The fingernail he bit is torn and bleeding. Noyce sucks it.

"*Do you feel angry when that happens?*" Fletcher asks.

"*Sometimes.*"

"*What do you do when you feel angry?*"

"*I hit and I hit, but I'm not allowed to hit.*"

From the corridor comes the sound of a suppressed sob. Fletcher feels his heart rate quicken.

"*Did you hit Charlie and Scott?*"

"*No!*"

"*Are you sure? It's important to tell the truth.*"

"*I only found them. I didn't know if they was pretending, but I checked them and they was still breathing.*"

Fletcher wants to ask more, he's desperate to, he'd love to squeeze a confession out of Noyce here and now, but they've got to do this properly or anything this man-child says won't be admissible in court.

"*Sid,*" he says, "*have you ever had a ride in a police car?*"

"*With lights on?*"

"*With a radio. A real police radio. Would you like to? You could come and see the police station where the detectives work and we could carry on talking there.*"

Sid jumps to his feet. "*Let's go!*"

Fletcher avoids Valerie Noyce's gaze as he walks out of the room with his hand on Sid's shoulder. He remains focused, turning possibilities over in his mind one after the other. If he's right in thinking he may have just been dealt a winning hand—and he's feeling *increasingly certain that he has—then he needs to use it as wisely as he can.*

"Sid's going to come down the station and have a chat with us," he tells Danny, who nods as if that was nothing special. Fletcher turns to Phil Noyce. "We would prefer it if one of you could come with him, if that's possible? If not, we'll make sure he has an appropriate adult with him at all times."

"We'll come," Valerie Noyce answers from behind Fletcher. She's as pale as a ghost.

"There won't be room for you both in our car, I'm afraid," Fletcher says. He feels as if a band is tightening around his chest as he says it, because it's not true and he hasn't got a Plan B if they call him out on this. "Do you have your own transport?"

Danny doesn't move a muscle as Fletcher lies. Phil Noyce nods in acceptance, and Fletcher scribbles down the address of the Southmead Station in a businesslike way even while his adrenaline surges in anticipation of what he wants to do next.

Downstairs in the parking area, they jog through the rain, Sid Noyce acting like it's a game. Fletcher gets into the back of the car with Noyce, and Danny takes the wheel. Noyce's parents climb into a beaten-up Ford Fiesta and Fletcher sees the taillights come on and off as they try to get it started.

"Where's the radio?" Noyce asks as Danny starts the ignition and the wipers slice across the windscreen.

"It's in the front. Built into the dashboard. Look." Danny turns on the radio and it obliges by crackling with speech. "Not many people get to see that," Fletcher says. Noyce leans forward to inspect the radio more closely. He reaches out to touch the handset that's clipped to the side. "Don't touch!" Fletcher says. Noyce snatches his hand back and looks upset.

"Sorry," Fletcher says. He mustn't lose Noyce. "We can't touch it now, we're just listening in case there are any burglars we need to chase. You're part of the team now."

"Which station?" Danny asks. They are closest to Trinity Road, but Fletcher needs as much time as possible in the car with Noyce. They could go the "pretty way" to Trinity—they've done that before plenty of times—but he thinks it's safer to head back to base.

"Southmead," he says. "I think Sidney would like to see the detective headquarters, wouldn't you, Sid?"

Danny's and Fletcher's eyes meet in the rearview mirror, and Danny nods.

IT'S TIME TO TELL

EPISODE 6—THE CASE AGAINST
SIDNEY NOYCE AND THE
SILENCING OF OWEN WESTON

A DISHLICKER
PODCAST PRODUCTION

"The jury had to decide: was Sidney Noyce a gentle giant or an avenging monster? He presented as the former in court, but the evidence against him piled up. Throw into the pot an inept defense and an aggressive and skillful prosecution, and what hope did he have?"

My name is Cody Swift. I'm a filmmaker and your host of *It's Time to Tell,* a Dishlicker Podcast Production. That's the voice of Owen Weston, the crime reporter who has mounted a long crusade to convince others that Sidney Noyce was innocent of murdering my best friends, Charlie Paige and Scott Ashby, in 1996. Owen is asking one of many questions about this case that have haunted him for twenty years.

Maya and I tried to secure an interview with the barrister, Robert Clay, who defended Sidney Noyce. He wasn't easy to find because he no longer works in the law. The most recent professional trace of him we discovered was a ten-year-old ruling by the Bar Standards Board, who fined and suspended him because he had, and I quote, "behaved in a way likely to diminish the trust and confidence which the public placed in him and his profession."

With a bit more persistent research we found a phone number for a Robert Clay who we thought might be the same man. He appeared to have settled on the south coast, where he works at a boatyard. I gave him a call:

"Hello. Is this Robert Clay?"

"Speaking."

"Hi, Mr. Clay, my name is Cody Swift. I'm working on a true crime podcast concerning the murders of my best friends, Charlie Paige and Scott Ashby, back in 1996. I believe you defended Sidney Noyce, the man accused of murdering them. I would love to ask you a few questions about Sidney Noyce's trial, if you're willing to talk to me."

"No. Not willing."

"But that's you? You were the barrister defending Noyce?"

"I was."

"Mr. Clay, it was alleged by a reporter at the time that your defense of Sidney Noyce was not as robust as it might have been. Do you have anything to say to that?"

"Absolutely no comment. Please leave me alone."

"Do you believe Sidney Noyce was innocent, Mr. Clay? Do you think you let him down?"

What you just heard is Robert Clay hanging up. I called back on more than one occasion, but it went to voice mail. I left messages, but he didn't return them.

We tried to track down the prosecution barrister to see what she had to say, but learned that she had passed away. She was close to retirement at the time of the trial, so it wasn't surprising news.

In the absence of interviews with the main players for the prosecution and defense, my primary resource for learning about the day-to-day machinations at the trial has been the reporting done by Owen Weston for the *Bristol Echo*. I'm a fan of his work. He maintains a steady, reasonable tone, he avoids sensationalism, and like a man after my own heart, he has clearly done his research. I also discovered that he won a prize for his coverage of the Noyce trial.

Owen Weston invited me to come and interview him at his home.

The drive to see Weston takes me north of Bristol beyond the suburbs and into the fringes of the countryside. His house is one of a row of bungalows built on a ridge overlooking the Severn Valley. He welcomes me warmly and shows me through the house into a conservatory, which has spectacular views across the broad valley toward Wales. The river glints below, a silver band edged by the green silhouettes of trees. Pockets of fog hover in dips and ditches, and skinny layers of clouds crowd the horizon. The scene is a held breath, a moment of stillness.

Weston is tall and slim with curly and abundant gray hair. I figure he is just on the far side of seventy years old. His shoulders stoop, but only a little. In the main, he seems physically fit, and a *Times* newspaper with completed crossword and sudoku puzzles tells me he is mentally fit, too. He has kind eyes and a gentle manner that put me at ease immediately. As we chat, I begin to understand that his nonthreatening demeanor is very likely one of the reasons Weston has persuaded so many people to talk to him over the years.

I jump right in with the question that haunts me most.

"Do you think Sidney Noyce killed Charlie and Scott?"

"I don't know if he did or not—he could have—but what I do believe is that the police did not treat him fairly and he did not get a fair trial as a result. You read my recent article, so you will know that I'm not the only one to have my doubts about Noyce's treatment. His solicitor expressed reservations, too."

"Can you talk about what she said?"

"Her name is Julie McDowell. She was the duty solicitor on the day Sidney Noyce was brought in, questioned, and subsequently arrested at Southmead Station by Detective Inspector John Fletcher. Full disclosure: Julie is a friend of mine. I got to know her well, as we had met each other at court on numerous occasions when I was covering stories. I had—still have—a lot of respect for her. She was present at the first interview with Noyce after they arrested him and she wasn't comfortable with what she observed."

"Why not?"

"Frustratingly, she wasn't able to put her finger on what exactly made her feel that something about the situation was off, but she described how she had the feeling that there was something going on behind the scenes."

"Such as?"

"Possibly something that had gone on between Noyce and CID, prior to her involvement. It's not unusual for detectives to withhold information from solicitors and muck about with disclosure and that kind of thing—everybody is trying to work the system to their advantage—but in this case she said John Fletcher seemed too eager to disclose, if that makes sense. He was trying incredibly hard to demonstrate that he was doing everything by the book, ostentatiously so."

"Could that be because of the nature of this case?"

"It could be, but Julie had worked on some big cases and she had never experienced anything quite like it before. That eagerness on the part of the police to demonstrate overtly that they are doing everything by the book, it's not unheard of, but it was unusual and it certainly wasn't associated with DI Fletcher. He had a mild reputation for being a bit of a maverick. He was certainly smart enough to work the system to get the results he wanted."

"The lady doth protest too much?"

"That's one way to describe it, yes, though I'm not sure how John Fletcher would feel about being described as a lady. It boiled down to the fact that Fletcher was working so hard to demonstrate that everything was tickety-boo, it made an experienced solicitor like Julie smell a rat."

"Did she have any evidence of wrongdoing?"

"If she had, she would have used it, but never underestimate a gut feeling when it's underpinned by years of experience and observation. Instinct can be very accurate."

"Did you find any evidence yourself?"

"I hate to say it, but where this case is concerned, I had to admit defeat for personal reasons, but I still believe there is more out there to be discovered and this might be the time to find it."

I'll come back to the reasons why Weston gave up investigating, because they are important, but I want to spend a few more moments considering Julie McDowell. Maya and I felt it was important to contact Julie herself. She has moved on from Bristol and now lives and works in Norfolk. Julie didn't want to record

an interview, but she sent us this statement by email. This is Maya
reading it out:

"I have an excellent track record as a solicitor. I represent
many of my clients in court. There are very few cases that
gnaw at me for years after they're over, but Sidney Noyce's
case is one of those. Something felt wrong at the time, and
still feels wrong. I was devastated to hear that he took his
own life. It brought a lot of the frustration I felt at the time
flooding back. Sidney Noyce was not a perfect man, but I
was, and remain, convinced he was not a murderer. A certain police officer twisted Noyce around his little finger. I
raised my suspicions, and had anybody pursued them seriously, I believe they could have been enough for the case to
be dismissed, but unfortunately the officer concerned was too
clever for that. In that situation, there is nothing you can do,
but to this day I continue to live with the sense that I, and the
justice system, failed Sidney Noyce."

Interesting, don't you think? To get a better idea of what Noyce
was up against at trial, I asked Owen Weston to summarize the key
evidence against him.

"The evidence against Noyce all added up nicely, up to
a point. A lot of people on the estate attested to the fact
that he used to spend time with you boys, and that you
three taunted him. A key witness described Noyce following Charlie and Scott down Primrose Lane. That was the
final sighting of the boys. She also described how Noyce
circled the block and how she heard him calling the boys.

That was contested by the defense because they claimed to have discovered that her story had changed since her original statement, but not effectively enough. What else? The bodies were discovered on a patch of land behind the dog track, a place that Sid is likely to have known because he spent time at the track. This location was also near Tesco, where Noyce worked. But even given all that, there was no doubt in my mind that reasonable doubt existed, because the bulk of what the prosecution had against him was circumstantial. Unfortunately, Noyce's barrister was unbelievably ineffective. I told his parents to make a complaint, but they wouldn't. They were scared of offending him and that it might damage Sidney's defense. But a good defense should have been able to cast reasonable doubt on each and every one of those things."

"What about the blood?"

"Ah. The blood. Yes. That's what swayed the jury in the end, of course, even though Noyce refused to say how it got there when they questioned him. I believe they judged him first and listened to the evidence afterward. Just like the police."

"Did you speak to any jury members?"

"It's illegal in our system. They're protected. I wish I could have. I would have given anything to be a fly on the wall in the jury room. That verdict got returned so fast, it was as if they'd agreed what they were going to say before they even went in there. I think it was the blood that got Noyce, though. I'd put money on that. It was by far the most damning piece of evidence. Even a good defense would have found it a challenge."

The tiny droplets of blood found on Sidney Noyce's trousers were enough to damn him because a forensic expert testified— albeit vaguely, according to Owen Weston—that the droplets appeared to have been transferred at the time an injury occurred. They constituted evidence that Noyce had been with the boys at the time they were attacked, and not afterward, as he claimed. Without access to the photographs of the spatter pattern, we are unable to draw our own conclusion or get them independently examined. The photographs remain archived in the police case files.

I had an important question to ask Owen Weston.

"If you don't think Noyce murdered Charlie and Scott, then who do you think did?"

"I don't know. I have theories, but I don't know for sure. Whoever it was put a lot of effort into stopping me reporting on the case."

"Can you explain what you mean?"

"Somebody tried to intimidate me. At first it built up slowly. When my first few articles about the case were published, I began to get silent phone calls. Infrequent at first, then daily, then a few times a day. Usually at my office number, but some at home, too. Then the threatening letters started. They went to the office at first, but we received one here, too. It said some horrible things and my wife saw it. I told her the best thing to do would be to ignore it and assured her everything would be okay. But it escalated quickly. I came down one morning to find that somebody had slashed my tires in the drive, and a few days later I was attacked in a lane near the courthouse."

"Did you consider stopping?"

"Not at first. I'm an investigative journalist. Intimidation is what you expect if you are doing your job properly, and I had my professional pride, but it took its toll on my family. My wife asked me to stop reporting on the case after the physical attack. She gave me an ultimatum. We had small children."

"How did they attack you?"

"A few punches to the abdomen, he slammed me against a wall. And this."

Weston pointed to the crooked bridge of his nose: an obvious break.

"Did you see who did it?"

"It was just one man, but I couldn't identify anything about him afterward except that he wore black boots and a balaclava. He took me by surprise, landed the punches where he needed to, very professional. It happened as the trial was coming to a close, so after the guilty verdict I stopped reporting, reluctantly, because I felt Sid Noyce needed somebody to continue to make a noise on his behalf, but you do these things for your family. The intimidation ceased immediately."

"Did your recent article trigger anything?"

"No, but it might. And so might the podcast. If you want to get to the bottom of this, look at other possibilities. Noyce was just one of many initial suspects, and once he was arrested, the police didn't examine the alternatives properly. In fact that is one of the single most notable things about this case: the early focus on Noyce meant that all other avenues of investigation were shut down too early."

The clips you've just heard are from an interview I recorded with Owen Weston before Maya and I received the packet of photographs. As soon as the photos arrived, I realized, based on my conversation with Owen, that they might be the start of a campaign of escalating intimidation. After the police, he was the first person I phoned. Owen had this advice to give me:

"If you plan to continue with the podcast, watch your backs. It's not a game. Whoever is behind this might be capable of murder."

Sobering words, and all the more so as another threatening incident has occurred since then and has been reported to the police. This morning, Maya lifted the lid of the laptop and was faced with a gruesome image. Our laptop wallpaper had been replaced with a candid photograph of Maya in the bathroom, the same photograph we were already sent a copy of anonymously. The photograph on our laptop had been doctored with a red line ripping across Maya's throat. It looked shockingly violent. A word in red capitals scrolled across the bottom of the screen: STOP. Maya slammed the lid of the laptop shut. When we opened it again later on, mustering our courage to face it again, we discovered the laptop had died and we weren't able to bring it back to life.

Fortunately, we are religious about backing up our work in progress via secure methods, so everything we have been working on is safe. Before this happened, you might have called our obsession with backing up a form of paranoia. Now it feels like a wise thing to have done. We have handed the laptop over to the police for analysis and bought a new machine to continue work on the podcast. To protect it and us, it will not be connected to the internet.

We would not advise any of our listeners to continue with a project in the face of intimidation, but I do not want to stop, because I am on a personal mission. Unlike Owen, I do not have small children or a wife who need me to stop. Maya and I are in this together and we have agreed we will keep going, because if somebody is going to such lengths to bully us, it is all the more likely that there is something to discover. In the next episode of *It's Time to Tell*, we'll be talking about who else could have been responsible for the murders. We're going to look into avenues of investigation the police apparently ignored and ask some more questions about why that happened.

Here are two clips related to what we'll be focusing on in next week's episode. The first voice belongs to ex–Detective Superintendent Howard Smail, the second voice to crime reporter Owen Weston.

"I was cradling Ms. Paige as I tried to help her sit down safely. It was the biggest mistake of my career, though of course I didn't know that at the time."

"Jessica Paige was unaccounted for between 22:13 and 23:25 on the night the boys disappeared. That's seventy-two minutes. So far as I could ascertain, this was never properly investigated. It was an unforgivable lapse on the part of the police and Noyce's defense team."

Felix invites Jess to lunch and she doesn't feel she can refuse. In the taxi on the way to the restaurant, Felix works on his phone while Jess watches London pass by. A notification pings.

"New episode of the podcast just dropped," he says. "Want to listen?" His thumb hovers over the play button.

"No!"

"Joking. Keep your hair on, darling. I think it's best if you don't, actually." He reads out the podcast title: "'The Case Against Sidney Noyce and the Silencing of Owen Weston.' Cody Swift likes his fancy titles, doesn't he? Makes him sound like Sherlock Holmes." He laughs, but Jess doesn't see the funny side. She's relieved when Felix slips the phone back into his jacket pocket.

The restaurant Felix has chosen is small and the other clientele are as groomed as he is. Jess feels a little underdressed by comparison, but she knows how to fake confidence and she holds her head high. The hostess greets Felix warmly and shows them to a private booth toward the back of the restaurant. Felix orders for them both without looking at the menu and Jess doesn't object.

There is a moment of awkwardness once champagne has been poured and the waiter has left. Felix wordlessly proposes a toast and their glasses chink. Jess thinks she can detect affection in his eyes. She sips. The chatter in the restaurant is a pleasant hum around them. Warmth, the taste of champagne and the smell of food encourage her to relax.

"I could get used to this," she says.

"Not too shabby, is it?" he replies. His gaze seems to fall on her in a different way from when they were in the office. Here the light is dimmer and kinder and they are close enough to each other that if they adjusted their positions, their knees could touch under the table. It is intimate in a way Jess finds familiar but unsettling.

What does he see when he looks at me? she wonders. She holds the fragile stem of her glass lightly. Sunshine pouring through the window hazes her view of the front of the restaurant. *A used woman? A has-been? Is it just me who feels the old spark we had, or is he sensing it, too?* She thinks there might still be a spark. She is certain there was one, back in the day. Felix had so many girls over the years, but Jess was the only one he visited at her flat, she's sure of that. They weren't like a normal boyfriend and girlfriend. He would often arrive very late at night and they would listen to music and fall asleep together on the sofa, his arm over her shoulder, just like she imagined a husband and wife would. Felix would drop his guard around her at those times. In the morning, he would tease a grumpy Charlie until he smiled. Charlie never liked to find Felix there when he woke up.

"You married?" Jess asks.

"Between wives."

"Kids?"

He shakes his head. She's not surprised. Food arrives, hidden underneath small silver domes. The waiter removes the domes from their plates simultaneously, and clouds of dry ice spill from the rims of pewter bowls and across the tabletop. The smoke dissipates quickly, revealing a tiny mountain of chopped flesh in each bowl, laced with dill and chunks of salt and pepper.

"Something wrong?" Felix asks once the waiter has gone.

"Pretentious, isn't it?" She can't be arsed to pretend.

"Pretentious as fuck."

She bursts out laughing. It's not what she was expecting him to say. This is a glimpse of the old Felix.

"Would you rather get a McDonald's?" he adds.

"Probably."

Now it's his turn to snort with laughter. Other diners turn to look. "That's my girl."

They tuck in, reminiscing about some of their old haunts and other safe topics, careful not to mention any unmentionables. Jess carefully monitors how much she is drinking, not easy to do, as the waiters seem ever present, topping up her glass with champagne. The portions of food are so small and delicate it doesn't take long to get through their first two courses. She's about to ask Felix if he's seeing anybody, given he's not married. She wants to know if he's bagged a celebrity girlfriend, but he speaks first.

"Can you get away for a bit?"

"Away?"

"From Bristol. Ideally for a few weeks. I think Cody Swift's podcast has a naturally short shelf life, and his interest in you has a shorter one. If you're not in Bristol, he can't get to you, and with a bit of luck the whole thing will have run out of steam by the time you get back home."

"Nick's on a shoot in Morocco," she says.

"*Operation Crusader*?"

"How did you know?"

"I've got a client on it."

She wants to ask who but knows better. Felix can make you feel special—he can make you feel like the center of his world—but no matter how special you feel, you never get to hear about the other people in his life, so you don't ask.

"You should go, if you can. Take the kid. I'll deal with our little problem here." He smiles.

It's an incredibly tempting idea, but Jess is skeptical. Wouldn't it be just too easy to disappear and leave everything with him? But on the other hand, God knows she'd give her right arm for an easy solution, and hasn't she been through enough tough stuff to deserve an easy ride in life sometimes?

A wave of tiredness flattens the adrenaline that's kept Jess going all day. She's not sure if she's feeling her age or the champagne. Both, probably. She glances at Felix. "I want to know what you're thinking of doing," she says.

"Do you ask Nick to tell you every detail of what he does when he's on a shoot? Do you ask Erica to describe how she studies for all those exams she's doing at school, or learns her lines for those plays she's in?"

Jess freezes. Felix's tone is friendly, but these are details about her daughter that Jess hasn't shared with him. She shakes her head.

"Then let me do my job."

"Don't hurt him."

"I heard you the first time. There's no need to be paranoid, darling."

"Felix—"

"Relax. What makes the world go round?"

She hesitates, then offers, "Money?"

"And what does Cody Swift need to keep his podcast going while he's not taking on paid jobs?"

"Money."

"Exactly. He's doing very well, as a matter of fact, but that doesn't mean he has enough of the green stuff. I happen to know somebody who is contributing some funds to the podcast, who may be persuaded to withdraw those funds over, maybe—what shall we say?—some editorial differences, perhaps?"

Jess is relieved. Money. Of course! She's fine with that. What was she thinking? Felix is respectable now, he's got a public profile. The things they did were so long ago. Water under the bridge for them both. Nobody needs to get hurt in the present day for them to get what they want. She tells herself to relax, that she doesn't need to be hypervigilant.

"Sorry," she says. "Thank you."

"Book yourself and the kid a flight to Morocco. Have a holiday. Spend some time with the other half. Treat yourselves. Don't worry about a thing."

She reaches for his hand and squeezes it. "Thank you." She means it because she wants to believe in the possibility that the different parts of your life can remain distinct, that old selves and new cannot bleed into one another.

Felix turns her hand over and draws a circle in the middle of her palm with the tip of his finger before letting go again. "You're welcome."

She pulls her hand back. She takes the starched napkin

from her lap and twists it with both hands. "Can I get a coffee?" she asks.

"Anything you like." He orders two espressos. She thinks he seems detached now, as if she's overstayed her welcome, but there's one more thing she wants to achieve in this conversation.

"Are you worried about the podcast?" she asks.

"Not in the slightest."

"But what if I . . ."

"What if you talk about what happened that night? Is that what you're going to say? After a nice lunch like this and a generous offer of help from me?"

"And what if I do?" She wants him to feel a tiny edge of threat from her, to know that he is not a hundred percent in control.

"You won't." He leans on one elbow. It's a relaxed pose, but threat laces the atmosphere and feels as familiar from the past as the tug inside Jess telling her she wants to be with him. "You're not that stupid."

"Aren't I?" she says. "Are you sure? A frightened woman can do some very silly things." It's the sort of thing he used to say to the girls who worked for him. He stares.

"I remember when Charlie died," he says. "Do you?"

She nods. Braces herself for the inevitable retaliation.

"What was that word you used when you talked about it afterward? Do you remember what it was? No? Shall I remind you?" he asks.

She shakes her head. It's a tight movement.

Felix licks his lips. "*Relief*, you said. It was a relief when Charlie died."

She raises her head and watches him watching her, sees

the curl of his lip, the set of his jaw, and the hardness in his eyes.

"It's time I went home," she says. "Thank you for lunch and for helping me. I appreciate it." She has to force herself to say it. His words have cut her to the quick, but she won't let him see that. He wouldn't have said them unless she'd rattled him, so she got what she wanted.

"Good girl," he says. "You're welcome."

He doesn't stand up. She feels his eyes on her back as she walks through the restaurant, toward the door. On the street she turns around to look back inside—hoping for something, though she's not sure what—but all she can see is her own reflection. She walks briskly toward the tube station.

It's true, what Felix said, though nobody else knows apart from them. Jess did feel relief after Charlie died—only at first, when she still didn't know which way was up—because it had been so difficult to look after him. Her memory of that feeling is the hardest thing she has had to live with.

letter is on the phone talking to a member of the fraud team who originally investigated Dale when a call from his elder son starts to buzz on his mobile. He picks it up but can only watch uselessly as the call goes to voice mail. He's been waiting for a call back from Andrew for what feels like weeks. Andrew is a Royal Marine. Earlier in the year he was on a winter training exercise in Norway, but Fletcher doesn't know where he's been since then. The radio silence has been especially tough for Fletcher because he knows Andrew is in regular communication with his mother. Andrew doesn't leave a message.

The fraud team struggle to help Fletcher. He gets passed from pillar to post while they try to find somebody who can talk to him about the case. "The problem is," says the old-timer they eventually put him through to, "there's nobody here any longer who worked on it. I was around at the time, but it wasn't my case. From what I recall off the top of my head, they worked bloody hard, but the money was untraceable and so was Dale."

"I can't find any mention of it in the file, but I heard Dale got divorced previous to disappearing. Could he have hidden some of the money that way?"

"Yes. He absolutely could have. We see that occasionally.

Money's almost impossible to trace after a divorce, but if you hide it that way you have to be sure you can rely on your ex to be willing to give it back later."

"So he might have had a sham divorce?"

"Exactly. Otherwise you might never see a penny of your money again! There has to be a lot of trust involved."

When Fletcher puts down the phone he feels pleased because it's a lead of sorts. After only a short time on the case he has already discovered something that seems to have been missed twenty years ago. This small success doesn't do much to mitigate Fletcher's irritation with himself for his slip of the tongue with Swift, though. He cannot believe he let down his guard and was stupid enough to suggest that the witness had seen Noyce walking away from the boys instead of following them on the night they disappeared. It is possible Swift will be like a dog with a bone on this one, and it was entirely avoidable. He sighs. Watchful waiting might be the best tactic, he thinks. No point in drawing more attention to it at this stage. Best to hope it goes away, and if not, he'll deal with it somehow. Cody Swift will not get the better of John Fletcher.

Fletcher cricks his neck before standing up and stretching. The office is quiet this morning. Danny is frowning at his computer monitor.

"The on switch is on the side," Fletcher says.

"You finally took Computing 101? Congratulations!"

Fletcher smiles. "What have you got?"

"The name of Dale's ex-wife. They divorced in June 1996, two months before he disappeared."

"Promising," Fletcher says.

"I know. That's what I thought at first, but now I'm not so sure. Meet Peter Dale's ex-missus."

"Are you having a laugh?" Fletcher says. The face on Danny's computer screen is a woman called Rhonda Street. She is the police and crime commissioner for Avon & Somerset. She was elected only three years ago but is known to be ambitious and has already flexed her muscles, gaining a measure of infamy by having at least one chief constable moved on since she's been in office. Her position is powerful and her remit is extensive.

Fletcher pulls up a chair beside Danny and lowers his voice, even though nobody else is around. "What do we know about her background?"

"She married Dale in 1995, so they didn't last long. No kids. She was working for a property business when they met and carried on working there throughout the marriage and afterward. It was a family business her dad built up. Seems to be totally legit. Her husband and kids run it now and do very well out of it, apparently."

"We need to find out if she profited from the divorce from Dale," Fletcher says.

"How?" Danny asks. "We can't take a detailed look into her affairs without permission. It's a fucking minefield."

"I'll have to speak to David," Fletcher says. Normally, he avoids Chief Constable Tremain like the plague, but Fletcher has dodged enough bullets in his years of service that he recognizes one when it's coming straight at his chest. He hasn't fought for his position in CID so hard and for so long that he's going to stand in front of it and wait for impact.

Fletcher heads up to Tremain's office. He gets lucky. "He's in," Tremain's assistant tells him, "but he's only got five minutes." She holds up her hand with the five pudgy digits spread wide to illustrate her point, as if Fletcher is simpleminded.

"Come in!" David Tremain has an unpleasantly high-pitched voice. Fletcher winces at the shut door but recomposes his expression before he enters. Tremain is sitting at his desk peeling the top layer of flaccid white bread off a cheese and pickle sandwich. He sniffs the filling. The smell is pungent even from where Fletcher's standing.

"Do you think the catering department is trying to kill us all?" Tremain asks, indicating the sandwich.

"Probably," Fletcher says. He doesn't care for small talk but knows he must make an effort with his superior officers. Tremain slaps the bread back on the sandwich and takes a big bite out of it. "Not too bad, as a matter of fact," he says. "What can I do for you, John?"

Fletcher fills him in on the situation with Rhonda Street. As he speaks, he observes Tremain's color rise and the rhythm of his chewing becomes increasingly mechanical. When Fletcher has said everything he needs to say, Tremain swivels his chair toward the window. Daylight filtered through a grimy windowpane settles on his features, graying his profile. He stays there long enough that Fletcher clears his throat.

"Leave it with me," Tremain says to the view.

"Are you sure, sir?"

Tremain swivels to face Fletcher and plants his elbows on the desk. His fingertips meet and his fingers slide neatly between one another. His knuckles whiten. "I'm sure. Does anybody else know about this?"

"Just Danny and me." The back of Fletcher's neck feels as if something is crawling there.

"Keep it that way. Not a word to anybody else. It's too sensitive."

"Should we—"

"What did I just say?"

Fletcher swallows. He and Tremain share a difficult history, and meetings between them are never easy. Fletcher particularly doesn't appreciate being spoken to as if he is a child, but it's something he has to endure from this man. "You said we would be keeping a lid on this," he replies.

"Exactly. Is that difficult to understand? Can you toe the line on this one?"

"No, boss."

Tremain raises an eyebrow and Fletcher explains, "I mean no, it's not difficult to understand, and yes, I can toe the line." His mouth tastes as bitter as if he's sucking lemons.

Tremain dismisses him. He picks up the phone before Fletcher has left the room. Fletcher exits, feeling irate and aggrieved, and of course Tremain's assistant has to rub in the humiliation by peering at him over her reading glasses as if he's something the cat has dragged in. Fletcher feels his anger rise. "Cheer up, darling," he tells her. "It might never happen." He winks. Guaranteed to annoy.

"Prat," he thinks he hears her say as he walks away. He turns around. "What did you say?"

She looks at him, head inclined cockatoo-like. "I said you're a prat, John Fletcher. Always have been, always will be. I'm fed up of you strutting about like you own the place when you passed your sell-by date years ago. The only time

I'll look forward to seeing you will be at your retirement party."

Fletcher is at a loss for words. He blinks and turns away. In the elevator he punches one hand heavily into the palm of the other. "Bitch!" he spits at the sliver of mirror that reflects a slice of his face. He hits the stop button and the elevator halts. He leans against the wall. *She's a nobody,* he tells himself. *Get over it.* He finds it harder to ignore Tremain's treatment of him, though, and it seems to take forever for the tremor in his fingers to begin to subside. *When,* he thinks, *will Tremain think I've laid on my back for long enough? Never?*

As he calms down, Fletcher wonders if he shouldn't make some discreet inquiries of his own about Rhonda Street, in spite of Tremain's instructions. It would give him some pleasure to subvert Tremain in some small way. As if it's meant to be, an idea of whom he could speak to dawns like a revelation. He straightens up and hits another button. The elevator lurches into life. Just before the doors open, Fletcher sinks his still-shaking hands into his jacket pockets and his features harden as he puts his game face back on.

Fletcher sweeps a dog-eared logbook and a few empty coffee cups off the back seat of the car and gets in beside Noyce for the drive to Southmead Station. He tries to smile and maintain a casual posture while the pressure of the gamble he's taking dries his mouth and creates a tension headache. He tells himself they are the symptoms of a man who might be about to chance his luck, but who knows that he is skillful and the odds are good. As they leave the estate they see a group of reporters huddled around Howard Smail and David Tremain at the far end. Good, Fletcher thinks. Let's hope Smail is kept there for as long as possible.

The traffic is fairly heavy, which pleases him because it buys him more time. Danny drives and leaves the talking to Fletcher. It's a well-rehearsed routine. Danny's not big on ideas, but he has always been willing to follow and execute a plan that Fletcher devised just as long as he gets to enjoy some of the benefits afterward.

"Can I see your badge?" Noyce asks. He's grinning like the cat who's got the cream. Fletcher begins to reach for his wallet, where his warrant card is tucked unobtrusively beside his bank cards, but has a better idea. "You should see Danny's," he says. "It's much smarter than mine." Fletcher always enjoys an opportunity to rag on his partner for the fact that Danny ordered a fancy official folder to keep his warrant card in. It's a smooth black leather case with the force badge printed on the outside. "In my jacket," Danny says and Fletcher finds it in the inside pocket, where he knew it would be. Danny loves to pull it out and flip it open with a flourish.

Noyce examines it as if it is a precious relic. He opens and closes the folder and turns it this way and that. He pulls the card out. It gives Fletcher time to think. His heart is thumping in his ears, but he shuts his eyes and runs through the situation in his mind. There's so much about Noyce that's screaming guilty at Fletcher. Noyce is obviously mentally limited, he's got a provocative history with the boys, and there's the red-hot and smoking fact that he admits to seeing the bodies.

Fletcher shuts his eyes and runs a scenario through his head. It's the one where they inform Smail that they've brought Noyce in as soon as they arrive at Southmead. Fletcher thinks he knows what will happen if they do that: Smail will take over and he, Fletcher, will be sidelined. Smail will probably describe Noyce as "my" suspect, and it's a short leap from there to "my" arrest. Fletcher will get no credit, and he badly doesn't want to spend the rest of his career as Smail's wingman. His career has been on a steep and successful trajectory thus far, and he wants to stay on it. He's made his name by putting in the hours, by going above and beyond, by holding his nerve, by keeping his processes to himself, and by making smart decisions that serve the interests of justice—as he sees it. He knows that if he does what he wants to do, there may be questions about this journey, but he thinks he knows how he will answer them. There is no time to waste. It is time to throw the dice. He turns to Noyce. "Sid, do you know that feeling of when you want something to be nice, but you're scared that it won't be?"

"Sometimes I do."

"After we've had a look around the police station, where the detectives work, I know some of them might want to have a little talk to you about Charlie and Scott."

Noyce's finger works around the rim of Danny's warrant card.

"They're really nice, but I want to tell you something about them because you don't know them as well as you know me."

"Stranger danger," Noyce says.

"Yes. Except they're not strangers, they're police officers." Fletcher works to hold his nerve. He needs to find the right angle to persuade Noyce of something before they arrive, but they're already well on their way to the station.

"Charlie and Scott got hurt by stranger danger," Noyce says. His eyes widen, and for a second they seem to Fletcher to be bathed in innocence. It startles him. He must gather himself and regroup mentally. Stick to the plan. It's the man's simple mind fooling him, he thinks. He has committed the worst possible crime, but he can't process it like normal people. Momentarily, he thinks of his own baby son, and the thought of anything happening to him is unendurable. He presses on. "What worries me," he says, "is that the other de-

tectives haven't seen what a nice bedroom you've got, so they might not understand that you definitely want to go home later today."

A small furrow appears between Noyce's eyes.

"Not many people are lucky enough to have a big telly in their bedroom like you," Fletcher says.

"It's just for me."

"That's nice. That's very nice. The thing is, I'm worried that you might not be able to get back to your room today if you give confusing answers to the detectives who talk to you. That's the problem with detectives, they ask a lot of questions, and if they don't understand the answers they can keep you at the station for a very long time. They don't mean to be horrible, they're just trying to understand your story."

"Tell the truth," says Noyce.

"Exactly. You're right. So before we get to the station I think it's a good idea if you and me have a chat about what the truth is. That means you will know what to say to the other detectives."

"Can I go home now?" Noyce says.

"Your mum and dad are meeting us at the station, so we'd better go there, don't you think? You will like it. You can look at one of the squad cars with the lights on it."

Noyce makes the sound of a police siren and Fletcher forces himself to smile even though he feels as if his head's going to split in two.

"Here's a question the detectives might ask you," Fletcher says. "They might say, 'Did you hurt Charlie and Scott?' What would you say to that?"

Noyce shakes his head. "I didn't hurt them. They were already hurt."

"I think you did hurt them."

"I didn't."

"But you left them there when they were all damaged and cut and bruised, with blood on their faces and flies buzzing. Isn't that the same as hurting them yourself?" Fletcher knows how this sounds. He could blame this vivid recitation of the boys' injuries on his memories of Scott's pulpy face and the blood pooling in Charlie's mouth as he cradled the child, but he doesn't. In this moment, he prefers to face up to his own capacity for cruelty because the end justifies the means. He wouldn't do it otherwise. He is using cruelty like the controlled cut of a sharp blade: just enough. Then stop.

Noyce recoils at his words but Fletcher continues: *"You hurt them, Sidney, you hurt them because you didn't help them. Do you know how many hours Charlie lay there for, hurting? And Scott? How many blows did it take to make his face like that? How many times did you hit him?"*

It feels to Fletcher as if the world has shrunk so nothing else exists except the two of them in the car, their hot breath and the possibility of a murder confession hanging between them. He takes Danny's warrant card back from Noyce. Noyce begins to shake his head, then bats at his own face. His knuckles make contact with his cheek, but only softly. He does it again with a bit more force. Fletcher seizes Noyce's hands. *"Sidney, the other detectives are not going to understand what you mean if you say you didn't hurt the boys. They're going to keep you in a room and ask you questions over and over until you tell them what really happened. They're not going to let you go home until they think they understand what the truth is, so it might be a long time before you see your bedroom, your television, or your family again. It could be questions, questions, questions all night long."*

"You're hurting me," Noyce says, and Fletcher drops his hands as if they were hot coals.

"Sorry," he says. "I didn't mean to. I'm very sorry, but you mustn't hurt yourself."

Noyce rubs his hands together in a circular motion that starts to annoy Fletcher when it seems like it's going on too long. He stares at Fletcher reproachfully. "Perhaps I did hurt Charlie and Scott," he says, "because I didn't help them?"

Fletcher's lips are dry as the desert. He licks them and nods slowly. Noyce mirrors his actions.

"Yes. The detectives will understand that. You hurt the boys. It's best to be honest," Fletcher speaks as calmly as he can manage.

"And I can go home after that if I say it?"

"They'll let you out of that interview room, definitely."

The radio crackles into life with a request for their location. Fletcher tenses and then relaxes when Danny ignores it. They don't want to broadcast the fact they're bringing Noyce in. Easier to claim later on that they didn't hear the request.

Fletcher debates pushing Noyce further—he wants this man-child to admit outright what he did, because Christ knows, he has to have done it—but this is as far as he thinks they can go for now. Even though Danny's taken a bit of a roundabout route, they're already in Henleaze. He checks his watch as Danny gives way at the round-about and flips the indicator for the right turn into Southmead, yards from the entrance to the station. It's fourteen minutes since they left the estate. He had fourteen minutes to own this case. He hopes he has done enough.

Erica throws a curveball regarding the Morocco plan: she doesn't want to go.

"What about *Guys and Dolls*?" she whines.

"Would it kill you to miss it?" Jess feels especially irritated because Erica doesn't have a big part in the production. She's in the chorus. It's fun, but it's not Broadway.

"Yes!" Erica's lip quivers. "This is *all* I've been looking forward to this holiday. It's the final performance and the cast party."

It's half ten in the evening and they're sitting in the car outside the hall where rehearsals take place. Jess struggles to control her temper and hold her tongue. She starts the car and they drive away in silence while Erica taps furiously at her phone and sniffs aggressively.

Whatever Erica was doing on her phone bears fruit quickly. Half an hour after they get home, Jess's notifications ping with an email from Olly's mother:

Please excuse if this is out of turn. Olly said you had an unexpected change of plans and are going away but Erica would like to stay here and finish *Guys and Dolls*. If you're agreeable, we'd be happy to have her to stay—separate rooms, of course! Then we could put her on a plane to join

you? Give me a ring if we can help. We're just thrilled about
the relationship! Erica is a gorgeous girl!

Jess reflects on her options. It's a good offer and it's going
to be hard to turn it down without telling both Nick and
Erica something's going on. She considers what it would
mean if she took up the offer. Taking Erica to Morocco
won't limit Erica's communication with her friends, not
if there's Wi-Fi, which there's bound to be, so if Erica's
friends hear about the podcast, then Erica will, too, wherever she is. Rehearsals could distract her from that, though,
perhaps more than being in the company of her parents in
Morocco might. That Erica wouldn't be staying at their
home while Jess is away means that if Cody Swift or his
girlfriend or any journalists call round, they won't be able
to get to her. They would be hard pushed to track her down
at Olly's house.

Jess wishes she could discuss everything with Nick, but
she can't have him finding out about her contact with Felix.
As she tries to think, the cat winds through her legs. "Then
there's you to deal with as well," she says.

By morning, her mind is made up. She will go, but she'll
let Erica stay. It'll be good for Erica, a tiny step toward in-
dependence. A safe step, the kind a normal teenager would
make. The cat can return to the rescue center temporarily.

A notification on her phone tells her that an email has arrived overnight. Sent at midnight, it's from an address that
looks to be Felix's private account.

Lovely lunch. Nice to catch up. Have a great holiday. Xx

It's a bland message, yet so riddled with subtext from yesterday that Jess doesn't know how to reply. She deletes it instead.

Before she has a chance to waver, she books herself a ticket to Marrakech leaving in twenty-four hours and calls Olly's mum to accept her kind offer, make arrangements for Erica to stay with their family, and get reassurance that Erica and Olly will be looked after and monitored appropriately while Erica is there.

When Jess tells Erica what she's done she's rewarded with a crushing hug. "Thank you soooo much," Erica says. She actually jumps up and down with excitement, then begins to throw her stuff into a bag. Jess says, "You're welcome, darling," and is pierced by the thought that Charlie never had one thing like this to look forward to. She can't remember him jumping up and down with excitement after the age of about seven or eight. He was too street smart. She suppresses an urge to snap at her daughter and tell her to calm down. *Erica's privilege is not her fault,* Jess thinks to herself. *You made Charlie one way, and you and Nick are making Erica another way. Don't blame her for that.* She knows, too, that she wouldn't want it any other way for Erica. For Charlie, she'd rewrite the whole book if she could.

By the time she's packed her own stuff, Jess feels both bolder and relieved about the podcast situation. Felix can handle everything here. He bloody owes her after all, so perhaps this won't become the crisis she has feared. Perhaps it's karma and she can actually relax because everything will be okay.

She reckons she'll surprise Nick in Morocco. She knows where he's staying and she thinks it might be fun to be there when he gets back to the hotel after a long day on set. She looks up the hotel online. It's got two pools, a "couples only" area, and the cocktail list looks promising. She crams the last few items into her suitcase and zips it shut.

"Mum?" Erica is in the doorway of her bedroom.

"Yes?"

"I packed. And I love you."

"I love you, too."

Erica blows her a kiss and disappears as suddenly as she appeared. Jess sits on her bed and wipes a tear from her eye.

didn't think you were a gossip."

Fletcher tugs at one of his earlobes. He's not sure how to respond. Dr. Mary Hayward is standing beside her hatch-back in the car park at Southmead Hospital. A red umbrella with a smart leather handle keeps the rain off her. As she waits for his answer, she smiles. She is teasing him. He gets it now.

"That's why I've come to you," he says. "Because I don't think you're one, either."

"Drink?"

The suggestion makes him feel absurdly happy. His exist-ing plan for the evening is the usual post-divorce void, and he can't think of a better way to fill it. He admires everything about this woman from her elegant ankles to the way she handles a dead body. They drive into the city center in con-voy and find a table upstairs at the Mud Dock Café, which offers an excellent wine list and expansive views across the floating harbor. Rain pits the surface of the water, shattering the reflections of the lit buildings and walkways that line its banks.

Mary orders a glass of red wine and Fletcher says he'll have the same. He wonders briefly if they're on a date, but he's not exactly sure how that's different from having a chat over wine just like they would over coffee. It was over coffee in her office that he learned Dr. Mary Hayward was an acquaintance of Rhonda Street. She mentioned it around the time of Street's election to her post.

"Why do you want to know about Rhonda?" Mary asks him.

"You were at Uni with her? Is that right?"

"I asked first."

He acknowledges she's right with a raised glass and she chinks hers against it. He sips his wine. It's very good. On the blackboard behind the bar somebody is chalking up the evening's specials. "Are you hungry?" he asks. He's thinking of the pot noodle rings on his table back home. The whole tableau in his dining room is unutterably glum compared to this buzzy place and his current company. She shakes her head and he feels a sharp twinge of disappointment. Back to business, then.

"Rhonda Street was married to our John Doe," he tells her and notes with pleasure her expression of surprise. It's hard to shock her.

"Peter somebody?"

"Peter Dale. You were right about the lucky charm. It didn't take long to ID him once we had that."

She taps the stem of her wineglass with a fingernail that gleams with polish. "I remember him," she says. "Good lord. How strange."

"You met him?"

"Only briefly. It was at their engagement party. He was holding forth and I was introduced to him, but we didn't exchange more than a few words."

"What do you remember about him?"

"Um. Height and weight as I described to you in the lab. My impression was that he was a slick sort of a guy. His hair was styled and he wore snappy clothes. I can't remember what, mind you, but I know that's what I thought at the time. Funny, isn't it, how you don't remember the detail but you do remember impressions? Rhonda was infatuated with him. It was a whirlwind thing. They met and got engaged within a few weeks. People were gossiping about that at the party, as they do. It didn't last, mind you. Do you know what? I think that's the first time I've worked on the body of somebody I met when they were living. It gives me a bit of a funny feeling."

She takes another sip of her wine and the liquid moistens her top lip. Fletcher watches her and takes in the modest plunge of her neckline. He thinks—but doesn't dare say—that this might be the first time he's seen her outside their work environment. He also thinks that she's a beautiful woman and that he wants her. It's not the same way he wanted his ex-wife when they first met. That was young, naive, and animal. They couldn't get enough of each other in the early days. That was something, but this is different. Mary Hayward is like the finest trophy in the cabinet. She is classy. You'd look forward to your day if you woke up next to her in the morning. He asks, "Are you still close to Rhonda?"

"No. We were never close. We had a mutual friend at University, so we hung out in the same crowd, but after we left, we lost touch for a while, as you do, when you all start working. I met up with her again when I came to Bristol, but I

didn't see much of her. We never got close. I was surprised
to get an invitation to the engagement party, if I'm honest. I
heard they had a quickie wedding, just friends and family. It
might have been abroad somewhere."

"Do you remember where?"

She shakes her head. Fletcher notices a mole the size and
shape of a beauty spot behind her ear. He takes another sip of
wine. He is beginning to feel warmed by it. "Did she have
money?" he asks.

"She did. She was noticeably better off than the rest of us
at Uni. Better clothes, money for going out whenever she
wanted, and her dad bought her a flat in her second year. An
investment property. It was very nice and the rest of us were
jealous because we lived in such cheap, nasty student flats.
The money came from the family business. She worked for
her dad when she moved back to Bristol."

Fletcher ponders this. It doesn't sound as if Street would be
motivated to act criminally by Dale's cash if she was already
comfortably off, but he supposes having money can breed an
urge for more of it.

"What about Peter Dale?" he asks. "Moneywise."

"He was pretty slick, as I said. He definitely looked mon-
eyed, though I don't know what his actual financial situation
was. He was certainly the type you could imagine flashing
around wads of cash, but I never saw him do that. Maybe he
was one of those guys who act rich when in actual fact they
haven't got two pennies to rub together."

"He had money," Fletcher said. "It wasn't rightfully his,
though. He conned a lot of people."

"I see. And finished up under the tarmac as his comeuppance?"

"Could be."

"I don't see Rhonda being involved in that," she says. "She was too straight."

"Why was she with him, then?"

She shrugs. "Infatuation? Sex? Those are powerful things when we're young."

Fletcher takes a sip of his wine to avoid meeting her eye. It's as if she's articulating the very same thoughts he had about his ex-wife earlier, and it feels curiously intimate. "Are you sure you don't want to get something to eat?" he asks.

He's dismayed to see her check her watch. "Oh, my goodness! No. I'm sorry. I haven't got time. I'm supposed to be meeting a friend at the cinema." She begins to gather up her bag and coat and Fletcher's disappointment is acute.

"I'll get this," he says as she riffles through her purse. He tries to smile graciously. He wants her to go because he fears his dismay that she's leaving is written all over his face.

"Thanks, John." She leans down and pecks him on the cheek. It's chaste, but he savors the feel of it as she walks away. When she's gone, he feels carved out. He orders another glass of the same red wine and a steak, cooked bloody, and watches the waiter clear away Mary Hayward's place setting. He tries not to think about whether she might be meeting a male or female friend at the cinema. He checks his phone. No personal texts or calls or emails. It occurs to him that Danny Fryer and Mary Hayward are the sum of his friendships these days, and he wonders how that could have happened. He puts his phone facedown on the table and looks around the restaurant, checking out the other punters while he waits for his food. He tries not to give the name *lonely* to the way he feels.

"Mr. Noyce is a voluntary attender," Fletcher tells the sergeant at Southmead Station. "In for a chat, aren't you, Sidney?"

Sidney Noyce nods, but he's not really listening because he's rubbernecking, even though Fletcher can't imagine what's so interesting about the dismal waiting area they are passing through. Fletcher settles Sid and his parents into one of the better interview rooms, which is to say it has a window, through which the storm-bruised glow of the winter sun is attempting to penetrate. Fletcher flicks the lights on and leaves the Noyces alone there. He asks Danny to bring them refreshments. He knows he will have to caution Noyce and that he is also obliged to offer him free legal counsel from a solicitor now that Noyce is being questioned at the station. Fletcher has given Noyce the spiel about being "free to leave" and able to ask questions at any time.

It's not easy working around the system, Fletcher thinks, but he believes he has it covered. Part of him relishes the challenge, but that doesn't stop his heart from pounding. Fletcher is aware Noyce will need an "appropriate adult" to be with him during questioning because his mental impairment is severe enough that any evidence gathered in an interview with Noyce on his own could be rejected by the court. Valerie Noyce is Fletcher's preferred "appropriate adult," and he thinks he can swing that because she is so eager to please. Noyce senior seems to be a gentle giant and not burdened with the smarts himself, so hopefully he will not object. Getting a solicitor in quickly could be tricky, and Fletcher wants it to be quick to minimize the chances of Noyce kicking off. Fletcher wants a solicitor present to ensure that this interview appears to be done with belt and braces. As he heads to the custody suite to see if any of the duty solicitors are lurking *and available, he gets a bit of luck: Julie McDowell is just leaving. She has a soft spot for Fletcher. They've worked together previously on a number of cases. Once, as they shared a cigarette in the shelter of the columned portico of the Bristol Crown Court, she invited him out for a drink. He declined the invitation—it wasn't that she wasn't attractive, but he was recently married—but he gave her enough eye contact to let her know he was tempted. Fletcher has always believed it is important to keep your options open.*

"Julie!" he says. "Are you free?"

She's burdened by a stack of files, but she frees a hand and fixes a loose strand of hair. "Free for what?" she says. "Are we finally having that date?" Fletcher holds up the back of his hand to her, fingers spread, and she pouts at his wedding ring. "Is it something boring, then?" she says.

"I've got a person of interest in and I want to interview him quickly. He's a voluntary attender, but he has special needs. It won't be in his interest to keep him and his family hanging around."

"His interest or yours?" she asks. She's no fool. She's good at her job, one of the best. She is exactly what Fletcher needs. He doesn't reply, and she sighs and shifts the weight of her files from one arm to the other. "Have they requested representation?"

"Not yet, but I'm going to strongly recommend that they do."

"You're being extremely helpful."

He ignores that.

"Come on, then," she says. "Lead the way!"

As she trots beside him on the way to the interview room, Danny meets them in the corridor and lets them know that the Noyces have agreed to Valerie acting as the appropriate adult. Fletcher can feel his stars aligning. He tries not to let his excitement show. When he introduces Julie to the Noyces, he notes that Sid Noyce is looking a bit agitated, but Fletcher's confident Julie is the right person to calm Noyce down.

Fletcher mainlines instant coffee while he waits for Julie to finish speaking with the Noyces. By the time she invites him and Danny back into the room, the atmosphere has shifted from earlier. Noyce is fidgeting as if he's waiting in the headmaster's office and Julie's expression has transformed from flirtatious to combative. That'll be because she's just realized she's got the prime suspect in the double murder on her hands, thinks Fletcher.

Once formalities are over and Fletcher is sure the machine recording the interview is working, he gives Noyce his best friendly smile. "How are you doing, Sidney?"

"Fine!" Noyce says and immediately slaps his hand over his mouth as if he's remembered something. His eyes swivel to Julie. She and Valerie Noyce look tense.

"That's great," Fletcher says. "Are you comfortable?"

Noyce's eyes bulge. He looks at Julie and she inclines her head slightly. "No comment?" Noyce says. Julie winks at him and he beams.

"How old are you, Sid?" Fletcher asks. "You don't mind me calling you Sid, do you?"

Noyce's lips curl in and then unfurl. Fletcher knows how hard it is to maintain a "no comment" interview even if you don't have learning difficulties. Julie gives a small shake of her head for Sid's benefit and he repeats, "No comment."

Attaboy, thinks Fletcher, but he leans back in his chair and frowns. Fletcher wants Noyce to think he's disappointed him. He asks a few more benign questions and Noyce answers "no comment" to each one. Each time he does, he seems to gain a little more confidence, grinning at Julie, who nods back at him reassuringly, and Fletcher glowers a *little bit more. Fletcher's got to hand it to Julie, she had only a few minutes to gain Sid's trust and she's done that. She would have made a good detective, he thinks.*

He asks a few more questions. They remain deliberately mundane, though Fletcher knows Julie won't let him get away with that for long. Fletcher is waiting for signs that Noyce is not finding it quite so much fun to give a "no comment" response. Fletcher keeps his voice flat. The questions are small and detailed. Boring. He needs to take time to work up to the interesting stuff. In fact, he wants to stretch time out, pull it like a piece of elastic right as far as it will go just before snapping. He's playing a delicate game, because if he takes too long or strays too far off topic, he runs the risk of Noyce becoming totally uncooperative or Julie stopping proceedings. She is already looking dubious.

Fletcher breaks off from questioning and falls silent. He spends a few moments pretending to consult his notebook. Noyce fidgets. Julie's eyes are narrow slits. Noyce throws his head back and stares at the ceiling. He lets out a big sigh. Now, Fletcher thinks. Step it up a gear now. He asks Noyce where he was on Sunday and what he did. He asks how Noyce knew the boys and what his relationship was like with them. He asks general questions and detailed ones. He speaks in a more upbeat manner. He maintains a friendly demeanor. He performs faultlessly. Noyce seems reenergized and comes back with "no comment" answers every time.

When Fletcher has worked through this first tranche of more focused questions, he peels the top page off a sheaf of papers he's holding and peers at the second one as if it has important notes on it. It doesn't. It's empty, but the gesture has the desired effect because Noyce scowls at the back of it. "Aren't we finished yet?" he asks. He sounds tired.

"We're just trying to get to the truth of this," Fletcher says. He chooses his words carefully, echoing what he said to Noyce in the car

earlier, putting emphasis on the word truth *and hoping it will jog Noyce's memory.* "That can take some time."

Noyce squirms in his seat. He hangs his head and his forehead collapses into a frown. Fletcher watches him like a hawk. It might be now, *he thinks.* Come on. *Noyce looks up. The lights have come on behind the eyes. Fletcher speaks before Noyce has a chance to. He wants to get the right question in at precisely the right moment.*

"Sidney, earlier you said you saw Charlie's and Scott's bodies. Can you tell me about that?"

Noyce looks elated. He knows the answer to this and he thinks it's his "get out of jail free" card. Fletcher is confident Noyce will ignore the "no comment" instruction and he hopes to God he's right because he's missed his moment if not. Julie can sense a shift in atmosphere. She moves her hand as if she's going to lay it on Noyce's arm but thinks better of it. Fletcher keeps his poker face on. It's out of your control now, honey, *he thinks. Noyce sits up as straight as if he has a rod in his back and meets Fletcher's eye firmly and with excitement like the kid in class who is certain of the answer to a math problem:* "I hurt them," *he says.*

Valerie squeezes her eyes shut and Julie looks as if she's been thumped.

"Can I go now?" *Sid says. He's smiling.*

"Just a couple more questions, if you wouldn't mind," *Fletcher says. He has to be very careful what he asks.* "Where were the boys when you hurt them?"

"At the back of the stand."

"Which stand?"

"The dog track."

"How did you hurt them?"

"I left them so hurt they were dying."

"Why did you do it, Sidney?"

"I'm not allowed to talk to them or touch them or follow them."

"And does that make you angry?" Fletcher is asking the same question he put to Noyce in his bedroom and praying silently that it produces the same answers.

Noyce nods.

"Can you give us an answer for the tape, please?"

"I get angry and sad."

"You told me there is something you do when you get angry, do you remember what you said?"

"I hit."

Danny looks at Fletcher, who nods. He wants to stop this before Noyce gets a chance to deny hitting the boys. He thinks they have enough for an arrest. Danny moves around the table toward Noyce and says, "Sidney Noyce, I am arresting you on suspicion of the murder of Charlie Paige and Scott Ashby. You do not have to say anything, but anything . . ."

As Danny reads Noyce his rights and Noyce's smile fades, first into confusion and then dismay, Fletcher sits back in his chair and feels absolutely satisfied. He meets Julie's eye and she gives a disappointed shake of her head. Does she sense a setup? He doesn't think so and he doesn't care. Noyce has only confessed to what he's done. His guilt is not in doubt for Fletcher.

Fletcher speaks into the tape recorder to say that the interview is over. He is so looking forward to telling Smail that he, Fletcher, has obtained a confession to the murders and has the suspect in custody.

Danny needs two burly officers to help him restrain Noyce and get him to the custody suite. He gets his tour of the jail now, Fletcher thinks.

IT'S TIME TO TELL

EPISODE 7—THE MANY LIVES
OF JESSICA PAIGE

A DISHLICKER
PODCAST PRODUCTION

"When I look in the mirror at the end of the day, I think, did you try to help somebody today? If the answer is yes, I can live with myself."

My name is Cody Swift. I'm a filmmaker and your host of *It's Time to Tell,* a Dishlicker Podcast Production. The clip you just heard is Jessica Paige in her role as tough girl Amber Rowe in TV soap opera *Dart Street.* In this episode, we're going to be asking: Who is the real Jessica Paige? Maya and I have continued our efforts to contact Jessica in the hope she might agree to an interview, but we have had no success, so you'll be hearing mostly from people who knew Jessica back in 1996.

"When they were little, we brought up our kids together, we did everything together, but Jessy turned into a party girl. Going out became like a drug to her. She never came out with us, though. The pub wasn't good enough for her. She was always off to some nightclub or restaurant. She showed off about it. Sometimes a car used to pick her up. But she never really talked about who she was with. She said she had a boyfriend, but I don't remember her mentioning his name. Me and the other girls used to think he was really rich. We were jealous of her. She started keeping to herself a few years before Charlie died, so that was when we drifted apart. It was like she thought she was better than us. I missed her and my daughter missed Charlie."

That's the voice of Kirsty Brown, another teenage mum who knew Jessy on the Glenfrome Estate. The next clip you'll hear is Doris Russo, who lived in the flat next door to Jessy and Charlie:

"I used to babysit for Charlie a lot. I sat for him for free, but Jessy asked me so often after a while I had to say no. It was stopping me seeing my own grandkids, and I didn't think it was fair on him, her being out so much. I didn't want to encourage it. I don't know how she managed after I stopped. She didn't have many friends on the estate. She kept herself apart. Charlie was a lovely boy, though. He loved to have a story read to him."

My mother, Julie Swift, has something to add:

"Scott's mum and I always used to say, Jessy loves Charlie but she doesn't know how to handle him. It was because she was just a kid herself when she had him, and she had no family of her own to help."

In the last episode of *It's Time to Tell,* crime reporter Owen Weston told us about a period of seventy-two minutes—which he referred to as "the lost hour" in one of his articles—during which Jessy Paige was unable to account for her actions on the night of Charlie's and Scott's murders. I asked Detective John Fletcher about this. You'll hear his voice first.

"In her statement to police, Jessica Paige claimed that she could not remember what she did between 22:13 and 23:25 on the night of 18 August 1996. She stuck to that story. Jessy Paige was seen leaving the Paradise Casino at 22:13 in a vehicle driven by an unidentified male. She arrived back at the Glenfrome Estate in a taxi just before 23:30. We never discovered precisely what she did during that period of time. Staff at the casino testified she was drinking heavily while she was there, and witnesses stated that she appeared to be inebriated on her return to the estate."

"Do you have any thoughts on what she might have been doing?"

"Your guess is as good as mine. She might have been having a good time."

"Did you consider her a suspect at any point?"

"She was ruled out as a suspect after Sidney Noyce's arrest because the evidence against Noyce was very strong. It would have been pointless and cruel to pursue lines of inquiry against Jessica Paige at that point. She needed to be left alone to grieve. Our job was to ensure that justice was served and the case against Noyce was as watertight as possible. We had our man."

Ex–Detective Superintendent Howard Smail has a different view.

"I know Jessica Paige is a liar because she lied about me. I think she did know what she was doing during the seventy-two minutes she was unaccounted for."

"Can you talk to us about that?"

"While John Fletcher was going rogue and bringing Noyce into the station for questioning without my knowledge, I was at the Glenfrome Estate with David Tremain—he was Detective Chief Superintendent then; he's gone up in the world since—and we were giving a press conference."

I remember the press conference. I watched it from our balcony. After the murders, me and all the other kids on the estate were kept inside. We became little ghostly faces behind windows. We looked out at the world with less innocent eyes and we felt afraid. Our families did, too. From our balcony it looked as if the reporters were swarming around the two police officers like flying ants that had just hatched from a crack in the concrete. Smail continues:

"At the end of the press conference, I was told that Charlie's mother, Jessica Paige, wanted to speak to somebody. David Tremain suggested that because we were already on site, it might play well if that person was me. The force was becoming a bit more media savvy back then. We were actively trying to demonstrate good relationships with the community on the estate, and a senior officer pressing hands personally is a good thing. Historically, the police were not welcome at the Glenfrome. You'll know that. So I made my way up to Ms. Paige's flat and I went alone because I had been assured that the family liaison officer would be in the flat with Ms. Paige. That was important, because you never met with a witness or possible suspect on your own. We always worked in pairs. When I knocked on the door of the flat I expected to say a few words of condolence and reassurance and listen to what she had to say before leaving her in the capable hands of the liaison officer. Job done. Except it didn't turn out that way. After I knocked on her door, Ms. Paige opened it herself and invited me in. I entered her hallway. It was a very cramped space. She began talking quickly and incoherently. She seemed manic. I asked her where Lynn, our liaison officer, was, and she told me Lynn had popped out to get some supplies. At that point, I knew I should leave the property and I tried to do so, telling Ms. Paige I would meet Lynn downstairs and return with her, but Ms. Paige grabbed my arm. I'll never forget it. She held me so tightly I'd have had to wrench my arm away to get out of her clutches. It could have hurt her. But before I could think what else to do, she collapsed and I caught her in my arms. She was absolutely distraught. It was the rawest display of grief I think I've ever seen."

Howard Smail and I were having this chat over Skype. On screen, he shakes his head in a gesture that is weighted with regret. The image pixelates and reassembles, and when it does he is looking directly at me.

"What would you have done?"

It's a no-brainer. Even my ten-year-old self was drawn to Jessy Paige. She didn't project the same sort of authority as the other adults I knew. It felt as if there was no distance between us kids and her, and that stirred something in me at the time. It wasn't something you experienced much as a kid. Not when and where I grew up. What did she stir in me? The beginnings of adolescence, maybe? Maya tells me that we feel lust before we have a name for it, and I know I felt jealous when I saw Jessy hanging off her boyfriend, but I don't think it was that. I think I was sensitive to Jessy's vulnerability even then. And her energy. She was the only adult I knew who not only didn't follow the rules but was brazen about it. It was intoxicating to me. The answer is easy: "I would have stayed with her and tried to comfort her."

Smail nods, as if that answer absolves him somewhat.

"I tried to move her to the sitting room and onto the couch, but she seemed to be in pain—walking was difficult for her—so I helped her sit down right there in the hallway. That's when the liaison officer let herself in and saw us there, when I was cradling Ms. Paige as I tried to help her sit down safely. It was the biggest mistake of my career, though of course I didn't know that at the time. At the time it felt like I was doing the right thing and I was relieved to see Lynn. She helped me move Ms. Paige to the sofa where she'd be more comfortable and Ms. Paige sat there with a soft toy, a teddy bear in her arms. I expect it had belonged to Charlie. She held that bear like it was a newborn baby and wept all over it. It was hard to watch. She made the allegation against me shortly afterward. If it had stayed as a 'he said, she said,' my career might have survived that, but unfortunately they had Lynn as a witness to our physical contact and somebody fed Ms. Paige the security code for the door to the police accommodation where I was staying and she claimed she had spent nights with me there. I was stitched up thoroughly. Sewn up tight. It was the end of my career. So I know she's a liar."

"But she seemed grief-stricken that day?"

"You can still be grief-stricken if you killed. Even if you did it on purpose."

"Are you implying that Jessica Paige murdered her son?"

"I'm pointing out that showing signs of grief is not proof of innocence. To love somebody is not a guarantee that you could not be driven to murder them if a particular set of circumstances occurred."

"Why do you think she lied about you and her?"

"To get the heat off her and whoever she was with that night. They never identified him. Some crucial evidence went missing in that respect. Ask John Fletcher about that."

I already know about the missing evidence from Owen Weston. The CCTV tapes from the casino were stolen from Detective John Fletcher's car on the night he was due to examine them. I have a question for Smail:

"Does this mean you believe Noyce was innocent?"

"No. I don't know if he was or not. But if I had been able to continue to run the investigation I would have slowed things down and pursued every line of inquiry until I was entirely satisfied that we'd gathered enough evidence that the case against Noyce was cast iron and we'd explored the other persons of interest. Jessica Paige was one of them. Here, this is what I wrote in my policy book on the morning before the press conference."

I watch as Smail riffles through the stack of photocopied pages.

"Here it is. 'Actions recommended: investigate Jessica Paige's movements during the seventy-two minutes unaccounted for. Paige asserts she cannot remember what happened during this period of time, possibly due to intoxication. Examine statements as to Paige's fitness as a parent and look into habits, lifestyle, and associates.'"

"Is seventy-two minutes long enough to make you suspicious of her? Really?"

"You'd be surprised what you can do in seventy-two minutes. And let's not forget, this woman went on to be a very successful actress. She knew how to be more than one person, even back then."

Owen Weston, during our conversation back in his conservatory, held a similar view. This clip is from the end of my conversation with Weston, by which time we were surrounded by yellowed copies of all the articles he published on the case back in 1996. I had picked up a clipping illustrated with a photograph of Jessy at Charlie and Scott's funeral. You'll hear my voice first:

"Jessy would never have hurt Charlie and Scott. I remember her."

"You remember a version of her, I'm sure, but you were ten years old. You had no idea what the adult world was like for somebody like her. How could you? How could any child? She would have presented very differently to the adults who knew her. A common comment about her was that she was hidden, guarded, that she only let people see what she wanted them to see."

I look at the grainy photograph. It's a picture of Jessy as grieving mother. She's in a black coat and her hair is piled on her head. She looks distraught. Weston says he remembers me from the funeral.

It's a comment that makes me catch my breath. Some memories are a warm bath you can slip into; others assault you. Scott and Charlie's funeral was one of the worst days of my life. I don't think I had truly accepted that my friends were never coming back until the hearses containing their coffins arrived at the estate. There was one car for each small coffin. Flowers were displayed on and around Scott's, so many that there were petals pressing against the glass. Charlie's had three bouquets on it; one of them spelled out SON.

Jessy stood alone beside Charlie's hearse while people crushed around Scott's mum and dad, my parents and me closest of all. By then, people were saying it was Jessy's fault the boys were dead, because she was supposed to be looking after them.

The undertaker held his top hat in his hands while everybody assembled. He placed it on his head before he started walking in front of the first car. The hat was tall and silky. He wore a black jacket with tails and a black cravat. In his gloved hands he held a walking stick that was dark and shiny. When he began to walk, the cars followed at a crawl and we followed on foot. The procession was big, and people along the route to the church joined us. Everywhere, there were faces in windows as we passed by. When we got to the church, not everybody could fit in. In the chaos, I slipped away from my mum and held Jessy's hand, just for a minute.

I have wondered since then why there was a joint funeral for Charlie and Scott. Mum had an answer:

"Annette Ashby felt sorry for Jessy. She said whether what happened was Jessy's fault or not, Charlie deserved a good send-off. And the Ashbys didn't want Scott to go alone. They got the boys plots next to each other at the cemetery."

In the next episode of *It's Time to Tell* we are going to share the findings of our investigation into "the lost hour." Meanwhile, if anybody listening has anything to share, please reach out via our website, timetotell.com. We would love to hear from you. And please continue to spread the word about *It's Time to Tell*. The number of downloads for the podcast are still increasing beyond our wildest expectations, and we are working hard to deliver quality content in return. However, we have sadly lost our private sponsor in the past few weeks, as we had some editorial differences. Maya and I felt that editorial integrity was our priority, so we severed the link. This does mean that your support for *It's Time to Tell* is as important as ever, and we have set up a link on our website if any listeners would like to donate. To deliver quality content we need as much support as we can get.

Last but not least, many of you have been in touch to express concern for our well-being after the intimidation we reported. Thank you all, and please rest assured, we are taking precautions and working closely with police.

Here are two clips that give you a flavor of what to expect in our next episode. This is crime reporter Owen Weston:

"The drive from Paradise Casino to the Glenfrome Estate would have normally taken about ten minutes on a Sunday night. What the hell was Jessica Paige doing for the extra hour, and why and where did she swap vehicles?"

This is forensic psychologist Professor Christopher J. Fellowes, speaking by phone from his office at Cambridge University:

"There are a number of scenarios that present themselves in a case like this, and one of them could point to a mother losing control, perhaps intending just to punish a child but going too far, as one example. Teenage mothers with no support can develop complicated relationships with their babies, as they are children themselves when they give birth. Resentment can set in, particularly when the child grows old enough to challenge their parent. A child on the cusp of adolescence can be very challenging for a mother who has not had time to grow up herself."

Jess drops Erica at rehearsal with a packed suitcase and instructions to offer to help Olly's parents with the dishes, not to spend too long in the bathroom, and to hang up her wet towels while she's staying at their house. Erica gives Jess a warm hug and tells her to have fun in Morocco but doesn't look back once she's got out of the car. As Jess drives home she wonders if she should feel uneasy that she hasn't met Olly's mum in person, but tells herself to get a grip.

Jess wants to leave her car in the driveway while she's away—it might fool any nosy reporters into thinking she's home, and frustrate them further—so she orders a cab to Bristol airport for her flight to Marrakech. Once she is through security, she sits at the gate with her carry-on bag tucked against her legs and listens to a voice mail from Felix.

"Hello, it's me," the message begins, and the familiarity of his voice and that phrase give her the goose bumps, as if she'd unexpectedly turned up an old keepsake. "Everything's fine. Like I said, I don't want you listening to the podcast, so please don't, but you should know that the most recent episode unfortunately did focus on you, which is why I'm calling because I don't want you to find out from anybody else. It is not what we wanted, but I have it in hand and I'll keep you posted. If Cody Swift or anybody else tries to approach you in the meantime, keep it zipped, okay? Talk to nobody. That's the message. Have a good holiday, darling."

Jess hangs up and takes a moment to think. She's rattled, for sure, but also relieved. Relieved that she can rely on Felix and relieved that she doesn't have to worry about this alone any longer. She made the right call contacting him.

To try to get herself into the holiday mood, she buys and flips through a magazine where one of the actors she used to work with on *Dart Street* has a six-page color spread about his new wife and his new baby. *Would I have wanted a life like his?* Jess wonders as she flicks through the glossy pictures. *Plastered over a magazine for everybody to judge?* She rests the magazine on her lap and looks out of the window. Planes and trucks taxi across the tarmac outside, and her reflection is faintly visible on the glass. *You're all right,* she tells this version of herself silently. *You have a quiet, safe life and a chance to be a good mother and a good wife. You have a husband who loves you and a daughter who loves you. You are lucky.* She closes the magazine and can't suppress a familiar throb of panic. *But would Nick love me if he knew everything? Would Erica? Nick knows almost everything about her, but not that she felt relief when Charlie died. It wasn't for long, but it was there, undeniably there. A few days of relief that she no longer had the responsibility for him, because she knew she couldn't handle him. But what kind of mother feels that? Only a monster. And Erica has so much to learn about me. If everything comes out, they might both think they're better off without me.*

All of this circles painfully around her head until she has boarded the plane and ordered a vodka and tonic to take the edge off. She soon drifts into a fitful sleep and doesn't wake until the pilot makes the descent announcement. She texts

Erica as soon as the plane touches down because her sleep was plagued by scrappy nightmares she can't remember in any detail, but they have left her feeling anxious. Sod the roaming charges. As the aircraft door opens and she's buffeted by the Moroccan heat, she hears a reply come through. Erica is fine and about to head out shopping with Olly. She tells Jess to stop worrying and finishes with a row of helicopter emojis to remind Jess that this style of parenting is not appreciated. "Have fun, darling," Jess texts back. She turns her face to the sun, feels the heat on her skin and in the air she breathes in, and tells herself to *relax*.

She takes a taxi to the hotel where the film crew is staying. It's just outside Marrakech. The hotel's surroundings are dusty and plain and Jess prepares herself for disappointment, but it's lush inside and more luxurious than she expected. There are palms and other exotic plants everywhere. In the reception courtyard, water trickles through a fountain and into a little pool where rose petals float. The receptionist offers her fresh mint tea. "Lovely," Jess says, but when the woman's not looking she adds three spoonfuls of sugar.

Once they've shown her up to Nick's room, she inspects his things, including a quick check of his pockets, and finds nothing untoward. She picks up a call sheet Nick has left on the vanity table. The day's filming is scheduled to end at seven-thirty, and travel time from hotel to set is noted on the sheet as twenty minutes. That gives her a little time to relax and plan the best way to give him a nice surprise.

Jess changes into her new bikini and dons a hotel robe. She hopes her fake tan, hurriedly applied last night, doesn't rub off on it. She texts Erica again to let her know that she's arrived at the hotel, but this time there's no quick response. Jess can see the message has delivered, though, so she tells herself to be patient. She puts her phone in her handbag and heads downstairs to find the pool area.

She orders a coffee from the barman and sips it as she sits on a sun lounger. She wishes she'd had time for a pedicure before traveling. It's not as warm as she expected, so she keeps her robe on and watches a man plowing lengths up and down the pool.

She can't get Felix off her mind, even here in Africa.

She and Felix bonded because they were both young and scrappy, she thinks, and willing to fight for better.

A few months after their first meeting, when Jess was in so deep a word or a look from Felix could electrify her, she began to struggle to get people to sit for Charlie while she went out. She was going to the club two or three times a week. Felix was paying for drinks, but not for child care. Charlie was her secret at that stage and Jess wanted to keep him that way. Her neighbor was getting fed up of being asked to help, and nobody else was volunteering. Jessy Paige wasn't a popular girl amongst the sort of people you'd want to babysit.

One night, she left Charlie alone, sleeping. When she made it back to her flat the next morning, Charlie was awake and dressed in his school uniform, sitting at the table with a bowl of dry cereal. His eyes were red and puffy, the imprint of a creased pillow slip looked like a scar on his cheek. "Where were you?" he said. "I didn't know where you were." The reproach in his voice and his eyes shamed her. Claustrophobia and the squalor of the flat settled on her shoulders like a heavy cloak and she screamed at him. "Shut up!"

Charlie stared at her. He was beautiful, she thought. Why was she shouting? Light came through the kitchen window and framed the back of his head, turning his mat of hair golden. His forearms were slender and strong. His face was bursting with feelings she couldn't cope with. He rushed past her and out of the flat, his face set hard to hold back tears. She called after him, but only her voice tracked him out onto the balcony. The rest of her was so exhausted she let herself fall onto her bed as if from a great height. When Charlie got home after school she cooked him something nice for tea and told him she wouldn't stop hugging him forever and she wouldn't go out again without a babysitter. A sweet smile made its way across his little face eventually, and his feisty limbs relaxed, but even so he had a way of looking at her after that night that felt as if it might suffocate her.

She began to leave him alone more often, but only after she was sure he was asleep. Going out stopped her losing her mind.

It was around that time when Felix first introduced her to a man he described as a "gentleman" in the bar at the Swallow Inn in the city center. She was addicted to Felix because he was the cord that connected her to the sort of life she thought she wanted. When the "gentleman" put his hand on Jess's thigh, she glanced at Felix, surprised, expecting him to stake his claim, but he averted his eyes. When the man said he needed some company upstairs for a while, Felix gave her a nod, and she knew what to do. She understood she had no choice if she wanted to escape the estate. When it was over, Felix was waiting for her downstairs. He handed her some cash and drove her home. It wasn't so bad, she thought, though it wasn't good either. But she liked the cash and she liked being wanted.

After that, nobody bothered with the bit in the bar downstairs. It was straight to the bedroom. She always walked into the hotel with Felix to look respectable, but he would leave her at the room door after making sure she went in. Felix sometimes gave her presents: her favorite a bracelet with a sparkling heart dangling from a silver chain. Once it was a new dress with a designer label. She got brave enough to tell him about Charlie eventually. "You're a dark horse," he said. He gave her a few extra notes. "Buy something nice for the kid." She got Charlie a popgun.

The night of the first sex party changed Jess. Felix took her to a private home for the first time, a mansion sitting squat as a toad behind electronic gates, lights on in all the downstairs windows, a fountain out in the front where no water flowed but a sheet of ice had cracked into shards. Inside, Felix parked Jess on a velvet sofa with a vodka and Coke in hand while he pressed palms. Strips of cocaine were being hoovered up from the low glass table in front of her by a pair of large nostrils. Their owner looked up with bloodshot eyes and sniffed deeply. Jess breathed out shallowly in disgust but knew not to let her revulsion show.

"You're a lovely girl," the man said. "What do I have to do to make you mine?"

She said nothing. Across the room, Felix had half an eye on her as always. The man stood up and offered Jess his hand. His breath stank and his paunch sagged. Felix inclined his head slightly toward her. The look in the man's eyes was frightening, but once again Jess knew what she was supposed to do.

The man led her into a private room where he did things to her that she didn't consent to until somebody banged on the door hard because they heard her sobbing. The man didn't apologize. He told her it was what she deserved.

"Excuse me?" Jess's eyes snap open. The voice comes from a man-shaped silhouette hovering over the sun lounger. Instinctively, she throws her hands up over her face and rolls her body away from him. She is braced for violence. This happens occasionally when she's startled. Nick makes light of it. He calls it her "ninja response" and holds her carefully until she feels safe again.

"I'm so sorry!" the man says and his flip-flop-clad feet back away a little. She wonders why she has a mouthful of white toweling and remembers where she is. She props herself up on her elbows.

"Are you okay?" the man asks. He perches on the edge of a sun lounger opposite her. "I'm really sorry. I didn't mean to startle you."

"I'm fine!" she says. Her hands grab at her robe as she tries to make sure she's decent.

"I just . . . I only wanted to ask if you were Jessica Paige?"

Crap, she thinks, *a groupie.* They appear now and then, though it's rare nowadays. He doesn't look old enough to have watched *Dart Street.* "You've got the wrong person," she says.

"Really? You look just like her."

"Really." Jess extracts her sunglasses from one of the pockets of the gown and puts them on. They're very large and very dark: a barrier. She hopes he'll get the hint, but he doesn't move. There's something off about him, she thinks, but she can't put her finger on it, though she doesn't always trust her judgment. She starts to count slowly in her head. If she gets to ten and he is still there she'll tell him where to go.

On eight he says, "I could have sworn . . ."

She doesn't reply. *Nine, Mississippi,* she counts in her head. *Ten, Missi*—

He stands up and clears his throat. "Okay, then. Sorry to bother you."

She doesn't react. Keep engagement to a minimum. As soon as he's gone, she gathers her stuff and walks smartly to the bank of elevators in the lobby. The heels of her sandals clack on the tiles. As she crosses the space, Nick enters through the main entrance doors. He stops in his tracks when he sees her. His jaw drops. Behind him a young woman barrels into the back of him and drops an armful of papers.

"Jess!" Nick says. "Is that you?"

The young woman giggles and touches Nick's elbow to get his attention. Jess assesses the moment, then delicately moves so one foot is in front of the other, toes pointed. She opens her arms wide and lets the gown part to reveal her bikini and her newly bronzed midriff.

"Surprise!" she says.

Nick crosses the lobby in three strides and lifts her up in a hug. Over his shoulder, Jess sees a little flicker of disgust—or is it disappointment?—cross the young woman's face. Jess gives Nick a kiss and then a lingering hug that doesn't end until the elevator doors have parted. *Don't ever leave me,* she thinks as they embrace. *Please.*

nnabel Collins would have to be willing to undergo a DNA test for us to prove she was related to Peter Dale. That's assuming she doesn't already know who her dad is, or think she knows." Danny is thinking out loud.

Fletcher hands him a mug of coffee, and Danny receives it with hands pressed together in a gesture of prayer. The bags under his eyes have developed folds since yesterday.

"Baby still teething?" Fletcher asks.

Danny nods. He's on his second wife and family and it's taking its toll. "I'm too old to do this again," he says, but Fletcher knows the photograph Danny keeps in his wallet—of his new, young wife and their beautiful baby son—tells a different story.

"For what it's worth, I think Rhonda Street could be in it up to her neck." Danny's voice is lowered. The office is busy around them.

"She didn't need the money."

"Is that what you think really, or is that David Tremain's line?"

"Why would you ask me that?"

"Hey! Relax. It's just a question."

"Do I look like somebody's stooge to you? Have I ever been? Don't insult me with such a *stupid* question."

Danny reacts as Fletcher knew he would: a deep blush rises. Danny has hated being called stupid since school days, when his dyslexia scrambled every line of text he ever tried to read or write and all the world except John Fletcher assumed he was as thick as two short planks. Fletcher feels unrepentant.

They turn their backs to each other. Fletcher is about to delve back into the Peter Dale files when his phone buzzes. It's a message from an unknown number giving a time and a place and no other information. There is only one man who ever contacts Fletcher that way. He stands and grabs his jacket. "I've got to go out," he says. Danny ignores him.

Fletcher follows the Feeder Canal toward the city center. He puts on the latest episode of the podcast as he drives. It's a hatchet job. Target: Jessica Paige. Even Smail's gotten in on the act all the way from the edge of the world, or wherever he's exiled himself to. Fletcher feels sorry for her.

The harbor water in the city center is glassy, reflecting the Bath stone and pastel-painted houses of Georgian Bristol terraced up the opposite side of the gorge. Fletcher loses the view to a concrete underpass, and when he emerges, he sees parkland ahead and makes the turn up a driveway into the Ashton Court Estate.

He parks beside the entrance to the deer park and walks toward the mansion house. He wonders when he last came here. It must have been over fifteen years ago, with his young family, on a visit to the hot air balloon festival. He and Mrs. Fletcher drank scalding tea and ate bacon butties while they watched the balloons go up en masse in the dawn rise. That was an almost perfect few hours, marred only by the baby grizzling on his mother's shoulder. Andrew was a toddler, and Fletcher remembers how wide the kid's eyes got at the sight of the balloons crowding the sky like a host of multicolored baubles.

Beyond the mansion Fletcher sees a pickup truck pulled up onto a flat area of tufty grass at the base of a steep incline. As Fletcher approaches, a man-sized basket is lifted from the flatbed of the truck, followed by a burner and gas cylinders. Two men have laid a folded balloon on the grass and are unfolding it methodically.

When Fletcher spots Felix Abernathy, he feels the usual boost of adrenaline and a crawling sense of trepidation. He trudges through the mud and tussocks, fighting the suction under the soles of his office shoes with each step. He's struck by the thought that his relationship with Felix has lasted longer than his marriage, and just like his marriage, has morphed into something different over the years.

Felix is observing the activity around the truck. He is wearing a waxed jacket and Wellington boots. Fletcher can't help admiring how the other man looks as if he was born to stand in the countryside and survey his surroundings, even though Fletcher knows the roots of his childhood were sunk deep into both concrete and disappointment.

Felix extends a hand as Fletcher approaches him. "Long time, my man," he says.

Fletcher shakes the proffered hand. "How are you?"

"Can't complain. You?"

"Yeah. Fine. It's good to be out of the office. What's going on here, then?"

"I'm thinking about using hot air balloons for a client as a bit of a PR stunt, something to anchor an event with, so I'm here for a demo."

"You going up?"

"Fuck, no! Would you?"

Fletcher squints at the balloon. "I think I'd like the views."

"You're a braver man than me," Felix says.

"I couldn't do it, though. I get vertigo." The balloon has been unfolded to its full extent, making an oval-shaped lake of fabric on the grass. A few people have stopped to look. "What can I do for you?" Fletcher asks.

"Cody Swift." Felix pronounces the name as if it were a disease.

"Ah."

"I believe you've talked to him directly?"

Fletcher nods an affirmative.

"I need you to provide him with a bit of information," Felix says. "There's been a turnup for the books, as it happens. A contact of mine has been able to identify the taxi driver who dropped Jessy Paige home at the estate on the night of the murders. I thought it might be useful for the podcast."

Felix has Fletcher's complete attention now. The identity of this driver was never known.

"How did this come about?" Fletcher asks, but Felix taps the side of his nose. He hands Fletcher a piece of paper. A name, address, and mobile number are written on it. "Here's your man. He needs interviewing and Swift needs tipping off. Nothing for you to worry about."

"Why don't you tell him yourself?" Fletcher asks, but the men are testing the gas burner. A bright column of flame flares noisily in front of them before dying back again. One of the balloon team approaches Felix as another backs the truck off the grass.

"What did you say?" Felix asks, and Fletcher repeats the question.

"Authenticity," Felix replies. Fletcher doesn't like the sarcastic edge to his smile. "I think it's better coming from you than anybody else. It won't be a problem, will it?"

Fletcher wants to refuse, and would like to question Felix more about his motives, because the timing of this feels very convenient for Jessica after the last episode of the podcast, but the moment when Fletcher had the leverage to turn this man down is long past. "No problem at all," he says.

Felix raises his hand in greeting to the woman approaching them and begins to walk toward him. He turns briefly back to Fletcher. "You going to stay and watch it go up?"

Fletcher shakes his head. "Things to do," he shouts. He holds up the bit of paper Felix gave him, even though he was trying to suggest he had things of his own to do.

"Good to see you, John."

As Fletcher walks away he hears Felix say, "Will the logo be in the same position on our balloon? I want it to be much bigger than that."

The woman's reply is indistinct.

"Tell me once again how this came about?" Smail says. He and Fletcher are standing in the middle of the office. Heads have ducked low in the cubicles around them, and phone calls are being conducted in murmurs or hurriedly brought to an end.

Smail hasn't smiled once since Fletcher informed him of Noyce's admission and arrest. He hasn't patted Fletcher on the back, thumped

his arm genially, or given him the tight sort of nod that passes for ap-
proval from some senior officers. Instead, he's interrogating Fletcher.

Fletcher feels his temper rising but dutifully begins the tale again.
Smail asks, "Why didn't you arrest Noyce before bringing him in?"

"I had an inkling he might have something of value to tell us, but
I wasn't sure what, and he was distractible at home. I thought a chat
at the station might help him focus. I had no idea we were looking at
a possible confession."

"Why did Noyce travel alone with you and Danny? He should
have been accompanied."

"I didn't realize he had such severe mental limitations. Honestly,
I just thought he was a bit thick, boss. I only realized when we were
chatting during the drive and he said he went to St. Jude's special
school when he was a kid. I took the appropriate steps to safeguard
him as soon as we arrived at the station. His mum acted as appro-
priate adult, and we arranged for a duty solicitor to be with him in
interview."

Smail's fingertips tap a slow rhythm of disbelief on his upper lip.
"Sometimes," he says, and his patronizing headmasterly tone offends
Fletcher, "we feel euphoria at the prospect of a solve, and that eupho-
ria can interfere with the appropriate reason or, shall I say, caution
we might expect a senior officer to exercise during an investigation. It
can obscure the fact that gray areas might exist in our process. Are you
sure that once the pretty pink smoke of this solve has blown away, we
won't find ourselves staring at a steaming pile of shit that is of your
creation?"

Fletcher flinches. He was expecting a handshake and he gets this?
This is not how Smail should be treating a man who has just handed
him a solve. His anger swells, and beneath it, he feels as if humilia-
tion has soaked every cell in his body. He is sodden with it. A public

dressing down will be hard to come back from. He says nothing in response, because he can't trust himself to keep his cool. Smail isn't finished yet.

"I think you may get away with bringing Noyce in alone, I think you will, though it won't just be me asking for an explanation. But what you will not get away with is not informing me immediately that you were intending to bring Noyce into the station, and not informing me immediately he arrived here. John, what the fuck were you thinking? You are working on my investigation and you undermined me. This investigation should have been concluded with due care and attention to every detail."

Fletcher has detached himself emotionally. It's the only way to get through this. He notes the way Smail's acne scars have flared redder than usual, and how his pupils look as hard and shiny as wet pebbles.

"Here's what we're going to do," Smail says. "I will take over the Noyce interviews from this point onward and for the time being—until we are absolutely certain that the case against Noyce is watertight— you will pursue our other ongoing lines of inquiry. You can start by looking through the CCTV tapes you picked up from the casino. I look forward to a report on my desk in the morning."

Fletcher burns with anger and frustration as he leaves the office with the box of CCTV tapes in his arms. He should be in the pub, raising a pint with the rest of the team. It should be the finest night of his career. On any normal investigation, it would be. This outcome is a car crash for him personally, and so far as he's concerned, that's down to Smail. He—Fletcher—needs to fix it.

He slings the tapes into his car and gets into the driver's seat. Rain is pissing down. The back of his neck feels damp and slimy where it's got beneath his collar. He can't face going home to the wife and baby. It would do his head in. There would be a row within minutes.

A sharp knock on the car window makes his head snap around. It's Danny. He gets in.

"You all right?" Danny asks. He's out of breath.

"I've been better."

"I've been told not to talk to you." They both smirk. That's never going to happen. "There's something you should know. The duty sergeant told me they spotted blood on Noyce's trouser legs. Not a smear, droplets, as if from a fresh wound. Sergeant said they've gone off for testing." Danny raises his eyebrows at Fletcher. "Good news, don't you think? You're right about Noyce. This is going to prove it. Don't let Howard Smail get to you." He claps a hand on Fletcher's shoulder and squeezes it briefly before getting out of the car.

Fletcher watches Danny jog back across the parking area and disappear back into the building. He feels buoyed by the news of the blood. It's not anything until it's tested, but he feels optimistic it will back up his case against Noyce. He doesn't want to leave anything to chance, though. Even if the blood is Noyce's and Fletcher is proved right, he suspects Smail might still try to keep him down and take the credit for Noyce's arrest. Fletcher needs to own this, or Smail could bury him so deep he might never resurface.

He considers his options, and one of them seems more attractive than the others. In fact, as he considers it, it doesn't just seem more attractive, it seems positively sensible. Fletcher puts the key in the car's ignition, slings his arms over the back of the passenger seat, and before he's backed out of his parking spot, his beautifully simple plan is almost completely formed.

One hour later Fletcher pushes open the door of the Coach and Horses pub near the arches on Cheltenham Road. Felix Abernathy is already seated at a table with a pint and a pizza that looks as if it may have spent time in a microwave.

"Felix."

"John." Felix doesn't get up. Fletcher orders a drink at the bar and takes a seat. "All right?" he asks.

"Been better." Felix cuts a triangle of pizza, picks it up, and concertinas it into his mouth.

Fletcher lowers his voice. "I'm hoping to come to an arrangement."

"Oh, yeah? I thought you might be wanting to tell me the tapes had been destroyed."

"They will be, but things have developed. I think we may both have a problem."

"Go on." Felix pushes his plate away and scratches his cheekbone with the back of his fingernails. "I'm listening."

"My superior officer has got a wrong idea about me. I've handed him this case tied up in a bow, but he's not satisfied. He doubts me." It hurts Fletcher to say that, but he needs Felix to feel as much threat as he does. "He's asking me to look into Jessy Paige's movements on Sunday night, since she has no alibi. He's not going to let it go and he is very interested to know who is with her on the CCTV tapes. He's pushing me for an identification, which is not what I want, and I don't think it's what you want either."

"You found who killed the boys?"

"Found him, arrested him, charged him."

"Who?"

"Just between us? Bloke called Sidney Noyce from the estate. He's backward. Mental age of a kid. He used to try and hang around with the boys, but they taunted him. He's confessed."

Felix takes his time lighting a cigarette before asking, "What's the officer's name?" He has the best poker face in the business, Fletcher thinks.

"Howard Smail. Detective Superintendent Howard Smail."

Felix's eyebrows rise fractionally. "Tell me about him."

Fletcher explains what Smail is like, how he works, how he has recently moved from a job at the Met in London and is living in a police-owned flat at the Blaise Castle complex while he waits for his family to relocate.

"I can work with the accommodation," Felix says. "There's a young woman I'm acquainted with who knows her way around that place. I'll need to talk to Jess. Off-camera."

"She's in a bad way."

"Don't worry about that."

"Can we rely on her?"

"I said, don't worry about it." Felix stubs his cigarette out on his pizza plate and stands.

"You going?" Fletcher feels a moment of panic, and just as they did when he was on the phone to Felix, his emotions surge unexpectedly. He is overwhelmed by the need for somebody else to feel what he's feeling. "Charlie Paige died in my arms," he says. He can't meet Felix's eye. He takes a long sip of his pint to cover up an unexpected wash of tears.

"John." It sounds like a warning, but Fletcher can't stop.

"He was still breathing when I found him. My god! Oh, shit!" His spittle flecks the table, and he snatches up a napkin to blow his nose.

"It's a fucking shame, John, but you need to hold it together. Deal with the tapes, get me access to Jessy, and I'll take care of my end."

Fletcher sits at the table for a few minutes after Felix has left and picks damp bits of napkin off his fingers. He's embarrassed; he doesn't know where that outburst came from. He exhales heavily. It's over now, and he has work to do. He is as certain as he can be that Felix

will fulfill his side of the bargain, and as his emotions subside, a feel-
ing of confidence straightens his back as he steps out of the pub.

Fletcher drives home via Feeder Canal. He pulls over in a deserted
spot, takes a roll of duct tape from the boot, and carries it and the
box of videotapes onto a small pedestrian bridge. The only spectators
are the pigeons residing in the window openings of an abandoned
warehouse beside him. He finds some stones and places them in the
box with the videocassettes and tapes it up. He heaves the lot over the
side of the bridge and watches it disappear under the murky water.
He knows it's deep here. He's seen a car brought up at this site, the
driver a bloated mess.

Back at his car, he removes a screwdriver from the glove compart-
ment and closes the passenger door. Standing outside the car, he
inserts the driver between the top of the closed door and the roof of
the car and levers it until he creates a crack in the door and visible
damage on the door's metal frame. Once he is satisfied it looks like
there has been a forced entry, he replaces the screwdriver and drives
home.

He arrives half an hour later. He takes a minute to compose him-
self before going in. His wife is pacing the sitting room with the baby
on her shoulder. The TV is keeping them company.

"Sorry I'm late," he says. He pecks her on the cheek. She smells
of baby sick. "I just need to make a quick call. Then I'll take him,
I promise."

Smail picks up quickly. Fletcher keeps it brief and Smail repeats
his words back to him, barely containing his anger. "You stopped at
Feeder Canal?"

"Yes."

"To investigate something?"

"I saw a man by the canal who seemed in distress."

"And while you were helping him, your car got broken into and the videocassettes were stolen?"

"And my wallet."

"Really?"

"I'm as gutted as you are, boss."

"Why would anybody steal a box of videotapes?"

"People will steal anything, boss."

"Did you make a note of the license plate we need to trace, at least?"

"I'm sorry, boss."

Smail sighs as if Fletcher couldn't possibly disappoint him any more. "We'll speak about this in the morning."

Not if I can help it, *Fletcher thinks. He says, "Of course, boss. Sorry, boss," but the line has already gone dead. Fletcher returns to the front room and sinks onto the sofa beside his wife. He yawns so heavily his jaw clicks.*

"Long day?" she says. She looks weary, too.

Never explain. *"Yeah. Busy." He reaches for the baby.*

She hands the child over and stretches. "Tea?"

"Thanks, love."

"Sandwich?"

"No. I got something in the canteen."

Baby Andrew nuzzles his head into the side of Fletcher's neck and falls asleep almost instantly. Fletcher relaxes under the warm weight of his child, feeling the little breaths the infant is taking. He'll wait to phone Felix and let him know the tapes are gone, he thinks. It'll give Felix a bit of time and extra incentive to put things in motion. He relaxes a little. If Felix keeps his end of the deal, he thinks, I'm made.

IT'S TIME TO TELL

EPISODE 8—THE LOST HOUR: FROM PARADISE TO BLACKHORSE LANE

A DISHLICKER
PODCAST PRODUCTION

"You'd be surprised what you can do in seventy-two minutes."

My name is Cody Swift. I'm a filmmaker and your host of *It's Time to Tell*, a Dishlicker Podcast Production. That was the voice of ex–Detective Superintendent Howard Smail, referring to the seventy-two minutes when Jessica Paige, mother of Charlie Paige, was unaccounted for on the night of Charlie and Scott's murders.

Here's a question for you: What do you think you can do in seventy-two minutes? I did a bit of unscientific research on the subject—by which I mean to say that I looked it up on the internet—and discovered that seventy-two minutes is almost how long it takes for the International Space Station to circumnavigate planet Earth. You could also brush your teeth for the recommended period thirty-six times, smoke twelve cigarettes in a row, and have an extremely long soak in the bathtub. These are based on average activity times guessed by me, but you get the picture. You can do quite a lot in seventy-two minutes. You could end a relationship. You could murder.

At the end of our last episode you heard a clip from forensic psychologist Professor Christopher Fellowes, who gave us a hypothesis about Jessica Paige's state of mind. We were going to let you hear more of that interview, but some dramatic events have overtaken us this week. I'll explain more later in this episode.

Professor Fellowes is not the only academic we've had contact with. The criminology department at the University of the West of England, based here in Bristol, got in touch with us offering to help in any way they could. I asked them to assist us in trying to re-create possible scenarios for how Jessica Paige might have spent her "lost hour."

Simon McKay, a third-year student, tells us how they went about it:

"Firstly, we had to rule out unpredictable behavior, that outlying scenario where Jessica Paige went for a random drive with somebody, got out somewhere unexpected, and randomly got in a taxi home. Not many people do that sort of thing even if they are drunk. We started with an assumption that Jessica Paige was engaged in what I would call 'normal' behavior. Basically, something that is predictable or might have an innocent explanation. We mapped out the various routes you could take if you traveled by car from the Paradise Casino to the Glenfrome Estate. We consulted a map of the city from 1996 to make sure we did this accurately. In teams, we drove each route, sticking to the speed limit. The fastest took us nine minutes. The slowest route took nineteen minutes. We drove the routes on a Sunday night after ten P.M., to mimic the traffic conditions as precisely as possible. We thought about differences between our drives and the one Jessica Paige might have taken. At that time on 18 August 1996, there might have been a tiny bit of daylight lingering, but not much, and it probably wouldn't have been visible on any of the routes you could take. Jessica Paige's journey would likely have been made in more or less complete darkness. It was hot, so there could have been a few people out on the streets. We narrowed down our routes to the two we thought they would have been most likely to take, based on them being fastest and most convenient. Along every route, we looked out for places where Jessica and her first driver might have stopped, places she might have been likely to arrive in one vehicle and leave in another. One was a dual carriageway, with very little opportunity for stopping, so unless she traded cars in a lay-by—hard to do in the time before mobiles unless she flagged the taxi down—we felt it was the more unlikely of the two routes. The other route was along a road called Blackhorse Lane. We consulted a colleague who specializes in Bristol history, and he told us that Blackhorse Lane was partly residential, but in 1996 there were shops and cafés along there, too, and in fact there was a popular pub called the Blue Door. It had a beer garden and it was open on a Sunday night. Above a shop opposite it was a taxi firm."

Simon and I discussed the worst-case scenario, that Jessica Paige had some sort of involvement in the murders of Charlie and Scott. I asked him a difficult question:

"If the fastest route from the Paradise Casino to the Glenfrome Estate took nine minutes, do you think Jessy Paige would have had time to get there, witness or be involved in the death of the boys, and then leave, change clothing or whatever she had to do, and arrive back later in a taxi?"

"It would be tight, though that depends on where she got into the taxi, but it would be possible."

Maya and I are incredibly grateful to this team of brilliant students for their research. We followed the lead they had given us and found that, unfortunately, neither the Blue Door pub nor the taxi firm exist there any longer. In the past twenty years a large part of Blackhorse Lane has been cleared to make way for a new housing development. This is an exciting lead, though, and we will continue to investigate and bring you what we find.

You might be wondering why we did not do this research ourselves and why this episode might not feel as put together as our previous ones. The reason is that at approximately 20:45 on Wednesday evening, Maya was assaulted on the street where we live.

About seventy-five yards from our front door, a man dressed in dark clothing and a beanie dragged her from the pavement and down an unlit alleyway leading to some garages behind the properties opposite ours. He threatened to sexually assault her and told her she had been, and I quote, "poking your nose where you shouldn't." He pushed her up against a wall and covered her mouth with a gloved hand. He held a knife to the side of her neck. Before anything worse could happen, he was disturbed by a car turning into the alleyway. He tried to drag Maya farther out of sight, but she managed to shake free of him and ran home. He didn't follow her. She sustained a cut to the side of her neck. Maya got the wound checked out at A&E and we reported the assault to the police.

I am racked with guilt. This happened because I involved Maya in the podcast. We went to bed that night very shaken. I could not sleep. I sat up and watched her resting. The inky light in our bedroom seemed to shroud her. I climbed in beside her and found she was shivering. I held her until she slept, but I knew I wouldn't be able to sleep. I thought about how I had risked my future to seek answers in my past. I couldn't help listening out for every bump and thump in the night. I feared somebody would try to break into our property and hurt us in our beds.

My state of mind was so sickly that something unexpected happened. I remembered something. A memory that I once buried very deep fought its way back to me. I tried to make it disappear. I opened my eyes and fixed them on the spidery cracks in the ceiling plaster and the once opulent but now peeling ceiling rose from which our junk-shop chandelier hangs. I imagined the chandelier's pale pink icicle drops tinkling in a breeze. I imagined each bulb being replaced by a flaming candle. I imagined that the cracks in the ceiling were the cracks in my mind. I ran out of things to imagine, which was when the memory I had been trying to push to the back of my mind began to play like an old-fashioned cine reel. I watched a scene that I hadn't seen for twenty years:

It is the afternoon of Sunday, 18 August 1996. I am wearing my Atlanta Olympics T-shirt and it is not ripped yet. Me, Charlie, and Scott are hanging round behind one of the towers on the estate in a dark alley around the back of the social club. Black refuse bags are heaped in a pile. Dirty nappies spill from one of them, and when we kick one of the others, we hear the sharp chink of empties. Charlie takes a look in the bag. There's a bottle of Napoleon brandy. He swigs the dregs and smashes the bottle. We have a pissing contest up the wall of the social club and Scott wins easily. I notice

the bag moving first and point it out to the others. Charlie jumps a mile.
"Fuck!" he says. "What is it?"

We approach cautiously. As we get closer, a corner of the bag bulges, as if
something inside is squirming. We scream and run out of the alley.

Sidney Noyce is there. "Hello, Scott," he says. He liked Scott the most
out of the three of us, probably because Scott was the nicest.

"Hey, Sid," Scott says. "Do you want to do something?"

We know he'll say yes. He always does. Charlie points down the al-
leyway. "Go and see what's in that bag." Sid nods. He's too stupid to be
afraid. We watch from the end of the alley. Sid pokes the bag first, and
we all recoil when it moves again. He's not bothered, though. He kneels
down and makes a rip in the plastic and we can't see exactly what he's
doing but he says, "Hello!" and when he turns around, he's holding a
little creature in his arms and smiling even more widely than before. The
creature whimpers.

"What is it?" I say.

"Puppy," Sid says.

The little dog is brown with a white flash on its tummy. It has a pink
nose and floppy ears. Its eyes are open and so is its mouth. It is panting
with shallow, noisy breaths.

"Are there any more?" Charlie asks.

"Just this one," Sid says.

Charlie puts his arms out to take the dog. When Sid hands it over, the
dog cries again and we see that there's something wrong. Two of its legs are
hanging down unnaturally.

"His legs are broken," Charlie says. "Some bugger left him here to die."
He's upset. Charlie loves dogs.

"What shall we do with him?"

"He's buggered," Charlie says. He spends enough time at the kennels
that he thinks he knows this.

"No!" Sid says. He tries to snatch the puppy back and the creature squeals.

"Sid!" Charlie says. "We have to kill it."

"We should take him down the vet," I say. I have only a scant idea of how to take care of animals, but I'm pretty sure about this.

"With what money?" Charlie asks. "Vet costs an arm and a leg." He kneels down and strokes the puppy, fondling its ears gently. "Who's going to pay for that?" He sounds angry and he's right. None of our parents have money for a vet. "He's too far gone anyway," Charlie says.

We go to the club to fetch water for the dog, but we can't persuade it to drink. Charlie gets upset when it begins to whimper.

"Sid," Charlie says, "you have to kill it. It's not kind for it to be alive." Sid shakes his head.

"You have to. You're stronger than me. You can do it quick."

"I don't want to." Sid steps back.

"Come on! Do you want this dog to suffer because of you?"

"I don't know how to kill it."

"I'll hold him. You squeeze his neck. Squeeze tight and don't let go."

"Go on, Sid." Scott pokes him in the back and I do, too.

Charlie cradles the puppy and Sid places a large hand on its neck. He begins to squeeze. Charlie screams and Scott and I jump as the puppy reacts reflexively. It wriggles vigorously for just a second and its head whips round, small teeth marking the inside of Charlie's arm. He bleeds. Droplets fall onto the hem of one of Sid's trouser legs as he kneels beside Charlie with his hand clamped on the puppy's neck until long after it stops moving.

"Let go now," Charlie says. "Let go now! That's enough, Sid. Stop!" Sid steps away. "Sorry, Charlie," he says.

Charlie is crying. His tears fall onto the puppy's fur. He strokes it for a few moments and we are all quiet, watching him, but he can't get over it. He is so upset he turns on Sid. "Fuck off!" he says. "Dog killer!" He *reaches for a crumpled aluminum can that has spilled from the bag and throws it at Sid. "Fuck off!"*

Sid looks at me and at Scott, but we never break ranks. "Fuck off, Sid," I say. "You've upset him now. Can't you do anything right?" Sid looks horrified. He reaches down to try to console Charlie, or maybe it's to give the puppy one last stroke. "Don't touch me!" Charlie shouts. "Never touch me or my friends! You're dirty! You enjoyed that! You're a dirty dog murderer." He's crying loudly now, and Scott and I go to him. Scott hugs him. "What bugger would hurt a dog like that?" Charlie says over and over again. When we look up again, Sid has gone, and later, before we go to the playground and sit in the concrete tubes, we try to bury the puppy in a patch of land near the estate, but the ground is too hard to dig, so we tear up big chunks of long grass and lay them on top of the puppy instead.

The memory of this scene plays again and again in my mind as I lie in the dark beside Maya. I realize that for the past twenty years I have been the only person who knows the true reason why the police discovered Charlie's blood on Sidney Noyce's trousers. Perhaps this is why I have felt so certain Owen Weston might be right about Sid's innocence. Perhaps it is why I am prepared to dig into alternative scenarios for what might have happened that night in spite of the intimidation.

I apologize for this podcast being a sort of extended monologue and reflection. Things have felt very personal this week, and very strange.

Maya has recovered physically from the assault and we are beginning to rebuild emotionally. We are not sure how this act of violence will affect the podcast going forward long-term, but we can assure you that we will be back next week with a new episode and another important development. We will not be cowed, because if there is one thing this attack tells us, it's that somebody has something to hide, and our next episode will look into that more closely than ever. Here's a taster from ex–Detective Superintendent Howard Smail:

"What I do know is that we were never able to ascertain who Jessica Paige's boyfriend was. We were obviously very keen to trace him, but he was an absolute mystery man so far as we could tell."

On the night Jessica arrives in Morocco, there's a dinner for the cast and crew at the hotel. At Nick's request, she is hastily added to the seating plan. She wishes she'd known it was happening because she would have delayed her arrival to avoid the social overexposure. Nowadays she avoids big gatherings.

Jess looks down the long, narrow table where the movie's cast and crew are seated. Swags of fairy lights hang overhead, and glazed tagine dishes have been set at regular intervals down the length of the table. As each dish is ceremoniously uncovered by the waiting staff, a cone of steaming couscous appears, topped with tender meat, fresh herbs, and gleaming crimson pomegranate seeds scattered as liberally as birdseed.

The woman sitting beside Jess is a young actress. As Jess offers her bread, the actress covers her plate with her hand and stares morosely toward the far end of the table, where the big-name cast members are sitting with the director and producers. Bursts of laughter issue from them and billow down the table's length. Their crystal and cutlery seem to glint more magically than anybody else's, steam seems to rise more dramatically from the dishes they have in front of them, and waiters cluster behind them as if drawn in by their power. It's an intoxicating sight for the young and hungry, Jess understands that, even though she's become immune to this brand of envy. She reaches for the bottle of wine and tops up her own glass and the actress's. "Have a drink, love," she says. "It'll do you good. Why don't you tell me everything about yourself? I want to know it *all*."

The tactic works like a charm on this vapid girl, who is not the beauty she supposes herself to be. Her features flirt with loveliness, Jess thinks, but shy away from it at the last moment. The actress takes the conversational bait and Jess is able to sit back and appear to listen to the energetic monologue. It includes a catalogue of insecurities about her agent, her prospect of auditions after this shoot is over, and her current role, then segues into a tiresome description of the drama teacher who saw her potential. Jess nods and mutters "uh-huh" and "amazing" between mouthfuls of the lamb, which is delicious, and little more is needed in the way of interaction.

Jess thinks of her own career break, which she owes to Nick. It was a year after Charlie died, six months after Nick had taken her under his wing. Jess had spiraled blackly out of control by then. Charlie, resented by her and badly cared for by her at times, had nevertheless been an anchor in her life when he was alive. After his murder, she floated—rudderless and defenseless—further into the worlds of others than she had ever gone before, and was used by them as if she were a rag doll.

The actress leans across Jess to top up her wineglass. Fairy lights dance in her eyes. She's enjoying her audience, Jess thinks, and makes an effort to concentrate better. Listening to the woman talk, Jess feels nothing but relief that she's out of the business. She'll never regret doing *Dart Street,* though.

In her time on the soap she discovered she was a good actress and threw herself into the punishing shooting schedule to obliterate the rag doll. Rebuilding herself was a shaky business, but it brought her a measure of self-respect, the first she had ever experienced. The job and Nick and their life together haven't been able to stop her looking back over her shoulder and feeling the drag of shame and guilt, but they have taught her to look forward, too, and imagine a different, better life.

Jess glances down the table to where Nick is sitting. He catches her gaze and winks. She smiles. Nobody else notices. Jess sips her wine. Without Nick, she would be nothing, nobody. She would not be a good person. That he will stop loving her is a daily fear. It comes on strong even as she sits at the garlanded table; she feels as if bitter juice has seeped into the joints of her jaw. She's grateful to be interrupted by the actress standing abruptly and raising her voice at a photographer who is working her way down the table.

"Please don't take pictures of me without warning me first," the actress snaps. "Is that going on social media?" *Careful,* Jess thinks, *or they'll cast you as a harpy.*

"Excuse me," Jess murmurs to nobody in particular. "I'm going to find the little girls' room." She follows signs for the restrooms and finds herself in a corridor where the floor is tiled in black and white and a swing door flaps back and forth, giving glimpses of a busy kitchen where sweaty men work fast and noisily.

Jess moves on a few paces and leans against the wall. The plaster feels cool against her backless dress. She eases her feet out of her punishingly high-heeled sandals and lets her toes spread on the cool tiles, enjoying the feeling of relief. She fishes her phone out of her bag and checks it. Nothing from Erica. She feels a twinge of concern. She tries to call Erica, but there's no answer and she leaves a short, upbeat voice mail to disguise her anxiety: "Call me, please, darling, when you get this. Love you!!"

She wonders if she should call Olly's mother and ask if Erica is okay. It's pretty much a taboo thing to do now that the kids are teenaged, but Jess doesn't care. She calls, but it goes to voice mail. Jess leaves a message saying she'd appreciate a quick text or phone call to confirm all is well back home. It'll infuriate Erica if she finds out, but Jess doesn't care. She has learnt in the bitterest way that if you don't look after your own, chances are that nobody else will.

When she returns to the terrace, the evening has progressed. A band has set up in a corner and they're tuning up. People are leaving the table and mingling. She feels a hand on her elbow and turns to see Nick.

"Thank god you're here," he whispers into her neck. "I'm so sick of this lot already, and it's only been a week."

Their faces are as close as they could be without touching. She can tell he's pretty drunk already, but she doesn't mind. She moves her cheek alongside his. She doesn't mention that she's worried about Erica. He's had a tough week. He deserves to let his hair down. The band starts to play. The lead singer is a pale-skinned woman with a burst of curly hair and lips that look bitten pink. She has a very decent voice. She starts with Adele's "Make You Feel My Love," and the smile Nick gives Jess melts her heart a little for the second time that evening. "Dance?" he asks.

Nick holds her close. After the first number the next tune is livelier, and his eyes light up in invitation. His tipsy enthusiasm infects Jess. She nods and he whirls her around the dance floor like a pro. Her sandals get kicked off once again. By the time they step off the floor later in the evening they're both flushed, riding high on the music and the rare treat of a grown-up night out. They grip each other's hands and walk shoulder-to-shoulder on the way back to their room.

When Jess gets her phone out in the elevator it's in the absolute expectation that she'll have heard from both Erica and Olly's mum. She's right on one count. There is nothing from Erica, but she has four missed calls from Olly's mum and a text that reads:

Tried to call you. I thought Olly and Erica at your house tonight and you off to Morocco tomorrow?

"No!" Jess says. "Oh, crap!" In the mirrored walls of the elevator an infinite number of versions of her say the same thing, all with the same smear of mascara under one eye. Jess tries to phone Olly's mum immediately, but the signal is too patchy to connect.

"We'll call her from the room," Nick says. "It'll be fine. Don't worry. It'll be fine," but he has paled. When the elevator doors open, Nick takes her by the hand and they jog down the corridor to their room. He fumbles with the key until she takes it from him and opens the door. Jess grabs the phone and is dialing when she hears him say, "What the fuck is this?" On a table in the corner is a huge basket of fruit. It's a cornucopia. It wasn't there earlier. Nick removes a small card from between a mango and a kiwi and tears it open and reads it aloud: "'Have a great time. Compliments of Felix Aberna- thy.'" He looks at Jess. She puts the phone down.

"What the fuck is this, Jess?" Nick can get cranky and foul- mouthed when he's had too much to drink.

"It's okay," she says. "Relax, darling, I'll explain."

"Fuck's sake, fucking Felix Abernathy."

He's slurring his words. He doesn't look like her dancing Romeo anymore. She needs to defuse this and she needs to call Olly's mum immediately, but before she can do either of those things she also needs to quell the feeling of dread that feels as if it's scraping out her insides.

"Felix fucking Abernathy! I thought we weren't going to call him." Nick's not so drunk that he's not getting close to putting two and two together.

"Shut up a minute, Nick, will you? Just shut up!"

His mouth drops open in surprise and he gets a look in his eyes that's a little bit nasty, but Jess turns away. More than anything, she needs a few moments to think.

letcher buys a disposable phone before he calls Cody Swift because he hasn't lost his instincts for self-preservation, though part of him wonders why he's bothering. Who would care, after all, if he lost his job now because of something like this? Would he? He's not sure anybody apart from Danny would notice.

Swift answers with a robust "Hello?"

"This is Detective Inspector John Fletcher."

"I'm sorry! Your number didn't come up on my phone." Fletcher doesn't react to Cody's comment about the phone number. Never explain. "What can I do for you, Detective?"

"This conversation is off the record, understood?"

"Understood."

"You know the official investigation into the murders of your friends was closed when Sidney Noyce was convicted?"

"Yes."

"I understand you have been looking into alternative theories as to who may have killed your friends?"

"I'm exploring some possibilities."

Fletcher suppresses a snort. Who does Cody Swift think he is? "In the last episode of your podcast you mentioned you're trying to discover more about the taxi that Jessy Paige traveled in on her way back to the Glenfrome Estate on the evening Scott and Charlie were murdered."

"Uh-huh."

"As you know, we were unable to trace the driver at the time of the investigation, but I have received some information identifying him. A man has come forward as a result of your podcast."

"Oh, wow! That's incredible! Can you share it with me?"

Fletcher shares the information Felix gave him and Swift laps it up.

"This is a big break for the podcast," he says. "Can I record something with you? We could discuss what this means for the case."

"That won't be possible. I am speaking off the record here. I don't think you need to specify where the information came from."

"Will the police be investigating this?"

"As far as we're concerned, the case was closed satisfactorily twenty years ago, and I don't believe this will turn up any evidence to challenge the original outcome, but if you find out anything significant as a result of talking to this man, then the police would love to hear it."

"Why are you telling me this?"

"I like you, Cody. I remember meeting you back then and I admire what you are doing now. Like you, I believe closure is important and I expect you need that as much as anybody else who was involved."

An Oscar-winning performance? Fletcher wonders. *A BAFTA at least.*

"Thank you so much."

"I look forward to hearing about it on the podcast."

"And you will! Thanks again. It's amazing to have your support."

"You're welcome," Fletcher says. He marvels at Swift's gullibility.

He takes the scenic route home via the Portway. The steep sides of the gorge tower on either side of him. A large boat takes advantage of the high tide to cruise into the center of the city. The suspension bridge is lit prettily above. Fletcher pulls into a lay-by and stops the car. He removes the SIM card from the disposable handset he used to call Swift and steps out of the car. He smashes both thoroughly underfoot and hurls the fragments into the river. He wonders how many others have used Bristol's waterways to rid themselves of unwanted goods and unwanted people over the years. More than many of us would care to know, he thinks.

As he contemplates the water's dark flow, he finds himself questioning Felix's reason for wanting to share the information about the taxi driver. *Why didn't I ask?* he thinks. *Have I been as gullible as Swift?* He feels confused and the irony is not lost on him, the way he raged at Danny when he thought he was being accused of being Tremain's stooge but was willing to turn up and do Felix's bidding without question. It's because Felix and I have an understanding, he reassures himself. We do favors for each other. Quid pro quo.

Still, he muses on Felix's motivations. Was it to take the heat off Jessica Paige? If so, why? Or could it have been to take the heat off Felix himself for some reason? Is Felix aware that Cody Swift has lucked out and is actually getting close to discovering something that could prove damaging to Felix?

Something Fletcher's not aware of? Perhaps Fletcher shouldn't have been so dismissive when Swift said he was pursuing leads.

The breeze coming off the water is chilly and Fletcher shudders. These thoughts are uncomfortable. If any of them prove to be correct, then Fletcher himself could have been wrong about Noyce's guilt, and that is a road he will never be ready to travel down.

Fletcher is buffeted by the slipstream from passing commuter traffic as he gets back into his car. His work mobile is ringing. He extracts the phone from his pocket with difficulty, and it takes him a few seconds to work out that the caller is Annabel Collins because she is speaking so fast.

"Can you repeat that for me, love?" Fletcher asks.

"My mother has given me something and it's a bit shocking. I don't want to say any more because, well, I want to give it to you in person."

"Where are you?"

"I'm at a concert. Our performance starts in twenty minutes. I had to rush here, but I've got it with me."

"I'll come."

"I won't be able to talk until it's over."

"Not a problem."

"We're at the Lord Mayor's Chapel on College Green."

Fletcher makes a quick call to Danny and leaves a message to explain what he's doing. He knows he should be with another officer when he speaks to Annabel Collins, but it's late and he doesn't want to disturb Danny's family evening or deal with putting things together after the row they had earlier. He could palm the job off onto another detective, but he feels it's a good chance to build a rapport with Annabel and maybe an opportunity to ask about her paternity. Besides, a concert is better than going home. Fletcher pulls out into the traffic and makes a U-turn at the first opportunity. The call has got him fired up. Action always feels good. *This is why I do it,* he thinks, and then, *Why am I continually reminding myself of that nowadays?*

"I'm pushing my luck," Danny says. His knee jigs up and down.

Fletcher stretches, then relaxes his fingers to combat his irritation with his partner and cracks a window open. There's a fug in the car. "Nobody knows I'm here. Who knows?" he asks, but Danny doesn't look reassured. Smail has reiterated to him as well as Fletcher that they are forbidden from partnering on this case.

They stare at the tower block looming in front of them where the witness called Sonya Matthews lives. It's half nine in the morning. Not many people are out and about, even though the weather's fine. The murders have cast a pall of fear over the estate, and news of Noyce's arrest hasn't spread widely yet.

"We don't need to do this," Danny says. "If we wait for the blood results they'll make the case against Noyce watertight."

Fletcher runs his fingers over his freshly shaved chin and cheeks as they watch a pensioner pass, pulling a shopping trolley behind her. Only one wheel turns. The other scrapes along the tarmac path. A white cat dozes in sunlight on the bonnet of a car parked beside them. There are no kids about anywhere. The play area is empty.

"I don't leave anything to chance," Fletcher says. "You know my rules."

"You should have told me before destroying the tapes."

"The tapes were stolen from my car."

"Really?"

"Yes, really. Do you think I'd lie to you?"

Danny shakes his head, but he looks confused. He's always playing catch-up, *Fletcher thinks. He's never smart enough to get ahead of the game.*

"But this is a risk. What if the witness doesn't play ball?" Fletcher's wound up so tight he thinks he might punch Danny if he doesn't stop complaining and start to focus. *He's in danger of becoming a liability.*

"She'll cooperate if we do this right. Trust me! Have I ever let you down? Have I? What? Are you chicken now? You know what, as soon as this is done, I'll leave you alone and you can go and suck up to Smail all you want. I can look after myself."

Two red spots are burning on Danny's cheeks. He raises his palms in submission. He sighs when they slap back down on his thighs, then checks his watch. "Where the fuck is she? Perhaps the information isn't good."

They are waiting for Sonya Matthews to return home after a night shift. According to a neighbor, this is the time she's most likely to appear. Fletcher squints into the side mirror and sees a woman in jeans and a hooded sweat shirt approaching the building they're parked in front of. "It's her," he says. Danny reaches for the door handle, but Fletcher puts a hand on his arm to stall him. "Are you on board?" he asks. Danny stares at him for a moment, then nods, and Fletcher nods back at him. "Let's wait until she's inside," Fletcher says. He wants this conversation to be as private as possible.

They give Sonya Matthews a few minutes after she's gone into the building—not too long, they don't want her to have time to get to bed—before following her up to her flat. She answers the door promptly. She's got the sallow skin and dark eye bags of the night-shift worker. She invites them in and puts the kettle on. The flat is similar to all the others they've visited, except it's got a small private balcony on one side. The balcony isn't big enough to put a table on, but a couple of foldout chairs are crammed into the space between the window and the balustrade, and there's a limp washing line above them.

"Do you mind?" Fletcher asks, indicating the door that leads out.

Sonya Matthews shakes her head. "Be my guest." She has a nasal voice that grates on Fletcher's nerves further, but he doesn't let it show. He opens the door and steps onto the balcony. "Where were you sitting on Sunday night?"

"That one." She points to the chair farthest away.

"Was it in this position?"

She shrugs. "Think so. I haven't moved it." She withdraws inside to put the kettle on. Fletcher sits down in the chair she indicated. Danny watches from the doorway. Fletcher looks around. He can see a fair way down Primrose Lane. He estimates he's about forty feet above it. There looks to be a reasonable amount of lighting at the entrance to the lane. If the lights were working, the witness would have had a decent view of the faces of passersby on Sunday night even if daylight was fading. He goes back inside. The door makes a suction noise as he shuts it. Sonya Matthews indicates with a wary gesture that they should sit.

"Can you remind me what you told the other officer you saw?" Fletcher asks.

"I saw the two lads who were murdered. I didn't know their names, but I'd seen them around the estate a lot. Tearaways, the pair of them, so I kept my eye on them. I didn't want a bloody egg chucked at me or something like that. They were walking close together, talking like they were plotting something. Thick as thieves."

Fletcher experiences a jolt of sorrow at this. This could be a description of Danny and him when they were kids. Sorrow is followed by *a rush of anger toward Noyce and Smail. Charlie Paige and Scott Ashby need justice, and Fletcher is determined to give it to them personally. He works hard to maintain his composure as he asks, "What did you see after that?"*

"I already told the officer all this before."

"We are just double-checking."

"I saw that man they call Sid the Village. Big lad. He's a few sticks short of a bundle."

"What was he doing?"

"Walking along behind the boys."

"How long after?"

She sighs. "Not long. Maybe five minutes at the most."

"Which direction was Noyce going in?"

"Same as the boys. Toward Tesco. Like I said before. And then he went back again."

"He doubled back? Are you sure?"

"'Course I'm sure! I know what I saw."

Fletcher's pager begins to buzz, but he ignores it. He takes a sip from the weak cup of tea she has put in front of him. She's taken her shoes off and tucked her feet up under her on the sofa. She cradles her mug with both hands and blows gently across its surface. The steam scuds away and disappears.

Fletcher reaches into his pocket and takes out a sheet of paper. He unfolds it slowly and Sonya Matthews watches closely. He casts his eyes down it as if he's reading it, even though he knows what's on it already. It's a short and simple document, detailing both the various government benefits Sonya Matthews and her partner have fraudulently claimed over the past decade and the likely prison sentence that could be attached to such a collection of misdemeanors.

"Here's the thing," he says. "Your testimony is very important to us, so important that we've come all the way over here today to double-check it. We have a strong suspect for the murders, but we need our evidence to be watertight to make sure he gets punished for what he's done."

"Right." She sounds cautious. That's good. Fletcher's been trying to gauge how clever she is. This will be quicker and easier if she's got a couple of brain cells to rub together. He puts the piece of paper faceup on the coffee table and pushes it toward her. She looks at it but doesn't move. Fletcher nods, encouraging her to pick it up, and she reaches for it. When she's read it, her eyes rove from Fletcher to Danny. She looks scared witless. "What do you want?" she says.

"It's very important that you remember correctly which direction Sidney Noyce was walking on both occasions that you saw him."

She swallows. "He was walking . . . behind the boys the first time?" she asks.

Fletcher nods. "And the second time?"

"He was going in the same direction?"

She's smart enough. It's a relief. "That's interesting," Fletcher says. "I expect Noyce must have walked around the block searching for the boys."

"But, Detective," she says.

Don't fuck this up now, he thinks. I need this. "Noyce is guilty," he says. "He's guilty as sin. He's a sick man. A pervert. You have done your community a big favor. When the other detectives return, I need you to tell them what you just told me. Tell them you were mistaken about the direction Noyce was going in when you gave your previous statement. They'll understand that you might have been confused. Perhaps because you were trying so hard to help when you spoke to them before?"

She nods. She looks more uncertain than Fletcher would like, and he wonders if perhaps he hasn't pushed the Good Samaritan angle hard enough. But then she says, "I think I might have heard Sid calling the boys. Calling after them."

Fletcher licks his lips to suppress his instinct to smile. "That is very interesting. Getting Noyce off the streets will save the lives of other kids, and that will be because of you. You. Do you understand?" She nods. "And this"—he takes the paper out of his pocket and holds it up—"will disappear." He crumples it up and she reaches for it, but he replaces it in his pocket. He extends a hand and she shakes it limply. He cups her sweaty fingers between both his hands.

"Thank you," he says. "Now, get some sleep."

Fletcher and Danny take the stairs down at a pace. The soles of their shoes slap and scrape on the concrete and the sounds echo. Outside, Danny says, "Are you sure she's not going to get a guilty conscience?"

"I'm sure," Fletcher says, but he isn't, not completely. He knows he's spinning more and more plates on this case, and he's beginning to feel the toll it's taking on him. He has a headache pinching at both temples and a loose feeling in his gut that tells him he's about to hit his limit in terms of how long he can run on his nerves. He's hopeful, though. Fletcher's ambition is grand, and he's spent his life reading and manipulating others. Rather an overdose of adrenaline and a chance at glory than three decades trudging through knee-high career shit.

As they drive away, the radio crackles with news for Danny. As Fletcher listens, he finally allows a smile to wrap itself around his face. It's news that the blood on Sidney Noyce's trouser leg matches Charlie Paige's rare blood type. The pattern it has made on the trousers indicates that it probably resulted from a live injury. It was highly unlikely to have been transferred in that way if Noyce only visited the bodies after the assault. DNA results are still to come but the team is optimistic it'll be a match to Charlie because of the rarity of the blood type. The news makes Danny smile, too.

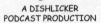

IT'S TIME TO TELL

EPISODE 9—FANCY MAN

A DISHLICKER
PODCAST PRODUCTION

"Jessy had a fancy man. I saw him once or twice coming and going, but he never said hello. He came and went at funny hours. She never talked about him much, neither. 'He's ever so busy,' she used to say. I think he might have spent the day with her and Charlie sometimes, but it wasn't very often. He was more a gentleman of the night, if you know what I mean."

My name is Cody Swift. I'm a filmmaker and your host of *It's Time to Tell,* a Dishlicker Podcast Production. That was the voice of eighty-year-old Doris Russo. She lived in the flat next door to Jessica Paige on the Glenfrome Estate.

When we asked other people about Jessica Paige's boyfriend back in 1996, we got a similar picture. At the end of the last episode you heard ex–Detective Superintendent Howard Smail describe him as a "mystery man," and here's a reminder of what Kirsty Brown had to say. If you remember, she was another young mother from Glenfrome Estate, and Jessy's friend. She is referring to Jessy in this clip:

"She was always off to some nightclub or restaurant. She showed off about it. Sometimes a car used to pick her up. But she never really talked about who she was with. She said she had a boyfriend, but I don't remember her mentioning his name."

And here's Annette Ashby:

"We never met Jessy's boyfriend. We knew she had one, because Charlie was always having to get out of the house to give them some time, but that was as far as it went. It could have been more than one boyfriend for all we knew, but I don't think it was."

So here's the thing: I have realized that I think I probably know as much—if not more—about this man than anybody else we've spoken to. I believe I met him once at Charlie's flat. He was there when I arrived, sitting on the sofa, long legs crossed. He was back-lit by the window, so his face was in shadow, but I remember he had thick black hair and he was smoking. Jessy sat on his knee and shared his cigarette. I wasn't used to public displays of intimacy, so it shocked me. I didn't know where to look. Jessy's boyfriend handed Charlie a few coins and told us to go out and get a soda and make ourselves scarce for a while. We scarpered, but as we did, he shouted, "Wait!" We stopped at the door. "What do you say?" he asked. Charlie looked blankly at him. I said, "Thank you." "Where's your manners, Charlie?" he asked. "You need to be po-lite like your friend." "Say thank you to Felix," Jessy told Charlie. "Thank you," Charlie said. Then we were gone.

Charlie mentioned this man to Scott and me a few times. He used to tell Scott and me about the man's fancy car and how he brought sweets to the house, and sometimes a present. Charlie liked him.

I asked Detective Inspector John Fletcher if the police had ever tracked this man down:

> "It would have been a priority if we had pursued our line of inquiry regarding Jessica Paige any further, but that was dropped—rightly so—once we had charged Sidney Noyce."

Maya and I decided to see if we could trace him ourselves. He might be able to shed light on the seventy-two minutes. He might be the man who was with Jessy Paige at the Paradise Casino. The problem is, I remember this man's first name, but not his surname. Maya and I scoured our interview transcripts from everybody who knew Jessy to see if we could find any further clues to his identity. There was one. Listen to the following clip carefully—we nearly missed the clue ourselves—it's the voice of Doris Russo, Jessy Paige's old neighbor and frequent babysitter for Charlie:

> "One night I went round to watch Charlie, and when I got there, Jessy was all dressed up ready to go out. She looked lovely, but she was upset because the boyfriend hadn't phoned her to say where to meet. So she starts ringing around places and she's getting more and more worried until she finds him. She puts the phone down, happy now, and she says, 'He was at Partridges. I thought he was.' And off she goes. But she wasn't fooling me. She had a wobbly smile on because she was embarrassed. He made a fool of her."

I looked up Partridges. It's still in business. It's a cocktail bar in the basement of the Leonard Lane Hotel. I went down there that evening and got lucky. The barkeep was a man in his fifties. He told me he'd been working at Partridges for thirty years. Here's our conversation. It's my voice you can hear first:

"Can I ask you a question?"
"Fire away."
"I'm looking for a man who used to drink here in the 1990s. He might have come regularly."
"I met a lot of drinkers in the 1990s."
"His name is Felix."
"Well, that narrows it down."

He squinted at me, assessing me.

"Why do you want to know?"
"I used to know him. I want to reconnect."
"Only Felix I remember was a youngster called Felix Abernathy. He was a good customer. I heard he got famous."
"Famous?"

I did an internet search for Felix Abernathy on my phone there and then, and the results piled in. I found a photograph and showed it to the barkeep.

"It's been a long time, but I reckon that's him."
"Do you remember him being with a woman called Jessy or Jessica?"
"I don't remember a Jessica. But two things I remember about him: he was never short of women and he never got drunk."

Felix Abernathy took my call. I was relieved and nervous. He is a very successful man with a significant public profile. He reminisced a bit about Bristol and the Glenfrome Estate. He showed an interest in the podcast and said that he remembered Jessica Paige and Charlie, though, unsurprisingly, he didn't remember meeting me. These are his words about the night of Sunday, 18 August 1996:

"I saw Jessy the night the boys were murdered. We'd had an on-again, off-again relationship at one point, but it had died out long before then, no hard feelings. We were just friends by then. A mate told me she was at the casino in a state because she'd been drinking heavily, so I went to pick her up. I had planned to take her back to her flat, but I didn't think her kid should see her like that, so I took her to one of her friend's houses instead, to sober up before she went home. It wasn't that late. Then I met a friend of mine at my local pub for a card game. I was trying to do her a favor. When I heard what happened later it was heartbreaking, really. Tragic. Charlie was a lovely kid. I tried to help her later on, after his death, because I heard she fell apart. I put her in contact with some friends of mine in the TV business and I was very happy when that worked out for her."

Felix told me that Jessy's friend lived somewhere near the estate, but he couldn't remember her name or the street she lived on. His exact words were "Somewhere off Blackhorse Lane," but he was unable to be more specific.

Maya and I discussed what this might mean. Blackhorse Lane

is so long that depending where Felix dropped Jessy, it was still possible she could have been on the estate for a period of time, left again, and taken a taxi back.

There are still so many unanswered questions about these seventy-two minutes, and only one woman who might be able to answer them. We decided to make another attempt to contact Jessica. Perhaps twenty years had jogged her memory? I waited once again at the animal shelter where she volunteers, but on this occasion she did not appear. I went inside. This is my conversation with the receptionist. Apologies for the sound quality, what you can hear in the background is the kenneled dogs barking.

"I'm looking for Jessica Paige."

"Never heard of her."

"Jessica Guttridge?"

Guttridge is Jessica Paige's married name.

"She's not in today."

"Oh, really? Did she call in sick or something? I thought this was her day."

"She's gone on holiday. Last minute. Lucky for some!"

"Do you know how long for?"

"I think it was a week, but it might have been two weeks."

Very frustrating news, and Maya and I wondered why Jessy had decided to take off at the last minute. A coincidence? We will be bringing you more on Jessica in our next episode.

And, yes, there will be one. Maya and I have been overwhelmed with the response to last week's episode of *It's Time to Tell*. Your messages of support in the aftermath of Maya's attack have been phenomenal and have given us the courage to keep going. Your generous donations have made it possible. The upswing in downloads and positive reviews has been dizzying. The *It's Time to Tell* community has made it very clear that you want more episodes, and you will have them.

Before we sign off, and start preparing for what we promise will be a big episode next week, you might be wondering what I did about the memory I retrieved in last week's episode. The memory provided an innocent explanation for why Charlie's blood was on Sidney Noyce's trousers.

I phoned Detective John Fletcher to tell him about it. His reaction surprised me. Here's a clip of our conversation. I've just described the events I remembered to him:

"Do you think you can do anything with this?"

"Generally, to reopen a case we would need new evidence or information."

"This clearly shows that one piece of evidence in the trial against Noyce was flawed."

"Really, this isn't even a police matter, because we would only reopen the case if Noyce's conviction was overturned by a court. This is a legal matter. You would have to convince a lawyer to take this on. It's not an easy matter. And ask yourself this: is a twenty-year-old retrieved memory of an event witnessed by a child going to be good enough to get you anywhere? A good solicitor will ask you the same question and give you the same advice, so take it from me and save yourself the money and time."

Maya and I took this on board. We believe the blood evidence is just one piece of the puzzle and we will find further evidence to prove Noyce's innocence. We are convinced of it. We are determined to do it in spite of the threats. In fact, the intimidation makes us believe, perhaps more than anything else, that there is more to discover. Otherwise, why would we be threatened? Here's a clip from our next episode. The man speaking has asked to remain anonymous:

"I didn't think anything of it on the night—she's not the first I've picked up in a bad way, and she won't be the last—and I was away on my holidays the next morning, so I missed the news about it and the police appeal. I didn't put two and two together until the wife told me about your podcast."

Jess opts for honesty. "Nick," she says. He's upright but gently swaying on the other side of the bed in their hotel room. "Listen to me. I have spoken to Felix while you've been away and I will explain everything to you, I promise, but Erica needs to be our priority right now."

Nick's eyes move toward the fruit basket and back to Jess as he processes what she's saying. "Call Erica," he says. He sits heavily on the bed. Jess starts by calling the landline at their home, not that Erica ever bothers to answer it. It rings seven times and then she hears Nick's voice as the message service picks up. Jess shakes her head at him. It's nearly midnight. She tries Erica's mobile again with no success and then Olly's mum. This time, there's an answer.

"Oh, hi! Hi!" Jess says.

"Oh, thank god!" Olly's mum sounds as frantic as Jess. "Are you home?"

"I'm in Morocco. With my husband."

"Olly and Erica said your husband would be home."

"Well, he's not."

"I'm sorry. I hope you don't think Olly has led your daughter astray. I had no idea neither of you would be there. It's very unlike him to tell a lie."

Jess tries to sound calm. "Well, they're teenagers, aren't they?"

"What shall we do? I could drive to your house and check on them, but I'm not sure I need to. I mean, whatever they're getting up to, they'd probably find another way to do it anyway, don't you think?"

Easy to say when it's a son, not a daughter, involved, Jess thinks. She's glad Nick can't hear this. He would fly off the handle.

"The thing is," Jess says, wondering how she's going to muster the politeness for this when she wants to have a screaming fit, "we'd be very grateful if you could pop round and pick them up. I don't want Erica in the house by herself."

"They are seventeen. And she is with Olly."

Jess shuts her eyes and pinches the bridge of her nose between two fingers. How to explain the terror that surges through her at the thought that Erica is not under the supervision of an adult? *Last time I left one of my children unattended, he was murdered,* she wants to say, but she daren't reveal this, even at this moment. "Yes, but Erica's only sixteen and we would be very grateful. Her dad's very protective. I'm sorry." Jess starts flicking through a mental Rolodex of contacts, wondering whom else she can ask to pop round to the house if Olly's mum won't do it. It needs to be quick. If Erica is at home, Cody Swift or the press might find her there.

"All right. I'll go now. What's the address?"

"Would you mind calling as soon as you're there?"

"Of course."

Jess gives her the address, hangs up, and relays the conversation to Nick. He glances at his watch. "Where does she live?"

"Stoke Bishop."

"She should be there in twenty minutes at this time of night. I'll kill that boy when I get my hands on him."

"Oh, for god's sake," Jess says, "they've probably already had it off in London. They're probably fine." This isn't how she feels—she is consumed by fear that harm will come or has come to Erica—but she finds Nick's drunken posturing to be pointless.

He stares at her with both anger and hurt in his expression. She wonders if his patience will break and he'll lash out. Only verbally, mind you, he's never raised a finger to her. *Don't you dare say anything about my past,* Jess thinks, and he doesn't. Nick is not a cruel man, or one to cast blame. Instead he says, "Why has Felix sent us a basket of fruit?"

"I don't know."

"You called him."

"I did. I'm not going to lie. You threatening Cody Swift over the phone was not going to stop the podcast, I'm sorry, but it wasn't. It's a job that needs Felix. He's got the contacts."

Nick bites his lip. He is sobering up. "What's he going to do?"

"I don't know for sure, but he said he might be able to squeeze their sponsorship." She's trying to give Nick as little detail as she can get away with. He plucks a mango from the fruit basket and holds it up. "This is an insult. How does he know we're here?"

"He told me to get away for a few days."

"So you're here because Felix told you to be?"

"No, I'm here to see you. The basket is a power play. It can only wind us up if we let it."

She grabs the fruit basket and dumps it in the corridor outside the room. She shuts the door and goes to Nick, putting her arms around his waist gently, affectionately. He doesn't reciprocate but neither does he move away. He checks his watch. "Try Olly's mum again," he says.

"It's only been a few minutes."

"Try Erica."

She does. No reply.

"If I get my hands on that Olly, I'll wring his fucking neck," Nick says. They wait in silence for a few moments. "Does Felix reckon he can shut down the podcast by squeezing sponsorship? Will that be enough?" Nick asks.

She nods, liking the feel of his shirt against her cheek. "I don't know. It's got to make it difficult for them, but Cody Swift is tough. People on the estate used to say his dad beat the crap out of him."

Nick sighs. "That's harsh."

"His home was harsh."

Jess could say more, but she doesn't want to think about Cody or Scott and especially not about Charlie, because her mind should be on Erica. Her fingertips play with the lacy hem of her dress and she feels extremely tired. Her phone rings. It's Olly's mum.

"I'm here, and I've rung the bell and banged on the door, but there's no answer. No lights on either."

"Shit," Jess says. "Do you think they've gone out?"

"I don't think so. I've phoned some of Olly's friends. They knew about this. They said Olly and Erica were planning to spend the evening and the night at your house."

Jess retches. The nausea comes from nowhere, hot and bitter and the exact flavor of her fear. Her daughter is missing. The podcast is threatening to open up old wounds that are deep and ugly, and Felix Abernathy is back in her life and already causing problems between her and Nick and knowing way more than he should about her family. She's not sure how much more of this she can bear.

"DO SOMETHING!" she shouts at Olly's mother. "Please!" And then, "Sorry, I'm so sorry. I shouldn't have shouted. That was uncalled for. I'm just feeling a little powerless."

How to explain why a missing child—even a teenager, even for what might turn out to be just the blink of an eye—feels like the end of the world for Jess?

There's a pause on the other end of the line. "Of course. I'll call you back with news. I promise."

She hangs up before Jess can respond and Jess begins to work, phoning other contacts, leaving messages online. Nobody has seen or heard from Erica.

Fletcher walks down Park Street toward the Lord Mayor's Chapel. The steep incline is hard on his knees. Traffic slows at the bottom of the hill, brake lights flaring. Pubs and restaurants are doing brisk trade.

He's been thinking about Peter Dale on his way over here and wondering if anybody will clamor for justice for him once they know he's dead. Perhaps he was too much of a bad man even for family to mourn. Perhaps, instead, his victims will finally feel that justice has been done: Dale's life in exchange for their collective financial ruin? One amongst them may be the killer. Might the unearthing of his body offer closure to the others and silence the old lament that some of them are no doubt still humming—if no longer singing—after all these years, the victim's lament whose chorus always asks, "Why me?"

It's luck, Fletcher wants to tell them. It's luck of the draw as to whether lightning strikes you and your family or not. The same applies to police investigations. Detectives don't just turn up at a scene, follow a trail, and discover whodunit. We need luck, too, he thinks, but—and here Fletcher smiles for the first time since this morning—there are ways of maximizing your chances of getting some.

The Lord Mayor's Chapel has frontage on the busy bit of

road opposite College Green, where council buildings form an ungracious semicircle and Bristol Cathedral squats. The chapel's facade is hemmed in by the modern buildings beside it, but stands out due to its age. The golden stone is pockmarked and stained by pollution and centuries of weather, but it describes three elegant pointed arches on the ground floor and forms delicate tracery above that dissects a vast stained-glass window protected from the pigeon shit and breakage by wire netting. To Fletcher, the chapel has the appearance of a secret building, one of those quiet, ancient places that nestles in the center of Bristol. Just like the river, these places exert a tug on Fletcher, making him think of lives lived over the centuries— good, bad, and ugly. He feels a part of that. He thinks he understands this city and knows its streets and its people. Just as he has traveled through this city's streets for most of his lifetime, thinking of them as veins and arteries, he feels as if Bristol has somehow got into his blood. Quid pro quo.

Fletcher turns the heavy iron handle on the chapel door and eases it open. The performance is under way. Annabel Collins sits at a harpsichord looking delicate in a black dress. The members of a string quartet are seated in front of her. Fletcher slips into one of the narrow pews at the back of the chapel. The audience is small but the music is exquisite, and for twenty minutes Fletcher loses himself to it.

At the end of the concert Annabel Collins spots Fletcher and makes anxious eye contact during the applause. As the audience stands, she makes her way swiftly down the aisle to greet him. She's holding a small box. Her face is drained of color. They move aside, away from the other audience members. A pair of stiff stone figures lie immortalized on a medieval tomb beside them. The stone is smoother in places where living hands have touched the figures. Fletcher shudders involuntarily at the sight.

"After you left the other day, Mum was very disorientated when she woke up," Annabel Collins whispers. "She was talking what I thought was a lot of nonsense. She was going on about Peter Dale. Talking about when they were lovers and then some of the people he harmed. Did he con some people out of money? Am I right?"

Fletcher nods and she continues, her words an urgent tumble: "I couldn't get much detail out of what she was saying, there was a lot of rambling talk, but she said Peter had a brother who was one of the people he conned."

This is news to Fletcher.

"Do you know the brother's name?"

"He was a half brother, apparently. Different surname. I forget what it is. His first name is Terry." The name rings a bell for Fletcher. There was a Terry amongst the list of Dale's victims, but no mention of a family connection that he can remember.

"Anyway"—Annabel Collins swallows laboriously as she gets to the point—"Mum has a box full of old stuff. She got obsessed with looking through it after you came round the other day. She got out an old tin I've never seen before. Inside it was this little box. She gave it to me. I think you need to see it."

She hands Fletcher the box. Her eyes are wide. Fletcher eases the top off the box. Inside, a layer of faded pink tissue paper obscures the contents. He removes it with his fingertips to reveal what's underneath, and Annabel flinches.

"Jesus Christ!" Fletcher says. He replaces the lid quickly. One of the audience members stares at him, but he gives her a look and she turns away. "Is that what I think it is?" he asks.

"I don't know," Annabel Collins says. "Mum said Terry gave it to her. She said it's Peter's."

Fletcher needs an evidence bag. There's one in his car. He also needs to get this to the lab. Unless he's very much mistaken, the object in the box is a mummified human ear.

He promises Annabel Collins he will call her and puts the box in his pocket. He steps out of the church onto Park Street and takes a narrow set of steps down to the warren of streets that used to be the medieval heart of the city. It's nearing midnight, and the acoustics of the empty streets magnify the clattering of his footsteps as he marches across the cobbles to his car.

FLETCHER ARRIVES HOME at midnight after dropping the box and its contents into evidence and making a few out-of-hours calls to be sure it gets expedited at the lab. If it wasn't so late, he'd go directly to re-interview Hazel Collins, but she will have to wait until first thing in the morning. He knows he won't be able to sleep, but at least there's nobody in the house to give him grief for pulling an all-nighter.

Most of the Peter Dale papers are still on his dining table. He pulls the ones he took to the office out of his briefcase and adds them to the top of one of the piles. He gets a desk lamp from his son's old room and sets it up on the dining table, where it throws down a bright cone of light. He makes a pot of coffee and begins to work through the papers. He has looked at each one once already, but he didn't know what he was looking for. This time, he's after anything he can find on Peter Dale's brother, Terry.

It's three A.M. when Fletcher makes a breakthrough, but it's not the one he expected. The notes tell him that Peter Dale's half brother was called Terry Taylor. He was scammed out of £40,000, the sum of his life savings plus money he had invested on behalf of his church's charity, for which he acted as treasurer. He was a bachelor who cared for their mother and lived in her bungalow with her. An internet search brings up an obituary for Terry just a few lines long, from five years ago. Fletcher learns he was unmarried, spent most of his life working on the railways, was an active member of his local church and local bowling club, and died of an unspecified cancer when he was sixty-four years old.

There's not much more to learn about Terry from the notes and Fletcher is about to give in to his aching neck and shoulders and lie down on the couch when something catches his eye. On the edge of the statement by Terry Taylor, the investigating officer has drawn an arrow from the sentence describing how Terry had invested some of his church charity's money. By the point of the arrow is the word *Lamplight*. Fletcher freezes. He thinks he's heard of this organization before, in relation to somebody else. Somebody relevant. He types as fast as he can, and a list of search results appears. He clicks on the first, titled "Lamplight Trust," and enters the website. His hands are shaking.

He clicks on the menu and then on "Board of Directors." He scans the names, but the one he expects to see isn't there. He curses, then remembers that this is a contemporary list and he is looking for a name from years ago. Stupid. He's not functioning because he's tired. He refills his coffee cup, drinks, feels his heart rate increase more than it should, and sits back down to search another way.

A few attempts later, he has found what he's looking for. Embedded in a newspaper article from 2003, a sentence reads: "Felix Abernathy, a member of the board of directors of the Lamplight Trust, said, 'I am here today to represent my late mother. This charity was founded by her ten years ago with the help of her church. She opened it because she found herself homeless for a time when we were children. I'm delighted to be in a position today to announce the opening of our first hostel offering beds for the homeless.'"

Fletcher absorbs what he's reading. He no longer feels tired. His neck prickles and he is suddenly aware that he hasn't drawn any curtains. Outside the street looks dark and still. He thinks he sees a fox slink between two parked cars, but it's hard to tell. He snaps the curtains shut and stands in the middle of the room, lost in thought.

Felix Abernathy is connected both to Dale's brother and to Charlie Paige. It's a coincidence Fletcher can't ignore. It's not a huge leap of logic to wonder if Felix was involved in all three murders. Fletcher's not quite sure how or why, but he feels this in his bones and he will find out, and when he does find proof that Felix is involved, the thought of the power that would bring him—Fletcher—is almost delicious. He wonders if Swift has made the same discovery. The thought troubles him, but might explain why Felix asked Fletcher to feed the information about the taxi driver to Cody Swift. Perhaps he wanted to distract Swift from another line of inquiry. Or is Fletcher just being paranoid? He reasons not. Felix has always been one step ahead of everybody. But Fletcher needs to be that step ahead now. His tired brain struggles to make sense of all the variables and their possible outcomes.

Fletcher looks at his watch: 4:00 A.M. He will try to sleep for an hour or two. He wants to see Hazel Collins first thing in the morning to find out more about Peter Dale's brother Terry Taylor and the ear. He will ask her about Felix, if she heard anything about him at the time of Dale's disappearance, if Dale himself had met him. There could be stronger connections. Fletcher will need to go it alone. Danny does not know the nature of Fletcher's connection to Felix, and Fletcher wants it to stay that way. John Fletcher dreams of having power over Felix Abernathy—it's been two decades since he felt he had any. He and Felix made a deal that felt fair once, but since Fletcher was held back after Tremain suspected he set up Smail, Felix has somehow held all the power. Above all, Fletcher needs to make sure Noyce's conviction remains secure. If Noyce is cleared, there will be further inquiries and Fletcher will fall. That cannot happen. Not now. Not after so long.

Fletcher lies down on the couch and pulls a blanket over him. He wriggles to get comfortable and stares at the ceiling. Things are a muddle, for sure, but he trusts he will be able to untangle them. He always has done.

"Cheers, mate!" Danny clinks his pint glass against Fletcher's, and Fletcher feels a sticky slop of beer wet his fingers. Fletcher's back and shoulders are sore from being slapped by his colleagues. The team investigating the double murders has packed out the back room of the pub and they're celebrating the news that murder charges will be

brought against Noyce. The blood evidence sealed the deal. They will drink hard before they rest and recover from the hours they've put in. It's what you do.

Some of the chat concerns the investigation, but mostly the lads are talking about Smail.

Fletcher kept away from the office when it happened, but he's getting the details now from a detective constable who has flappy ears and loose lips: "The allegation is that Smail was inappropriate with Jessica Paige when he went to see her—on his own—and that they'd had a previous relationship. She came forward. Smail absolutely lost it."

Fletcher feigns surprise. "Seriously?"

"He denied it, but apparently she knew the code for the lodgings at Blaise." The DC's eyebrows are halfway up his brow.

That's a nice touch from Felix, Fletcher thinks. Very nice. An allegation of inappropriate behavior is good, but suggestion of a previous relationship is genius, and feeding Jessica the code for the police accommodation was the icing on the cake. Felix must have got it from one of his other girls who'd been there previously. Fletcher smiles when he thinks how it makes Smail look so much guiltier.

Fletcher wants to ask more about Smail, but a round of "For He's a Jolly Good Fellow" has broken out and he's getting jostled because it's his solve they're celebrating. He sees Danny on the edge of the gathering and tries to bring him into the middle so they can stand shoulder-to-shoulder on this because it's a victory for both of them, but Fletcher gets caught up in the melee and finds himself at the bar. Danny has dropped out of sight. Fletcher's not worried, though. He's not Danny's babysitter. He downs what remains of his pint in one gulp and slams the empty glass down. "Who's keeping up with me?" he shouts. "Come on!"

There is radio silence from Olly's mum and Jess feels like she's going out of her mind.

Nick has sobered up fast. They sit together on the bed and wait for news about Erica. Jess searches online for flights back to the UK leaving tonight or tomorrow. This is the first time she's ever had a scare with their daughter. It's the first time she's ever left her in anybody else's care without constant text contact. She feels as if life is getting its revenge on her. She feels as if she was allowed to have a daughter only for a while, but of course it had to end. She doesn't deserve children. She proved it with Charlie, so why should it be different now she has Erica? She's been living a fantasy. Nick holds her as she sobs and he mutters reassurance over and over until his words sound as meaningless and strange to Jess as a foreign patois.

"Don't overreact, darling. They'll be out having a lark, I remember what I was like at their age," and so he goes on until she can't stand it anymore. "Stop! I'm giving it another hour, then I'm going to the airport. Don't argue with me."

"All right. But there's no flight until nine A.M., so be sensible. And I'm coming with you."

She strips off her dress, scrubs her makeup away, and puts on jeans and a vest top. They're not sleeping clothes, they're clothes she can travel in, clothes she feels like a mum in, un-like that dress and those sandals. She packs everything she unpacked earlier back into her case. When she's done what she has to do, Nick holds her tighter. He whispers, "I listened to the podcast."

She pulls away from him so she can see his face. In the half-light, Nick looks as if he's both there and not there. His breath is still musky with wine, but his voice is steady and sober.

"You never did tell me what you did for those seventy-two minutes," he says.

She catches her breath. "What do you mean?" But she knows. There was much made of the seventy-two minutes her movements were unaccounted for by a reporter at the trial.

"Don't you think it's time?" Nick says.

"I don't want to lose you."

"You won't lose me."

"I'll lose you and I'll lose Erica."

"Jess. Listen to me. Whatever it is, you will not lose us. We love you. We love you so much. Don't you think it's time to tell me?" Jess knows an ultimatum when she hears one, even if Nick doesn't yet know he's giving one. His desperation for her to be straight with him feels palpable. *It's now or never,* she thinks.

"I was at a casino," she said. "The Paradise. I wasn't sup-posed to be there because Felix arranged for me to be some-where else."

"With a man?" Nick knows what Felix did and how Jess worked for him.

She shakes her head. "At a clinic. I was pregnant. I didn't

know who the father was. I always took precautions, but something hadn't worked. It was a problem, obviously, and Felix arranged to have it taken care of. He could do that. He had people who would do things out of hours and on the quiet. There was a doctor who would open the clinic on a Sunday night for Felix, as a favor."

"Did you not want the abortion?"

"I wanted it and I didn't want it. I was scared of it and scared of being controlled. I didn't want the baby. I was struggling enough with Charlie, I knew it was a bad idea, but I hated being told I couldn't keep it, like it wasn't my decision. So I didn't turn up at the clinic when they told me to. I went drinking at the Paradise. I was such a stupid, fucked-up person that my response to not wanting an abortion was to go drinking. That's how stupid I was, Nick. That's who I was! I wanted that baby so much and I could have damaged it." She stares into his eyes, searching for condemnation, but seeing only pity.

"What happened?" he says.

"Somebody told Felix I was there. He came to get me and took me to the clinic anyway. He was so angry." She feels Nick squeeze her hand a little tighter.

"Why didn't you tell anybody?"

"Because I was scared. They threatened me. The doctor shouldn't have been performing abortions out of hours. They told me it was more than my life was worth to speak about it."

Nick mutters something angry, but Jess isn't sure what it is.

"Felix was so mad at me for not showing up, he dropped me there and left me. The nurse took pity on me. Her husband was a taxi driver, and he dropped me home while they cleaned up the clinic. Everybody thought I was drunk when I got back to the estate, and maybe I was a bit, but mostly I was hurting and faint from the procedure. They rushed it."

"You poor girl." She sees Nick's eyes are welling up, too, and it makes her cry all the more.

"Erica must never know!" she says.

"I'm not going to tell her and you don't need to tell her, but if she ever finds out, I expect she'll understand, or she'll try to, at least. Have faith in Erica and me, Jess. I know you don't believe it, but we love you."

The screen of Jess's phone lights up as a text appears. It's from Olly's mum:

Found them. Both safe. Going to collect them. Will call when we're home.

Jess angles the phone so Nick can read it.

"She's okay," he says. He holds Jess and she lets herself cry. They are tears of relief. When her eyes have dried, she lies in Nick's arms, exhausted, and a thought begins to nag: *He believes I've told him everything, but what if he knew I was relieved when Charlie died?* She turns to him.

"I love you, Jessica Guttridge," he whispers. "My poor, beautiful girl."

What if he finds out? Should I tell him?

She puts her hand on his cheek and prepares to whisper the words that could break her marriage or unburden her forever. But before she can, the phone rings. It's lying between them. They both fumble for it. Jess gets there first. Her hand shakes as she answers. It's Olly's mother.

"They were at a midnight showing of *Rocky Horror Picture Show,* would you believe it? Fishnet stockings and all, and that's just Olly. They're with me at my house now. We're about to go to bed. Do you want to speak to Erica?"

Jess is so overwhelmed with relief that she can't do more than murmur "thank you" and pass the phone to Nick. He finishes the conversation and talks to Erica. Afterward, neither Jess nor Nick is able to sleep. Jess stares at her packed bag on the floor of their room and knows she'll be on her way to the airport tomorrow morning, regardless.

IT'S TIME TO TELL

EPISODE 10—GHOST

A DISHLICKER
PODCAST PRODUCTION

"What do you do after something has knocked you down in life? Do you become a ghost of your former self, forever held back by it, or do you move on and try to rebuild by learning from what happened? To rebuild is possible. I am proof of that. I've probably had a happier life than I would have done if I'd been allowed to stay in the police service."

My name is Cody Swift. I'm a filmmaker and your host of *It's Time to Tell,* a Dishlicker Podcast Production. That was the voice of ex–Detective Superintendent Howard Smail reflecting on the passing of time. Before I get down to the business of this episode, I have a short personal note: I am bringing you this episode of *It's Time to Tell* on my own. Unfortunately, Maya has stepped away from the podcast. She tried to carry on after the assault, but she feels she needs time alone, somewhere she feels safe, to recover. I respect her decision. Having Maya working alongside me has been a privilege, but I won't lie, it has also put a strain on our professional and personal relationship. Her departure is the right thing for her. For me, it's a personal blow.

However, I intend to carry on without her, regardless of the risks. I feel I am too close to some kind of resolution to stop. To walk away now would leave too much unfinished business for too many people.

Yesterday, I took a trip to the center of Bristol, where I met a man who, after twenty years of silence, got in touch as a direct result of listening to this podcast. He has asked to remain anonymous, so when you hear his voice, it will sound a little distorted. I met him, at his request, in a diner near the University buildings. Students sat at booths around us and you may also hear some bangs and crashes from the kitchen as we talk. It's my voice you will hear first:

"Can you tell us about yourself?"

"I'm a taxicab driver. I've been doing the job for forty years."

"Here in Bristol?"

"Yes. I'm born and bred."

"Can you explain why we're here?"

"I heard the podcast and I realized I had something to tell you."

"Go ahead."

"I was the driver who dropped Jessica Paige back at the Glenfrome Estate on that night."

"The night of the murders?"

"Yes. But I didn't know it was her. If I had, I would have told police. I didn't think anything of it on the night—she's not the first I've picked up in a bad way, and she won't be the last—and I was away on my holidays the next morning, so I missed the news about it and the police appeal. I didn't put two and two together until the wife told me about your podcast, and I listened to that episode about Blackhorse Lane."

"Where did you pick her up?"

"Near the bus station in the center. As I recall, she was sat on a bench. I was waiting at a red light and she approached the car. I had my Out of Service light on, but she begged me, saying she didn't feel well and she had to get home to her kid."

"You took pity on her?"

"I did. She showed me some cash, too, so at least I knew she could pay."

"How did she seem?"

"In a bad way. She was pale and sweaty and propping herself up on the side of the car. She had trouble talking."

Do you remember what time it was?"

"I'm going to say around quarter to eleven, something like that. Fifteen minutes after we set off, we was almost at the edge of the estate, and I had to stop to let her out to be sick. I thought about leaving her there, we were so close, but she was crying and you wouldn't do that to your own daughter, so I let her take her time. I even got out and asked her if she wanted to go to the hospital. She said no, she just wanted to be home, and I gave her a few more minutes. She got back in after that and I drove her to her door. There were people there, so I left her because I had to get home. We was on a flight out to Málaga at five o'clock the next morning, so I never saw the news about the murders or any of the appeals the police made. I never made the connection until now."

I shared this report with my criminology students, who previously studied the routes between the Paradise Casino and the Glenfrome Estate. They mapped out the new route after further consultation with the driver, taking into account what Felix Abernathy told us, and had this to report. This is Simon McKay, a third-year student, once again:

"We looked at the route and the timeline and we concluded that everything made sense. Whatever she was doing, it's likely that Jessica Paige was not near the Glenfrome Estate at any time during those seventy-two minutes."

It is such a relief to hear this. Whilst I have tried to retain a professional detachment during the investigation into Jessica Paige, it hasn't been easy. I liked her too much for that. To find out that she had had some direct involvement in the murders of Charlie and Scott, or had even witnessed them, would have been terrible. I plan to continue to delve into who her associates were, but I want to change tack. In the clip at the beginning of this episode, Howard Smail mentioned the word *ghost*. It reminded me of something. I asked Smail about it: "Do you remember DI Fletcher reporting that Charlie spoke a word to him as he was dying?"

I asked because I remember Fletcher quizzing me about it the very first time he interviewed me, but when I mentioned this to Fletcher during our recent conversations, he denied it. Smail riffled through his policy book.

"I'd forgotten this, but I do have a note of it. It's on a list of possible avenues of inquiry. It was low priority."

I even tracked down Fletcher's partner, Detective Sergeant Danny Fryer, who interviewed me back in 1996. He couldn't talk to me about the case on the record—he said the police were keen that I had a single contact, and that was John Fletcher—but he did confirm this point. I wasn't recording him, but his response when I asked about it was something along the lines of "I remember John mentioning it to me. He was really cut up after the boy died in his arms. You don't get over something like that. We never knew what it meant, though. Didn't we ask you about that in the interview?"

DS Fryer's response made me even more curious that Detective Inspector Fletcher claimed not to remember this. How could you forget?

I thought about it a lot. I thought about all the things it could mean. Did Charlie know he was dying? Did he think he'd seen a ghost? Did he think DI Fletcher was a ghost? The answer came to me when I went back to revisit the site where my friends' bodies were found.

It's a different place now. The old stadium where the dog track was situated has been torn down and replaced with a massive IKEA. I stand in the car park in the spot where I think the bodies might have been. I brought two bunches of flowers with me, one for each of my friends, and I lay them at the base of a streetlamp and take no notice of the furniture shoppers who give me funny looks. In a corner of the car park a police tape flutters around a hole in the ground. I can see the towers of the Glenfrome Estate from where I lay the flowers, but I recognize little else apart from the old social club in the corner. It looks identical, even after all these years. I had no idea it survived the redevelopment. I go in, order a drink, and nurse it at the empty bar.

The barman is chatty. I ask if he remembers my dad, though he looks a bit young. He says no, but he reckons there are blokes still drinking in the club that would do. He asks why I'm there so I tell him. He has a tip for me:

"If you want someone to tell you about the dog track, that's Len. He used to be a steward. He's in there."

"In there" is a room on the other side of the bar where six pool tables are set up and men are playing on two of them. Len is an old-timer with white hair and a lively laugh. We take a seat at the edge of the room while his companions continue their game. Len talks about his time working at the dog track and paints a picture of the place that brings memories flooding back for me. He remembers Sidney Noyce and the murders. Here's a clip from our conversation. You'll hear Len's voice first, and you might hear some background sounds of the games being played around us.

"Sidney Noyce was a gentle lad. It was hard for any of us who worked with him at the track to believe he was violent. He was very good with the dogs, and although he wasn't the sharpest tool in the box, you never had to tell him anything twice where they were concerned. I remember the morning the bodies were found. Hot as hell. I was stewarding."

"Charlie was still alive when they found him."

"I heard that. Doesn't bear thinking about. To think we were just feet away from him all morning."

"He said something to the officer that was with him. I've been trying to find out what it might mean."

"What did he say?"

"Ghost."

"*Ghost,* did you say?"

"Yeah."

"You need to talk to Bill Felter."

Len makes a call and tells me he will come with me because he hasn't seen Bill in years. I drive us onto the motorway and out of the city toward Wiltshire and the countryside. We pull off the motorway after twenty-five minutes of driving, into rolling chalk hills. Len directs us down a narrow country lane and before long indicates that we should pull off down a ridged concrete driveway that leads to a small farm. We park beside a chain-link fence enclosing a dilapidated yard. We can hear barking dogs even before we get out of the car.

A man in blue overalls crosses the yard toward us. A crow lifts from a fence post as he passes and lands on the chimney stack of a small, unloved redbrick home. The man shakes Len's hand and introduces himself as Bill Felter. He takes us on a quick tour of the property. A stable building has been converted to dog kennels. Len looks at the dogs with a critical eye before petting each one. I find it hard to see them penned. I am moved by the apparent frailty of their limbs and their liquid eyes. I think of Charlie. "I like their soft ears," he told me once, "soft as cotton wool." I remember how he used to fret if he thought one of the dogs wasn't happy.

After the tour Bill takes us into his kitchen and we talk. He makes strong tea and offers us biscuits from a chipped tin. Len tells him about Charlie's last word. This clip is the conversation that followed between Bill and Len. You'll hear Bill's voice first:

"*Ghost*! Was it now? Goodness me. I didn't know."
"It's got to be to do with one of your lot."
"Yes, I suppose you're right."
"Did you have a runner that morning?"
"Might have done. I can check."

"Don't tell me you've still got the program."

"I keep them all. We can't all have a memory like yours."

Len chuckles as Bill leaves the room to search for the race program. It doesn't take Bill long. He returns within minutes, holding a booklet. He has folded it over to expose one particular page, and he hands it to me. The date at the top of the page is Monday, 19 August. It lists the dogs running in the morning races. That is, the dogs that may have been running as Charlie took his last breath. I run my finger down the names. Here and there Bill has annotated it with results. I don't know what I'm looking for until I see it. In the 11:05 race a dog called Ghost Chaser ran. It took first place at odds of nine to one. Len leans over to take a look.

"That's it. All Bill's dogs run under the kennel name Ghost. I knew it had to be one of his. Makes sense, don't it? Fancy keeping that all these years, Bill."

"How else do you remember?"

"Fair enough."

Len is pleased with himself, and I want to thank him but I find myself lost for words. Tears run down my face because all I can think about is how I reckon Charlie heard the race starting and heard the name of the dog on the PA. You could hear it a mile off. He always stopped to listen if we were passing and the races were on. When I've composed myself a little, I ask what Ghost Chaser looked like. Bill answers swiftly:

"Brindled. White sock, left hind leg. I never forget a winner."

Charlie loved the brindled dogs the most. The men fall silent. One of them puts a hand on my shoulder and leaves it there until the shaking subsides and I am ready to drive Len and me home.

Ghost Chaser won the race as Charlie died, and Charlie knew. I'd like to think it distracted him from his suffering.

I'll be back next week with a new episode of *It's Time to Tell*. Meanwhile, here's a clip from ex–Detective Superintendent Howard Smail to give you food for thought:

"What's the worst case of all? One involving kids. Why? Because it involves kids. The majority of detectives I knew had to work hard to build up emotional armor in that job. We did it the difficult way: by being thrown in the deep end on tough cases and working out afterward how to deal with how we felt about what we'd seen. There was very little psychological support within the force back then, so it was a sort of DIY job, but sometimes our defenses weren't strong enough. Every man I knew had a bad day sometimes, but John Fletcher was different. It was as if he arrived on the job complete with a heart of steel, and from what I've heard, he's never shown any cracks in it to this day. That's not healthy. Now I'm not necessarily talking about John Fletcher, I'm talking about any human being, but you have to ask yourself: how much can one human being take before they break?"

Fletcher wakes with a start because the doorbell is ringing. It's daylight, which means he's overslept. He has a sour mouth and he isn't awake enough to ask who is there before he opens the door.

"John! I was about to let myself in!"

His ex-wife is holding a set of keys. Her gaze travels up and down Fletcher and she recoils a little. He stands aside to let her in. "What do you want?"

"I left you a message to say I was coming to collect Theo's walking boots." Her perfume washes over him as she bustles past.

"He can't get them himself? You spoil him."

"Don't start."

"How's Andrew?" he asks, but she doesn't hear him. She has stopped in the doorway to the kitchen. "John! Oh my god! What kind of state are you living in?"

Fletcher stands behind her and sees it with her eyes: dirty crockery and cutlery piled in the sink; garbage overflowing from the bin; a pan lined with burnt baked beans abandoned on the stove; a frying pan so black and dirty he can't even identify what he last cooked in it; spills and grease on every surface. She turns to face the entrance to the sitting and dining rooms.

"Don't go in there!" he says, but it's too late. He sits on the stairs while she takes in the chaos. He's been sleeping under blankets on the sofa for weeks. The dining table is ruined. A red wine stain darkens the carpet.

"This is worse than a student house!" she says. "You need help."

"Take whatever you need and go," he mutters.

"We have to get this sorted before we sell it, John, you know that, don't you? And look at the state of you!" There is irritation all over her face and, worse, pity. He can't stand it. "Lock up after yourself," he says. He turns away from her and walks out of the house. He doesn't care that he hasn't changed or showered since last night, or was it the night before? He ignores her calls. He needs to get away. He needs to see Hazel Collins.

HAZEL COLLINS OPENS the door and peers at Fletcher. "You again, Detective? You'd better come in."

Fletcher is impressed she remembers him. He wouldn't have put money on that. He follows her into the sitting room, and Hazel sinks into the high-backed armchair she occupied last time Fletcher was here. He takes the chair beside her, as before. Two used mugs are on the coffee table. Otherwise the place looks and feels as still as a museum.

"Would you like more tea?" Hazel asks. "I'm afraid you'll have to make it yourself if you do. Annabel's rules: no kettle boiling while she's out."

She thinks I never left, Fletcher thinks. *No point in contradicting her.* He declines the tea. "Where is Annabel?" he says.

"She's at a rehearsal. She'll be back later."

Fletcher glances at a carriage clock on the mantelpiece. It's a quarter to ten.

"I saw her concert last night," Fletcher says.

"The Bach?"

"She played beautifully."

"She plays Bach very nicely, but she prefers the Romantics. The young love to express their emotions, don't you think, Detective?"

Fletcher blinks. "I suppose so. Look, Ms. Collins, Annabel gave me something at the concert. Something she got from you."

"What's that, dear?" Sunlight reaches into the room and picks out drifting dust motes above Hazel Collins's head. She squints.

No, Fletcher thinks just as he's about to answer, *this is the wrong tactic.* He needs information from her before he challenges her about the ear. Where has his judgment gone? He assumes a light tone. "Actually, I'll talk to you more about that in a minute, but I'd like to chat about Peter Dale first. You said before that you and Peter were lovers?"

"Saucy!" Her fingertips flutter across her chest until they locate her string of pearls.

"Did you ever meet Peter's brother, Terry Taylor?"

"Terry wasn't Peter's brother; he was his half brother. They had different dads."

"Did you ever meet Terry?"

"I met Terry, all right. He was a pest, always phoning to ask about his investment. He turned up at the office more than once. He was a very fussy man, and he didn't know how these things work. It used to wind Peter up."

"They didn't get on?"

"Terry annoyed Peter."

Her eyes travel the room in an unfocused way and Fletcher fears she's going to drift into an absent state. Her fingers pluck at the pearls. "Didn't we talk about this already?" she asks. "I'm getting muddled."

Fletcher tries a different tack. Her mind is scattered, so perhaps scattered questions might work. "Does Annabel know Peter Dale is her dad?"

She blinks. "Can you pass me my glasses, please, Detective?"

He picks up a pair of glasses from the coffee table and she slides them on clumsily. Behind the lenses, her eyes look startlingly large.

"Now I see you!" she says. "It wasn't you that came before, was it?"

"I can assure you it was me. I came with Detective Fryer."

"He's a lovely man."

"Yes, he is. Ms. Collins, please try to concentrate for me. Does Annabel know Peter Dale is her dad?"

"No."

Fletcher's excitement quickens. He was right about Annabel Collins's paternity. "What about Peter? Did he know you were pregnant before he died?"

"No. Peter was embarrassed about me. I would never have told him about the baby being his because I knew he didn't want me. Not as a proper girlfriend to take out in public. I was no spring chicken and no beauty either. He was randy, though. He couldn't keep it zipped up when we were together. I knew I served a purpose for him and I wasn't saying no because it wasn't like I was getting any other offers."

"Did you love him?"

"I wanted a baby. I didn't care who gave me one. Peter was a means to an end. To be honest, I thought I was too old to get pregnant, I thought I'd missed my chance, so it was the loveliest surprise when I discovered I was." Her fingers release the pearls and she lays her palm flat on her stomach. The sunlight has moved out of her eyes and plays on the side of her face. Her skin lies in tissue-paper wrinkles and Fletcher can see her scalp beneath her coiffed hair, but her gaze is sharper than ever. *I'm just going to ask her outright,* Fletcher thinks. He has a feeling this is a good moment.

"Is that why you killed Peter? Because you didn't want him to know about the baby? Or perhaps it was because you wanted the money? You knew how to access his money, didn't you?"

"I didn't kill Peter. Not me." She smiles, apparently unshockable. Fletcher's not buying it.

"Do you remember what you gave Annabel yesterday?"

"I don't remember giving anything to Annabel."

"Last night Annabel phoned me. She was upset and asked me to meet her because she had something she wanted to show me. Do you know what she showed me?" There is no change in Hazel Collins's expression. "She showed me a box. It contained something that appeared to be a mummified ear. Annabel said you told her that the ear was Peter's. Can you explain that?"

At first Fletcher wonders if Hazel Collins is choking. A sound that is part wheeze, part cough begins low in her throat before swelling. He half stands up to help her before he recognizes the mirth in her eyes. She is laughing at him.

"Ms. Collins!" he says. "This is a very serious matter."

"Oh, my darling," she says when she's able to talk. "Has Annabel gone and given you Peter's ear? She's such a drama queen."

"You gave it to her," Fletcher says. "In a box."

"Well, I was reminded of Peter after you detectives came the first time, so I was having a look in a trunk of his stuff that I keep. I never told Annabel it was her dad's stuff. I meant to, I probably should have done years ago, but the moment never seemed right, especially with what Peter did to all those people. It would have upset Annabel. She thinks she was conceived in a one-night stand."

"The ear, Ms. Collins. You need to tell me about the ear."

"Oh, of course. Peter studied anthropology at University. He was especially interested in voodoo. He told me he bought the ear on a trip to New Orleans when he was a student and smuggled it home. It's a voodoo relic, or something. I always thought it was a fake. But it's not Peter's actual ear. It didn't come off his head."

Fletcher is rigid with embarrassment. He is thinking of the ear being fast-tracked through the lab at his request. He'll be a laughingstock if it's fake, but she might be lying.

"Annabel said that Peter's brother Terry gave you the ear. Why was that?"

"Annabel is wrong. The only things I've got of Peter's is the stuff I packed up from his office. Terry didn't want it and I didn't know who else to give it to. I thought I might give it to Annabel one day if I ever told her who her dad was, but it didn't come to pass. Did I say that already? Sorry if I did. Annabel says I repeat myself too much. I'll tell you something for free, Detective. Life doesn't always turn out how you think it's going to."

She yawns. Her ribs rise and fall. Fletcher thinks they look fragile, like birds' bones. He suppresses a shudder. There's no trace of amusement in her expression now, just fatigue. Fletcher knows his time is running out. He says, "Do you know who killed Peter Dale?"

"Well, it was Terry." She frowns. "We just talked about this. You have a terrible memory. I think it's worse than mine."

"Terry killed Peter?"

"Yes, dear."

"Peter Dale's brother, Terry Taylor, murdered Peter?"

"That's what I said. Terry found out Peter was going to do a runner with all the money. Don't ask me how Terry found out, but he did. He turned up at the office on a Saturday. Peter had asked me to come in and work, so we were both there. I heard them have a terrible row and both stormed out of the building. I didn't know what happened after that, but on Monday morning when I got to work, Peter didn't turn up but Terry did. He wanted access to the money. But he was in a terrible state."

"Because he had murdered his brother?"

"Yes. He broke down."

"Why didn't you make a report to the police?"

A smile plays at the corner of her lips. "Money, darling. Filthy lucre. I had a baby to provide for. Me and Terry came to an arrangement about the money, and later that day I called the police to say Peter had gone missing. It was so easy. He's dead now, Terry is. Brain tumor. So he got his comeuppance in the end."

Fletcher knows he should stop this interview now and caution Hazel Collins, but he has one more question he is desperate to ask. "Did you ever meet a man called Felix Abernathy while you were working for Peter?"

"No."

"Are you sure?"

"Felix who?"

"Felix Abernathy."

"Was he in the newspaper?"

"He might have been, but what I want to know is, did you ever meet him? Or do you know if he was close to Peter or Terry?"

"It's a fancy name, isn't it? I don't think I met him, though. I'd remember if I met somebody called Felix."

Fletcher grimaces. Her mind slips so easily between fantasy and reality. He feels his hopes of some leverage over Felix fade, but there will be other ways he can look into the connection he believes is there. He checks the time, but the hands on the carriage clock on the mantelpiece haven't moved since he arrived. He gets his phone out. It's gone ten-thirty. He has two missed calls from his ex-wife plus five missed calls and a message from Danny.

"Excuse me," he says.

"You're excused, darling. I'd always excuse a handsome fellow like you."

He stands in the bay window, in the sunlight, and pays scant attention to a hot air balloon drifting over the suspension bridge. He kneads his forehead. The sunshine warms him, and within the long shadow he's throwing across the room, Hazel Collins's eyelids droop. Danny's message is curt:

Fletcher is to call him asap. Fletcher dials and Danny picks up on the first ring. "Where are you, mate? I've been trying to track you down for hours."

Hazel Collins's mouth has dropped open. Fletcher thinks she's asleep but he drops his voice anyway. "I'm at home," he says. "I'm sorry. I wasn't feeling well last night and I overslept this morning. What's happening?"

"I went round your house. You're not there, John. I saw Jean. She said you walked out this morning. She's worried about you."

"There's nothing to worry about. I went to the doctor. Tell me what's going on."

"I interviewed Hazel Collins again this morning. DC Banks came with me because I didn't know where you were."

"What?" Fletcher says.

"Hazel Collins? You remember? The old lady?"

Fletcher looks at the sleeping woman before he says, "Yes." As Danny continues to talk, Fletcher takes in the empty mugs of tea in front of her. Two of them. He had assumed they had been used by Hazel and Annabel, but they must have been for Danny and the DC. Hazel was right when she said she'd only just talked through everything. She mistook Fletcher for Danny.

Danny says, "She linked the cases."

Fletcher sits down hard on the piano stool. "Which cases?" he says, but he knows. His mouth is suddenly dry.

"Peter Dale and the double murder: Charlie Paige and Scott Ashby. Dale was murdered by his half brother, Terry, and the boys were murdered because they stumbled on the scene."

"Christ," Fletcher says.

"We need to talk. Where are you, mate?"

Fletcher swallows. He can't admit where he is. It would be professional suicide, even to tell Danny. "I'm at my doctor's surgery. Where do you want to meet?"

"I'm still in Clifton. I was hoping to grab Annabel Collins for a chat when she gets home. Where's your doctor?"

Fletcher feels as if somebody has stepped on his grave. He steps back from the window of Hazel Collins's flat and peers out carefully. Outside, he sees a man walking up the pavement, phone to his ear. It's Danny. With him is a young man in a sharp suit. He must be the DC Danny is working with. They get into a car parked directly across the street from the flat. There's no way Fletcher can leave without being seen.

Fletcher's not sure he can count the ways his career has probably just broken. He turns and looks at Hazel Collins. Her head has lolled so far forward you might think her neck was broken. To have come all this way and be brought down by this witch, he thinks, is not something he can allow to happen.

"I'll call you back," he tells Danny.

Detective Chief Superintendent David Tremain has a red-wine birthmark on his face and Fletcher is surprised at how livid it looks close up. He is standing in front of Tremain's desk. He has been summoned with no explanation and has already endured ten minutes outside Tremain's office in the company of his assistant, who was date-stamping letters with a ferocity and volume that seemed designed to take Fletcher's post-celebration hangover to a critical level.

Fletcher can guess why he's here.

"Detective Inspector Fletcher," Tremain says, and Fletcher tenses at the use of his rank to address him, "something has taken place and we shall need to keep it under wraps."

"I am aware of Howard Smail's departure, sir."

"Oh, you're aware of it, are you?"

"Yes, sir. Some of the men were talking about it at the pub last night." Fletcher senses danger. Tremain still hasn't asked him to sit.

"In public," Tremain says, "I shall be praising your work on the case. I shall praise the way you identified Charlie Paige's and Scott Ashby's killer and brought him in. I shall let the public know that the departure of Howard Smail from the force is an unfortunate incident, which has been dealt with immediately and robustly, and that the police service does not tolerate such behavior. I shall offer the proper apologies where they are due, in particular to Ms. Jessica Paige."

Fletcher blinks. It doesn't feel safe to say anything. He's not sure where this conversation is going, even though his sluggish, hungover mind is trying its hardest to work it out. He wishes more than anything that a terrible urge to puke wasn't convulsing his gut. He is wearing yesterday's suit and there is a beer stain reeking on the cuff. He kipped on the floor at Danny's pad last night. Tremain looks immaculate from top to toe. His eyes are glassy with contempt. "In private," he continues, "I would like you to know one or two things, and to remember them."

Tremain walks around his desk until he is standing very close to Fletcher. Fletcher sways but doesn't step back. He swallows with difficulty, his tongue thick and tacky in his parched mouth.

"Firstly," Tremain says, "Howard shared with me some of his doubts about the way you have worked during this investigation. While it seems in the end that the result you so aggressively *sought was the correct outcome, neither he nor I approve of your methods. I cannot state that strongly enough. No! Don't interrupt me. Listen!"*

Tremain leans closer still. Fletcher avoids eye contact. His gaze roves around the room until it settles on the photographs on Tremain's office wall. It takes him a moment to understand why he recognizes a few of the faces in one particular photograph. Is that? he thinks. It can't be. There is a photograph in which Tremain stands with his wife and another couple. The man very much resembles Howard Smail. Fletcher is gripped by a feeling of dread so intense it's as if somebody has placed a cold hand on the back of his neck. He squints at the picture. The women look like sisters, or could they be mother and daughter? Oh, dear god, *he thinks,* whichever it is, I'm finished. How did I not know about this?

"Look me in the eye!" Tremain bellows. Fletcher tries but finds he needs to step away to do so. His back is only inches from the wall. "Secondly!" Tremain says. Fletcher can see right inside his mouth, where metal fillings lurk in abundance. He blinks at them. He wonders how the hell he got here. He thinks he might be in shock. Tremain talks on relentlessly. "You and I both know the allegation against Howard is untrue. I don't know how you did it, but I will move heaven and earth to find out, and until I do, I will keep you so close to me that you won't take a breath without checking in with me, you won't go for a shit without getting my authorization. I will own you! Do you understand me?"

Fletcher's heart is hammering. He nods. It's not enough for Tremain. He puts a hand on Fletcher's chest and shoves him backward against the wall.

"I said, do you understand?"

"Yes, boss," Fletcher replies. *He can hardly say the words. He feels winded.*

"Howard Smail is a good man and a fine detective. He is worth ten of you. Twenty of you! What's he worth?"

"Twenty of me."

"Get out of my office."

IT'S TIME TO TELL

EPISODE 11—WRONG TIME, WRONG PLACE

A DISHLICKER
PODCAST PRODUCTION

"Yesterday, we received new information regarding two historic investigations from a member of the public.

"The significant information concerns the 1996 murders of Charlie Paige and Scott Ashby and the 1996 disappearance of businessman Peter Dale.

"Peter Dale's remains were recently discovered buried in the Eastville area of Bristol. Until their discovery, Peter Dale had been presumed to have absconded abroad, after perpetrating a sophisticated financial scam in 1996.

"In the light of this information, police are appealing for members of the public to come forward if they knew a man called Terence (Terry) Taylor who died in 2012, aged sixty-four. Terry Taylor was closely involved with St. Giles' Church in Kingswood, and Peter Dale was his half brother."

My name is Cody Swift. I'm a filmmaker and this is the final episode of *It's Time to Tell,* a Dishlicker Podcast Production. The clip you just heard is a statement issued to the press by the Avon & Somerset police department.

Events, it seems, have overtaken this podcast and taken me, for one, by surprise. The question that remains is this: How to make sense of this new revelation after everything I've learned during the making of this podcast? In this episode, I'll try my best to do that, so we can all process this together.

I called Detective Inspector John Fletcher to discuss the development, but was unable to reach him. I persisted and eventually got a call back from Detective Inspector Danny Fryer. In the following clip, you'll hear his voice first:

"Thank you for your patience. DI Fletcher is currently on leave."

"Can you give me any information about Terence Taylor, and what this means for Sidney Noyce's conviction?"

"I'm unable to comment on an investigation that is ongoing."

"Is Terence Taylor a suspect in the murders of Charlie and Scott?"

"I'm unable to comment on specifics. I can say that as of yesterday we have reopened our investigation into the murders of Charlie Paige and Scott Ashby."

I phoned Howard Smail to see if he could help me interpret events. Here's what he had to say:

"Reading between the lines of the press release, Terence Taylor is a suspect in all three murders."

Is it going too far to speculate that that person who came forward might have been listening to *It's Time to Tell*? I'd like to think so.

Owen Weston had this to say:

"I am a hundred percent certain this means Sidney Noyce will be exonerated at some point down the line. You must remain vigilant until police have concluded their inquiries, though. Your personal safety is still a priority. If Terence Taylor committed all three murders and he is dead, somebody out there must still have a stake in this and care enough about it to threaten you."

Noted.

So what am I feeling in the aftermath of this news?

I'm pleased for Sidney Noyce's mother, Valerie. I wish I could turn back time so she and Sidney could avoid the heartbreak of his stigmatization and conviction for a crime he did not commit. I wish he hadn't ended his own life. But I hope his exoneration might bring Valerie a measure of relief. A very small measure, given what she's been through, but a measure nonetheless.

I am also plagued by a question: If Terence Taylor murdered my friends, how could that have happened, and why? Smail and Weston both posited that the boys might have stumbled across him committing an act of violence against his half brother. Weston was quick to research Peter Dale. These are his findings:

"Dale was reported missing two days after the boys were murdered. His half brother was one of the people he ruined financially. If the boys interrupted Terence Taylor while he was either in the act of harming his brother or of disposing of his body, it might have been enough to get them murdered."

The thought sends a chill through me. What are the odds of Charlie and Scott being randomly killed in this way? What are the odds of them being in the wrong place at the wrong time?

Professor Christopher Fellowes, forensic psychologist, has a handle on the statistics:

"If you look at the data published by the Office for National Statistics between 2014 and 2016, it shows that in 64 percent of homicides where the victim is under sixteen years of age, the victim is acquainted with the person who harmed them. In the vast majority of these cases, it is a parent or a stepparent who commits the crime. Only 11 percent of victims in this age bracket are murdered by a stranger. In real numbers, that translates to between one and nine homicide cases in each year over the past decade. Not many."

"So it's rare."

"Yes. But it happens."

I asked Howard Smail if he had come across anything similar in his career.

"It's your worst nightmare as a detective, because it's the crime where the perpetrator got lucky. He killed a man, or possibly a man and two boys in this instance. He disposed of their bodies; he went home. He did not leave a trace; he did not arouse suspicion. Nobody saw him; nobody discovered Dale's body; police assumed Dale had disappeared abroad; the investigation veered off elsewhere in the case of the boys. For Terence Taylor, if he is guilty of triple homicide, it was a perfect storm of luck. In a case like this, you have nowhere to turn if you're investigating. To solve it, you need somebody to come forward with information. It's the only way. Otherwise you risk what happened here: a miscarriage of justice and a murderer getting away with his crimes. What you hope is that it doesn't take twenty years for somebody to come forward. But better late than never."

And that is why this is the final episode of *It's Time to Tell*. It feels abrupt to me, and it may to you also, but the police have a new lead and they are investigating it. It is time for me to step away and wait for the results of their inquiries. I do this out of respect for the police investigation and also because it's time I prioritized my personal safety. Valerie Noyce's advice to me to get on with my life will not go unheeded.

I am dedicating this final episode of *It's Time to Tell* to the memory of my two best friends, who I still miss every single day, and to the memory of Sidney Noyce. Rest in peace, my brothers.

Sidney, I am sorry. I am sorry for the way we treated you and sorry for what happened to you. You were, as they said, a gentle giant, and you did not deserve any of it.

Scott and Charlie, on the day you were murdered I ruined my brand-new and beloved Atlanta Olympics T-shirt and that small piece of bad luck saved my life. In fact, it wasn't bad luck, but the best luck I've ever had. The night you disappeared, Mum took the ripped T-shirt away to clean and fix it and I put my Newcastle United shirt back on, my beloved Magpies shirt, the one that was my pride and joy before the Atlanta shirt arrived. Do you remember how you were jealous of it, Charlie? Do you remember how you told me Arsenal was a better team, Scott? After they told me you were dead, I refused to take that Newcastle shirt off because it reminded me of us. It felt like part of you was still with me when I wore that shirt. My parents had to pry it off me when I finally grew out of it, but I kept it and I have it still. It is cleaned and carefully folded and stashed in a drawer. It is perhaps a clumsy metaphor for some of the ways in which we carry on after a tragedy, but neither of you ever judged me when we were kids and I'd like to think you never would have if you'd had a chance to grow up.

I missed you at school. I missed you during the school holidays. I missed you whenever I ate a 99 Flake ice cream. I missed you at graduation. I missed you whenever I read a comic. I missed you the first time I went to the pub, when I went traveling, when I went to University, when I got my first serious girlfriend, when I got the first job I was proud of. I missed you every time I saw a fancy car or motorbike that you would have loved. I have missed you so much, I still miss you, and I'm so sorry you never had the chance to grow up.

So what is next? How do I carry on?

Well. Here's the thing. The answer is in the skies.

Look up, Bristol! Look to the skies!! Look to the heavens!!! Look out of your windows right now and over the next twenty-four hours, and if you can't do that or you're not in Bristol, or you're catching up on this too late, here's a hashtag to search for. It'll let you know what's happening. Just search for #awaitthedate.

I will see you then.

I cannot wait.

#awaitthedate

Fletcher hurries through Hazel Collins's flat to the back door and lets himself out into the garden. It is surrounded by stone walls. They are taller than Fletcher. A wheelbarrow is beside one of the rose beds, full of mulch. Fletcher tips the muck out and props the barrow against one of the walls. He climbs onto it and struggles to get a grip on the top of the wall as the barrow wobbles beneath him. He tries to lever himself up onto the wall but can't. The effort makes him pant.

After two more attempts, he manages to scrabble up. The top of the wall is littered with shards of glass set into a concrete channel and Fletcher curses as he cuts his hands. He hears a shout from behind him. Somebody has seen him. Below to his right is the road. He sees that he has caught a break: he is out of sight of Danny's car. There is another shout, louder this time. He wobbles. He crouches and tries to lower himself over the edge of the wall, but the glass cuts into his hands and he drops.

He feels his ribs snap as he hits the pavement. He cannot move. It is agony to breathe. He sees somebody approaching from the far end of the street. *Leave me alone,* he thinks. After a few seconds, he manages to reach for his phone. His fingers are bleeding. He ignores two women who are crossing the road to help him, concern all over their faces. He ignores the voices coming from behind the garden wall. He tries to call Felix. Felix will fix this. He finds Felix's number and taps it. As he puts the phone to one ear he's aware that the other feels hot and sticky. Blood. As Danny rounds the corner, alerted by the commotion, Fletcher clasps a hand to his ribs and listens to a message telling him that the number he has dialed is no longer in service.

J ess watches out of the window as her plane breaks through the clouds and lands at Bristol Airport. She has never been so glad to see the familiar landscape, fields plump from overnight rain and new leaves softening the strict winter outlines of trees and hedges. A gentle drizzle falls as she walks down the steps from the aircraft to the tarmac. Her face feels swollen after her night of visceral remorse and fear, and the dampness is a salve.

She takes a cab directly to Olly's house, where Erica waits, contrite as a chided puppy. On the journey, Jess has been full of words she wants to say to her daughter: righteous, angry words about responsibility and boundaries and more. They get lost in the hug Erica gives her on the doorstep. "I'm so sorry, Mum. I'm really, really sorry. I never wanted to interrupt your holiday. I'll make it up to you, I promise." Erica has even made a card, just like the ones she laboriously forged for Jess when she was a little girl. *Sorry,* it says. The edges of the letters bleed into a beautiful, intricate design.

On the way back into the city, traffic is at a standstill in the queue to cross the suspension bridge. The cabdriver huffs and cranes his head out of the window to see what's causing the delay. After fifteen minutes of stop and start, they finally reach the toll barrier and crawl onto the bridge.

"Look!" Erica says. The cause of the delay is filling the sky. Where the limestone walls of the gorge taper abruptly, giving way to the once marshy plain where the city now hugs the riverbanks, a cluster of hot air balloons is visible, drifting serenely upward. There are an unusually large number of them, so many it looks as if they might have been popped out by a bubble machine. Every driver stops to rubberneck. Traffic on the Portway, in the bottom of the gorge, is also at a standstill.

"They're all the same," says Erica.

Each balloon has a picture of a greyhound on it. "Aren't they lovely?" Jess says, keeping her tone bland, but she shudders, because Charlie loved greyhounds. It is something Erica doesn't need to know.

"Dishlicker Channel," Erica says, reading the text on one of the balloons as it floats close and above them. "'Await the Date!' Sounds so cool!" She takes her phone out and snaps multiple pictures. "I wonder what it's for. I'm going to look it up."

Erica taps at her phone and Jess flinches as a cyclist weaves between the traffic, dangerously close to their vehicle. The balloons are making her uneasy. There are so many of them, and all identical. It's not usual, even for Bristol.

"This is it!" Erica says. She reads from her phone:

Bristol-based Dishlicker Productions are launching a new venture in style by flooding the skies of Bristol with hot air balloons for the duration of a two-day event!

After the phenomenal success of their Bristol-based podcast *It's Time to Tell,* Cody Swift of Dishlicker Productions is bringing you a new online TV channel specializing in reality TV and true crime.

Swift said, "We are passionate about our new TV channel. Reality TV is an incredibly popular area and we think we have something to add. We want to bring the stories people want to the people who want them. We plan to dig deep into real lives and make Dishlicker Channel the face of quality modern online television. We are going to bring to Dishlicker Channel the biting stories, high production values, and top-class journalism we've already become known for in a very short space of time."

PR guru Felix Abern . . . Abernathy . . .

Erica stumbles as she tries to pronounce Felix's name. She's never heard it before. Jess doesn't help her out. Her mind is racing.

. . . helped to launch the project. "I've been involved since meeting Cody Swift via his phenomenally success-ful podcast *It's Time to Tell*. He is an extremely talented individual. It's been my pleasure to design the launch of what I know will be a thrilling and successful new ven-ture. It's a new era in television, and Dishlicker is at the forefront."

Bristol—look to the skies today and tomorrow! The rest of Britain—look to the skies this coming week! Dishlicker Productions is coming to you in style and they have a question for you: Do you know *The Date*?

Here is Cody Swift, your host of the podcast phe-nomenon *It's Time to Tell*, with a teaser: "Folks, look out for *The Date*. It's a new production to launch Dishlicker

Channel. It's going to blow *It's Time to Tell* out of the water. This is the future, folks. You need to decide whether
you are with us or not. What's the only way to know for
sure? #awaitthedate."

"Oh, my god," Erica says. "How come I haven't heard of
this? It sounds so cool, and it's got, like, thousands of likes."
She holds her phone up to show Jess. Animated balloons with
greyhounds on them cluster across the screen, closing in and
obscuring the text beneath, and Jess shuts her eyes as three
words appear in huge type: AWAIT THE DATE.

"Mum," Erica says. "Mum! What?"

"Sorry," Jess says. "I'm sorry, darling. I was looking. I felt a
tiny bit faint for a moment. I think it's the travel."

Erica falls quiet, tapping on her phone. Jess stares out of the
window at the balloons above them, as the full extent of what
Cody has been up to dawns on her, piece by piece. Or, she
corrects herself, what Cody *and Felix* have been up to.

At home she drops her luggage on the floor of the hallway.
She pauses only to get a glass of water before she uploads the
podcast onto her phone.

"I'm having a nap," she says to Erica. "Tired from the
travel."

"I'll make supper!" Erica always cooks for her parents when
she's feeling contrite. It suits Jess today. Jess shuts herself in her
bedroom and sits on the bed. She puts headphones in and
presses play on the first episode of the podcast.

Cody Swift's words swill around her, dirtying her home.
She begins to weep as she listens. They are hot, stinging tears
and they fall silently.

By the end, she thinks, *I've been played. We all have.*

The podcast has been nothing more than a publicity stunt for Cody Swift, directed by Felix Abernathy. The audacity and cruelty of it stun her. There are so many lies.

She plays some of the episodes again. It is when she hears the final episode for the second time that her head snaps up. She blinks. She rewinds the episode and plays it again, and then again. At first the memory it invokes is just a tease. She rewinds one particular line. Cody says:

> "The night you disappeared, Mum took the ripped T-shirt away to clean and fix it and I put my Newcastle United shirt back on, my beloved Magpies shirt, the one that was my pride and joy before the Atlanta shirt arrived."

She listens again. In her mind what she sees at first is no more than a flash of black and white picked out in the darkness by a streetlamp, a blur, a few sensations, but it slowly comes into focus. Jess, twenty years ago, is trying to hold her hair back out of her face as she vomits. The cabdriver has wound down his window and is looking at her with resignation as she crouches beside the road. She is so sore and her body feels empty. She recalls the sounds of her retching and the driver's voice as he asks if she's okay. She hears the fast panting of somebody running. A boy. In a black-and-white shirt. He flashes past, a shadow in the corner of her eye, but definitely there.

"No!" she says out loud to the room. But she thinks, *Could it be? Of course it could.*

In her office, she rummages in a cupboard until she finds the old Rolodex where once she neatly inscribed her contacts from her acting days. She reminds herself of the name of somebody she used to know and googles it to obtain up-to-date contact details. She makes a phone call. It lasts for thirty minutes. After she hangs up, she goes downstairs.

"Erica," she says, "we're going out."

Her daughter is in the kitchen, at the stove. "What?" she asks. "Can't I stay here?"

"No. I want you with me."

"What about this? I've made arrabbiata." It's Jess's favorite. Erica holds a wooden spoon and the red sauce drips from it onto the glossy surface of the hob.

"Turn the heat off and put a lid on it. It'll keep."

"Are you okay, Mum?"

"I'm fine. Get ready. We're leaving in twenty minutes."

Jess selects an outfit from her wardrobe. She showers quickly, blow-dries her hair efficiently, and applies her makeup expertly. She considers her reflection in the mirror and unfastens one of the buttons on her silk blouse. *Knockout,* Nick would say if he was here. She feels incredibly calm. She feels ready for what she needs to do.

ow's the pain?" the nurse asks.

"Fine," Fletcher says. "When can I go?"

"You hit your head, so the doctor wants to get it scanned."

As soon as she's left the room Fletcher tries to shift upright so he can swing his legs over the side of the bed. It's not possible. He feels as if he has hot pokers in his side every time he breathes, let alone moves. He's propped at an awkward angle when Danny lets himself into the room.

"Where are you planning on going?" he asks. He remains standing until Fletcher has rolled himself properly back onto the bed, then takes a seat.

"I shouldn't have gone to see her on my own," Fletcher says. "I—"

"John. It's over."

"No, no, I—"

"Stop, John. Just stop."

"She's an old woman, her statement about Peter Dale's brother won't count for shit."

"It's checking out."

"Fuck!" Fletcher says. It causes an intense rush of pain.

"Everything is going to be unpicked."

"Nobody knows what we did."

"*I* know what you did."

"What?"

"What on earth makes you think I'm going to go down with you?"

Fletcher is lost for words at first. "I've looked out for you for forty fucking years," he manages.

"Really?"

"Yes."

"Is that how it seemed to you?"

"Yessss." The word is a wheeze. The pain is excruciating.

"Maybe you did once, back in the day. Maybe you did look out for me. But that was twenty years ago. Honestly, for the past two decades, I've propped you up, and I can't do it anymore. I've had no thanks, you've cut me no slack. You still always behave as if you are the smartest person in the room. I am invisible to you. I have two families to support, I am trying to do a good job, but all these years I have been made to feel like an extra on the John-fucking-Fletcher show."

"Danny!" Fletcher gasps, but it's not the final betrayal. He can do nothing but watch helplessly as the expression in Danny's eyes morphs from angry to cold. It coincides with the clip of footsteps in the corridor outside. The door opens and Danny stands. "Sir."

David Tremain enters and Fletcher scrabbles with bandaged fingers to pull the sheet up over his sagging hospital gown, desperate to cover the wiry gray hairs sprouting on his pale chest and his bruised arms.

"Hello, John," Tremain says. "I very much wanted to be here for this. Thank you for waiting, Danny."

"Sir."

"Can you make sure we get some privacy, please?"

Danny nods and steps out of the room. Fletcher feels as if he's drowning. Tremain sits down on the end of the bed and Fletcher winces as the mattress sags.

"So," Tremain says, "you have a choice. You offer me your resignation, effective immediately, and when investigators come asking, you tell them everything you did to Sidney Noyce and Howard Smail, or I ask DI Flynn back in here and he will charge you with an offense connected to the recent death of Hazel Collins."

"I didn't touch Hazel Collins."

"Her daughter found her dead in her chair when she got home this morning. Fortunately, it was after the ambulance had collected you. Only you, me, Danny, and a commendably ambitious young DC know that you were alone in her flat with her, subjecting her to harassment. Would you like to keep it that way?"

"You wouldn't want that kind of publicity."

"I'm going to be getting bad publicity anyway over two historic investigations, and I believe you know what I'm referring to. If I can be seen to act decisively and weed out a very bad seed, it might help to mitigate that."

Fletcher lets his head fall back onto the pillows. He shuts his eyes. A fog is rolling down.

"They say you're probably concussed, John, but I suspect the cogs are turning nevertheless. You should bear in mind what the relative judicial punishments might be for the offenses we're discussing."

Fletcher makes a final try. If he's going down, Felix should, too. "Felix Abernathy is involved in these murders. I have notes. I wrote it down. I found a connection last night."

Tremain laughs. "Give up, John. Small fry like you will never take down a man like him. Felix Abernathy was nowhere near the estate when the murders took place."

"How do you know?"

Tremain smiles. "Your naiveté astounds me. Are you a total fantasist? Did you think you were the only person to have good contacts? Always the puppet, never the puppet master. How has that been for you over the past two decades?"

Tremain stands, straightens his jacket. "You realize I lost a brother-in-law as well as a fine colleague after you ruined Smail? It broke my wife's sister." He leans over Fletcher and pats his ribs hard. Fletcher cries out in pain. "Let Danny know what you want to do," Tremain says and leaves the room.

Fletcher's final humiliation comes in the form of fat, childlike tears that roll down his cheeks unstoppably. He doesn't think he has cried since he cradled Charlie Paige in his arms. Orange poppies—so bright—begin to crowd his vision. When the nurse reenters the room he sees only a smudge.

"Your colleague said you might need some more pain relief?" she asks.

His only response is a groan that sounds helpless even to his ears.

Jess parks beside the arches beneath the Temple Meads station forecourt.

"I won't be long," she says to Erica. "Then I'm going to take you somewhere nice because I want to have a talk."

"You're being weird, Mum. What's going on?"

"Give me twenty minutes. Then I'll explain everything, I promise."

Jess gets out of the car and her heels clatter as she crosses the cobblestone courtyard. She walks past an artisan bakery built into the arches. It is shutting its doors for the day, but a few hipster types linger on the benches outside. She approaches a trendy set of offices converted from an old warehouse. Jess can't see a huge slice of sky because the courtyard is hemmed in by buildings, but even so she catches a glimpse of two Dishlicker balloons drifting by. Yet more balloons have filled the skies this afternoon; people gathered on the station's forecourt are gazing at them. The Dishlicker stunt has made national news.

The Dishlicker Productions office is easy to find. Their greyhound logo is emblazoned across the floor-to-ceiling glass at their entrance. A young man lets Jess in. He is working on the ground floor at a glass desk alongside an androgynous colleague. They both wear the tightest drainpipe jeans. Each has a tiny laptop open in front of them.

"I'm here to see Cody," Jess says. Her confidence is absolute. She doesn't have to fake it. "I'm Jessica Paige. It's time I told him something."

She watches with amusement as Cody's assistant fails to disguise his surprise before jogging smartly up a spiral metal staircase that threatens to snag his coltish limbs. She doesn't bother to wait, but follows him up.

Cody Swift is sitting behind a large desk in a room that has a wall of glass overlooking the cobbles and some of the station's more impressive wrought-iron Victorian architecture. It's not quite Felix's setup, but it's not bad. Cody is on the phone, but hangs up when he recognizes her. As she crosses the space toward him, he takes on a wary expression, as if they were two boxers entering a ring.

"Thank you," Cody says to the underling, who takes the hint, although he looks as though he would dearly love to witness their exchange. "Would you like to sit?" Cody asks. He looks uncertain. His chair scrapes noisily on the polished concrete floor as he stands and gestures toward the seat on the other side of his desk.

"No, thank you." Jess feels heady, but poised. Adrenaline is coursing through her.

"How can I help you? It's so lovely to see you."

Cody is trying for good manners. Naturally. *Nice try,* Jess thinks. An image of a younger Cody runs through her mind: freckle-nosed, sunburned, and fierce, accepting coins from Felix in return for a drug delivery made on the estate, and haggling for more.

"Here is fine," she says.

"Do you mind if *I* sit?"

"Do what you like."

He eases himself back down into his seat.

"Where's Maya's desk?" she asks.

"What?"

"I thought you and Maya worked together. I was wondering where she sits?"

"She works at home." His smile is plastic. "Anyway, she's moved on."

"I've done some homework," she says. "I've listened to your podcast, and there's something I want to ask you about."

"Go ahead."

"Newcastle United. The Magpies."

"What about them?"

She almost smiles at his response, because a sweet little furrow has appeared in his brow, just like it used to. It means he can't see where this is going yet. *Good.* "In the podcast, you said you went back to wearing your Magpies shirt after your Atlanta Olympics shirt got ripped."

He seems to relax a little. "Sure."

"What color was the Magpies shirt?"

"I beg your pardon?"

"You heard me."

"Black and white stripes."

"So it was the same one you wore all that summer? The one you wore when you came round my flat? The one Felix used to compliment you on?"

"Probably. I can't remember."

"Well, that's a relief, because now I know I'm right." Jess smiles, big and broad, and like the immature little toerag he is, Cody Swift takes his cue from her and relaxes further. "Okay, well, I'm glad to help."

Jess walks to the window and gazes out. A shadow from a Dishlicker balloon travels across the cobbles. "Are you sure you don't want to check with Maya? About the shirt?"

"I don't think so." He looks confused.

"Shall we phone her?"

"I told you, she's moved on."

"Where did you say she worked again?"

"Maya works at home. Worked at home."

"She worked at home when you have this lovely office facility here? Really?"

Jess turns around and moves to take the seat in front of Cody. She doesn't hurry. Cody's not so jumpy now; in fact he looks like he might be getting pissed off. "Did you have something to tell me? The podcast is technically over, but we could do a special addendum. Your story? It's not too late. I'm sorry if we came down a bit hard on you in some of the episodes, but this could be a chance to put your side of the story across in your own words."

"I think I'd be more comfortable talking to Maya. You know, woman to woman." His Adam's apple is sharp, Jess thinks, as she watches it travel up and down his throat. "Can we call her?" she asks. "Now?"

"She's moved on."

"Surely she'll take my call to help you out? I really would be more comfortable talking to her."

Cody's eyes flick sideways.

"You did that when you were a kid and you were lying," Jess says.

"Did what?"

"Maya doesn't exist, does she? You always were a little liar. I think you've made up a girlfriend even though you're supposed to be all grown up now."

Cody blinks. Jess presses on: "Do you know how I know you made her up? Because nobody in their right mind would be skanky enough to do this podcast with you, knowing the real reason why you were doing it. You're the lowest of the low. You've used us all to set up a bloody business. Nobody like that gets a lovely, supportive girlfriend like *Maya,* because a person who does something like that is very, very hard to love."

Cody leans forward. There's some fire in his eyes now. "You're right. She doesn't exist. The podcast needed a personal story to add a bit of threat. We, I, thought it would be stronger that way. Turns out it was a good call, don't you think?"

"*We* being you and Felix? I love how you fudged that in your podcast. Never met him before? My ass. You used to follow him around like a shadow whenever you got the chance. You did jobs for him. I remember."

"Felix speaks very highly of you."

"Fuck you."

"Hey! I was only—"

"No. Shut up. It's time you stopped blabbing and listened, Cody. I saw you the night Charlie and Scott were killed. You were wearing your Magpies shirt and you snuck out of your flat when everybody thought you were in bed, and nobody noticed you'd gone. 'Course you did. When did you ever do what you were told? What did you see?"

"I was at home asleep."

"Bollocks. You could have snuck out easy as pie. Your bedroom was by the front door. I haven't forgotten that. Who was supposed to be watching you? That hippie from next door who was so doped up she could never see straight? I bet she was passed out before your parents ever left the building. She was never going to check on you. Probably Julie and your dad didn't either because of the search and all the worry. What happened, Cody? Were you with Charlie and Scott? Did you go out and find them?"

His eyes rest hard on Jess in a way that is probably supposed to intimidate her but doesn't because she knows Cody Swift is a coward. "Were you with Charlie and Scott when you saw somebody doing something they shouldn't have been doing? Yes! I've heard about that. I've heard it wasn't poor old Sid Noyce that was a murderer. Did you see trouble coming? Is that what it was? Did you scarper before the man saw you and leave my boy and Scott behind to be hurt? Is that why you were running so hard and so fast? *Because you left them there?* Then you let Sidney Noyce go down for something he didn't do?"

"You're hysterical," he says. "Calm down."

She laughs. "You must think I was born yesterday. I can see in your eyes I'm right. Who else would be running for his life down Blackhorse Lane in a Magpies shirt that night? *I saw you*. Make no mistake. I *know* I did. I only hope you can live with yourself."

"I hope you can live with *yourself*." It's a pathetic retort.

Jess stares at him as his cheeks flush. "Oh, I can live with myself, thank you very much," she says. "And no thanks to you." She uncrosses her legs and stands. She walks to the staircase and takes a step down, then turns back to him again. "I forgot!" she says. "There *is* one more thing I wanted to say."

His face is a snarl.

"I've given an interview to the BBC. A very salable interview." She checks her wristwatch. "In fact, it's probably airing right about now."

Cody Swift stands. His chair falls backward.

"You might start to hear from people in a few minutes," Jess adds, "because I opened up to them about what we just discussed. *It's Time to Tell,* I said to them! It's time they knew who the real Cody Swift is. You're going to be on everybody's lips, my darling."

"You c—"

"Oh, Cody!" Jess interrupts him. She puts a finger to her lips. "Language! And here was me thinking you had such lovely manners."

A smile creeps across her face just as the blood is draining from Cody's.

"Aren't you afraid?" he asks. "Of what people might think of you? Of what Felix might do?"

"I'm not," she says. "Finally. I'm not."

Before Cody can find a single word to answer her, his phone begins to buzz and clatter. Notifications scroll across its screen. His computer pings and his landline rings just as the reception phones do downstairs. He looks from the screens to the landline to Jess and back again.

"In fact, you can give my regards to Felix," Jess says over the noise of the phones, and as she makes her way down the staircase with her head held high, projecting all the elegance she ever learned to mimic, she thinks she might have just given the performance of her life. Out on the cobbles, she pauses to retie her trench coat tightly around her waist and she thinks, *You deserve it, Cody Swift, you little shit.*

As she crosses the car park, Erica watches her from the car. Jess smiles, raises her hand, and wiggles her fingers. Erica smiles and waves back. Jess takes a deep breath. *It's time,* she thinks, *for a very grown-up talk.*

ACKNOWLEDGMENTS

Warmest thanks to Helen Heller, Emma Beswetherick, Emily Krump, Liate Stehlik, Cath Burke, Jen Hart, Molly Waxman, Lauren Truskowski, Julia Elliott, Jeanie Lee, Aimee Kitson, Stephanie Melrose, Thalia Proctor, PFD agency, Camilla Ferrier, Jemma McDonagh, and the team at the Marsh Agency. Special thanks must go to Leo MacDonald, Mike Millar, and the whole crew at HC Canada, who gave me such a wonderful welcome, and also to the publishers, editors, and translators of the international editions of my books.

Thanks, too, to all the terrific sales teams and booksellers who we all depend on. To the book bloggers, readers, fellow authors, and other amazing bookish people I have had the pleasure of getting to know via social media: Thank you all. Your support and our interaction often make my day.

Special thanks to Elsie Lyons for the stunning cover design.

As ever, I relied on my two retired detectives to advise me

on police procedure and other related things. Thank you both; you make such a difference.

On the home front, huge thanks to my writing partner, Abbie Ross, who makes everything more fabulous, always, and to my friends and family who unfailingly offer support and encouragement in so many ways. It means a lot.

Jules, Rose, Max, and Louis: You are the best support team. Thank you, love you, couldn't do it without you.

Insights,
Interviews
& More . . .

Meet Gilly Macmillan

Courtesy of author

GILLY MACMILLAN is the bestselling author of *What She Knew, The Perfect Girl,* and *Odd Child Out.* She grew up in Swindon, England, and lived in Northern California in her late teens. She trained as an art historian and worked at *The Burlington Magazine* and the Hayward Gallery before starting a family. Since then, she has been a lecturer in photography and now writes full-time. She resides in Bristol, England. ᔕ

Creating a Fictional Podcast

The idea to include a podcast in *I Know You Know* emerged from a conversation between my agent and me. I was planning a novel about a fictional cold case based very loosely on a real case I had read about, and I hoped to include a character who was the mother of a young murder victim. I wanted my fictional case to be an infamous one, which had sent shock waves through a community because it involved the murder of two children.

My agent and I were discussing the best way to tell the story. We asked each other questions: What if the victims' best friend comes back to Bristol to look into the case twenty years later? What if he looks into it partly because he wants to put some demons to rest but also because he wants to create his own true crime podcast? What if the podcast itself is cut through the book? That was an "Ooh!" moment. When both you and your agent get excited, you know you might be onto something.

I was already a regular listener of a wide range of true crime podcasts but had never tried to write anything like them before. True crime podcasts feed into my novels in many ways, not least in providing inspiration. For example, something a retired detective said in ▶

an episode of *Australian True Crime* gave me the idea for John Fletcher, the detective who plays a central role in *I Know You Know*.

As preparation, I revisited some of my favorite podcasts and studied how they were put together. Some were professionally produced and very slick. Others were more of a mom-and-pop production where sound and edit quality was patchy. Regardless of production quality, the podcasts I found most compelling were the ones that gave a voice to the people directly touched by the crime: victims, witnesses, law enforcement officers, suspects, and others. This format excited me, because I felt it could translate effectively into a novel, allowing me to introduce short direct quotes from a variety of characters.

The narrator of the podcast was important, too. I was especially intrigued by podcasts in which the narrator emerged as a character in their own right, so as the series progressed you could get a flavor of their personality and learn to trust them and understand what the investigation meant to them. An effective example of this is the first series of the Canadian podcast *Someone Knows Something*, where narrator David Ridgen returns to his childhood home to investigate an unsolved missing child mystery. Thoughtfully, Ridgen wove his personal story into the narrative. All of this gave me lots of inspiration for Cody's approach to *It's Time to Tell* and brought home how much of an editorial hand the creator of a podcast has in how they present a story.

I also noticed how each podcast has a distinct identity, or brand. This led me to think about how Cody would have created an identity for his podcast. I felt it would probably be closely tied to the story of his friends' murders. As the bodies of his friends were discovered near a greyhound racing track, this felt like a good starting point for a logo. I enlisted the help of my family (many of whom can draw, whereas I cannot!) to sketch a greyhound. The design team at HarperCollins improved on this.

The name of Cody's production company needed careful consideration. I thought it should be distinct and memorable, but not too formal. Sticking with my theme, I researched alternative words for *greyhound* and came across *dishlicker*. It stood out immediately because it was fun, descriptive in a slangy way, unusual, and had a bit of a cool factor that might appeal to Cody.

When deciding on the name of Cody's podcast, once again I was inspired by something I had heard in a real podcast: a detective saying that often the only way a cold case can be solved after a long period of time is for somebody to ▶

Creating a Fictional Podcast (*continued*)

come forward with information they'd been holding back. *It's Time to Tell* sprang to mind.

As I began writing the podcast, I thought carefully about how to write what is effectively a transcript of something that is intended to be listened to, and how to make it feel true to that format but also readable within a novel. I couldn't use any of the bells and whistles podcasts typically include—such as atmospheric sound effects or music—so everything compelling about *It's Time to Tell* has to come from the page. I had to cut down on the level of detail you might expect in some podcasts. For example, a transcript of one episode of *Serial* runs around ten thousand words (one-tenth of a novel), so I knew episodes of *It's Time to Tell* had to be short and sweet by comparison, or I would have either no room for my other characters or an epic six-hundred-page novel on my hands.

Creating *It's Time to Tell* was a challenge, but a fun one. I hope you enjoyed reading it. If you're interested and you've got the stomach for it, I cannot recommend true crime podcasts enough. Here are a few of my favorites:

Serial
Australian True Crime
Someone Knows Something
A Killing On the Cape
Missing & Murdered ❧

Questions for Discussion

1. *I Know You Know* shifts perspectives between multiple characters. How did the changing points of view shape your experience reading the novel?

2. How is motherhood defined throughout the book? What kind of mother was Jessica Paige? Do you think it is a parent's role to give a child freedom or shelter them?

3. Think about the friendship between Charlie, Scott, and Cody. Why do you suppose they became so close? Do you believe the boys brought out the best or worst aspects in one another?

4. Sidney Noyce was used as a scapegoat for a crime he didn't commit. Did his fate give you a new perspective on the challenges mentally ill people face during criminal trials?

5. We see only Cody Swift's point of view through his podcasts. How did this affect your ability to anticipate the ending? ▶

6. What do you think is the novel's message about the binds of family, friendship, and community? Why do you think the community rallied to support some characters and not others?

7. Did you feel any sympathy for Jessica Paige when she said she felt some relief after Charlie's death?

8. What do you make of Fletcher's understanding with Felix? Do you think his willingness to bend the rules made him a better or worse cop? Do you think Fletcher got what he deserved in the end?

9. Why do you think Cody Swift decided to dig into the murders of his childhood friends if he had something to hide about that night as well?

10. Do you think there is ever an objective truth, or is a story always framed by its narrator? By the end of the novel, did you feel you'd discovered the real truth?

More from Gilly Macmillan

ODD CHILD OUT

"Subtle, nuanced writing and a compelling, timely story taut with tension—*Odd Child Out* is a hugely satisfying and thrilling read. Highly recommended!"

—Shari Lapena, *New York Times* bestselling author of *The Couple Next Door*

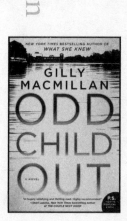

How well do you know the people you love . . . ?

Best friends Noah Sadler and Abdi Mahad have always been inseparable. But when Noah is found floating unconscious in Bristol's Feeder Canal, Abdi can't—or won't—tell anyone what happened.

Just back from mandatory leave following his last case, Detective Jim Clemo is now assigned to look into this unfortunate accident. But tragedy strikes, and what looked like a simple case of a prank gone wrong soon ignites into a public battle. Noah is British. Abdi is a Somali refugee. And social tensions have been rising rapidly in Bristol. Against this background of fear and fury, two families fight for ▸

their sons and for the truth. Neither
of them know how far they will have to
go, what demons they will have to face,
what pain they will have to suffer.

Because the truth hurts.

"Literary suspense at its finest."
　　　　—Mary Kubica, *New York Times*
　　　　bestselling author of *Pretty Baby*

"A wonderfully addictive book with virtuoso plotting and characters—for anyone who loved *Girl on the Train*, it's a must-read."
　　　　—Rosamund Lupton

Zoe Maisey is a seventeen-year-old musical prodigy with a genius IQ. Three years ago, she was involved in a tragic incident that left three classmates dead. She served her time, and now her mother, Maria, is resolved to keep that devastating fact tucked far away from their new beginning, hiding the past from even her new husband, and demanding Zoe do the same.

Tonight Zoe is giving a recital that Maria has been planning for months. It needs to be the performance of her life. But instead, by the end of the evening, Maria is dead.

In the aftermath, everyone—police, family, Zoe's former solicitor, and Zoe herself—tries to piece together what happened. But as Zoe knows all too well, the truth is rarely straightforward, and the closer we are to someone, the less we may see. ▸

More from Gilly Macmillan (*continued*)

WHAT SHE KNEW

"A nuanced, completely addictive debut."

—*People*

In a heartbeat, everything changes . . .

Rachel Jenner is walking in a Bristol park with her eight-year-old son, Ben, when he asks if he can run ahead. It's an ordinary request on an ordinary Sunday afternoon, and Rachel has no reason to worry—until Ben vanishes.

Police are called, search parties go out, and Rachel, already insecure after her recent divorce, feels herself coming undone. As hours and then days pass without a sign of Ben, everyone who knew him is called into question: from Rachel's newly married ex-husband to her mother-of-the-year sister. Inevitably, media attention focuses on Rachel too, and the public's attitude toward her begins to shift from sympathy to suspicion.

As she desperately pieces together the threadbare clues, Rachel realizes that nothing is quite as she imagined it to be, not even her own judgment. And the greatest dangers may lie not in the anonymous strangers of every parent's nightmares, but behind the familiar smiles of those she trusts the most.

Where is Ben? The clock is ticking . . .

Discover great authors, exclusive offers, and more at hc.com.